FIRE AND INK

CHOCTAW TRIBUNE SERIES, BOOK FIVE

SARAH ELISABETH SAWYER

RockHaven Publishing
P.O. Box 1103
Canton, Texas 75103

Scriptures taken from the Authorized King James Version, Holy Bible. Used by permission. All rights reserved.

This is a work of fiction. Names, characters, places, and incidents are fictitious or used fictitiously. Any resemblance to real persons, living or dead, is coincidental and unintentional.

Editors: Lynda Kay Sawyer, Catherine Frappier

Cover Design: MiblArt. Frisco Line time table image, C. C. Roberts Collection [(SP-2005-08)], Special Collections and Archives, Missouri State University Libraries.

Author Photo by Lynda Kay Sawyer

Print ISBN: 978-1-956043-10-5

LCCN: 2023915486

To Carole Ayers
I think Mr. Don would have enjoyed this one, too.

For this is thankworthy, if a man for conscience toward God endure grief, suffering wrongfully.

For what glory is it, if, when ye be buffeted for your faults, ye shall take it patiently? but if, when ye do well, and suffer for it, ye take it patiently, this is acceptable with God. (1 Peter 2:19 KJV)

CHAPTER 1

March 1895
Fort Smith, Arkansas

The sickening thud of a trap door releasing echoed in Matthew Teller's mind. Even hours later, the sounds disturbed his focus as he shoved another stack of papers to the side on the dusty work-table in the basement of the Sebastian County Courthouse.

Matthew had come to Fort Smith to research, but there happened to be a hanging scheduled and, as a newspaper reporter, Matthew attended. What he witnessed haunted him, distracted him from his task—he was there to find the documents he needed to dismantle the legal claims of the town of Dickens, Indian Territory.

Matthew stood and pulled another file folder from the metal cabinet marked "Choctaw Nation 1889." He sat again at the wooden table and flipped the file open. Somewhere in these records could be the evidence he needed to prevent one of the town's founders, Christopher Maxwell, from filing for annexation. If the annexing went through, the town of Dickens would technically no longer be in the Choctaw Nation, chipping away at yet more of the tribe's sovereignty.

There was nothing useful in that folder and Matthew added it to the growing stack to refile when he finished. Keeping sharp records wasn't a priority in Indian Territory nor in Arkansas. Matthew had already dug through records at Tuskahoma, McAlester, and Little Rock. Nothing on the founding of the town of Dickens. No records of the survey, no copy of the lease that Sam Mishaya signed to turn over the parcel of land to the founders of Dickens. Nothing about Dickens. It was as though the town didn't exist.

If only it didn't. How different Matthew's life would be.

He opened a new folder, sounds of the trap door ringing in his mind again, filling his senses.

A chill swept over him and he shook his shoulders. That wasn't the first hanging he'd witnessed. Probably wouldn't be the last.

When he opened the folder, the swish of dusty air tickled his nose. But something else caused the hair on the back of his neck to stand up.

Someone else had entered the basement.

Before Matthew could turn, cold metal pressed against the back of his neck. The unmistakable cock of a revolver sounded close to his ear.

Matthew didn't flinch. A deep, haunting voice whispered, "Boy, you sure ask an unhealthy amount of questions."

There was a sting of familiarity in the voice, but Matthew couldn't place it. He slowly spread his hands on the table as though surrendering, yet he was poised to push upright. If he had a chance, he'd go down fighting whoever this was.

The muzzle of the gun pressed hard against his neck. "You sit nice and still and listen."

The man paused, then drawled, "If you don't quit poking your nose around, you're going to wind up with more troubles than you or your ancestors ever saw."

Silence stretched, giving Matthew a chance to weigh the gravity of the words. The man went on, "Give me a nod to let me know you understand what I'm saying."

Mindful that he was a heartbeat away from death, Matthew lowered his head, the muzzle following his slight movement.

There was a chuckle in the man's next words. "That's good, boy. Real good. Now you sit quiet and you keep on sitting for ten minutes."

The muzzle loosened its hold on Matthew. He listened for retreating footsteps. None.

Then the man's voice came from the stairwell. "From now 'til the day you die, boy, you won't know when I'll be watching."

The next sound was the door at the top of the basement closing.

Matthew let out his breath in one puff, stirring dust on the table. He glanced over his shoulder to make out the rows of files, shelving, and stacks of boxes that filled the basement. The only light was the lamp attached to the wall near the back where Matthew was working. The man had come and gone as soundless as a shadow.

He didn't know who that man was, but he knew who must have sent him—the man wanting to annex the town of Dickens.

Matthew turned back to the folder. He would use the ten allotted minutes to continue his investigation.

He flipped through three pages, mindful to keep his senses sharp while focusing on the papers. The courthouse would close soon, closing off his opportunity to overturn every rock in that basement.

A stamp on one of the pages caused him to slow. It was for the county that held Dickens. A few pages later was a sheet of paper that caused him to freeze more than the muzzle of the gun.

Laying on the table before him was a letter addressed to a

man named John Bellanger, a resident of Fort Smith. But throughout the letter were mentions of the town of Dickens.

Most notable—the letter was signed by Christopher Maxwell.

~

Ten minutes after the man in the basement threatened him, Matthew emerged from the Sebastian County Courthouse that also held the jail and the old fort barracks.

The sun outside looked like it was doing its job, but it wasn't. Cold wind slapped Matthew's face as he passed the gallows. The chill of death would stay with him the rest of the day. He couldn't shake it, but he had to keep his focus.

The document he copied from the basement indicated that John Bellanger lived outside of Fort Smith, down near the river. It was close enough for Matthew to make the walk in the late winter sunshine.

Traversing the road out of Fort Smith, he observed each man he passed, and looked over his shoulder more than once. He should wait a few days before following this lead, but he doubted the shadow man would go away any time soon.

He slowed by the white picket-fence gate that held the address for John Bellanger and did a final check up and down the road and the pasture across the way. No sign of anyone watching.

Matthew picked up his pace and entered the open gate into Bellanger's yard, following the gravel path to the front door. He knocked but heard no sound inside. Going around the modest home, Matthew saw a man sitting by a small barn on a stool, repairing a plow harness. The man looked up at Matthew, eyebrow raised.

Matthew knew his expression was as tense as a hangman's, so he offered a relaxed greeting. "Are you John Bellanger?"

The man stood and Matthew noted the old Springfield rifle

leaned against the barn wall. The man lowered the harness to the ground.

"Who's asking?"

Matthew offered his hand to shake. "Matthew Teller."

There was little else he could add about who he was without raising the man's suspicion.

The man shook his hand cautiously. "Yeah, I'm John Bellanger. What can I do for you?"

"I'm writing a story about the founding of Dickens in Indian Territory."

Bellanger blanched, and Matthew knew he'd come to the right place. He also knew it would be difficult to get the answers he needed from this stranger.

Bellanger licked his pale lips. "What makes you think I know anything about it?"

Matthew reached into his pocket and pulled out a copy he'd made of the letter. "Seems you conducted the survey of the town site and were paid by Christopher Maxwell. This letter was presented during the filing. Do you know Maxwell personally?"

Chickens near the barn squawked and a woman peered from around the corner, feed bucket in hand.

John Bellanger frowned. "You go on in the house, honey. We got business to talk."

She hooked the bucket on a peg and headed for the house, looking long between the two men. When she closed the door behind her, John Bellanger turned to Matthew with such a dark expression, Matthew would suspect he was the shadow that threatened him in the basement. The voice didn't match, but his words were no friendlier.

"I got nothing to say to you, Teller. And if you know what's good for you, you won't have nothing to say about that town in any newspaper, either. Now get off my place."

Matthew gave a quick nod. "Have it your way. But the truth always comes out, Mr. Bellanger. Willingly or unwillingly."

Matthew turned and went around the house to regain the front walkway to the road. Gravel crunched beneath his boots. He barely heard the soft voice behind him.

"Mr. Teller?"

Matthew jerked to look over his shoulder, mentally kicking himself for not being aware that someone was on the porch. He just might end up dead before the day was out.

Mrs. Bellanger came down the steps, glancing to the side of the house that obscured them from sight of her husband. She rushed up to Matthew and grabbed his arm.

Her words tumbled out in a breathy whisper. "You need to go to the Palace in Hot Springs. It's where all this started, and it won't end until someone does something. I don't want my John living with that survey hanging over his head the rest of our lives."

She took a quick breath and squeezed Matthew's arm hard. "But take care. Men have died because of all this."

She released Matthew's arm and ran back into the house. Matthew turned and continued his brisk walk to the gate, not wanting Bellanger to see him hanging around.

The Palace. Matthew had been there before and would take her caution to heart.

He turned onto the main road and felt a prickle on the back of his neck. He looked over his shoulder.

The road was empty.

CHAPTER 2

U.S. Marshal Daniel Garvin clenched his revolver, cocked and aimed at his opponent. "Don't do it."

The outlaw was frozen in the middle of throwing his saddle onto a sorrel, caught off-guard by Daniel's sudden appearance. The flash of determination in the outlaw's eyes told Daniel his plea of *don't* was useless.

The man threw his saddle toward Daniel, blocking his view. Daniel jumped to one side to regain his sight on the outlaw. Before the saddle hit the ground, the man had his Colt .45 in hand and was drawing a bead on Daniel.

Daniel squeezed the trigger on his Colt. His aim was sure and the bullet hit its mark.

In one foul moment, another human life ended.

There was no stopping death.

Two months as a Choctaw United States Marshal, and this was the second man Daniel had killed. He'd only hunted two.

Gun still in hand, Daniel stood by the body of the outlaw he'd come to arrest near Skullyville, Indian Territory. The man was breaking camp in the woods when Daniel drew down on him.

The outlaw lay in a crumpled heap, face down. A sad end to

an ill-lived life. Wanted for robbery and murder, most lawmen wouldn't be bothered about ending that kind of life. In fact, one old timer advised Daniel to, "leave outlaws in the brush where alibis don't count."

Daniel removed his hat and bowed his head, listening to the sounds of the forest surrounding the outlaw's camp. He rocked back on his heels, then forward again. In the same motion, he twisted around, flinging his hat behind him and bringing his Colt up, cocked.

His hat flew at the face of the man who'd come up behind him. The large black man easily batted the hat away, his smile grim.

"That was good shootin', Dan."

Daniel relaxed, lowering the barrel to aim at the ground. Marshal Bass Reeves was the closest he had to a friend of the marshals in Fort Smith. They'd ridden together for Daniel's first month before Bass turned him loose to track down wanted men on his own. Daniel managed to stay alive. He couldn't say the same of his quarries.

Daniel holstered his gun. "I suppose so."

Bass Reeves dropped the reins of his trusty bay and helped Daniel search the outlaw's belongings. They found loot from a recent robbery.

Daniel pulled his leather gloves on over his numb hands and finished saddling the horse. He and Bass wrapped the man's body and hefted him over the sorrel. They tied the body in place for the sixteen-mile ride to Fort Smith.

Stepping back, Marshal Reeves gripped Daniel's shoulder. "Don't let killing get easy. You won't be a lick of good for nothing."

Daniel nodded. He couldn't imagine death ever being easy. Not since he buried his wife, Daisy, and their baby last fall.

The two marshals mounted, and Bass shifted in his saddle to

open his saddlebag. He withdrew a folded sheet of paper and handed it to Daniel.

"I come to give you this." Bass tapped the crisp paper. It was a new warrant. "I was tracking that man, but you know the territory he headed into real good. I gotta git on back to Fort Smith to testify at a trial. I'll take our friend here with me."

A gust of icy wind whistled through the woods and Daniel held the warrant open with both gloved hands. He read the description of the crime and jerked his head up to meet Bass' eyes.

His mentor shook his head, rubbing gloved knuckles on his horse's neck. "Son, you gonna see more of the worst of mankind than you ever wanted on this job."

Daniel crumpled the warrant in his fist. He'd have to fight to keep a cool head while tracking someone accused of killing a woman. "You say the man is headed into familiar territory?"

"Yep. He ain't likely to leave Indian Territory, but he's making tracks south, deep into Choctaw country."

Daniel slowly spread the warrant out again and stared at the details of the crime. He wanted to catch this man, but he hoped he didn't have to face his own past to do it. Daniel hadn't spent much time among his people since October.

He did miss them. And he missed the family he'd married into, especially his closest friend and cousin-in-law, Matthew Teller. Matthew was the only one he could still face after the fever that took Daisy and the baby.

There was no stopping death.

CHAPTER 3

$\mathscr{I}$n the Enterprise Hotel restaurant, Matthew sipped coffee while holding a copy of the *Dickens Herald*, reading rapidly. It was Saturday, and businessmen, travelers, and families jammed every table. Matthew didn't normally read his rival's newspaper in public places, but since the *Dickens Herald* had gone to a daily edition to match the *Choctaw Tribune*, Matthew had to snatch every chance he could. He needed to know what Christopher Maxwell was printing more than ever now after the shadow man threatened him three days ago in Fort Smith.

Matthew wouldn't be at the restaurant at all, but he needed to make time to meet Daniel for the noon meal. Daniel had left a note at the shop that morning while Matthew was out, asking to meet at the restaurant. Since it was the first time Daniel had been in Dickens since last fall, Matthew figured it was important.

Matthew had many things on his desk that needed tending after the trip, and time was an unrelenting task master. But lunch was the least he could do for his cousin-in-law.

Daniel had been out of town when Matthew was in Fort Smith, and he hadn't seen him for a month, not since Daniel's first successful apprehension of an outlaw. Or lack thereof, depending on one's point of view. The man was dead, killed by Daniel while resisting arrest.

From the corner of his eye, Matthew caught sight of a tall, sapling thin figure making his way through the circus of tables. Daniel reached Matthew's table and threw his long leg over the back of the empty chair. He landed with a thump and grin. "There's a rumor you're buying the town lunch today."

Matthew took a gulp of the cooled coffee. "Don't you believe it."

"How are you, Matt?"

"Fine, last I checked. You?"

"Fair enough."

Matthew didn't buy it. "How about the truth, brother?"

Daniel sighed, his jovial facade dropping off. No longer the fresh-faced, awkward boy who married Uncle Preston's only daughter a few years ago, Daniel looked haggard and aged.

"Always stuck on the truth, aren't you, Matt? Don't let it get you killed someday."

Daniel unfurled the napkin at his place setting and tucked it in the collar of his shirt. "Why do you risk so much for truth? You're only one man, and not one responsible for the whole Choctaw Nation."

Matthew folded the *Dickens Herald*. He was only halfway through, but it was time to focus on his cousin. "Have you ever heard how important one nail is?"

Daniel crossed his arms on the table, leaning forward. "You always tell a good story."

"It's more of a proverb. It goes, 'For want of a nail, the shoe was lost. For want of a shoe, the horse was lost. For want of a horse, the rider was lost. For want of a rider, the battle was lost. For want of a battle, the kingdom was lost. And all for the want of a nail.'"

Matthew sat back in his chair, using his thumb to crease the familiar newspaper edge as he'd done thousands of times with the *Choctaw Tribune*. "One person not doing their job can cost the whole war. Or, from the other perspective, one person doing theirs can turn the battle and save the kingdom."

Daniel smiled, features softening, and Matthew knew he would be all right in body and soul. Not all the way today, but someday.

"That's why I like talking to you, Matt. You've got answers that makes sense of life."

Matthew tossed the newspaper to the empty chair beside him. "I'm not always right."

"I've never known you to be wrong."

Before Matthew could list his failings, young Glenrose Jessop came to their table. She was dressed in the hotel's uniform, a light gray wool dress covered with a lace-trimmed apron. She'd recently gone to work as a waitress, taking shifts after school and Saturdays, and was blossoming in the public atmosphere. Matthew's cousin, Peter, had noticed lately. Peter took nearly every evening meal at the hotel these days.

A writing pad and pencil in hand, Glenrose addressed the men with a naturally sweet lilt to her Texas drawl. "What can I get for you, Mr. Teller, and Marshal Garvin, ain't it? We got a ham steak special today."

Daniel smoothed his napkin over his shirt. "Yes, ma'am. But I got to ask—do you have any ham from the left side of the hog?"

Matthew rested his elbows on the table and steepled his hands in front of his mouth to hide the smile sprouting there. Daniel was gearing up to pull off a story on the girl.

Glenrose flushed, her pencil touching the tablet, then lifting away. "I, um, I'm not sure. I can check if it's mighty important."

Daniel spread his hands wide as though preparing to impart great wisdom. "Well, young lady, back when I worked on a ranch, I watched those pigs scratching. Most of them are right hoofed, of course, and they use their back right foot to scratch with. It stands to reason that side builds up a lot of muscle, and that's no good for eating. That's why I always order ham from the left side of a hog."

Glenrose slowly nodded as she stepped away from the table. "I'll check."

When she left, Matthew shook his head. "I can't believe you did that to her."

Daniel shrugged, grinning. "When I started at your uncle's ranch, I didn't even know which end of a branding iron was hot." His lips turned down and he twirled the knife on the white tablecloth. "With a gun, I sure do."

Matthew settled back in his chair. This could be a long conversation, but at least Ruth Ann was working at the newspaper shop today. He saw less of her in there these days as she prepared to wed her fiancé, Benjamin Nakishi-Dunn.

Matthew still hadn't gotten accustomed to the idea of his baby sister getting married. That life change would take her from the *Choctaw Tribune* and to her new life in McAlester. Benjamin practiced law out of the Tobucksy County Courthouse there.

Matthew didn't know what he'd do without her in the shop. No one could replace Annie when it came to running the newspaper.

But there was time to figure it out. The wedding wasn't until June, and Daniel needed him in the current moment. For such a young man, his brows creased deep. Matthew understood that feeling—the heaviness of life and death.

"When I got your note this morning that you were in Dickens, I figured something bad happened," Matthew said. "You haven't been here in awhile."

Daniel stared at the knife, catching glints of sunlight streaming through the large picture windows. He spoke low.

"I killed a man a few days ago. Had the drop on him, figured sure he wouldn't try to fight, but he did. No chance of just winging him. I shot him dead. Dead."

Daniel blinked and rubbed a hand over his mouth. "I haven't brought a man in alive yet. After the first, one of the old timers started calling me Dead Man Dan."

"That's rough."

Daniel sighed heavily. "No wise answers?"

Matthew pinched his lips together. He'd liked Daniel from the time they met, but after helping rescue Daniel in the Red River bordering Uncle Preston's ranch, they were bonded for life.

Matthew vividly recalled that Christmas Eve and the look of life and death in Daniel's eyes as the young man clenched the rope wrapped around his chest in the rising floodwaters where he was trapped in quicksand. Matthew was in a wagon stuck in the river, holding onto the rope. The rope wasn't doing any good. Daniel was sinking in the quicksand.

Still, he looked straight at Matthew and said, *"Please don't let go."*

Matthew hadn't. He never would. But all he could offer Daniel now was his compassion.

The mood was broken when Glenrose Jessop came back to the table, carrying two plates ladened with ham steaks, mashed potatoes, and peas. She gave Daniel a sweet smile.

"Yours came from the left side of the hog, and there's only an extra ten cent charge."

Daniel eyed the ham as she walked away. Matthew chuckled. "You had that coming."

Daniel smiled as he cut into the thick ham. "I know you're busy, but I'm glad you could meet me today, Matt." He heaved in a sigh. "Two days ago, Bass Reeves turned a warrant over to me, and I tracked the man to here. But it's hard being in the area again, you know?"

"I do."

Daniel rested his knife and fork against the plate and met Matthew's eyes. "Still, I reckon it's like you said, just being that one nail. If I can do my part to make Indian Territory a civilized place to live, that's a life worth living. I want this man, bad, Matt. Bad enough to track him here. He's suspected of killing a woman in Fort Smith Wednesday night." He clenched his jaw.

Matthew's mind wandered to how he was still in Fort Smith Wednesday night, watching shadows. "You said it happened in Fort Smith?"

"At a little farm outside of town. The husband was away, Bass said. The killer…he violated then strangled her to death."

Matthew swallowed the bile that rose at the back of his throat. He didn't envy Daniel his job. "You'll get him."

Daniel tapped his knife on the edge of his plate. "I'll try to bring him in for trial, but I know partly what Mr. Bellanger is feeling."

Matthew went cold. "Did you say *Bellanger?*"

Daniel's eyebrows furrowed. "Yeah, John Bellanger, near Fort Smith. It was his wife. You know him?"

Matthew's tongue lay thick in his mouth. "I met him a few days ago. Wednesday to be exact."

Daniel's eyebrows bunched together again. "Did you see his wife?"

Matthew hesitated, measuring his words. "Briefly. Bellanger was involved with Christopher Maxwell, and the other men who founded Dickens."

"So, you talked to Bellanger and his wife on Wednesday before she was killed?"

"She told me to go to the Palace in Hot Springs, but to be careful. Men have died over what I'm investigating."

Daniel's jaw twitched. He shook his head. "You're always stuck on finding the truth, even if it kills you. Well, you might be called to testify after I bring the suspect in. Anything else happen while you were in Fort Smith?"

"Nothing worth mentioning." *Other than a man threatened to kill me.* Matthew didn't say the last part aloud.

He had no way of knowing if the shadow man was connected

to the murder of Mrs. Bellanger, but it was a sharp coincidence. Once Matthew figured out what Maxwell was doing, it could connect him even. But there was nothing useful in that for Daniel. He needed to stay on the killer's trail and bring him in—dead or alive.

Daniel accepted Matthew's vague answer as he picked at his ham steak. Then he pushed away from the table. "I best get back to asking questions, see if anyone in town knows anything. I lost the trail near here—too much population."

Matthew agreed with that sentiment. Too many settling in his people's nation.

Matthew stood with Daniel and clasped his cousin's shoulder. "God go with you, brother."

Daniel half-smiled. "That would be nice."

He started to reach for the tab Glenrose left with their food, but Matthew snagged it. "Some rumors have basis in truth. And like you said, I'm stuck on that."

Daniel chuckled softly as he returned Matthew's handshake. "Just don't let it get in the way of staying alive."

After Daniel left, Matthew finished eating while he tried to read the *Dickens Herald*. But he couldn't concentrate, thinking of how fearful Mrs. Bellanger looked a few days ago. Now she was dead.

Matthew rolled up the *Dickens Herald* and tucked it under his arm. He'd finished reading later.

He left enough money on the table to cover both tabs, plus a tip and the extra ten cents for Glenrose.

Matthew wove his way through the tables and to the hotel door. When he pulled it open, he nearly bumped into a well-dressed woman coming inside.

It was Dorothy Maxwell, Christopher Maxwell's young wife.

She looked up in surprise, then her eyelids lowered coyly. She wore heavy rouge and lipstick, a fur wrap covering her shoulders.

Matthew stepped back from the door, allowing a wide berth for Mrs. Maxwell to enter.

"Thank you, Matthew Teller. You are a true gentleman." Her voice was honey smooth as she breezed through the door and swept off her wrap. She wore a purple silk dress that dipped distractingly low in the front. "Won't you join me for a cup of coffee and dessert?"

This wasn't the first time she'd given Matthew this sort of invitation. The worst was last December at a community Christmas party. She'd been drinking, though no one would outright say it, especially since alcohol was illegal in the Choctaw Nation. At one point, she trapped Matthew against a wall, and he had to escape to the other side of the room.

Now, Matthew tipped his hat briskly. "No, ma'am."

He exited and closed the door securely behind him. He wondered if Christopher Maxwell was putting his wife up to harassing him to agitate his rival. If so, it was working.

CHAPTER 4

The family was at the Teller home when Matthew arrived after closing up the shop. His mother, Della, was in the kitchen with Ruth Ann as they prepared dinner while Peter and Benjamin Nakishi-Dunn wisely waited in the living room. Peter had his boots propped on the coffee table. Matthew decided to leave it up to his mother to whack him with a spoon if she wanted.

The rules around the box house had gotten more lax over the past several months. There was still the shadow of grief over the passing of Daisy and her baby. Matthew got on to Peter when he needed it, but overall, he found himself leaving his cousin alone to grieve in his own way over his sister's death.

Peter hadn't lost his jovial spirit, but it was subdued. There was something else going on beneath the surface, and Matthew suspected it had to do with the girl working at the hotel restaurant. Matthew would alert Uncle Preston about it soon. The father and son needed to talk.

Matthew wished for a chance to talk to his uncle, too, but Preston's grief was so deep over the passing of his only daughter that there was an unspoken consensus in the family to not burden him with personal troubles.

But there was someone tonight that Matthew could talk to about the recent events.

Matthew didn't take off his coat as he went to stand by the fire to warm his hands. Benjamin was settled on the couch by Peter, reading that day's edition of the *Choctaw Tribune*. Benjamin folded it as he looked up at Matthew.

"How was your trip to Fort Smith?"

Matthew flexed his fingers to take in heat from the fire. Instead of answering, he asked Peter, "Stock been fed yet?"

Peter slapped his forehead. "You know, Matt, I clean forgot that Ruth Ann isn't taking care of the animals this week. Too busy sewing on a new dress, I suppose."

Peter winked at Benjamin, who took it in stride as he stood. "I'll give you a hand, Matthew."

Matthew nodded, his respect for Benjamin going up a notch. He understood Matthew's hint at having a private conversation.

To avoid disrupting the work in the kitchen, Matthew and Benjamin went out the front door and around the house to the barn.

Matthew waited until they were inside before he said, "When I was at the courthouse in Fort Smith, a man put a gun to my head."

Benjamin halted by the stalls and stared down at him; he was several inches taller than Matthew. It wasn't until Matthew met Benjamin that he wished he had a more imposing frame. But Benjamin never used it to intimidate. That was probably why God hadn't given one to Matthew.

Benjamin looked him up and down as though checking to see if he was hurt. "What happened?"

Matthew took up the pitchfork to toss hay into Falama's stall. The stallion was antsy from not being out on a good run in awhile. Matthew understood the feeling. Too much train riding for him and not enough time in the saddle.

While he pitched hay and Benjamin scooped grain, Matthew relayed the shadow man's threat, then the brief encounter with the Bellangers. He ended with how he learned Mrs. Bellanger was killed the evening after he was there.

Benjamin said nothing as they finished feeding the horses. Matthew leaned against the edge of the stall, resting his hands on the top of the pitchfork. "I would appreciate if you didn't mention this to the family. You and Ruth Ann have good things to talk about, not the trouble her brother is getting into."

Benjamin smiled. "Just this once, brother. Once she and I are married, I will not be able to keep secrets."

Matthew chuckled. "Fair enough."

Benjamin sobered and rested his large hand on Matthew's shoulder. "Are you well?"

Matthew started to reply with a quick *yes*. But Benjamin's probing gaze didn't allow that. He wasn't talking about the threat or Matthew's work or the investigation. This was about Daisy.

He swallowed, surprised at the burn in the back of his throat. Tears. Hadn't he shed them all at the *yaya*? Hadn't everyone? Tears flowed like a flooded river that day.

But his focus was keeping Daniel on his feet. Focused on taking care of the family's grief. Matthew didn't give in fully to his own then. Same as when his father and—at the time he believed—his brother were killed. Daisy's passing was another time he set aside his own grief, but here it was, roaring in his ears and causing his eyes to mist.

Matthew stabbed the pitchfork into the haystack and jammed his thumb and finger over his closed eyelids, drawing in a deep breath. This wasn't the time to grieve, not with his future brother-in-law to witness his undoing.

Matthew dropped his hand. "We grew up together on the

ranch. Daisy and Annie were close. But I'm all right, it's everyone else I worry about."

Benjamin squeezed Matthew's shoulder with the strength of the athlete he was. "God knows your grief, too."

That nearly did it, but Matthew held on and simply nodded.

He never thought there would be a man in the world he would trust his baby sister to. But this Benjamin Nakishi-Dunn was a good man. He was the one.

Benjamin released his grip, his expression still solemn on his dark-toned features. "On the other matter, I know your investigation is important for our nation, but do not make it personal. It is difficult to win a case that way."

Though this wasn't a pleasant topic, Matthew gladly accepted the shift of focus. And considering Benjamin was the finest lawyer in the territory, Matthew respected his advice. But it was hard to define the burning in his heart to tear this town out of Christopher Maxwell's schemes.

After securing the barn, they headed for the kitchen door, passing the new cellar doors that sat beside the stoop. Benjamin and Peter had helped Matthew dig the cellar for Della before cold weather set in. She appreciated being able to store the food she brought home from the ranch.

Coming into the kitchen, the men were immediately scolded by Ruth Ann for letting cold air in over her freshly baked pie. At least, she scolded Matthew. Benjamin could get away with anything.

Matthew didn't mind the glow emanating from his sister since she returned from D.C., but he did feel a stab of sadness at the thought of her leaving the *Choctaw Tribune*. He'd set out to do the newspaper on his own, but he'd never have made it without her. Someday, he needed to tell her that.

While Matthew and Benjamin were in the barn, the Levitts had arrived for dinner and Matthew greeted Mr. Levitt and Beulah as they came in from the living room.

Della quietly nodded for Matthew and Benjamin to clean up at the wash basin as she placed a pot of *tanchi labona* on a thick woven mat on the table.

Matthew noticed his mother cooking more traditional dishes of their people in recent months, like this hominy mixed with pork roast. Della went about her work quieter than usual.

Daisy's passing was hard on her. She'd spent weeks with her ailing niece and baby, and was at their bedside when first the baby, then Daisy, slipped away. And Della was still grieving Philip being in prison, and the separation from her only granddaughter, Nita.

The Tellers had made several attempts to contact Kat Russell, Philip's former girlfriend. But with him in prison, she had sole rights to their child and seemed bent on cutting her Choctaw relations out.

Family was a complicated thing.

After everyone settled at the table and the blessing was given by Benjamin, the conversation turned to the joyful topic of the wedding. Dominated by Ruth Ann and Beulah, there was plenty to discuss with having a ceremony at the church then a traditional Choctaw one at Uncle Preston's ranch.

At a break in the two young women's chatter, Peter declared, "If it causes all this fussing, I won't never get married."

Ruth Ann rolled her eyes and Matthew noticed she had pretty curls framing her face. Normally after a day's work at the *Choctaw Tribune*, she didn't bother with fluffing up for dinner. But things had changed.

"Is that why you spend so much time at the hotel restaurant, always asking for a certain waitress?" Ruth Ann teased Peter.

Peter held his hands up in defense, but the teasing continued into dessert.

The chatter sounded like a lot of chaos to Matthew, but that was partly because he wasn't trying to follow along. His mind was on his investigation and the fact that a woman killer could be nearby. There was no way to bring that delicately into the conversation, but the women needed to know sometime.

It wasn't lost on Matthew how quiet Della remained after she dished out pie for everyone but herself. Since Philip's trial and sentencing, his mother had retreated into herself.

When she sat again, head of the table to his right, he caught her hand and held it. She let it rest there awhile before withdrawing to refill Ruth Ann's teacup. The three of them sat close at every meal.

Beulah asked Ruth Ann something about trimming for her dress. Ruth Ann gasped in the way Matthew recognized when something she deemed vital caught her attention.

"I forgot! I left the samples in the telegraph office. I'll run over and grab them so you can—"

"No!" Matthew hadn't meant to bark the word, but out it came.

Everyone turned their attention to him. He steadied his voice, keeping his tone firm. "No women should go anywhere alone, especially after dark." He glanced at Benjamin, who nodded that Matthew should go on. He didn't have to tell them about the shadow man, but they did need to know about the other threat.

"Daniel's in the area tracking a…a very dangerous outlaw. Besides, this town is getting bigger every day and we don't know everyone anymore." He eyed his sister. "Not that there weren't dangers even when we did."

Ruth Ann's gaze dropped to her half-eaten pie. Neither she nor Matthew had told anyone about the time she brought a late-night dinner to the old shack that served as the first *Choctaw Tribune* office. Christopher Maxwell had cornered Ruth Ann in the dark and by the time Matthew came out to see what was going on, his sister was flushed and flustered. She looked that way now with her fiancé seated beside her.

Time to change the subject.

"We have to stay involved with the growth of this town,"

Matthew said. "I spoke with Mr. Bates this morning and he declined my recommendation to run for mayor. He's too busy with the store and says being on the city council is enough for him."

This wasn't a much better topic, but Ruth Ann looked relieved at the turn. Then she frowned. She'd always been fond of Mr. Bates and had made the suggestion that Matthew ask him about running for mayor this summer. "I wish he would reconsider."

Beulah chimed in her agreement. "Mr. Bates is just what this town needs. Mayor Higgins is, well, he's such a fragile old gentleman, and it is wise for him to retire from the position early. We need someone with strength who can lead this town in a new direction, and not one that includes annexing," she ended firmly.

Matthew couldn't agree more, but he didn't need to bring his passion and troubles to the dinner table.

He met Ruth Ann's gaze across from him and felt a fresh wave of uncertainty. How could he continue the fight without her?

She must have understood because her expression came alive with a fire he hadn't seen in awhile. That could mean disaster or triumph for them. He'd welcome either as long as they faced it together.

"Matt, I just had the most brilliant idea, and don't you dare try to talk me out of it," Ruth Ann said in one breath. "Our people need the truth like never before, and with the Tobucksy County Courthouse trying so many cases dealing with our sovereignty, we're missing stories everyday." Her eyes flashed brilliantly with delight and determination.

"After the wedding and with Benjamin's support, I want to start a branch of the *Choctaw Tribune* in McAlester."

CHAPTER 5

Christopher Maxwell shoved another log into his white marble fireplace, bringing the flames ablaze again. It was past midnight, but he could be in the parlor for awhile. He didn't like having meetings in his home, but with the expansion of the *Dickens Herald*, he no longer had total control over his employees.

Total control was something he was determined to regain.

If not for Matthew Teller, the portrait of Christopher Maxwell's life would be perfect: Thaddeus Warren, Jake Banny, and Josiah Carter would still be under his thumb as they ran Dickens exactly how he wanted. Their establishments and investments would be secure and profitable. All his plans would have set him up for dominance the remainder of a long and happy life.

But along came Matthew Teller.

Uncovered Thaddeus Warren's sordid past and caused him to flee town. Shot Jake Banny deader than a doornail, pardon the Dickens' pun. Infused Josiah Carter's backbone with enough gumption to start over in St. Louis with his young bride. And set Christopher Maxwell's investments back to the point of no return.

Actually, the stock market crash of '93 had done that.

These were all things Christopher could overcome. He had solid relationships with new investors and plenty to tempt them with in Indian Territory. Timber and coal. Land galore. Progress with new technology like the telephone. And there was his personal favorite on the cusp of becoming a reality in the next year.

But there was Matthew Teller.

The stubborn publisher of the *Choctaw Tribune* was the reason for this clandestine meeting in Christopher's own home, an incriminating location. But his hired man had insisted on it.

There was only one person in the house to overhear the conversation, and she wouldn't be coming downstairs. Not on her own two feet. Dorothy was either in bed asleep or nursing the bottle she kept in the nightstand. He didn't care which.

The flames popped, but Christopher detected light tapping on the window to the right of the fireplace. A tree branch? No. Something else.

He went to the end table by the red velvet sofa and picked up the pistol he had laid there. He tucked it in the waistband of his trousers under his evening coat and went to the window. This wasn't the normal way to let people in his house. But this was no normal person.

Christopher turned down the gas lamp before unlocking the window and raising it silently. The curtain blew out straight from the cold wind and Christopher took a step back. He blinked and the dark window produced a black boot and then, almost magically, an entire man had slipped through the window and stood in his parlor.

The man, dressed in solid black, pulled the window closed, hat shadowing his face.

Christopher growled, "You were supposed to kill Matthew Teller. Why didn't you? And why did you kill Bellanger's wife?"

The man moved to the fireplace and pulled off his black gloves. He pocketed them and extended his hands to the warmth. His posture spoke of his cockiness which Christopher despised.

When he'd brought this man into his plans, he knew there was no way of controlling him. He was a killer who picked his own targets and timing.

But that didn't work in Christopher's schemes. He needed Matthew Teller out of the way before his next announcement to solidify control of Dickens and secure it for his cautious investors.

It was time for the original plan he set in motion years ago to come to fulfillment. There was no one to stop him. No one but Matthew Teller.

The black-clothed man took his time rubbing his hands together and turning them this way and that. When he spoke, he drew each word out like he enjoyed the taste of them on his tongue.

"You ever read the Bible, Chris?"

Christopher never allowed anyone to call him *Chris*. But he was more annoyed with the man's stupid question. "What does that have to do with you not killing Teller in Fort Smith?"

The man turned his back to the fire, facing Christopher. His eyes were in the darkness, shadowed by the brim of his hat. "Even if you haven't read the Bible, you go to church on Easter Sunday, don't ya?"

Christopher pressed his lips tight. The man smiled. "At some point, I'm sure you heard the story of the Romans crucifying Jesus Christ. You ever stop to think why they did that, Chris? After all, crucifixion wasn't the most efficient way of putting someone to death. They could have done it easy, cut off his head like John the Baptist. But no. They took their time, putting spikes through his flesh, then lifting him up in disgrace for the whole world to see. He hung there for hours in shame."

The man leaned to one side, relaxed as his coat opened enough for Christopher to see the six-gun tied low.

"The point of the crucifixion wasn't simply death, Chris. It was torture. But it wasn't just the physical torture that got to Jesus Christ. Imagine, the Son of God stripped naked and hung on display for the world to see."

A chill went through Christopher. He crossed his arms to not show it.

The man pushed his hat up his forehead enough for Christopher to see his brown eyes. They gleamed with delight. At the same time, they shimmered in pain. This man was a wild animal preparing to rend apart the creature that had wounded him.

The man smiled. "I don't intend to just kill Matthew Teller. I intend to crucify him."

CHAPTER 6

It was freezing when church let out Sunday morning. No one lingered as the cold wind attempted to rip away hats and scarves as the mixed congregation headed for horses, buggies, or the short walk to their homes in Dickens. The First Baptist Church of Dickens sat on a little hill in an unpopulated section of town with a field around it and a cemetery to one side. That was populating, too.

Staying near the warmth of the church's stove, Matthew watched his family go on out, taking turns to shake the pastor's hand. Benjamin would look after Della and Ruth Ann until he needed to return on the afternoon train to McAlester.

Through the open doorway, Matthew noticed Peter mounting up and riding south, but not on the road to the family ranch. He disappeared most Sundays lately and no one questioned where he went. Not yet.

But that wasn't why Matthew held back to speak privately with Pastor Rand. The conversation at dinner last night had kept Matthew awake in his room most of the night.

He wouldn't dream of talking Annie out of her bold declaration to start a branch of the *Choctaw Tribune* in McAlester. Her idea kindled a fire in him, a feeling of freshness and starting over. But too much of the past weighed him down, memories of the opposition he faced when launching the newspaper. That opposition wouldn't let go even now.

Matthew watched until Pastor Rand shook his last congregates's hand and snuggly closed the door. He turned and caught sight of Matthew, grinning in surprise.

"Well, Matthew Teller, don't want to face that frosty weather just yet?"

Matthew waited patiently by the stove while Pastor Rand gathered hymnals and carried them into the back room of the church that also served as a schoolhouse for white children in the area. There was talk of building a bigger school. This one was filled to capacity.

They may have to add on to the church as well, but there was enough room for now. New churches were being built as other denominations established their place in Dickens. Matthew didn't imagine going to any church except Pastor Rand's. He trusted him for sound spiritual wisdom, and that was what Matthew needed today.

Pastor Rand finished with the hymnals and went to the pulpit to re-stack the papers from his sermon. He had his routine that he went through after services, so Matthew only helped him move the pulpit to the back corner of the room, leaving everything ready for school the next morning.

Pastor Rand motioned to the pew nearest the stove and sank onto it with a heavy sigh. "How exhausting are Sunday sermons on a cold day like this. It takes a lot of heat to light a fire under people!"

Matthew sat next to him. Pastor Rand folded his hands in his lap. "What can I do for you, Matthew?"

Matthew waited a few more moments, letting his heart settle, then said, "I want to talk to you about tearing this town apart."

Pastor Rand raised his eyebrows. "I could use a few details before offering counsel."

"I don't mean literally, but if Christopher Maxwell is successful in annexing Dickens, it will effect tribal sovereignty. We are already facing one of the greatest challenges my people have known, what with Senator Dawes pushing forward with his census."

Matthew ground his fist in his palm. Pastor Rand was a white man, but he was vocal in his support of tribal sovereignty. In private, the two men knew it was a battle the nation would ultimately lose.

Still, Matthew had a personal stake in the fight. Yet Benjamin was right—he couldn't make it personal.

But how could he separate the two?

Matthew kept his fist pressed into his palm. He wanted to strike something but met Pastor Rand's gaze instead. "There were four men who started this town—Josiah Carter, Thaddeus Warren, Jake Banny, and Christopher Maxwell. Carter is in St. Louis, Warren in prison, Banny..." Matthew didn't need to say the rest. He'd killed Jake Banny himself.

"That leaves one, Christopher Maxwell, and I've always suspected he was the leader ever since I worked for him at the *Dickens Herald*. He doesn't have to share control with anyone else now. I have to stop him from filing to annex this town."

Pastor Rand had held Matthew's gaze steady through his discourse. He asked quietly, "Is it justice or revenge you're seeking?"

Matthew broke eye contact and leaned forward to rest his elbows on his knees. The answer should be obvious, but it wasn't, not even to himself.

"How can you know?"

Pastor Rand rubbed his hands together. "Have you forgiven those men for what they've done to you?"

Matthew stared at the pastor's hands that weren't afraid of

physical labor yet remained gentle in guiding his flock. Matthew likely needed the shepherd's crook used on himself more than not.

He sighed. "I can't honestly say I have. My only excuse is that I could never prove the things they did—burning down my print shop, and later, having me shot."

"What about what you know for certain, all they've done to your people, and that Maxwell is still trying to do?"

Matthew interlaced his fingers to keep from balling his hands into fists. He thought he'd overcome his battle with offering forgiveness when he forgave his brother Philip. Wasn't all of this supposed to be behind him?

"No. I have not forgiven any of them for anything."

Pastor Rand settled a hand on Matthew's shoulder, warming it beneath his coat. "You need to forgive before you seek justice, otherwise you can be certain it's revenge. If you first forgive, no matter the outcome in the battle, the war has been won."

The war has been won. Was forgiveness the nail he was in want of to save the kingdom?

Pastor Rand went to his pulpit in the corner, coming back with his Bible. He had the book open and started reading as he retook his seat on the pew. His voice didn't change from his conversational tone.

"But I say unto you, Love your enemies, bless them that curse you, do good to them that hate you, and pray for them which despitefully use you, and persecute you; That ye may be the children of your Father which is in heaven: for he maketh his sun to rise on the evil and on the good, and sendeth rain on the just and on the unjust."

How easy it was to read those passages when Matthew was growing up. He never had enemies until he started the *Choctaw Tribune*, never had one who cursed him, hated and persecuted and despitefully used him. Christopher Maxwell had done all the above.

Love, bless, pray. How impossible that seemed, especially with all the real work he had to do each day.

God knows.

Matthew rubbed his chin with his interlocked knuckles. "It's not what I wanted to hear, but what I needed, I guess. Thank you."

They stood and Pastor Rand walked Matthew to the door. Matthew stepped outside in the frigid air, turning back to shake the pastor's hand. Pastor Rand held on a moment.

"One more thing, Matthew, about tearing apart this town. Be careful you are not doing what God did not give you to do."

CHAPTER 7

"Lance! Lance Fuller!"

Peter rounded the old Warren home so fast he felt his horse's hooves slipping beneath him. His father would tear him up for riding a horse so hard, but this was an emergency.

The trusty little mare regained her balance as Peter pushed her to the front porch.

The door swung open and Glenrose Jessop hurried out. She'd changed from her Sunday dress to kitchen clothes, a large apron covering her blue gingham dress. She stared wide-eyed at him. "Peter Frazier! What on earth is the matter?"

Peter gulped cold air, mindful he'd never see his jacket again. No time to mourn that if he wanted to keep himself from being buried six feet under.

"Where's Lance?"

Glenrose gripped the porch rail. "He's at the school getting ready for tomorrow. What happened?"

Peter leapt off his horse and looked around, clenching the reins in one hand. Not much cover in the yard. "I gotta hide. I got real live gunmen after me!"

Glenrose gasped. "Get inside, then. Hurry!"

Peter turned toward the stairs, but still held his reins. "They'll see my horse."

Glenrose beckoned at him with both hands. "Bring her in, too!"

Peter stared up at Glenrose on the porch, her cute little freckled face all tight with concern and bravery. He made up his mind right then he was going to marry this gal someday.

Peter tossed the reins at her which she caught and used to guide the horse's head in while he urged the mare on from behind to climb the stairs. Once they cleared the doorway and barged into the foyer, Peter kicked the door closed and followed Glenrose as she led his horse straight into the fancy parlor.

He gulped, wondering if Amarillo was home. She'd shoot him for sure, what with his horse soiling the rug with muddy hooves.

"What if…"

"Shhh." Glenrose put one finger to her lips and hurried to the double front window. Peter had to say, he didn't mind being protected by this little gal.

She glanced out then quickly undid the heavy burgundy drape on one side and let it fall, covering part of the window. Peter did the same on the other side. He peeked through the middle of the drapes, but Glenrose pushed him back.

"There are men looking around out front. Stay quiet."

They stood stock still a few minutes, then Glenrose peeked through the drapes again.

She breathed a sigh of relief. "They're leaving."

Peter came up behind her, but not too close. Glenrose's older sister, Amarillo, was the feisty one in the family, but Glenrose could take care of herself. She just proved it.

She turned and looked up at him. "What did you do, commit a crime?"

Peter ran his tongue over his teeth, stalling. "Define 'crime.'"

He had probably broken more than one law that day by

gambling *and* doing it on a Sunday. But this was the only day Peter had to himself with no one asking where he was. Lance Fuller's shadowed past was the reason Peter had run to him for help instead of Matthew. Besides, those men didn't know who Peter was or where he lived, and he planned to keep it that way.

Glenrose frowned at his answer, then looked beyond him and gasped. He turned to see his horse munching on a small table doily.

The mare took the doily in her teeth and lifted her head, pulling the cloth out from under teacups and whatnots. They crashed to the rug and one teacup busted in half.

The young people rushed up to the horse, succeeding in spooking her backward. The horse kicked the sofa, breaking one leg. The horrific crash echoed in the room.

"What in the name of heaven is going on here!" a man's voice shouted from the foyer.

Peter grabbed his horse's bridle and rubbed a calming hand down her face as she snorted. He dared to look over his shoulder. Lance Fuller was planted in the parlor doorway, glaring at the horse. Glenrose snagged the mare on the other side of the bridle to keep her from skittering forward. At least Glenrose was between Peter and Lance.

Peter stammered, "I, um, I came to call on Glenrose."

She whipped her face around to glare at him, blonde ponytail flipping into her face. Peter kept his attention on Lance.

Peter swallowed hard. "You're going to shoot me, ain't you?"

Lance dragged a hand down his face and held it over his mouth, tapping one finger against it. His eyes flamed. "Not without giving it careful consideration first. Now get that horse out of here."

Peter and Glenrose kept the horse between them as they awkwardly maneuvered out of the parlor and to the front door.

Once outside, they clattered down the steps. When they halted, Peter ducked to look at Glenrose beneath his horse's head.

"Don't say nothing about those men being after me, would you? I don't want Matthew finding out what I did."

Glenrose planted her hands on her hips. "The way I see it, you're still in trouble with me. What did you do exactly?"

Peter stayed hunched down. It was better to keep the horse between him and Glenrose. "Well, I might have heard there were gamblers down by the Red River, and I might have bet them that I could jump thirty-three feet."

Glenrose closed her eyes. "You didn't."

"Hey, everyone around here has seen me do it so I needed fresh game. I didn't really plan on taking their money, but they were so surly, well, I figured the wealth of the wicked is laid up for the righteous, ain't it?"

Glenrose shook her head. "And then you did it—you jumped one-third of three feet, took their money, and now they wanna kill you."

Peter twisted his mouth. "Well, when you put it that way...I best get out to the ranch for a few days. Don't tell on me, please? Matthew and Daddy wouldn't be happy to hear I was gambling."

Glenrose sighed. "Promise me you'll stay out of trouble?"

Peter grinned and straightened to talk to her in front of his horse's head. "The next trouble I'm getting into is asking you to marry me."

Glenrose rolled her eyes and pushed the horse toward him. "Go on, now. I got to get the house cleaned up and get the noon meal on the table before Amarillo gets back from the Levitts."

Peter tipped his hat to her, mounted, and rode away from Dickens in the opposite direction of those men.

At least Glenrose didn't know the real trouble he was in.

CHAPTER 8

inter wouldn't let go.

Remnants of Sunday's storm lingered in the overcast sky. Sharp winds gusted through town as Matthew mounted the steps of the Dickens depot. The southbound train let out a long whistle, alerting the depot of its arrival.

This train carried the eastern newspapers he subscribed to, and he liked meeting at least one of the six trains that came through Dickens each day. There was always news or excitement with each train's arrival.

Today might prove an exception, though. Through the window of the depot, Matthew noted only a few people waiting to catch this train. They huddled around the stove, leaving the platform clear of activity.

The wind blew leftover rain droplets like needles through the air and into Matthew's face. He tucked himself under the depot's overhang and shoved his gloved hands in the pockets of his heavy overcoat, rocking back-and-forth on his heels as the train rumbled into the station.

After writing all morning, the short stroll to the depot was refreshing. But he needed to get back to the newspaper office right after he picked up the mail. It was the first day of the work week and he had to focus on the next step in his investigation—a trip to Hot Springs, Arkansas and the Palace. Today, he was making sure Ruth Ann had everything she needed to get the daily out while he was gone.

But the trip wasn't truly the next step he must take.

After his conversation with Pastor Rand, Matthew knew he had to consciously forgive the men who had built this town. Matthew might as well get started while the train engine puffed slowly by, brakes screeching and smoke belching from the stack.

The first man he could forgive was Jake Banny. But how did he go about forgiving a dead man? And there wasn't much Matthew could do to bless Jake Banny. Maybe he could take flowers to the man's grave when the weather warmed.

The train came to a stop and, out of habit, Matthew scanned the passenger cars lined up with the depot platform. It didn't look like anyone was disembarking. The waiting passengers inside the depot darted out and up the steps of the closest car.

Matthew sidled to the mail cart where porters were offloading sacks of mail. One of the boys handed Matthew a bundle addressed to the *Choctaw Tribune* and the Teller's home address across the road from the depot.

He thanked the boy and moved under the overhang to scan headlines on the top of the newspaper bundle. He knew most of this news thanks to their AP subscription that Ruth Ann obtained in D.C. last summer. But there was still something special about reading eastern newspapers with their sprawling banners and three-inch headline type.

The train whistled and chugged away. Matthew looked up, realizing he was standing in the cold when he could take the newspapers back to the office to read. He turned toward the steps situated at the other end of the depot but froze at the sight before him.

Under the marble gray sky, mist spitting from the clouds, two female passengers had disembarked from the train and now stood on the platform. They huddled together, staring at Matthew. He knew them both.

One was a young woman, sickly thin. The black veil over her face didn't hide her gaunt face, and her sunken eyes were worse than the last time Matthew had seen her.

Moving his gaze from those eyes, he looked down at the little girl who clutched the young woman's skirt, using the material like a bandanna to shield her nose and mouth from the wind. But those little eyes peeking above the fabric… soft and brown and fearless. A painful reflection of his brother's eyes.

Matthew slowly approached the mother and daughter pair.

"Miss Russell. We weren't expecting you."

Awkward words, but Matthew had to assume that Philip's old girlfriend, Kat Russell, and their little girl, Nita, were there to see the Tellers. Why else would they come to Dickens? Yet Kat Russell had made it clear that she didn't want her little girl around the Choctaw side of her family.

A carpetbag rested on the platform by them, indicating a short stay. Matthew waited for Kat to respond as he clutched the bundle of newspapers to keep from reaching out to his niece and frightening her. He was a stranger to her.

Kat's gloved hands hung loose at her sides, a white handkerchief balled in one. Her voice was raw and dull when she spoke. "I've come to find a home for my little girl."

Matthew twisted the newspapers, instinctively looking down at Nita, who didn't flinch.

Kat went on. "I'm sick, real sick. The doctor called it tuberculosis. I'm supposed to be in a hospital right now, but I had to come find a place for her. I don't want my mother to know nothin' about anything."

Matthew couldn't take his eyes off Nita's round face. The little girl captured and wouldn't let go of him with those precious brown eyes.

So many questions swirled in his mind at Kat's declaration, about what it would mean to take little Nita into their home and into their lives. But he didn't need to ask anything before he gave the family's answer.

"She's welcome with us. We'll raise her right."

Kat sucked in a deep breath, immediately causing a tremendous coughing fit that nearly sent her to her knees. She pressed the handkerchief to her mouth over the veil. Matthew stepped closer, reaching to take her elbow, to support her somehow. But she pulled back. Nita buried herself deep in her mother's skirt, but her upturned gaze didn't leave Matthew's face.

Kat's eyes overflowed with tears, and she spoke between gasps. "Raise her right? Like you were raised, that what you mean?"

She finally caught her breath and glared at him. "I hated you, Matthew Teller. I always thought if Philip hadn't had such a strict upbringing and an angel for a brother, we could settle down and everything would've been fine. But we were both fools."

Matthew swallowed back a flood of words, things he wanted to say to Kat Russell about her part in ripping the Teller family to pieces. She had as much to do with his daddy's death as Philip. But he set his jaw and let her speak her mind.

Kat took a trembling breath. "All that don't matter now. I just need to know my little girl will be cared for just like you said. After seeing your family at the trial and how gentle you all were, I guess I knew this was the place to bring her."

Matthew wanted to shout at this woman for all she had cost their family. All she had cost him. But her words about his family struck him and he couldn't say anything. Here was another person for him to figure out how to forgive.

He leaned down to pick up the carpetbag. "Come over to the house. Mama will welcome you."

Kat choked out a laugh and shook her head fiercely. "You

don't hear too good. I got tuberculosis. Besides, best I don't see no one else. I'm staying right here until the next train."

She tugged her skirt away from Nita, leaving the little girl's ruddy face bare, exposed to the cold wind and mist.

Nita craned her neck to look up as Kat said, "This is your uncle. He'll take care of you, so you go on with him."

Kat stepped toward the depot. Matthew wondered if the little girl would follow after her mother. But after a few moments of gazing into Nita's eyes, Kat turned and fled inside the depot.

Nita stood shivering, staring at the closed door. Her light gray shawl was no protection against this weather.

Matthew dropped the mail and carpetbag to the wet platform and shrugged off his overcoat. He swung it over Nita's head and draped it around her shoulders. She didn't move. He noticed the hem of her dress was fraying above her worn boots. His mother would sew a new dress for her right away, and he'd take her to Bates General Store and get new boots.

What else did she need? Matthew's heart pounded with a feeling he'd never experienced. He would get her anything, do anything for her.

Matthew squatted in front of Nita and pulled the large coat up under her chin. He fastened it as snugly as he could. She finally looked at him. He tried to smile steady and strong.

"Nita, I'm your uncle Matthew. You're going to live with me and my mama, that is, your grandmother, and your aunt Ruth Ann. We have a warm home across the road from here. Why don't we get you by the fire now?"

The little girl's nose had started to run, and Matthew reached in his pocket for a handkerchief. He carefully wiped her reddened nose like he did for his second cousins on Uncle Preston's ranch.

But this was nothing like that. This was his niece—Philip's little girl. The one he promised his brother he would look after, and teach her about her Choctaw heritage.

It was time to fulfill that promise.

Matthew picked up the carpetbag and mail in one hand as he straightened. He held his other hand wide open to Nita.

She looked at it a long moment as if considering her entire little life. Then she tucked her hand in his and squeezed tight in a way that made Matthew wonder if she would ever let go.

Lord, I forgive Kat Russell.

The Texas Pacific train engine jerked into motion before Matthew was able to sit down. He landed hard and straightened his coat and hat. In Paris, Texas, he'd nearly missed his transfer from the Frisco to the Texas Pacific. His mind was back home in Dickens as he fought guilt of leaving Nita after she'd had only one night in her new home.

Matthew watched the Paris train depot slip out of sight, replaced by dead pastureland. The train chugged toward Texarkana where he would switch to the Frisco line again to reach Malvern, Arkansas. From there, he'd take the Hot Springs Railroad to his destination. Hot Springs wasn't an easy place to reach, especially with everything currently on his mind.

After he'd taken Nita to the box house and made sure his mother was all right as she sat on the floor and rocked Nita in her arms, Matthew had rushed to the newspaper office to let Ruth Ann know she was on her own for the daily. She was shocked about the arrival of Nita, and he didn't scold her for immediately hanging up her apron and going home. Matthew told Caleb Gentry, his longest-term employee, to do his best with the daily. Matthew headed to Bate's store and bought boots, a bed frame, and a mattress.

By the time he set up the small bed in the attic bedroom near his mother's and made another trip to the store for three new bolts of cloth, it was late afternoon. But he didn't regret the slim daily that went out, nor did he care about the gossip circulating in town about the newest addition to the *Choctaw Tribune* family. Owning a newspaper made the Tellers public figures. Matthew only cared about settling Nita in and making sure she hadn't caught a cold on the damp depot platform.

But the following morning, the urge to take down Maxwell settled in Matthew's gut once again. He had to stay focused on that if they wanted to raise Nita in a town that was firmly within the Choctaw Nation.

Still, guilt settled heavy on him as he recalled the way Nita looked up at him from the living room floor where she was curled with her thin arms around her thin legs. Still in her night-gown in the early morning hour, she watched him prepare to leave. Didn't her mother at least give her a rag doll to hold close?

He'd knelt to kiss Nita's forehead, her brown eyes hollow and sad, like she believed he was abandoning her the way her mother had.

Her look ripped at his heart, but he had to stay on this trail until he reached the end. Wherever that might be.

Matthew opened his satchel and pulled out the letter to Philip he'd started that morning while waiting for his train. This draft was his second attempt. The first he'd tried to write late last night by the light of the fire. It was filled with all the things Matthew wanted to say to Kat, wanted to say to Philip about the past six years, and what led them to today. He wondered if he could ever truly forgive his brother.

Nita had crept into the dark living room and stood watching him. Matthew laid aside the letter and slid from the sofa to the floor at her level. Nita climbed into his lap and fell asleep. He carried her to bed, then returned and tossed the angry letter in the fire.

Today, Matthew was trying to write the letter again with the sweet image of Nita fixed in his mind. He didn't know if Philip was aware of Kat's illness or that she had brought Nita to the Tellers. The last letter the family had from Philip was at Christmas, and he didn't write one directly to Matthew. It was hard for Matthew to figure out what their relationship was now.

As he wrote to the irregular sway of the passenger car, questions flooded back to Matthew. How were they going to raise Philip's daughter with Ruth Ann marrying and Matthew constantly in the newspaper's business? With the income from the *Choctaw Tribune* doing well so far this year, maybe Matthew should talk to his mother about cutting back on sewing to give her plenty of time with her granddaughter. Since Matthew gifted Della a sewing machine at Christmas, she was busier than ever with her business.

But there was also the constant danger for anyone who was close to Matthew. The shadow man was out there somewhere, and Maxwell wasn't going to let up on his schemes. Maybe they should move Nita to Uncle Preston's ranch where she would be safe and surrounded by her Choctaw kin.

Yet the thought of Nita not being in their home burned a hole in Matthew's heart. She belonged with the Tellers. She *was* a Teller.

Matthew added that to his letter, but the train jerked around a sharp curve, causing his pencil to streak across the page. He'd need to recopy the letter before sending it, if he could steady himself enough.

He had to sway with the rocking passenger car, but there wasn't a rhythm he could fall into. Life was that way.

Matthew had been to Hot Springs three years before when Christopher Maxwell sent him to cover his first front page story for the *Dickens Herald*. Instead, the events in Hot Springs were the catalyst for Matthew to start his own newspaper. The events made the first headline article in the *Choctaw Tribune.*

On that visit, Matthew had met the editor of the *Hot Springs Daily Tribune* and immediately liked the man. Their acquaintance was short-lived, and Matthew didn't want to visit the office of the deceased editor.

There was a boy hanging around the depot looking for work and Matthew hired him with instructions to go through a set of dates in archived newspapers, searching for the names of *Maxwell, Carter, Warren,* and *Banny.*

But there was one place Matthew would have to face himself.

The Palace looked the same with its green trimmed terraces and red canopy top. But entering the place brought a rush of unpleasant memories for Matthew even though it looked considerably different. Before, it was still in repair after a rival gambling hall ransacked and tried to burn the building. Now, the green and black damask wallpaper appeared pristine, no signs of smoke damage.

The place was packed with people, too. When Matthew entered the back gambling hall before, it was wholly empty except for the manager who threatened to have him shot if he didn't leave.

The Palace Casino, as it was now called, nearly folded after the owner lit out for New Orleans. Back then, Matthew was sure Thaddeus Warren, Jake Banny, and Christopher Maxwell all had a vested interest in the Palace, but he never discovered what it was. When Mrs. Bellanger urged him to go to the Palace for answers, Matthew knew it was a key piece in the puzzle he missed before. And a dangerous one. She was dead.

Matthew made his way to the gambling hall, packed wall-to-wall with blackjack tables, roulette wheels, and poker tables, most of them filled despite it being early Tuesday afternoon. With gambling illegal in Arkansas, the establishment saw business seven days a week.

Matthew wove through the tables and air filled with cigar and pipe smoke. Bottles of liquor and shot glasses were scattered everywhere. If Dickens were annexed, did Christopher Maxwell intend to establish something like this there?

Matthew came to a halt by one of the blackjack tables closest to the back. He angled himself to see all the activity of the gambling hall.

The dealer asked if he wanted to join the game. Matthew hesitated. Maybe he should so he wouldn't stand out in the crowd.

But his daddy taught him a man could lose everything in the time it took to flip a card. And Matthew didn't want the distraction of pretending to gamble.

He gave a low wave of his hand to the dealer and moved on down the wall. He came to a dark alcove that held a closed door. He casually stepped backward into the space, felt for the doorknob, and twisted. Locked.

Before he could slip out, he saw a man in the corner of the hall, gaze sweeping his direction. He halted on Matthew and squinted. Matthew recognized him as the manager who threw him out before.

Matthew made long strides to leave the alcove, cutting straight through the middle of the gambling hall. From the corner of his eye, he spotted two powerfully built men angling his direction.

Matthew made it out the huge arched doorway before them and exited the Palace into the chilly sunshine of Hot Springs. He didn't stop until he was near the county clerk's office, out of breath and looking over his shoulder. No one followed.

Matthew slowed his breathing and entered the title office. Since he was known in the Palace, he needed a different angle.

Inside the title office, Matthew asked to look at the purchase records for the land and building where the Palace sat.

He scanned the public documents. It contained no familiar names, but he jotted them down anyway, then settled at one of the tables to look through several titles in the town to see if Maxwell's name popped up.

After two hours of searching, Matthew determined that Hot Springs was yet another dead end in his search, unless the boy he'd hired to go through newspapers had turned up anything.

He found the boy snoozing outside the *Hot Springs Daily Tribune*. Matthew gazed at the picture windows, the printing press serving as a background for the white lettering on the glass. The editor's name was different. That sent a painful reminder through Matthew that he had chosen a hazardous occupation.

Matthew nudged the boy's boot. He awoke with a start and jumped to his feet, blinking rapidly. "Say, you took a long time, mister. Shoulda told you I can't read, but I know my numbers and letters and found one of the names you gave me. I cut out the article for you."

The boy offered Matthew the clipping, which he took with the thought of how he needed to hire a capable assistant for trips like this.

He quickly read the article and raised his eyebrows. The boy did well.

The article, dated October 1892, was about the freight office in Hot Springs. It had shipped a crate of "linens" that actually contained illegal whiskey smuggled into Indian Territory.

The article named Josiah Carter as the recipient.

"That story mean something to you, mister?"

Matthew nodded. "It means I need to make a trip to St. Louis."

～

Matthew didn't know why he hadn't visited Josiah Carter before now. Carter knew everything the founding men were up to when they created Dickens. He was one of them, though the weak link. They used him for a scapegoat when their illegal whiskey running was uncovered.

Visiting Carter would dredge up more unpleasant memories for Matthew, not to mention the awkward business of Carter's young mail order bride who'd briefly been in Matthew and Ruth Ann's care. Maybe that was why he hadn't made visiting Carter a priority.

Besides, Carter would surely rather forget his time in Dickens.

But if there was a story that connected Josiah Carter with Hot Springs, Matthew needed to dig into it. Since Carter had the whiskey shipped from Hot Springs, he might know of the connection there with Christopher Maxwell and the Palace. And maybe he knew of the connection with John Bellanger and his survey for the Dickens townsite. Which led Matthew's long train of thought to the root of the future of his people.

Matthew turned his thoughts to the Dawes commission and Chief Jefferson Gardner, who staunchly ignored the commissioners who were conducting a census throughout the Five Civilized Tribes of Choctaws, Cherokees, Chickasaws, Muskogee Creek, and Seminoles. Of those, the Choctaws were most closely tied to the Chickasaws. The two tribes had a long history going back to the origin story that Choctaw and Chickasaw were two brothers who parted and became distinct nations. For decades, the tribes were intwined legally until the 1850s when a treaty gave the Chickasaws back their own nation instead of being a subset of the Choctaw Nation.

Because of the closeness of their languages, Matthew was fluent in Chickasaw. He loved words, loved languages, studied them in college before being pulled back home after the ambush that left his father dead.

Maybe he could return to his passion of foreign languages someday—if his life ever settled from the constant turmoil of pursuing truth at all costs.

During the train ride, Matthew became acutely aware of the dying day. He had a berth in a sleeper car since he wouldn't arrive in St. Louis until early Wednesday morning. If he kept the meeting with Carter brief, he still wouldn't be back in Dickens until early Thursday morning. That meant Ruth Ann would have to run the shop three days instead of one.

She would not be happy, not with working on wedding plans and helping outfit Nita in clothing for her new life.

At least Matthew wasn't physically present for Annie to whack. Still, she already knew when he was on an investigation like this, he wouldn't stop until he ran his lead to ground.

At least he had put in advertisements in newspapers throughout the territory, trying to solicit new employees. He needed to train at least three—one to replace Ruth Ann when she left, and two to go with her to McAlester and the new shop she was determined to open.

At the next stop, he would send a telegram alerting her of the change in plans. He would ask his sister to kiss Nita goodnight for him. He'd told his niece he'd be back that evening.

How many promises would Maxwell cause him to break?

CHAPTER 10

annot work. Jailed in Paris. Will resume soon.

The telegram wasn't signed, but it didn't need to be. Christopher Maxwell crumpled the message and threw it in his office stove at the *Dickens Herald*. He slammed the stove door shut, but burning the telegram wouldn't change facts. The man he hired to get Matthew Teller out of his life was sitting in jail in Paris, Texas.

Whether the man was arrested for a prior warrant or fresh trouble, Christopher didn't care. He needed Matthew Teller taken care of before Christopher announced his bid for mayor in May. That would really set young Teller off. If he were still alive.

Christopher couldn't do the deed himself. It was too risky. And he'd had his fill of paying outlaws to carry out his dirty work only to botch it like Cub Wassom when he missed a clear shot at Matthew Teller's heart.

Christopher would have to wait on the man he'd brought in because of the personal grievance the man had against Matthew Teller.

Opening his desk drawer, Christopher drew out a bottle of brandy. He didn't drink at home, didn't want Dorothy to have the pleasure of knowing what he consumed or when. If he wanted to stay late at his office, like this evening, and drink alone, that was his prerogative.

He poured a shot and sat at his desk, picking up the second important telegram he'd received that day. Only this one was unofficial.

A few months back, Christopher had taken over an abandoned shack in the woods north of Dickens. It was a quarter of a mile from the train tracks, just the right location to discreetly run a wire from the telegraph line to the shack. He stationed one of his most trusted employees in there to intercept messages when Matthew Teller was out of town.

That was how Maxwell had known Matthew was in Fort Smith and was staying the night there when Mrs. Bellanger was killed. It was how he now knew Matthew Teller was headed to St. Louis, probably to see Josiah Carter. And Teller had asked his sister to kiss Nita goodnight for him.

If Christopher's man wasn't in jail, he would send him to St. Louis to make sure Matthew Teller never saw the little girl again.

But Teller was like a cat with nine lives. He was going to survive another day.

Teller had been a thorn in Maxwell's side from day one. When the young man came to work in the *Dickens Herald*, Christopher saw an opportunity to turn the head of a young Choctaw and get him woven into his web. But Matthew Teller stayed aloof. Christopher should have known the young man was learning the newspaper business with the intent of becoming his rival.

Christopher couldn't be certain that Matthew Teller had planned all along to open his own paper. The spark happened when Christopher sent Matthew to Hot Springs, Arkansas, to investigate the wrecked Palace—an illegal gambling hall that Christopher had a vested interest in.

He'd sent Matthew Teller there to test his integrity. The young man showed what he was made of. He came back with the truth and started his own newspaper just so he could print the real story. He hadn't stopped since, despite continuous opposition from the leading townsmen.

All of those men were gone now except Christopher. He didn't regret that. He was on the cusp of owning this town and there was only one stubborn Choctaw in his way. Teller's press was too powerful these days.

But Dickens was Christopher's town. His private kingdom.

All he needed was for the annexation to go through. His investors were anxious about the large sums of money he wanted them to invest in a town sitting on land belonging to the Choctaw Nation.

Part of gaining final control of Dickens was winning his bid for town mayor. He'd be hard pressed to do that with Teller enjoying decent influence in the town.

But he didn't want Teller to turn up dead too close to the mayoral announcement. Everyone knew what rivals—enemies— the newspaper publishers were.

Christopher was going to have to handle Matthew Teller in another way for now.

Blackmail.

The idea formed in Christopher's mind as he sipped the brandy with images of a pretty Choctaw girl on his mind. Yes. It was perfect with Matthew Teller gone a few days.

Christopher would enjoy this stunt. Ruth Ann Teller was an attractive young woman.

CHAPTER 11

The St. Louis Union Station became the largest in the world when it opened the year before. Tracks and service areas were all located on one level in the cavernous building, passengers navigating elbow to elbow. The station alone could overwhelm anyone unaccustomed to large cities.

It wasn't Matthew's first time in St. Louis, but it still wasn't easy to make his way through the station after his train arrived early Wednesday morning. At least he didn't have luggage to bother with and wouldn't worry about his rumpled brown jacket and trousers. He hadn't slept well in the Pullman car, but he wanted to see Carter before breakfast.

He knew the man's home address from marking it enough times on his *Choctaw Tribune* subscription. It surprised Matthew that Carter was still a subscriber. Maybe Carter used the daily edition to start the cook stove each morning.

Matthew boarded an electric streetcar and told the address to the operator who informed him which stop to get off.

It wasn't hard to find Carter's house, a modest but stately two story white and blue frame house squeezed between homes on each side. Matthew noticed smoke rising from the chimney. Good. Someone was up early.

He knocked, and a few minutes later, the lace curtain over the glass window on the door fluttered. Then the door swung wide open.

"Well, if it isn't Matthew Teller, the Choctaw reporter himself!"

Matthew stared at the matronly woman a moment before realizing it was Viona Blake Carter.

Her unruly red hair was tied up neatly in a bun, and her waistline had thickened. Viona had grown quite, well, motherly looking. Two toddlers hung onto her skirts. Twins, and it appeared she was expecting at least one more child now.

Matthew smiled, feeling a sense of relief at how settled Viona was. "It's been a while, Mrs. Carter. I should have sent a telegram first, but I need to speak to your husband."

Viona motioned him inside. "Pssh, no Mrs. Carter to me, Matthew Teller. But Joe is out of town on business, so he is. He'll be back later this morn. Why don't you take breakfast with me and the babies?"

"I appreciate it, but I have some other business to tend to. I'll meet him at his freight office later."

Viona, green eyes bright, let him go with an admonishment to return for a real visit to the family soon.

Matthew ate breakfast at a nearby hotel, then wandered the business district. Passing a general store, something in the picture window caught his eye. It was a wooden Noah's Ark, a toy he wouldn't have taken a second look at a few days ago.

He went inside and bought it, having the lady behind the counter wrap the box in pink and white floral paper.

It had been a few hours since Matthew visited Carter's home, so he headed for the man's freight company.

Josiah Carter's freight business in St. Louis was grand by comparison to what he had run in Indian Territory. Three stories showed rented offices and storage space while the bottom floor was entirely a warehouse large enough to drive freight wagons inside.

Matthew got directions from a worker to Carter's office on the second floor. Up the stairs, the door was open, and Matthew ducked inside with a quick knock to find Carter scratching figures in a ledger book.

The man looked up when Matthew entered. His expression wasn't hostile. Carter looked scared.

He laid aside his pencil and rose slowly. "Matthew Teller. My wife said you were in town."

Matthew offered his hand to shake. The man hesitantly took it, his hand limp.

"Halito, Mr. Carter."

Carter looked stricken to hear the Choctaw word after being out of Indian Territory for awhile now. Matthew wondered if Carter's first wife, who passed some years before, had spoken her language in their home.

Carter recovered enough to nod and sit again. Matthew sat across from him, settling the pink and white package and his brief bag on the floor beside the chair.

Carter gripped his hands together on the desk, twiddling his thumbs. "Mrs. Carter said you had something to talk to me about?"

Matthew drew in a deep breath and plunged in the only way he knew. Headlong.

"Christopher Maxwell filed to have Dickens annexed. Doing so would take the townsite out of the Choctaw Nation. He wants control of the town. I want you to help me stop him."

Carter jerked back in his seat, eyes wide as though Matthew

had slapped him. Then Carter sprang to his feet and paced the room. He stopped by the window overlooking his freight yard behind the building.

"I guess I always knew this day would come."

He turned back to face Matthew, beams of morning sunlight shifting around his form.

"I am still beholden to you for how you and your sister took in Viona when I was too much of a coward to face her. You gave me the most wonderful gift of my life and I'll never forget that."

Carter looked down, then at Matthew square in the eyes. "But I don't want to lose them because of you."

Matthew didn't blink. "What you mean is, you don't want to lose them because of the man who burned down my shop and had me shot?"

Carter shoved his shaking hands in his trouser pockets. "You think I wanted any of that? It was my own building that...that we burned. Yes, I was part of it all. I signed that townsite lease with Sam Mishaya even though I knew it would hurt the tribe. Those men used me and my freight office to haul whiskey into the Choctaw Nation. I stood by quiet when they made plans to burn down your newspaper office. But I wouldn't have gone along with...how they hired Cub Wassom to shoot you. I left all of it behind when I moved out of that cursed town."

Carter halted, probably from the dark look Matthew felt coming over his face, a fury rising in him. He made no attempt to tamp it down as he asked, "Who were those men, exactly? I want to know for sure."

Carter closed his eyes, his head trembling. "The fire is the only thing I know for sure on what happened and who planned it." He opened his eyes but didn't meet Matthew's as he spoke slowly. "It was Thaddeus Warren. Jake Banny. Christopher Maxwell. And me, because I didn't take a stand against them. But Jake Banny did the actual deed."

Matthew gripped his knees, wondering again if he was supposed to forgive a dead man.

Several minutes passed before Matthew looked up at Josiah Carter. The man stood stock still, eyes wide as if facing an executioner.

That was exactly what Matthew felt he was. He could file charges against this man for damaging his property and trying to destroy his business. At the least, he could run a front-page story about the man's past and spread it to the St. Louis newspapers. The man's business and family life would be sullied, maybe ruined.

Matthew rose from his chair, clenching his fists, wanting to hold onto his right to be angry with this man. Then he slowly unclenched his fists.

"I forgive you, Mr. Carter."

Carter let out a gust of air, pulling his hands out of his pockets, shoulders sagging. His eyes watered.

"That's good of you, Matthew Teller."

Matthew swallowed, feeling like a piece of himself had escaped. It was a piece he didn't need.

He had one more hard question to ask. "If I can unravel this, I may be able to have Maxwell's lease stripped and him kicked out of the Choctaw Nation. Maybe even land in prison, like Thaddeus Warren. But I need to know, will you testify against Maxwell?"

Carter shriveled, turning to stare out the window again. He mumbled, "I can't lose my family..."

Matthew couldn't argue Carter into this. Mrs. Bellanger was dead and Matthew didn't want Viona and her children in danger because of him. Still, he pressed in for one last piece of information.

"Carter, I came across a story that connected your freight company in Dickens with shipping whiskey from Hot Springs. I know Christopher Maxwell has ties to the Palace there and..."

Matthew didn't need to finish. Carter jerked back around, sweat breaking out on his forehead. He looked for all the world like John Bellanger had.

Carter pulled a handkerchief out of his pocket to wipe the moisture from his forehead. "Lord knows, I wish I had your courage, Matthew Teller. But I'm telling you right now—stop digging. You'll break your shovel. Or dig your own grave."

CHAPTER 12

The world was silent. But Hannah Stillwater could see things. She could see love and hope. Bitterness. Anger. Sadness. Regret.

That last emotion was on her employer's face as he shook his head, making it difficult to see the words he said.

"I'm sorry Miss Stillwater, but…"

She didn't need to read his lips to know what he was saying. She was fired. Regrettably. He hoped she understood.

She did.

When he finished speaking, Hannah nodded, bracing against the desire to defend herself as she stood beside her typist desk. There was a stoic posture people assumed about all Indians, including her people, the Chickasaws. Hannah assumed that posture now to guard from her fear showing.

"I do understand, Mr. Shaw. I will clean my desk out at the end of the day."

He twisted his mouth, still looking regretful. "I'm afraid this is the end of your day, Miss Stillwater. We simply cannot have an employee who falsified information on her application."

Hannah gripped the edge of her desk, determined not to

scream to the world that she was not a liar. But the world wouldn't hear her, no more than she could hear it.

Mr. Shaw stepped back, tipped his head in apology, and left for his own desk near the door where he managed the six typists at the law firm in Paris, Texas.

Hannah sat down stiffly in her rolling chair and began opening desk drawers. Mr. Shaw regretted letting her go because she had the highest output of all the typists each and every day. She was fast because she was focused. Sounds couldn't distract her, and she had no social life. The law firm was losing a good typist and Mr. Shaw knew it.

What he didn't know was how devastating it was for Hannah to lose her job. It cost money every time she had to move to a new town to start over. Money was something she had little of.

By late afternoon, Hannah was exhausted as she settled at the secretary desk in her room at the boarding house. This day had started well. How could it have ended so badly?

The answer was simple. Her former teacher, Jackson Thomas, learned her newest place of employment and sent a scathing letter to the law firm. He claimed that Hannah Stillwater never attended college and she was notorious for falsifying her records and stealing from employers. She was little more than a vagabond.

Hannah knew the contents of the letter because Mr. Shaw showed it to her, along with a letter that featured her college's letterhead, a warning to potential employers that this student was dismissed for cheating and misconduct.

Jackson Thomas had lied. The college had never employed him.

Since Mr. Shaw hadn't offered to let her explain, Hannah hadn't told her side of the story. It hadn't worked with her previous two employers when she pleaded with them to believe that her former teacher was exacting unjustified revenge against her.

Ten years ago, Jackson Thomas was fired for using a ruler to whip her hand for using sign language with a visiting friend. It wasn't his first offense, but it was the one he was finally caught in. No one witnessed how he whipped Hannah for even making friends at the school that was filled with hearing students. He believed in segregation of deficit children and capable ones and despised her being there through her teenage years.

In recent years, she learned he was advocating in favor of eugenics—a theory fast gaining popularity in this golden age just prior to a new century. Eugenics was a term coined by Francis Galton, British explorer and natural scientist, heavily influenced by his cousin Charles Darwin's theory of natural selection. Wealthy men were backing studies on how to eliminate people like her from walking the earth through Social Darwinism. Among their biggest pushes was forced sterilization of anyone who was imperfect—like Hannah.

That drove Jackson Thomas to track her since she had graduated college, attempting to isolate her from society whenever he could. In the last letter she read that he sent her, he stated the greatest thought terrorizing his mind was that she would marry someday and reproduce "defects" like herself.

Now, letters from him went straight into the fire, unopened.

Now he had cost her the job at the law firm, leaving her to scour the newspaper for job listings in her room at the boarding house. She still owed the last week's rent.

Her heart sank lower with each column she read. Nothing matched her skills and experience.

Then her eyes landed at one near the bottom of the page.

Wanted: Typesetter for the Choctaw Tribune *newspaper. Dickens, Choctaw Nation, Indian Territory. Must be experienced and able to*

work under pressure. Fluency in the Choctaw language a benefit.
Contact Matthew Teller, publisher.

Hannah sat up straight, reading the advertisement again. She could fill all the requirements perfectly.

She snatched a blank sheet of paper from the desk and took up a pen, poised to write a letter of interest. But could she afford to wait for an answer? Her funds were depleted. It had taken all her pay the past two months to cover expenses, and also debts, after her last position she'd had to leave early. She had just enough to pay her debt at the boarding house and buy a train ticket to the next job. Or a train ticket to her family's home on the Blue River in the Chickasaw Nation.

Hannah bowed her head over the blank paper and blinked back tears. Going home wasn't an option.

She wouldn't fail. She was Chickasaw. Her people were unconquerable, and so she had to be.

Hannah clipped out the advertisement and tucked it in her reticule before setting it aside. It was time for her favorite task of the day, and she wouldn't neglect it, not even today.

She pulled out her writing tablet from the drawer and settled it in the center of the desk, adjusted her lamp to compensate for the fading daylight, and gazed out the window to drink in the sunset. It flowed through her like a healing oil to soothe the day and take her to another place.

The sunset was breathtaking, marigolds and rusts captured for a moment in the cerulean sky. A smile tugged up the corners of Hannah's lips and she placed the tip of the pencil to the page as peace returned to her soul. She continued writing on the scene where she'd stopped last night.

The sunset was God's way of saying to her, "You worked hard today. Here's something beautiful."

ednesday's daily barely went out, but it did and Ruth Ann released a sigh of relief when the last employee left the shop and she settled at the typesetting desk. Why she had thought of the idea to push the *Choctaw Tribune* to a daily, she couldn't fathom, but it was working.

Yet what a struggle it was to get it all done, now more than ever. She had two wedding ceremonies to prepare for, a new shop to open, and making her niece a part of the family. It was overwhelming.

Not to mention how much Matthew was gone these days! Ruth Ann fussed and fumed yesterday after receiving his telegram that he was going to St. Louis. She was supposed to travel with Beulah to Paris today to shop for her trousseau.

Yet what Matthew was doing was vital for their peoples' future, and she'd let him off the hook. Just this once.

The ads he placed for typesetters produced two candidates in the shop that day, and she wished Matthew were there to conduct the interviews. Neither applicant had even worked at a newspaper before, and Ruth Ann politely turned them down. She didn't feel right about them, and she doubted anyone could fill the position. They needed a second Matthew.

Now it was growing dark and Peter had objected to going to the box house before Ruth Ann, but she insisted he leave with the others so she could have an extra half hour to finish setting type on the next day's headline story. She wanted to slip away in the morning as soon as Matthew arrived. She and Beulah were supposed to sew a lace covering on the arbor for the church ceremony.

Ruth Ann promised Peter she would be home in time to eat supper. He made a halfhearted attempt to stay but Ruth Ann assured him it was more important for him to go home and see after Della and Nita.

Nita needed her family's arms around her now, although the little girl hadn't warmed up to them yet, except for Matthew. Ruth Ann noticed the way the little girl had watched the front door during dinner last night, waiting for Matthew to come in, even though Ruth Ann told her he wouldn't return for a few days.

If only Nita could be raised in a home with two loving parents, the way Ruth Ann had.

She halted setting type, a thought striking her, and she spent a few moments dwelling on it. Then she quickly went back to work. She could think about it later.

Ruth Ann managed to finish right when the Grandfather clock on the Levitt's side of the shop chimed six times. She stretched as she rose from the typesetting desk and went to pull down the nifty gas chandelier Matthew had added. He and Mr. Levitt worked on it over Christmas break and Ruth Ann appreciated the abundant light it gave them throughout the shop, especially that winter. It was a simple piece, but gave the newspaper shop a classy look. Ruth Ann extinguished the chandelier and the remaining gas lamps throughout the shop.

Matthew had installed a low wall around his desk and two visitor chairs, which gave him a designated office space. Pausing to straighten Matthew's cluttered desk before blowing out the lamp beside it, a smile tickled Ruth Ann's lips. When they launched the shop in McAlester, she'd have her own desk that she could keep as tidy as she wanted.

Not to mention her own home with Benjamin. Oh, if only the days would hurry by! June 1 was so far away from mid-March.

Ruth Ann was tidying the telegraph office—Peter left it so messy these days—when a tap on the closed window drew her attention. She turned to see a well-dressed man standing in the grayness of evening. He was holding up a slip of paper, his expression urgent. She recognized but couldn't place him. There were so many new people moving into town.

Ruth Ann cracked the window to say, "I'm sorry, but the telegraph is closed for the day."

"Please, ma'am, I have an emergency." His tone was gruff but sincere. Where had she seen him before?

Cautiously, Ruth Ann opened the window and he offered her the paper as he said, "My sister is having a baby and I need to reach her husband in Tuskahoma. He works at the sawmill there, comes home weekends."

An image jumped to Ruth Ann's mind of Daniel pacing the floor at Uncle Preston's house while Daisy was upstairs, crying out in labor pains before giving birth to their precious child.

Sharpness stabbed Ruth Ann's heart, catching her off guard and a tiny tear slipped out. How could her beautiful cousin Daisy be gone from this earth?

Ruth Ann took the message, written in pristine penmanship, which matched the man's business attire. "I understand. Let me see if I can catch the operator at that station."

After taking the man's payment, Ruth Ann swiftly sent the message off through the sounder. It clacked with confirmation.

"Sir, your brother-in-law should have your message soon. I do hope things go well for your sister." She started to close the window, but the man put his hands on the frame.

"Could you wait for his reply? I need to know if he's coming by horseback or if he can catch the night train. I will pick him up in my buggy."

Beyond the man's frame, the sky was growing darker. Matthew warned Ruth Ann not to be out alone at night, and the streets were already deserted because of the cold teeth still clenching back spring. It would reach freezing tonight if she didn't miss her guess.

But the man didn't move. Ruth Ann sighed. "I can only wait a short time. I'm expected at home now."

While the man waited at the open window, Ruth Ann warmed her hands at the extinguished fire in the lean-to's stove. The fire at home would feel much better without the unease in the pit of her stomach.

Not able to stand still, Ruth Ann retrieved a writing tablet from Matthew's desk and settled by the sounder to jot down article ideas for the next edition.

Minutes ticked away and Ruth Ann checked the timepiece she kept in her shirtwaist. It was twenty minutes past the hour. Peter would come looking for her soon, but there was no sense in worrying everyone.

It was mostly dark outside now except for the new gas street-lamps. Ruth Ann went to the window. "I'm sorry, I really must close up now. I'm sure your brother-in-law will make his way to you soon."

The man looked at the darkened sky, gave a curt nod, and strode away without a word or glance back.

Ruth Ann watched him disappear then closed and locked the window. She hurried to the main shop and wound her red scarf around her neck before swinging her coat on. A hot meal and long night's sleep awaited her.

She locked up the shop and crossed the street to head for the box house just in sight down the road. She was nearly to Bates store when a voice stopped her.

"Good evening, Ruth Ann."

She swirled and stared at Christopher Maxwell who appeared behind her. Had he been waiting between the two buildings that she passed? The uneasiness in her stomach flared with alarm. She should've been more alert.

But this was Christopher Maxwell, not a random outlaw in the territory. She'd faced down this man more than once.

"Mr. Maxwell. I'm on my way home for supper."

He came around in front of her on the dirt street, underneath the lamp post in front of Bates store. Ruth Ann turned in a small circle to follow his every move. He had his scheming smile in place.

"This will only take a minute, Ruth Ann, dear. I wanted to congratulate you on your plans to open a second newspaper in McAlester. Fine business move."

How had he learned of it so quickly? "Thank you. Good evening."

Ruth Ann started to step around him, but he held out a hand to block her. "I understand you'll be the publisher there. Seems your brother is giving you a bit of license for once. Perhaps we can work together, you and I."

Annoyance filled Ruth Ann's chest. "Mr. Maxwell, you know good and well I would never have any part in anything you concoct. Besides, Dickens has grown large enough for our two newspapers to get along, if you would let them. Otherwise, please leave us alone."

She stood her ground, wanting him to walk away.

He didn't, instead taking a step closer. "If you don't want to talk business, let's make this personal."

Before Ruth Ann could flinch, he jerked her into his arms and pressed a hand over her mouth.

Ruth Ann's scream stuck in her throat. She tried to kick Maxwell in the shin, but he held her too tight. And too close.

He whispered, "Dear Ruth Ann, don't you remember how I

took care of you in that mob in Paris? I can take care of you in McAlester, too. We could enjoy a cozy arrangement that not even your nosy brother would know about."

In the fuzziness that clouded her mind, Ruth Ann heard several clicks as she pushed against Maxwell with all her might. She hated that he was so strong.

Then Maxwell released her with a shove.

Ruth Ann staggered back, breathless as she grabbed onto the lamp post to steady herself. She couldn't bring the scream back up her throat as she looked around the empty streets for help, and spotted the well-dressed man who sent the telegram standing not far away. She gasped as she finally made the connection of who he was. One of Maxwell's employees! He held up a Kodak camera, and nodded at his boss.

He'd been lying about his sister and brother-in-law, and Ruth Ann played right into the charade. How could she have been so foolish!

Maxwell grinned and picked up Ruth Ann's scarf that she hadn't realized dropped in the struggle. He offered it to her.

"Thank you, Ruth Ann, dear. That's all I really needed."

He tossed the red scarf at her feet and tipped his hat. "Tell your brother there is something all towns have in common. They all have a road going out of them."

CHAPTER 14

Weary from the twenty-hour train ride, Matthew came down the steps of the passenger car to land with a thud on the wood platform of the Dickens depot. Briefcase in one hand and Nita's package in the other, he stretched wide and breathed in deeply of the crisp late morning air as he gazed around the familiar platform.

To his surprise, activity at the depot slowed. Boarding passengers watched him and the station master stared out the depot window at him.

Then the moment was broken, and everyone seemed in a hurry to go on with their business. Matthew tucked the package under his arm and rubbed his eyes, wondering if his imagination was running wild. He didn't normally draw attention, but people seemed struck with his arrival.

Maybe Christopher Maxwell printed a story that Matthew was dead. Again.

He exited the platform and glanced at the box house across the street. While his heart longed to see Nita, he needed to go straight to the print shop and get to work. He would eat lunch at home.

Reaching the cross street, Matthew could see through the picture windows of the *Choctaw Tribune* and Levitt Repair shop. Strange. The place looked abandoned.

He pushed through the door, the bell over it loud in the quiet shop. It was empty of everyone except Peter in the telegraph office and Caleb Gentry, who barely looked up from slamming the lever on the printing press. The telegraph sounder clicked. Peter glanced over his shoulder at Matthew but then went back to work taking down the message. He said, "It's been a bad morning, Matt."

Matthew frowned as he strode over to Gentry, who kept steady on operating the press.

"What's going on? Where's Ruth Ann?"

Caleb slammed the lever again. "We might miss today's edition, but I'm going to get this advertisement flyer out, even if she gave me the day off."

Matthew's eyes popped and he nearly shouted, "The day off?"

Gentry hefted a stack of completed advertisements and carried them to the worktable. He squared up with Matthew. "You best read this morning's *Dickens Herald* before you light into her. Her lawyer fiancé is on his way here by train."

Matthew strode over to his desk, where he saw a crumpled copy of the *Dickens Herald*. He didn't want to read whatever Maxwell had printed that caused Ruth Ann to shut down the entire *Choctaw Tribune* office and was bringing Benjamin down from McAlester. But he had to.

He dropped his briefcase and package on the desk and picked up the newspaper to see the single headline above the fold:

Choctaw Tribune Publishers Playing Loose With Privileges

By the time he finished reading the article, he was shaking so hard, the words blurred. He had never read such a vile article in his life.

Matthew shoved open the front door of the box house, letting it bang into the wall. He halted, chilly air gusting into the living room as he dropped his satchel and package.

Ruth Ann was curled on the sofa, a quilt wrapped around her as she leaned back against Beulah. Della sat in her rocking chair, sewing. They looked up at Matthew's abrupt entrance, but it was Nita who jumped from where she was sitting on the floor by Della's rocker. She ran to him, arms outstretched. Matthew bent to scoop her under the arms and settled her on his hip. She was so tiny for a five-year-old. So innocent.

Matthew closed the door and came around the end of the sofa, swinging Nita around to where he could cradle her in his lap as he sat by Ruth Ann. Nita kept her arms around his neck, both warming and calming him. A school slate was on the chest table in front of the sofa, the alphabet scrawled across it.

Matthew looked at his mother's red eyes, then turned his focus to Ruth Ann as Beulah stroked his sister's hair. Beulah's lips were pinched as though she was holding in a string of curse words.

Matthew tried to keep his voice under control. "Ruth Ann, tell me exactly what happened last night."

"Nothing."

The way she wouldn't look at him told Matthew she wasn't giving him the full story.

He pressed in. "Then why did Christopher Maxwell run a front-page story saying you met him on the street and propositioned him?"

Ruth Ann squeezed her eyes shut and Matthew regretted his bluntness. This was his sister, not someone he was interrogating for a story.

Nita tightened her grip around his neck and Matthew softened his voice. "Just tell me what happened, Annie."

Beulah shifted and used both hands to pull Ruth Ann's hair back. Her movements were snappy as she tied a kerchief over the unbrushed hair. "I will tell you what needs to happen. That Christopher Maxwell needs to be oiled and feathered."

Ruth Ann opened her eyes, her lips twitching with a smile. "Tarred and feathered, my friend."

Matthew remained silent.

Ruth Ann met his eyes, then looked down. "I stayed to set some type after everyone left. Now, don't lecture me, Matt, or I'll never make it through the story."

Matthew took a sharp breath when she mentioned being alone at the shop. He should have given her more detail about the dangerous man Daniel was tracking in the area.

Ruth Ann drew a shaky breath. "When I was coming home, Mr. Maxwell stopped me and said he wanted to talk business. Of course, I told him straight out there was no business for us to discuss. That's all, Matt. He made up everything else."

The rest of what Maxwell put in the article wasn't true either.

If Nita wasn't clinging to him, Matthew would put a fist through the wall as he recalled the contents of that hideous article. Maxwell must have already written it and had it ready to go even before the encounter with Ruth Ann. The *Dickens Herald* got it out first thing that morning.

The article started off with the accusation about Ruth Ann. Then the article targeted Matthew. Specifically, Matthew visiting Viona Carter.

It questioned whether there had been a relationship between the two before she married Josiah Carter, and insinuated the relationship could be ongoing in the present, with Matthew's recent trip to St. Louis.

Then came the worst.

The article attacked the Teller family's integrity and morality, printing in black-and-white Philip's escapade with Kat Russell and how he was now in prison, and that his illegitimate child was living with the Teller family.

Matthew had mustered all his strength to come home first instead of going directly to Christopher Maxwell and beating the living daylights out of him.

Nita flipped one corner of Matthew's shirt collar, playing with its limpness. He'd worn the same shirt for three days. She stilled and laid her head on his shoulder.

Her presence was the only thing keeping him from committing murder. At least, it felt that way.

Matthew had gone to St. Louis and forgiven one of the men who had done him great harm—only to come home and find his dedicated rival doing something unforgivable.

Who would the town people believe? Matthew had worked hard to earn a reputation as a newspaperman from there to D.C., but Dickens was always shaky ground. Mostly a white town that knew and respected Christopher Maxwell years before Matthew ever opened the *Tribune*, losing credibility and advertisers was a real prospect.

None of that was his greatest concern at the moment.

Matthew searched Ruth Ann's face, aware of how she wouldn't look directly at him as she leaned against Beulah, who rubbed her shoulder. Ruth Ann's face seemed swollen, probably from crying. But was that a bruise on her cheek?

"Did he put a hand on you, Annie?"

Ruth Ann raised her eyes to meet him, fire and determination in them. "Nothing happened."

"Then why did you close the shop? We need to get a counter story out right away. We can't let lies get that kind of head start on truth."

Ruth Ann's eyes melted with tears. "I couldn't do it, Matt. I just couldn't do it."

Matthew gently hefted Nita off his lap to her feet. She had a hearty look in her eyes, a look that came straight from Matthew's own father. Yet she was confused as she stared at him. He stroked back bits of hair that had come loose from her sable brown braids.

"Everything's going to be all right, Little Bear."

Matthew wished someone could give him that same assurance.

God knows.

He left the house and headed back to the newspaper shop. Benjamin would be at the house soon to look after Ruth Ann. Meanwhile, between Matthew, Caleb Gentry, and Peter, they would get the daily edition with the truth out by evening.

Matthew was going to take it to Christopher Maxwell and cram every word down his lying throat.

It was midnight when Matthew arrived at Christopher Maxwell's house. It took the staff at the *Choctaw Tribune* all day to print and distribute a single page daily edition, which focused on countering the slander in the *Dickens Herald* article. Matthew had personally distributed it, reminding him of the early days of the *Choctaw Tribune*.

Why were they still fighting the same battles and the same enemy?

Matthew strode up the porch steps and hammered on the door. The interior was dark, but his presence wouldn't be unexpected. The only thing Maxwell could be surprised about was that Matthew, along with Benjamin, hadn't come to his newspaper shop to shoot him.

Benjamin, rigid but calm, had remained at the Teller home until evening before leaving on the night train. He had a case at the Tobucksy County Courthouse the next morning, and Ruth Ann insisted he not neglect his clients. That she was fine, everything was fine.

Matthew pounded with his fist again on Maxwell's door and didn't stop until a light showed inside. In the silence, he heard heavy footsteps approaching.

Matthew stepped back, wanting to have maneuvering room in case Maxwell opened the door with a shotgun. He braced when the lock clicked and the door opened.

Christopher Maxwell stood there in an evening coat and slippers, but it didn't look as if he'd been in bed.

Matthew held up the daily. "Had one more delivery to make."

He flung the newspaper in Maxwell's face. Maxwell jerked his head, smiling as the newspaper fluttered to the floor. "I appreciate the personal service. It seems you and your sister do that often these days."

Matthew took a step toward the man and noted how Maxwell glanced off to one side. His right hand was hidden behind the door and Matthew suspected it held a gun.

Matthew ground his next words out slowly. "If you ever, *ever*, go near my sister again, I will do more than write a story. Do you understand?"

Maxwell cocked his head. "You had a lot of potential, Matthew Teller. But you're in a losing fight. Your tribe is a thing of the past. You need to let go and move on, or you'll sink with the ship."

Matthew clenched his jaw. "Let me tell you this, Maxwell—you will not annex this town, even if I have to be the only thing standing in your way."

He turned and headed for the steps, wondering if he would get a bullet in the back. Instead, he got final words tossed at him.

"You should be grateful your sister is moving. It will save her from the heartache you always bring anyone you know."

CHAPTER 15

Christopher Maxwell closed the front door quietly, but he'd been foolish to hope that Dorothy wouldn't wake and come down the stairs.

She barely made it to the bottom without breaking her neck, both hands gripping the rail as she slinked down like the intoxicated cat she was.

Dorothy halted and glared at him. "That was Matthew Teller, wasn't it? I'm sorry he didn't shoot you."

Christopher met her at the last step as she staggered off it, still holding the rail. He tucked his small pistol into the pocket of his evening coat.

"Go back to bed, Dorothy."

She hissed, "It's true, isn't it? You and that Indian girl. Don't think I'm ignorant. I know she's not the only one."

Christopher didn't bother answering. He'd thought to use the photographs in this morning's article, but they didn't turn out well. Still, he might send Matthew copies, make it clear that he had enough evidence to disgrace Ruth Ann before her wedding. Maybe he would save the photographs to release the day of the wedding. In any case, he had them for when he needed for blackmail. They were an ace in the hole.

He wasn't ready for his wife to see them, anyway.

Pushing off the rail, Dorothy straightened and sneered at him, her breath sour. "How would you like it if I flung myself at Lance Fuller? Or better still, handsome Matthew Teller? Maybe I'd like a man not old enough to be my father."

Christopher stared into her eyes a long moment. She didn't take the warning.

His right hand flashed out to clutch her throat. Her eyes bulged, the only reaction she could make.

She belonged to him. Just like this town. There was nothing under heaven that Matthew Teller could do about it.

Dorothy clawed at his hand, face ghostly white as she gurgled for air. Christopher said quietly, "I don't think you would ever, *ever* do that."

He released her and she crumpled onto the bottom step. He went around her and up the stairs as she sobbed.

Hannah Stillwater stared at the clerk through the caged window at the Paris depot. The bars made it hard to read his lips, so surely she saw the wrong price he gave for the train ticket to Dickens, Indian Territory.

She swallowed. "Sir, I'm deaf. Could you please write the price down for me?"

His eyes widened and he fumbled for a piece of paper. He scrawled out numbers and slid the paper to Hannah, his eyes filled with pity.

That was the hardest emotion to witness in someone's expression. People didn't need to feel sorry for her, only be willing to communicate with her differently. Not everyone was willing.

She glanced at the paper. The clerk's handwriting was harder to read than his lips, but it did confirm she saw the price correctly. Nearly a full dollar more than she planned! Worse, she'd already been short for the ticket after paying her bill at the boarding house. She sold her summer lace gloves to a fellow boarder for the difference she thought she needed.

Maybe there were coins in the bottom of her reticule?

Hannah set the small purse on the counter, aware of impatient travelers behind her, waiting to buy their tickets at the busy station. At least she couldn't hear their grumbling.

She quickly emptied the bulky pieces from her bag onto the counter, including a small book, *On the Blue River by T.A. Paige*. No hidden money in the bottom of her reticule. She opened her coin purse again just to make sure. Yes, it was empty.

The clerk reached through the opening in the cage and hesitantly tapped the back of her gloved hand. Hannah looked up and he smiled sheepishly. He slipped another piece of paper to her, along with a silver dollar.

I'll buy your book.

Hannah was startled, then relaxed. He knew it was her book, but he didn't know it was *her* book. He had frightened her for a moment. She only wrote novels under a pseudonym, an identity her publisher assumed was accurate.

"Thank you."

He opened his mouth to say something, but then just nodded and gave her a ticket to Dickens.

As Hannah settled on the train, she kept her gaze roaming the passenger car. She preferred looking at the scenery, but she had to keep her sense about her when in public in case someone tried to get her attention. Besides, watching people and their conversations always gave her good story material.

Too bad that material didn't provide her a stable income. At least her personal copy earned her enough to hopefully get to her next place of employment. If she didn't get the job at the *Choctaw Tribune*, she would have to wire her father for a train ticket home. She couldn't imagine anything worse.

A short while later, Hannah disembarked at the Dickens depot. It wasn't as crowded nor as large as she'd expected. Not that she minded a smaller town after coming from Paris, but with Dickens boasting two newspapers, both delivering a daily, she thought it would be quite sizable and busy this Friday morning.

She asked the station manager for directions to the *Choctaw Tribune*. He frowned, but gave them to her in short, clipped sentences. Enough for her to figure out the general way, though his stiff attitude left her wondering about the newspaper's reputation.

But the view from outside the large picture windows of the *Choctaw Tribune* showed a thriving business as Hannah approached. White lettering adorned both windows, announcing the building as the *Choctaw Tribune* Newspaper and the Levitt Repair Shop.

She paused across the street to observe the structure and its contents, so she knew where things were, leaving her free to focus on conversations once she was inside.

Beyond the block lettering, a cast iron printing press was set toward the back of the room. A desk with a low wall around it was positioned in the middle of the right wall, facing the shop. Closest to the front entrance, a door led from the shop into a telegraph lean-to that boasted its own window and sign. On the left side of the shop was a small desk and several woodworking projects, including a Grandfather clock and a set of kitchen table chairs.

Hannah's attention went to the people inside the building. An older man with fine, thin hair at the back workbench was dwarfed by a taller, blonde-haired young woman. Perhaps the Levitts who ran the repair business?

There was a white man operating the printing press, which surprised Hannah. The newspaper's advertisement said it preferred someone fluent in Choctaw, so she assumed it was run by Indians.

Shifting to her left, Hannah spotted a young woman seated at the desk, head bent, writing. Her dark complexion was easy to distinguish even from across the street.

That was all she could see from there. It was time to go in and apply.

Hannah took a fortifying breath, checked the street for traffic, and crossed rapidly. When she pushed open the door into the shop, she was immediately struck with the familiar smells of ink and paper. If only this would be her new home.

The blonde woman at the back of the building looked over her shoulder and Hannah glanced up to see a bell over the door. Her presence was known.

Hannah smiled at the young woman but hoped she wouldn't call a greeting. Hannah was too far away to make out her lips clearly.

Thankfully, the desk was only a few short strides away. She spotted double swinging doors in the low wall and pushed through them without looking down so she could keep her focus on the young woman behind the desk, who looked up at her approach.

Hannah greeted her with a smile and quick words. "Good morning, I am Hannah Stillwater and I'm here to apply for the typesetter position you advertised."

The young woman raised both eyebrows, probably surprised a woman had come to apply. Or maybe the position was already taken? Yet the typesetter cabinet positioned against the wall near the printing press was empty.

Hannah had a feeling something else bothered the young woman. Dark circles rimmed her otherwise pretty dove-shaped brown eyes and her hair was pulled back in a severe bun. Still, she smiled as she rose.

"I'm Ruth Ann Teller, one of the *Choctaw Tribune* publishers. Do you have typesetting experience?"

"I worked at my college's newspaper, and I am fluent in Choctaw and Chickasaw."

The woman, Ruth Ann, closed her eyes and exhaled. Hannah could tell it was a deep sigh of relief by the rise and fall of her shoulders.

When Ruth Ann opened her eyes, her lips were soft as though she were whispering. "Am I glad to meet you, Hannah Stillwater."

Then Ruth Ann did what so many did that caused the greatest challenge in Hannah's life. She turned her face away.

Ruth Ann motioned to the empty typesetter desk, and Hannah didn't know if she was instructing Hannah to go over there, or making a different comment.

Ruth Ann turned back to Hannah as though awaiting a response.

Hannah kept the confident smile her mentor had taught her. "Miss Teller, I'm deaf, but read lips accurately. Otherwise, my deafness gives me excellent focus when doing work like typesetting, and enables me to work well under pressure."

Ruth Ann Teller's face went through the usual expressions—confusion, surprise, bewilderment. To Hannah's relief, Ruth Ann's expression ended with a soft smile. "So you know what I'm saying just by watching my lips?"

Hannah nodded. "I can also read them in Choctaw or Chickasaw if you would like to test me."

Ruth Ann's head lilted to one side. "*Chahta chia ho*? Are you Choctaw?"

"*Ki'yo, Chikasha saya.* No, I am Chickasaw."

Ruth Ann switched back to English. "It is truly good to meet you, Hannah Stillwater. Let me show you the typesetting cabinet and explain our process."

Ruth Ann led the way to the cabinet, motioning toward her left at the press operator who didn't pay them any mind. Ruth Ann halted and turned back to Hannah, looking sheepish.

"It may take some time to remember that I need to face you when speaking. I was saying that this is Caleb Gentry, our press operator. He likes to stay focused as well."

Keeping her face toward Hannah, Ruth Ann motioned toward the two people at the back bench. "I'll introduce you to Beulah and her father, Mr. Levitt, when they finish. They're fine people."

As she spoke, Ruth Ann stepped backwards to draw even with the typesetting cabinet. Hannah imagined this young woman knew every square inch of the print shop. Hannah needed to learn it that way, too.

Ruth Ann motioned to a narrow door beside the cabinet. "That's a dark room we added to develop photographs. Matthew does those. I ruin them nearly every time!" A hint of amusement lit her eyes, but it didn't quite chase away the shadows.

Ruth Ann put a hand on the typesetting cabinet, still facing Hannah. "This was primarily my job when my brother started the newspaper. But we have so many stories to write with a daily that's mostly what I do now. But I really need to get these set in Choctaw. As you can tell, we are short-staffed, so if you are available to start right away, we could use you."

During the long flow of words, Hannah noticed Ruth Ann's speech slowed and her lips widened. She was thinking through what it took for Hannah to read lips, and also speaking louder. Hannah didn't mind. She was focused on calming the flutter in her stomach. It seemed as though Ruth Ann Teller was hiring her on the spot.

She went on, "Besides being short-staffed, I am opening a new branch of the *Choctaw Tribune* in McAlester. Of course, that leaves this one in worse shape and we will be hiring on more workers. Still, it's long hours and you will have to work with my brother Matthew, but…"

Ruth Ann's shoulders relaxed and genuine respect layered her tired expression. "You'll get accustomed to his ways. He really is a kind man, but if you ever truly need to capture his attention, stick a story under his nose. That will do it."

Hannah's heart skittered. She was sure she'd secured the job. Now it sounded like she had a greater hurdle to overcome with Mr. Teller, who placed the advertisement that summoned her there.

Ruth Ann turned to the cabinet then quickly back. "I was

saying, why don't you start setting type on this story in Choctaw? That will save me a great deal of time, and my brother should be back soon. We had…an incident that set us behind, and he was out late last night."

The shadow came to Ruth Ann's eyes again, and Hannah recalled the frown the station master gave her when she asked about the *Choctaw Tribune*.

But then Ruth Ann blinked, and the shadow was gone. "Matthew will make the final decision, but as far as I'm concerned, you're hired."

Hannah wished she could close her eyes and take in the moment of relief. But her eyes were her connection to the world, and she learned long ago to always keep them wide open.

CHAPTER 17

The smell of bacon was faint when Matthew opened the back door into the kitchen after dressing in his lean-to bedroom. It was well past dawn, well past time for him to be at the newspaper office. He rarely slept so late, even after a late night of writing, but fatigue was catching up with him. Even the extra few hours of sleep left him feeling more tired than when he went to bed. Here was another Friday, the end of another week of feeling he was a month behind.

A plate of eggs and bacon were on the back of the hot stove and Matthew used one of his mother's pads to transfer the plate to the kitchen table. He was already late starting the day, but a quick breakfast would see him through the whole day. He had advertisers to visit first thing.

Yesterday when making rounds to deliver the daily, he encountered the Enterprise Hotel manager Blane Johnson, who acted hesitant when Matthew mentioned his advertising renewal was coming up. Ruth Ann had worked hard to earn that account, and the thought of losing it to Maxwell burned Matthew to the core. Maxwell was not going to win.

Matthew took a final gulp of food and coffee and shoved

away from the table, scraping the chair legs soundly across the wood floor.

A tiny gasp came from the doorway leading from the living room to the kitchen. Matthew barely caught a glimpse of little eyes before they disappeared behind the wall.

Nita.

How long had she stood there watching him without his noticing her?

Matthew walked softly to the doorframe to see her huddled on the floor against the wall, looking up at him. The events of the past few days had frightened her, not to mention the way he'd broken his promise to be there for her.

Matthew held a hand out to her, like he'd done at the depot, and she slowly rose and took it. Her hand was cold despite the warm room with the fire heating it. She wore her new boots and an orange plaid gingham dress, light for the current weather. But spring was coming.

The sewing machine clacked where Della was working in her room. She hadn't noticed Nita's absence, or perhaps she had and wanted Matthew to fulfill his role as her uncle and one of her guardians.

Advertisers would have to wait. Matthew tugged Nita's hand and led her to the mantle. He retrieved the family tintype in its gold frame and knelt by her, holding it to where she could see as she leaned against his knee.

"Little Bear, this is your family. Your grandfather, Jim Teller, went to Heaven before you were born, but he was a good man and took good care of his family. This is your aunt Ruth Ann, and your *pokni*, your grandmother Della." Matthew's thumb traced over each face, his heart swollen with a love and longing he couldn't fathom.

Nita pressed a finger under his image and looked up at him, brown eyes so earnest and sure. He nodded. "Yes, that's me, some years ago."

Then Nita pressed a finger over the last face in the photo and Matthew thought his heart would burst with pain. Did Nita remember her own father?

"This, Little Bear, this is your daddy." Matthew's throat closed up. Nita waited for him to continue. She was a patient little thing. That would serve her well.

Matthew lowered the photograph to his knee, staring at the family as they were. They were fragmented, but held together by their mother's love, like a patchwork quilt keeping them warm and whole.

Matthew took a long breath. "Your daddy made some bad decisions, and he can't come home right now. But you'll meet him one day, I promise."

It was one promise Matthew had to keep.

He shifted Nita to the side and stood to set the photograph back on the mantle. "Come over here and let's practice your letters."

For a half hour, Matthew sat on the sofa next to Nita, helping her write the alphabet. Then he wiped the slate clean and wrote his name and Preston Frazier's Ranch. He handed her the chalk.

"Practice writing this, Little Bear, because that's home for all of us. I want you to always be able to find your way home."

She tried to copy it, but her hand slipped, and Matthew noticed they were swollen from gripping the chalk so hard and long. He understood that cramped feeling.

"Here." He set the slate aside and went to the door where he'd dropped his satchel and package from his trip. He retrieved the pink and white striped package, smudged and crinkled, and handed it to Nita, who never took her eyes off him. "I brought you something from St. Louis."

When she hesitated, he lowered to one knee beside the sofa and tore the paper away. He opened the box and lifted out the wooden Noah's Ark. The individual pieces inside rattled.

Nita remained still on the sofa, so he opened the ark and

lifted pieces out one by one, lining them up in a haphazard row on the floor.

Nita slid from the sofa and onto her knees by the ark. She reached out and touched the painted boat with one finger, then slid a donkey to rest next to a pig. Scooting back, she sprawled down on her stomach and shifted the donkey to sit beside its mate. Her sock covered feet raised in the air behind her and she hooked them together at the ankles as she rested her chin on one hand while moving the animals around with each other.

Her eyes were so bright and alert, and Matthew knew he could sit there and watch them all day.

But he couldn't. He had to stay focused.

Matthew pushed open the door to the *Choctaw Tribune* office, nearly taking the bell off its hook in his fury. After his long morning at home, he'd visited two advertisers. He managed to keep one of them. That was the better way of thinking about it, especially since the one he kept was the Enterprise Hotel.

The shop was nearly empty, and Matthew realized he'd arrived in the middle of the lunch hour. That didn't explain why there was a woman he didn't know at the typesetting cabinet.

The telegraph sounder was going off and Peter was taking down a message while chomping on a sandwich. He didn't look up at Matthew's entry in the shop. Neither did the woman in a calico skirt that covered the high stool at the typesetting cabinet. She continued setting type in the composing stick, not acknowledging him.

Matthew frowned. The woman must have responded to their listing for a typesetter. He didn't mind another woman working in the shop, but she could at least introduce herself, especially since Ruth Ann insisted he make the final decision on new hires for the Dickens office.

Matthew strode over to the typesetting cabinet, skirting the low railing around his desk. He came up behind the young woman, who didn't even look over her shoulder at him.

"Excuse me, but I think we should be introduced. I'm Matthew Teller, publisher of the *Choctaw Tribune*."

The woman kept setting type, head bent intently over the composing stick. Her sable hair was held in a neat bun by a shell comb without any of those Gibson girl curls Ruth Ann had taken to wearing. He guessed this new woman was fashionable yet practical, and wholly focused on her work. He respected that, but didn't appreciate being ignored.

Matthew stepped closer, towering over her shoulder. "Ma'am, I said I'm Matthew—"

The woman shifted to tie the type pieces to remove them from the composing stick. The movement caused her face to turn enough for Matthew to get a quick look.

It didn't last long because the woman leapt to her feet, hitting the cabinet and knocking the composing stick off. It clattered to the floor, the pieces flying everywhere.

Matthew stared at the mess. Ruth Ann had done nearly the very same thing the first time he had her set type. She later ruined his good printing paper when they were on a tight deadline, leaving him to print that edition on brown butcher paper.

Surely this woman wouldn't commit a comedy of errors like that before she finally settled in. Matthew couldn't afford trouble beyond what he caused.

The woman dropped to her knees and scooped type pieces in her hands. "I'm sorry, sir, I didn't know you were there."

Matthew rubbed his hand over his mouth, trying to hold in the fatigue, frustration, and straight-up heartache of his life.

"Did my sister hire you—"

"I'll have this cleaned up in a moment," she interrupted, sweeping her palm across the floor and gathering the type to drop in her apron she used as a bag.

She stood, apron holding the tiny metal pieces. Matthew held his hand tight under his jaw, not wanting words he'd regret to come out. They definitely needed to work on their communication if she was going to work in his shop.

"Let's try this another way. Who are you and what are your qualifications for working at my newspaper?"

The young woman stared at him intently. Shockingly so, then he realized why her gaze was so startling. By her hair and skin, he judged she was an Indian. But her eyes…he'd never seen anything like the combination of dark skin and hair with eyes the color of a clear, deep blue sky reflected on a lake.

The woman relaxed her shoulders with effort. "You must be Matthew Teller." A lisp in her tone made his name sound almost musical. "I have newspaper experience, and Miss Teller wanted me to set type for a story in Choctaw for you to review. I was starting on another one that was here, too."

Matthew glanced at a completed article set in a chase on the flat stone next to the cabinet. "That's impressive, but I'm more interested in how you conduct yourself in my shop, like ignoring—"

The woman cleared her throat loudly. "Mr. Teller, I understand you want to test my abilities, but I cannot read your lips if you turn your face away completely."

Matthew looked up sharply. "Are you normally so prone to interrupting people?"

She stared at him, then realization settled in her blue lake eyes. She calmly opened her apron over a small bowl on the typesetting cabinet. The pieces clattered into it. She turned back to Matthew and looked him straight in the eyes, making him want to apologize for his abrupt tone. But he waited and let her speak.

"I'm sorry, I assumed you already spoke with your sister." Her voice was clear despite its lisp. "I am Hannah Stillwater, citizen of the Chickasaw Nation, and I am deaf."

Matthew dropped his hand, staring into her eyes, repeating her words in his mind.

I am deaf.

Here he thought she was the rude one. He never felt so foolish in his life.

Then his feelings turned to amazement at how she would know what he said without hearing him. He'd never thought of anything like that.

Matthew took in more of her features—the roundness of her nose and the way her eyebrows arched in anticipation of observing his words. He connected her prim and proper physical appearance with the tremendous odds she'd overcome to find herself standing in a newspaper shop. *His* shop.

The bell over the door rang and a voice called, "Matthew!"

Ruth Ann came up beside him and motioned at the young woman. "I see you've met Hannah Stillwater. I told her you'd make the final decision on hiring…"

Matthew noticed that though she was speaking to him, Ruth Ann kept her face turned toward Miss Stillwater. Ruth Ann sounded hesitant, unsure, and he knew it was because he was red-faced from being ready to explode only moments before.

After the incident this week, he could only pray his sister's confidence in her work wasn't shattered. He'd learned long ago that occasional praise brought out better results in her than constant critique. He thought they were past a lot of things, but hiring a deaf employee was a new test.

For being the one who should show the most nerves, Hannah Stillwater was a calming presence as she watched the siblings to catch who was speaking.

Matthew rubbed his chin as Ruth Ann looked over the finished chase. She turned to face Hannah Stillwater.

"Fine work, and swift, without error." Ruth Ann gave Matthew a tentative smile. She wouldn't feel hesitant if she knew what a fool he had just made of himself.

He dropped his hand from his chin. "Miss Stillwater, you are hired."

A wash of relief splashed her dark complexion, but Miss Stillwater quickly masked it and nodded. "Thank you, sir. I promise not to be so clumsy in the future."

Matthew flushed as his sister shot an accusing glare his way. "I owe you an apology, Miss Stillwater, probably more than one. I'll make sure I don't sneak up on you again."

Ruth Ann touched the young woman's arm to get her attention. "I told you he's actually a kind man."

Smiling and looking more like the strong Choctaw woman she was, Ruth Ann asked, "Will you join our family for dinner, Miss Stillwater? We're having other guests, and I know our mother would like to meet you."

Matthew hadn't known they were having guests. He'd thought to spend the evening writing articles, and being the devoted uncle he should to Nita.

But inviting Hannah Stillwater to dinner was Ruth Ann's best idea of the week. Matthew wanted to know about her previous newspaper experience, and how in the world she'd developed into such a remarkable individual, one who could read lips and be patient with a beast like him.

"Please join us, Miss Stillwater," he said. "I'd like to ask…"

He halted, realizing she wasn't looking at him and didn't know he was speaking. Ruth Ann nodded her head toward him and Miss Stillwater quickly turned. She had a becoming smile.

"Just wave when you're speaking to me, Mr. Teller. It's like saying my name."

Matthew figured he'd find himself waving often in the near future.

CHAPTER 18

Once again, Matthew was in the barn on a Friday evening doing chores with Benjamin before dinner. But they couldn't talk openly. Nita had trailed Matthew to the barn and helped feed the animals by throwing hay in his stallion's stall, one tiny fistful at a time.

In a few stolen moments, Matthew asked Benjamin about suing Maxwell for his slanderous article. Benjamin wasn't optimistic about their chances in court and warned it would make things dirtier.

Matthew wasn't sure how to feel about his future brother-in-law's reaction to the incident. Not surprisingly, Benjamin had been angry, but levelheaded when he came the day the article was released. He reminded them to consider the source, and that the article would soon fade from memories, though he admitted damage was done.

After the stock was fed, Matthew carried the lantern out of the barn in one hand while Nita tucked her hand in his other. Her hand was cold, and he squeezed gently. Her fragile, fine frame was like a baby bird, but she had a fierce soul. She was a Teller, after all.

Benjamin closed the barn doors against the chilly night air, then turned to Matthew, his deep brown eyes nearly lost in the darkness as he spoke softly. "Will you do something for me, brother?"

Matthew tightened his grip on the lantern handle, wondering if Nita could make out the words of Benjamin's deep voice. Matthew couldn't recall Benjamin asking anything of him since he arrived in Indian Territory, except permission to court Ruth Ann. Benjamin's grave expression hinted that this request was as serious.

Whatever he was going to ask of Matthew would be hard, but fair. Matthew nodded his agreement without knowing what the request was. He trusted Benjamin like few other men.

Benjamin glanced down at Nita and placed a hand on her bare head, covering it against the cold. Then he met Matthew's gaze. "Will you discontinue your investigation until after the wedding?"

Matthew gritted his teeth. *Never.*

But Benjamin knew Christopher Maxwell would take every opportunity to ruin Ruth Ann's happiness until she was married and safely away in McAlester. Matthew had caused her enough grief in her young life.

"I'll wait."

Benjamin let out a soul-deep breath, and Matthew knew it was as hard for him to ask as it was for Matthew to agree.

"Remember, brother, you don't always have to tell your side of the story," Benjamin added quietly. "Time will."

Nita slipped her free hand up to nudge Benjamin's hand on her head. He removed it, stroking smushed hair away from her forehead. Nita grasped his hand and Benjamin released his smile that was never far away.

With Nita between them, the men headed inside the box house and Matthew knew there would be no scolding about the mud they tracked in.

Matthew just wished Hannah Stillwater had accepted Ruth Ann's dinner invitation. She declined and left the shop shortly after to get settled for a stay at the Enterprise Hotel where she would board until she could make other living arrangements.

Matthew couldn't comprehend his disappointment at her reticence to join them. He chalked it up to one of his failings as a human being. Maybe he scared people into his bidding more than not these days.

They entered the kitchen and Ruth Ann took charge of getting Nita washed up for dinner while Della and Beulah set food on the table. Matthew wove between them as he shrugged off his coat, Benjamin behind him. At the doorway to the living room, he halted, causing Benjamin to bump into him.

In the living room was Peter and Mr. Levitt seated on the sofa, carrying on a conversation with Hannah Stillwater, who perched on the edge of Della's rocker.

She rose, causing Mr. Levitt to stand as he greeted Matthew and shook Benjamin's hand.

Matthew motioned between Benjamin and Hannah. "Miss Stillwater, this is…" his voice was gravelly, and he cleared his throat. Then he remembered she couldn't hear the roughness anyway and a thought struck him. He could speak without a sound and she would be the only one in the room who would understand him. That could come in handy.

He finished introducing Miss Stillwater and Benjamin just as Ruth Ann stepped to the doorway to call them all into the kitchen for dinner.

While Peter led the way, Matthew gave Hannah a little wave to make sure she looked at him when he said, "I'm glad you changed your mind about coming this evening."

Her smile didn't quite reach her eyes. She was a stalwart individual, but he knew he made her nervous. He could understand after the way he acted.

"I was going to take dinner at the hotel, but your sister caught me coming down and asked again for me to join you all," Hannah Stillwater explained as she nodded for Matthew to proceed her into the kitchen so she could watch where she was going while watching Matthew in case he spoke. "Miss Teller wanted me to meet the rest of your family and her fiancé. I wasn't sure it was entirely appropriate, since I am now an employee...something I greatly appreciate."

Matthew smiled, trying to ease the tension between them. He'd never thought of himself as an overbearing boss, but he never worked with a female except his sister and occasionally Beulah. He wasn't always successful at reading emotions, something he learned was a key skill early on with Ruth Ann in the *Choctaw Tribune*.

They joined everyone at the table and Matthew found himself seated at the opposite end from Hannah Stillwater.

After grace, Beulah launched into excited chatter about the wedding. Matthew was grateful for her crisp manner in the awkward setting. It was the first time of having Nita seated at the Friday dinner table, across from Matthew and between Ruth Ann and Benjamin. Benjamin dished small servings onto her plate, her eyes down in her lap where she cradled a rag doll Matthew recognized. It had belonged to Ruth Ann when she was a little girl.

Matthew couldn't take his eyes off Nita for the longest moment. His brother's little girl, being surrounded by the love and protection and care she should have known all her life.

A touch on the back of his hand brought his attention to his mother, and he nodded before straightening from his slouch and began dishing up his own plate. He couldn't go through those files in his mind and heart, or he'd lose it right there at the table.

Thankfully, Beulah successfully pulled Ruth Ann from the slump she'd been in since the encounter with Maxwell. Soon, Ruth Ann was giggling at Beulah's descriptions of ludicrous weddings that had taken place in history. Beulah prodded Benjamin into describing weddings he attended in D.C.

Matthew had trouble keeping his gaze off tender Nita's face. He didn't want to crack, so he turned his attention to the end of the table with Mr. Levitt, Peter, and Hannah Stillwater, wondering how she could follow along and even take part in this setting with so many lips to read. Despite the back-and-forth and up-and-down of the table conversation, she seemed to be keeping track.

At one point, she watched Beulah and Mr. Levitt closely and smiled to herself. That wouldn't have been so remarkable except that Matthew noticed they had switched to Russian and were sharing a joke.

Mid-way through the meal, Ruth Ann waved at Hannah. When Hannah raised her eyebrows in acknowledgment, Ruth Ann asked, "Hannah, there is a novel with a beautiful description of a Chickasaw wedding ceremony, perhaps you've read it? *On the Blue River* by T.A. Paige? You would almost think a woman had written it."

Matthew was glad Ruth Ann drew Miss Stillwater into the discussion. They all sensed she didn't want to be the center of attention at dinner on her first night in Dickens.

Matthew just wished Ruth Ann had chosen a topic besides novels.

Hannah Stillwater didn't seem comfortable with the topic either. She blinked then nodded. "I am familiar with the book."

Matthew noted how she raised her voice enough to be heard by Ruth Ann down the table, but not too much. How had she mastered how loud or soft to speak when conversing with people?

Ruth Ann motioned at Matthew. "I hope you're not as opposed to novels as my brother is. He doesn't care for fictional stories. But I find there can be as much or more truth in fiction than true stories when it comes to human emotions."

Matthew had to respond. "There's nothing more powerful than the press except God Almighty." Belatedly, he turned his face toward the end of the table as he continued. "Entertainment might have its place in the world, but to me, fiction is a waste of good words."

He was aware that Hannah Stillwater caught everything he said, then she looked down at her plate. He felt as though she had exited the room.

Then she looked up and glanced around the table to make sure no one was speaking before she said, "I suppose there are enough words to go around in this family."

Everyone chuckled and Peter chimed in, "You oughtn't live in a town named after a novelist, Matt."

"I wish I didn't."

An uncomfortable silence filled the room. Ruth Ann cleared her throat. "*On the Blue River* was the finest novel I've read. The heart of a true story beat in that fiction." She sighed. "Sadly, I lost my copy in the train wreck returning home from D.C."

Her gaze drifted to Benjamin, pain in her eyes, and Matthew recalled Ruth Ann's dramatic account of the terrifying accident. He knew she hadn't exaggerated one word.

Matthew turned back to his plate, catching Hannah watching him from the corner of her eye. It was hard to know if she was simply following the conversation or if she was looking at someone for another reason. Beulah regained her attention and returned the conversation to weddings.

Who knew there could be so much to talk about with a one-day event?

After the meal, Ruth Ann directed everyone to the living room for coffee and cookies. Matthew held back, busying himself with helping his mother arrange cookies on a platter. Nita was under his elbow, and he slipped her a chocolate chip one. She gave him the tiniest smile he'd ever seen.

Behind him, he heard Hannah speaking quietly to Ruth Ann

before leaving the kitchen last. "If you don't mind, Miss Teller, I'm going to return to the hotel now. It's been a long day."

Matthew looked over his shoulder to see Ruth Ann grip Hannah's wrist, alarm in her eyes. "You really shouldn't walk to the hotel alone."

Turning just enough so that Hannah could still see her face, Ruth Ann said to Matthew, "Matt, you need to walk Hannah back to the hotel."

Hannah's eyes widened. "Oh, that isn't necessary. I'll be fine."

Matthew dusted cookie crumbs from his fingertips. He caught his mother's eye. She gave him a meaningful look.

"Ruth Ann's right, Miss Stillwater," Matthew said. "It won't take long. Nita, would you like to come with us?"

That satisfied the need for having a chaperone and Della took the cookie platter to the living room, though she paused to give one to Hannah, who still seemed hesitant. Matthew wondered if it was because he was her boss, or she just didn't trust him in general. Had she read the slanderous article by Maxwell? There was more than one copy of that *Dickens Herald* edition floating around the *Choctaw Tribune* office. Peter thought it would be useful for wiping muddy boots.

Whatever her hesitation, Hannah relented and took a few moments to bid everyone good evening. She gathered her coat, hat, and winter gloves while Matthew bundled Nita for the evening walk.

Outside, he wasn't sure how they would carry on a conversation. Other than the streetlamps, there were too many shadows between the box house and the hotel for her to see his face well.

Even though she didn't know how quiet it was, Hannah Stillwater must have sensed the awkwardness and filled the silence as they walked with Nita between them.

"I look forward to working at the *Choctaw Tribune*, Mr. Teller. Your sister is very kind and I know all will miss her, but I'm happy for her and Mr. Nakishi. It's a bold venture, opening another branch in McAlester, but I have no doubt she will succeed."

She glanced over at Matthew, and he figured if he partially turned his face while still watching the shadows for danger, she'd be able to read his lips.

"Annie's the best. Most of the time."

He smiled to let her know he was teasing. She smiled back. Good. They were starting to communicate. Might as well get the worst over with.

"Miss Stillwater, I need to ask if you read the erroneous *Dickens Herald* article accusing my sister and I of…unscrupulous activities."

Hannah turned away from looking at him and gave a short nod. "I did." She looked at him again. "I know what it's like to be falsely accused."

Matthew puffed out a breath. Hannah had a good sense of judgement. But he'd just as soon change the subject. "I wanted to ask you something about this evening. You seemed to catch an exchange between Beulah and Mr. Levitt, but I'm pretty sure they were speaking Russian."

Hannah nodded. "I learned some Russian from a classmate at college in the east. With all the European immigrants, there were several languages to pick up—French, German, Russian. I mostly love the languages the Bible was written in—Aramaic, Greek, Hebrew. But please don't look so impressed." Hannah laughed softly. "I know a bit of several languages but I'm only proficient in a few."

Matthew couldn't help but be impressed. "How did you learn to read lips?"

He wondered if the question was too personal, but Hannah Stillwater didn't seem to mind. "It was pure necessity, Mr. Teller. When I was in the Wapanucka Female Institute in the Chickasaw Nation, speaking was the way people communicated. I did have a teacher who helped me learn to speak better. I didn't think I would survive childhood." She gave a light laugh, but Matthew knew the depth of the experience must have cut deep.

"Your folks didn't send you to a school for the deaf?"

"No."

She didn't offer to elaborate. They were halfway to the hotel on the empty streets. Nita swung her arms loosely from side to side and Matthew wondered if she was cold or just bored. He paused and squatted, beckoning her to climb onto his back. She did, hooking her little legs around his waist, arms going around his neck as he lifted. Hannah tucked Nita's skirt modestly under his arms.

When she stepped back, he said, "The fact that someone can read lips is fascinating. I wouldn't mind trying to learn myself."

She looked at him as she resumed walking, curiosity on her face. "Very few people are interested in how I communicate. But if you want to learn, you can start by observing people's lips when they speak. Many words look the same, so you must decipher enough in an entire sentence to understand what was said."

They were almost to the Enterprise, so Matthew slowed his walk, hefting Nita higher from where she was slipping. Her head rested on his shoulder, and he wondered if she was drifting off to sleep. "So, you could be somewhere like the hotel restaurant and eavesdrop on any table?"

Hannah Stillwater laughed as they mounted the steps and turned to face him fully. "That would be rude, Mr. Teller. But I must confess I've done it."

Matthew shook his head. "Every time you say 'Mr. Teller,' I don't know who you're talking to. You can just call me Matthew or Matt. It's up to you, Miss Stillwater."

He hoped she would offer to allow him to call her by her given name. Instead, a shadow crossed her face and the brief connection between them was lost.

"Thank you for seeing me here, Mr. Teller. Goodnight."

She disappeared inside the hotel.

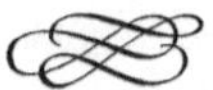

CHAPTER 19

*M*atthew unbuttoned the collar of his shirt to let heat escape before he started sweating. Late May brought warmer weather that clung to the air in the darkroom where he developed photographs for the daily edition. The dank air appropriately matched the photographs which showed angry springtime weather ravaging Indian Territory.

Tornados had sprouted with dire regularity the past two months. One hit Springstown just that week. Matthew went to do a report on the damage and help out their old friends, the Barnes. Pepper Barnes' home took damage, but neither he nor his pregnant wife were injured.

In nearby Antlers, Sissy Barnes, or rather Coxwell now, resided. After a whirlwind Christmastime romance, she'd married a businessman named Leonard Coxwell before the new year.

When Matthew asked Pepper how the newlyweds were doing, Pepper gave a clipped answer about Matthew minding his own business.

Matthew carried a pocket Kodak camera in his briefcase these days and it came in handy to document news events. Those were the photos he developed now for the tornado story. With the flashlight on the camera, he could even take photos indoors.

He'd already enlarged the tornado photos and now saw the current image taking shape on the paper he agitated in the silver gelatin tray. Once it reached the right density, he lifted it carefully to the stop tray, agitated it again, then on to the rinse tray it went before he picked it up by one corner and hung it to dry on the line by his worktable in the darkroom.

As the next image became visible in the tray, Matthew made out Daniel's grim face. He stood beside his horse, rifle butt resting on the ground by his boot, six gun visible at his side. Matthew asked Daniel to pose the last time he saw him a few weeks before. Daniel hadn't found the woman killer he'd been tracking and was being assigned to another outlaw trail. He hadn't wanted to give up the search. Matthew didn't want him to, either.

At least Matthew hadn't heard from his own shadow since that encounter in Fort Smith.

When he finished with the bath tray, Matthew hung Daniel's photo with the others. The process of developing photographs took time away from writing news stories, but Matthew benefited from the quiet moments in the darkroom. No one bothered him once he hung the "Do Not Enter" sign on the door. If only he could hang one on the town of Dickens to keep Christopher Maxwell out.

Matthew had kept his word to Benjamin and placed his investigation on hold, throwing all his energy into preparing for Ruth Ann to leave one shop and start another. The wedding was only days away, so she was hardly there anyway. He needed more employees, which turned into an impossible task after Maxwell's slanderous article.

For reasons unknown, Hannah Stillwater stuck with them

despite sour looks cast at the *Choctaw Tribune* employees by townspeople. She didn't seem bothered by it, and Matthew knew he needed to take care of this loyal employee. He had precious few.

He hung the last photo to dry and opened the door to the brighter interior of the *Choctaw Tribune* office. He blinked in the sudden light, then stepped to the typesetting cabinet occupied by Hannah Stillwater. She looked up, focused on his face to see what he was saying.

"Miss Stillwater, can you set a photograph with the story about the Springstown tornado? I'll have the halftone plate ready soon."

She cocked an eyebrow. "Of course."

Matthew's gaze drifted down to the article block next to the desk where she worked. It was the front page with the tornado article included, already locked in and ready to go. He'd forgotten to tell her he might have a photo for it.

"Never mind, we need to stay on schedule. I'll just give the picture to Pepper."

"It's no trouble to reset the page with the image, Mr. Teller. I can stay late this evening."

He shook his head. "It's not important. I don't want to hold you up."

Even as he said it, he realized he was holding her up as she gave him her full attention. She couldn't work and talk at the same time the way he often did when Ruth Ann was setting type.

He gave an awkward wave toward the typesetting cabinet as he stepped away toward the idle printing press. Caleb Gentry was away on lunch. With the telegraph sounder silent, Peter sat at Matthew's desk, eating.

Matthew frowned. His cousin making himself at home was normal, but something was amiss with Peter. Matthew sensed it, and it didn't solely pertain to Glenrose Jessop. Peter was missing most Sunday afternoons, disappearing to parts unknown until late evening.

But this wasn't the time to question Peter. Matthew hated for the press to be idle for long, and an order for an advertisement flyer awaited printing.

CHAPTER 20

Matthew drove the crowbar under the plank lid of the enormous box sitting in the middle of the room in the McAlester *Choctaw Tribune* office. He'd rented a space near the Tobucksy County Courthouse, and it was time to stock it with equipment. It wouldn't be as large as the shop in Dickens but there was room for them to print truth in one of the hotbeds of the Choctaw Nation.

There was a dentist office on the second floor of the building. An appropriate metaphor. Getting the truth out of a story was like extracting teeth sometimes. Matthew used the box lid to take out his anxiousness about getting back to investigating Christopher Maxwell as soon as the wedding was over.

Matthew had just gotten the lid off the crate when Benjamin entered the shop, dressed in work clothes instead of the suit he normally wore. Benjamin had shown his versatility many times over, not being afraid to lend a hand butchering hogs on Uncle Preston's ranch or distributing newspapers when they came up short of help in the McAlester area. Benjamin may have been a big city lawyer in Washington, D.C., but he was still an ordinary Choctaw boy. He was the right man for Ruth Ann.

It didn't hurt that Benjamin had purchased one of the finest houses in McAlester, a grand three-story mansion with six guest rooms that would house his crew of in-laws when they came to visit.

Matthew laid aside the crowbar and shook Benjamin's hand. "Halito. Chim achukma?"

Together, they lifted the heavy top piece of the press and set it aside. They analyzed the largest piece, the base, and agreed it would be easier to knock out the rest of the crate walls rather than lift it out.

As they hammered away with the crowbar and an actual hammer, Matthew said, "It was a miracle we were able to save the original printing press we still have from the fire at the first shop."

Benjamin knocked the last board on one wall free. "Ruth Ann told me what happened, but she spared the details. It is a traumatic memory for her."

Matthew levered the crowbar, splintering wood instead of pulling a plank loose cleanly like Benjamin had done. Things tended to get splintered when Matthew started yanking and pulling.

Maybe Ruth Ann hadn't wanted to talk much about that night, but Matthew did now. "Mr. Levitt is the one who sounded the alarm. He'd been out taking a walk and spotted our building on fire. I was out the door and in the flames before Ruth Ann got down the stairs, I guess. I had to save the press. I knew if I could save it, I could save the *Choctaw Tribune*. Wouldn't have made it without Mr. Levitt helping shove it through the doorway. It shouldn't have made it. Like I said, it was a miracle."

It was also miraculous how they hadn't been burned alive. And that Matthew hadn't shot Jack Banny on the spot and gotten himself hung. It was certain now that Banny—the hotel owner and illegal whiskey runner—was responsible for burning down the newspaper.

Matthew wondered again if he needed to forgive a dead man.

He and Benjamin finished removing the box walls and piled the boards close to the door. They dragged the printer base from the wood crate and settled it where Matthew had marked for its location. He'd gotten there early that morning and spent a few hours accessing the room and tacking pieces of paper to the floor where the various implements would go.

Ruth Ann would have her own desk near the front door to handle advertisers and subscribers that came in. The printing press was set on the backside of the middle of the room near the typesetting cabinet. Tucked in the other corner at the far back was a little desk facing the wall. Ruth Ann could use that for writing or whoever else was writing extra articles for the McAlester version of the paper. It was a small room, but having a dedicated space just for writing was important.

They hefted the top piece onto the base and Benjamin handed Matthew the appropriate screws while Matthew worked them in one at a time. He reached to take another screw, but it wasn't there. He looked up and found Benjamin studying him.

"Your first shop getting burned; is that what is driving you to try to eliminate the town of Dickens?"

Matthew rested his hand on the coolness of the press handle. The presence of the machine was already emitting the familiar smells of a newspaper shop in the room. Matthew had gone into the newspaper business to print truth. He hadn't reckoned on coming to love the paper and ink of the press so much. It was moments like this when he questioned if part of his drive to take down Maxwell was more related to them being business rivals in the same town or even going back to when Christopher Maxwell stunted Matthew's newspaper journey with his bad experiences at the *Dickens Herald*.

But no. This was more about blood and ink, not paper and ink.

Matthew met Benjamin's eyes. "Our people had everything

taken from them in Mississippi. My grandmother buried her parents on the trail. She and all her generation poured their sweat and blood on this land to rebuild the Choctaw Nation. It's been every generation's responsibility to fight for our nation. I may not win, but I have a duty to fight."

Benjamin handed him the next screw. "Yes. We do."

Matthew took the screw and twisted it in the hole to get it started then used the screwdriver to tighten it. He tightened it so hard he nearly stripped the head.

Benjamin chuckled. "As long as the fire is burning in you, we may as well talk about resuming your investigation into Christopher Maxwell. Whenever you are ready, I will commit to handle the legal matters of the case, even if it means losing the second case of my career."

Matthew grunted. "The Teller brothers are hard to win for, aren't they?"

Benjamin chuckled softly and Matthew grinned but kept his eyes down. "How do you feel about marrying my sister? I don't mean my sister in particular, well, of course I do. I mean you getting married in general."

Benjamin rolled the next screw between his fingers. "Marriage isn't something I have thought about in general. Only with a specific woman. When I met Ruth Ann, I felt God bringing us together. Marriage was more the default than the intention." Benjamin gave Matthew a sidelong look. "Is there a specific woman who has you asking these questions?"

Matthew snagged the screw from Benjamin's large hand and went to work adding it to the press as Benjamin chuckled.

"If you want to ask more questions, you may. But I have an important one also for you today."

"What's that?"

"Ruth Ann and I have been talking about Nita. She will be a young woman before Philip is released from prison. How would you feel if Ruth Ann and I legally adopted her?"

Matthew halted before he stripped the screw head. Tension had enveloped his body when Benjamin brought up Philip, but he released it in a long breath.

If Ruth Ann adopted Nita, that would make Matthew Nita's maternal uncle. Which, according to Choctaw tradition, meant he would be responsible for her upbringing.

He had already wanted to assume that role with her as Philip's daughter, but this made it even more special. He'd miss having Nita at their home in Dickens, but this could be another healing piece for him through an ancient Choctaw tradition of the mother's brother being responsible for the upbringing of her children.

"I think that would be a fine thing, provided Philip and my mother agree."

Matthew and Benjamin finished assembling the press, the first component in the McAlester *Choctaw Tribune* office. It also symbolized the first piece of a new chapter in their lives.

Benjamin and Ruth Ann's wedding was the next week.

CHAPTER 21

It was that quiet, early summer kind of evening when things settled after dinner, but the day wasn't done yet. Ruth Ann knelt on the floor next to the vanity in the attic bedroom she shared with her mother and now, her precious niece. Alone, she carefully emptied the vanity drawers into a crate, packing the last of her belongings except what she needed to prepare for her wedding ceremonies the next day.

Her heart and stomach were in such a flutter, she hadn't eaten a bite at dinner and excused herself early to pack. The rest of the family and guests, the Levitts included, had retired to the living room. Ruth Ann was grateful. She needed a few moments alone after the swirl of preparations and excitement.

She was terrified.

Not about marrying Benjamin. No decision in her life felt more right, aside from her salvation; and giving herself to the work of the *Choctaw Tribune*. She didn't know what frightened her.

The drawers were empty now, save for one item tucked into the back. She smiled as she tugged out the journal wrapped in her daddy's shirt. She held the shirt to her nose, inhaling the faded scent of her daddy's hugs. He was still there, mixed with the smells of the leather journal Matthew gave her for her eighteenth birthday, right before he egged her into working with him in the newspaper business.

She had long ago filled the journal. She'd written her first story for the *Choctaw Tribune* between its covers and never stopped, even though she had made a mess of her first attempts to work in the newspaper. She ruined an entire edition before she started gaining her rhythm.

"There are three ways of doing things, you know."

Ruth Ann snapped her head up, surprised she hadn't heard Matthew ascend the staircase to lean against the wall of the attic, a soft smile on his face. It was so rare she saw him smile these days. The intensity of his work consumed him.

But none of that was in him now. He was there for her on her final evening before her new life began.

She cocked an eyebrow at him. "Oh? And what are those three ways?"

She knew what he meant, but she wanted to hear it again. Wanted to hear the story of how their adventures all began.

Matthew pushed away from the wall and reached out a hand to help her from the floor. She shifted to sit on the bed beside him, on her quilt, the only thing she hadn't packed that she would take with her into marriage.

Matthew didn't tell the story. He kept looking at her, his smile sinking. He was thinking about Maxwell, she knew, and how the man had accosted her. She wished she could talk about it, tell him what happened. But not now. Not until after the wedding. It was Benjamin she needed to tell first.

"It's all right, Matt." That was all she could say to set his mind at ease.

He clamped a hand on the back of his neck. "No, it isn't. I haven't even gotten you a wedding gift."

Ruth Ann chuckled. "You've given me a newspaper shop in McAlester."

He grinned at the floor. "I used to say there were two ways of doing things—right and again. You taught me the third one: Annie's way." He dropped his hand and met her eyes, somber. "Thank you. For sacrificing living on Uncle Preston's ranch and going on this venture with me. I couldn't have gotten this far without you, Annie."

The dam holding back her emotions threatened to break behind Ruth Ann's eyes. If only she had one more day with her brother, the way it was before. Just two crazy Choctaw kids trying to make a difference in their world. They hadn't known the personal victories and devastations they'd face along the way.

The pressure and grief over Philip's situation and trial had showed all the cracks in her relationship with Matthew. Then the Almighty healed them.

She squeezed his hand, throat hot. "We've been through a lot together."

Matthew snorted. "Yeah. And most of it was my fault."

Ruth Ann leaned into his shoulder, tears spilling out with her giggle. "Oh, Matt."

She blinked and noted a bulk in his shirt pocket. "What's this?"

Before he could answer, Ruth Ann slipped the newspaper clipping from his pocket. She saw the word *Maxwell*, and snapped the clip open.

Matthew snatched it away, but not before she recognized the style of the *Dickens Herald*, Maxwell's name, and *bid for mayor*.

She gasped. "Christopher Maxwell is running for mayor?"

"You weren't supposed to see that."

Ruth Ann had wondered why that day's *Herald* edition had escaped her notice. She had insisted on working in the newspaper the day before her wedding, taking in the moments one final time and making sure all was ready for her departure.

Matthew must have hidden the *Herald* to keep from upsetting her.

Too late.

"Matt! Let me see that. Maxwell announced this today on purpose, didn't he? Knowing my wedding is tomorrow!"

Matthew tightened a corner of his mouth, still not giving her the clipping. "It was next to the congratulations on your upcoming nuptials."

"Oh!" Ruth Ann jumped to her feet, spilling the shirt on the floor as she paced to the attic window and back. "That man! I say we write a full front page spread tonight and publish a special edition tomorrow listing the true achievements of Christopher Maxwell. We cannot allow him to become the elected mayor of Dickens!"

Matthew's soft smile returned. "We have a wedding tomorrow."

Ruth Ann sank onto the bed, her stomach in yet more knots. "I cannot believe I'm leaving you to face everything on your own. I won't be around to rescue you."

She folded her hands in her lap, trying not to clench them and reveal the depths of her fears. "Be careful, Matt. Just…just stay away from Maxwell. He's…I think he's more dangerous than we ever thought before."

She said too much. Matthew went rigid, still seated on the bed next to her. "Tell me what happened, Annie. Everything."

"No, Matt. Please. Let us go through the wedding…and Nita's adoption." Her heart lightened, and she hoped her brother's followed suit. She touched his arm lightly. "We *have* been through a lot, and there is more ahead. But like the past, the future will have its bright spots; its times of hope and joy and peace."

Matthew scooped their daddy's shirt from the floor where Ruth Ann had dropped it. He whispered, "I hope he's proud."

"I know he is." Ruth Ann placed her hand over her brother's. "I know I am."

CHAPTER 22

The day of his baby sister's wedding came as a shock to Matthew. Even after months of knowing it would come, the all-consuming planning, stocking the new print shop, and Ruth Ann's last night in the box house, the moment that Matthew stood as Benjamin's best man still jarred him. He could hardly breathe as he watched Uncle Preston prepare to walk Ruth Ann down the grassy aisle of the brush arbor set up outside the First Baptist Church of Dickens.

Throughout the early morning hours, Matthew had followed orders of getting food packed, the buggy ready for the drive out to the ranch, and even washing the breakfast dishes, though only he and Peter actually ate. He hadn't seen the bride—no one had except her mother and Beulah—until this moment.

Ruth Ann wore a new, deep red dress in the traditional French style their people had adopted decades before. Red—homma—for their mother's clan. She'd spent weeks sewing the ruffles and doing the diamond embroidery, adding the ribbons flowing down her back last. She carried a wildflower bouquet loaded with bluestars, red columbines, blue indigos, hyacinths, yellow sundrops, and the striking plains coreopsis with its yellow petals and bright red centers.

Hair folded up in the old way, a wildflower crown adorned Ruth Ann's head like an angel's halo, allowing Gibson girl ringlets to frame her heart-shaped face. Her eyes glowed with tears as she clenched Uncle Preston's arm as though he were the only thing keeping her on her feet. Matthew wondered how Benjamin was standing so calm.

There wasn't a building in Dickens that could've held the crowd. Every chair on the lawn was filled, and people lined the aisle another dozen yards. It seemed most of the town had come to see the female newspaper publisher get married. More so, Ruth Ann was a beloved writer and human being. This was also a farewell gathering before she moved to McAlester.

They were all familiar faces of family, friends, employees, and acquaintances, but Matthew couldn't take his eyes off his sister as everyone rose to their feet. Beulah played a song on her violin as little Nita, the flower girl, walked up the aisle, chin high as she tossed flower petals, her gaze roaming with a glint of curiosity in her eyes.

She met Matthew's eyes and his heart turned to softened clay. He'd miss her, too, when she moved to McAlester, but they were bonded together in spirit for eternity.

Ruth Ann and Uncle Preston moved in step with the music at an excruciatingly slow pace. Matthew got his bearings enough to realize Benjamin was leaning forward on his toes.

Matthew whispered, "Be still, brother. She will come to you."

She did. Ruth Ann and Uncle Preston stood before Pastor Rand. The music faded. Beulah set aside her violin to take her place as the Maid of Honor. Pastor Rand asked, "Who presents this young woman for marriage?"

"Her mother and myself, her uncle."

Uncle Preston handed Ruth Ann off to Benjamin with a final look that reminded the man that Preston's role in her life wasn't ending. Benjamin nodded and Matthew watched as the world disappeared from around the couple, unconscious of everything Pastor Rand said until they reached the vows that Benjamin and Ruth Ann had written themselves.

At the end of Pastor Rand reading the vow, Benjamin squeaked, "I do," causing a ripple of laughter. Matthew chuckled. Benjamin was human after all.

Drawing up tall and clearing his throat, Benjamin repeated in his naturally-deep voice and with a grin, "I do."

Matthew's gaze drifted to Hannah Stillwater, seated a few rows behind his mother. Matthew wished he could convey what all was said since her view of the pastor was blocked. He'd have to fill her in later if she wanted.

When Pastor Rand pronounced Ruth Ann and Benjamin husband and wife and presented them to the crowd as Mr. and Mrs. Benjamin Nakishi-Dunn, Benjamin and Ruth Ann shared their first kiss. The crowd erupted in a cheer. The couple skipped up the aisle together, hand in hand, playful, as Matthew escorted Beulah down the aisle behind them. The rest of the groomsmen and bridesmaids—his cousins—fell in behind them. Matthew caught his mother's eye. He had escorted her to her chair that morning and she looked at peace now.

Matthew broke away to fetch the Teller buggy. There was a flurry as most people prepared to load up and head to Uncle Preston's ranch for the second ceremony and the reception.

Matthew helped his mother into the front seat of the buggy and Nita hoisted herself onto the back seat. He glanced around to make sure the bride and groom were ready. He smirked as Benjamin handed Ruth Ann into a small, two-seater carriage. Clever man.

"Uncle Matthew?"

Oh, how he adored those words. "Yes, Little Bear?"

Nita scooted forward as Matthew snapped the reins and started them down the road. "Why are people crying?"

Matthew looked to his mother to answer, but she just smiled softly, her own eyes watery still. He would do his best. "Well, it's because people are happy when a couple gets married. And, well, sometimes people get so full of happy, it spills out of their eyes."

"Oh."

Nita accepted anything Matthew said like it was the gospel. He needed to guard his words.

With the brisk step of the horses and excitement of the day, it didn't feel long before they were pulling into the wide yard in front of Uncle Preston's two-story log cabin.

The Grandmother sat on the porch, rocking and watching. She had had a bad spell recently and the family thought it best if she only went to the second ceremony. Thankfully, the Grandmother agreed. She was the matriarch and would have decided for her own self whether or not she would go.

In the rocker next to her sat an elderly full-blood Choctaw man, quietly rocking and watching, too. Reverend Willis Folsom, someone the Grandmother had known in the years following the Removal.

He and his village had crossed the trail on their own in 1834. Willis Folsom credited the miraculous journey to his friend Tushpa's father, Kanchi, who prayed for them. The entire band committed to follow the way taught in the Bible, no matter where the journey took them.

Though Kanchi had not survived the trip, his legacy lived on in Tushpa and Ishtaya, who later took the name Willis Folsom.

The Grandmother and Reverend Folsom remained seated while people exited buggies and wagons to head for the traditional summer house a short distance from the cabin. Made of pine posts and cypress clapboards for the roof, the "house" had no walls, a rectangular pavilion large enough for almost everyone to find shade in.

Once everyone gathered, Uncle Preston and his oldest son, William, helped the Grandmother down the steps, Reverend

Folsom behind them. Peter carried her rocking chair and set it up in the center of the pavilion.

Matthew stood close, his mother at his side and Nita in front of him. He rested his hands on her shoulders.

When the Grandmother was seated, Ruth Ann went to her and grasped her knotty hands in her own. They looked deep into one another's eyes for a time as everyone fell silent.

Time passed slow, then the Grandmother beckoned to Benjamin. He knelt in front of her, not minding the dirt floor on the knees of his pristine trousers. She took his hand in her shaking one and joined it with Ruth Ann's, covering them both with hers.

Reverend Folsom came behind the couple and draped a blanket over their shoulders, drawing the couple close to one another, and signifying the unification of two families. Reverend Folsom blessed their union in Choctaw and English. The Grandmother bent to kiss their clasped hands, then released the couple with her blessing.

Peter let out a whoop. Several others joined him, Matthew included, a jubilant release of so many emotions.

Nita jumped, staring up at him, eyes popping and mouth forming a precious O. Matthew laughed and scooped her up as the whoops continued. This was her first experience in her father's culture and Matthew wanted it to be among the best memories of her life.

Ruth Ann and Benjamin were herded out of the pavilion and encircled by family and friends. Matthew carried Nita to join the circle. He wouldn't want any other partner for this dance.

Benjamin bowed to Ruth Ann as though they were in a ballroom in Washington, D.C. She laughed and curtsied, some secret memory between them. Benjamin held up his hand, pinky offered to Ruth Ann. She intwined her own in his.

Matthew settled Nita on her feet, tugging her skirt to straighten it. Staying bent, he held his pinky out to her. She cocked her head, curious, and looked to her aunt and new uncle. Without taking her eyes off them, she held up her small hand and Matthew hooked her pinky and held their locked hands high in the air.

Circling the couple, the rest of the family and friends partnered up. To one side of the circle, Uncle Preston had retrieved his chant sticks. Striking the sticks together, he created a rhythmic *clack, clack, clack*. The cadence of his chanting guided the dancers as they began to move in a counter circle to the couple.

Matthew tapped his right foot toward Nita's opposite toe, then did the reverse with his left. She gave him a suspicious look, as though he was testing the limits of her trust. He grinned and that was all it took. She began imitating him as they exchanged footsteps, toe to opposite toe, while he slowly angled backward to keep them in the circle of dancers moving around the couple.

In the center, Ruth Ann and Benjamin also added the footwork, but stayed in place, facing one another with enough love to last a lifetime shining in their eyes.

Tuned into the chant, Matthew kept his grin as he whooped along with the others in the dance and twirled himself and Nita in a fast circle, pinkies still locked as they switched places. She stumbled and crashed into him. He righted her to continue the dance, gently guiding her backwards. Nita giggled as she matched his steps. Matthew lost his breath. It was the first time he'd heard her laugh. What a marvelous little laugh.

After a series of exchanges, a final whoop ended the dance. Nita looked disappointed it was over. "Uncle Matthew?"

"Yes, Little Bear?"

"What was that?"

He knelt on one knee in front of her. "It was the Choctaw wedding dance, one we've done as a people for many, many years to celebrate a marriage." He held up his pinky, locking with hers again. "This represents the talons of eagles, who we believe mate for life. It shows the forever bond between your Aunt Ruth Ann and your Uncle Benjamin."

Nita tightened her hand into a fist, pinky still hooked in his. "*You're* my uncle."

How would he ever let this little girl go? "I am, Little Bear. And now you have a second uncle. That's a good thing. Your uncles will always protect you."

Nita didn't move, her eyes searching his face for the truth. He didn't blame her. How much she'd suffered in her young life! Her father in prison. Her mother abandoning her. Matthew wanted to hold her close and never let go. The very thought chafed his soul.

Yet being raised by Benjamin and Ruth Ann was for the best. Benjamin would be able to understand the depth of her pain better than anyone. His own father was still in prison, sent there when Benjamin was a small boy. And Ruth Ann would be an outstanding mother for Nita.

It's for the best. Matthew kept trying to convince himself, even as Nita clutched his hand, warming him all over. She pulled him toward the newlyweds. Matthew caught his sister for a quick hug, her smelling of rose perfume.

Nita stared up at Benjamin who towered over her. He stooped and picked her up, lifting her high in the air as she kept hold of Matthew's hand. Nita looked down at Matthew from her position in the cerulean sky. An understanding passed between them. She trusted both her uncles to take care of her.

Benjamin brought Nita down for a snuggle with Ruth Ann before they were engulfed by family and friends lining up to congratulate the couple. Under the pavilion, Beulah began playing lively music on her violin while children danced.

Matthew tugged Nita away and released her to play with her second cousins around the pavilion. He caught sight of Hannah Stillwater speaking with Reverend Folsom and the Grandmother. Hannah was kneeling in front of the Grandmother's chair, hands clasped on her lap, intently watching her face as she took in whatever Pokni was saying.

It would be hard to hear anything under the pavilion with the music and shrieks of the children. That was one advantage Hannah had, Matthew thought, as he headed for the food tables. Time to get to work.

Still, his mind was on Hannah, thinking about the Choctaw wedding dance, the chanting, the chant sticks, and now Beulah's violin. How did one describe music with words to someone who'd never heard it?

Matthew helped bring food from the kitchen and set it out for the feast the bride's family had prepared for the guests. Mountains and mountains of food! There was no danger of sending anyone away hungry.

As Matthew carried a kettle of *pashofa* to the table, he noticed a buggy coming up the road at a fast clip.

He paused, trying to make out who it was and if they were bringing urgent news from town. It wasn't until the buggy halted and a couple hastily unloaded that he realized it was Sissy Barnes and her husband, Leonard Coxwell.

In the sea of faces, Matthew hadn't realized Sissy had been absent from both ceremonies, though the rest of the Barnes family was there. In fact, Pepper Barnes strode toward the couple now. It looked like sharp words were exchanged between Sissy and her brother, but Matthew wasn't close enough to hear. He turned back to the tables and settled the pashofa in place while the Coxwells joined the reception line.

Matthew had heard gossip that Sissy and Leonard Coxwell made a good match—on paper. Coxwell was a successful white businessman like her father. But in the few times Matthew had encountered him, he found Leonard Coxwell to be a man who kept his words few and demeanor formal.

The courtship and marriage last Christmas were a whirlwind and, as far as Matthew knew, Ruth Ann and Sissy hadn't seen one another much since. That was odd for the two who were close friends for so many years. He had expected Sissy to be a bridesmaid at Ruth Ann's wedding. But Ruth Ann simply said Sissy wasn't well. Nothing more.

Their salutations for the married couple were brief, and Matthew noted a pained look on Sissy's face. He also caught Ruth Ann's raised eyebrow in his direction. Even on her wedding day, his sweet sister was concerned about her friend, and she wanted Matthew to step in.

Matthew angled to intercept the couple who strolled toward the food tables, looking like they stepped out of a fashion catalog. Matthew hardly recognized Sissy as the hard-riding, straight-shooting, yet feminine eldest daughter of Robert Barnes except for her dark skin and hair that contrasted her white husband's.

Matthew stepped into their path. "Halito, chim achukma?"

Leonard Coxwell halted, bringing Sissy to an abrupt stop as she clung to his arm, more for support than fashion to Matthew's eye. Coxwell had a well-groomed look about him, even his expression. He was trying to place Matthew without appearing ignorant.

Recognition came to him, and he offered his hand to shake. "Teller. How are things in the newspaper business?"

"Well, thanks. How are things in your business?" Matthew didn't know what Coxwell's business was, an oversight on his part. Any white businessman in the Choctaw Nation was of interest to this newspaper reporter. If he recalled correctly, Coxwell was an investor of some sort. Which set off alarm bells in Matthew's mind now. In his experience, white investors generally meant bad news for his people.

"Doing well, thank you." Coxwell offered nothing more and Matthew felt a prickle on the back of his neck. Few businessmen passed an opportunity to brag on their success.

"Very well, in fact," Sissy inserted, her voice raw and cracked. Leonard Coxwell glanced down at her, but she kept her eyes on

Matthew. "Leonard is preparing for a business trip to Washington, D.C. I know what a fine time Ruth Ann had there. You should see it yourself, Matt. I just had a thought…why don't you go with Leonard? A body shouldn't make such a long, dull trip alone."

Leonard Coxwell stiffened, tightening his arm around Sissy's hand. She didn't flinch, but Matthew felt rocked back on his heels. "I, uh, I don't know that I could get away, what with starting a second newspaper office in McAlester and all."

"A second one?" Sissy's voice was hoarse, but there was a softness to it. She still didn't look at her husband. "I always knew you'd make good, Matt."

Matthew shifted to look around for an escape. Sissy Barnes never talked to him like this. Familiar, yes, as childhood friends. But it hadn't sounded quite like *this* before.

Leonard Coxwell interjected, "I think Eliza has a fine idea. It's a long trip and she is not well enough to journey with me. I would be pleased to have you along. I may even find the time to introduce you to influential people while we're there."

Sissy gave a tight glance up at her husband and Matthew could see the whites of her eyes streaked with red lines. She hadn't missed the condescension in his tone either.

Matthew stopped her response with a simple, "Thanks for the invite. I'll think about it."

His answer surprised them all, but he meant it. Leonard Coxwell wasn't an ideal traveling companion, but he had business dealings in the Choctaw Nation and connections in Washington. Those were things Matthew wanted to learn more about. Besides, there was someone he needed to face in D.C. What he didn't need was one more monumental task added to his workload. When would life ease up on him?

The afternoon stretched on with eating, eating, and more eating. Then Melinda and Mary, cousins-in-law, spread a king size quilt on the ground for Ruth Ann to sit on, framed from behind with the backdrop of the lake. People brought wedding gifts, piles and piles of them. It was a good thing Benjamin hadn't finished outfitting their home in McAlester.

Daniel came to stand by Matthew as the gifts were opened, appropriately swooned over, and taken away for the next present as Melinda streamlined the process.

Daniel said quietly, "It's quite an affair, getting married."

Matthew nodded absently then snapped his head over to look at Daniel. To really look at him and see the longing and pain in his eyes. It wasn't so long ago that Daisy had sat on that quilt and received adoring congratulations from the family.

"Daisy would have loved this," Matthew said. "She and Ruth Ann were close."

Daniel turned away. Matthew looked back to Ruth Ann and Benjamin to see Uncle Preston standing several feet behind them. He was watching Daniel.

The father and son-in-law hadn't spoken since Daisy and the baby's burial. Matthew should have made sure he spent more time with Daniel in those following months, let him know he was still part of the family. Daniel didn't have anyone else.

With the stream of gifts continuing, Matthew slipped away from the laughter to walk up the hill to where his father lay resting beneath a mature oak tree. They had removed Philip's headstone after discovering the bones they buried there didn't belong to the eldest Teller son. They put a small wooden cross for the outlaw they had mistakenly buried in his place.

Matthew knelt by his father's grave and dug away the grass from the headstone that had grown with the spring rains and warm sunshine. The Teller family had undergone many changes in the past six years. Their father's death. Moving into Dickens. Philip's return from the dead.

And now.

"Well, Daddy, your baby girl got married," Matthew said quietly. "Uncle Preston walked her down the aisle for you.

Philip's little girl is here, too. Your granddaughter. I'm going to look after her the same as Uncle Preston has done for Annie. You don't have to worry about either of those girls."

Matthew remained squatted by the grave for a time. Then he shifted to lean against the oak, legs stretched in front of him, arms crossed, and fighting sleep.

In the yard, William and Beulah struck up duel fiddling, and the dancing started. Matthew preferred watching from a safe distance.

His gaze drifted back to a lone figure standing apart from the crowd. It was Hannah, her attention on the dancers, a soft smile on her face. She shifted away to look around her, a habit Matthew noticed her doing often.

Hannah was always aware of her surroundings, alert to what she couldn't hear. Matthew should have stayed closer to her today, made sure she didn't get lost in conversations with too many lips to read at once. But she seemed content.

As she looked around, she spotted him on the hill.

Awkward, Matthew lifted one hand off his crossed arms and waved. Hannah's smile softened more, and she lifted her hand almost imperceptibly to return the gesture.

The dancing went on and on. Matthew leaned his head back against the oak tree. He knew what was coming.

In the midst of one of the dances, Ruth Ann, who was with Peter, broke away and ran toward the tall white pole with streamers flying in the breeze. She glanced back with a grin as wide as the sky. Benjamin whooped and chased her.

Barefoot, she made a hearty effort at reaching the white pole before he could catch her. There was no danger in her succeeding. Benjamin, the six-foot-tall football athlete, had slipped off his dress shoes when he spotted her doing the same earlier.

He caught Ruth Ann around the waist several yards before the pole and swung her around as they laughed.

Matthew smiled. The last piece of the Choctaw traditional

wedding, where the bride makes a run for the pole and the groom must catch her first, was complete.

Ruth Ann and Benjamin, hand-in-hand, ran back to the party, grabbed their shoes, and dashed for the two-seater buggy. Ruth Ann kissed her mother and the Grandmother on the way, then Ruth Ann made a quick turn to look at the loving figures casting well wishes and applause at the couple.

Matthew stood and their eyes met. Ruth Ann was crying and smiling, and he was too. He lifted his hand in a high wave. She blew him a kiss as Benjamin swept her into the buggy.

Matthew never thought there would be a man in the world he could trust to send his little sister away with. But there they went, off to start a brand new life together.

Matthew wasn't sure he was ready for the next phase of his.

CHAPTER 23

The woman killer was close. Daniel sensed it in the marrow of his bones.

He slowly walked down the boardwalk of Eagletown, eyes darting back-and-forth across the dirt street taking in the unfamiliar faces about that morning. Three men loaded a freight wagon at a lumber mill. A pair of men played checkers on a pickle barrel in front of the General Store. A man sat in a chair tipped against the post office wall, leather visor over his eyes as he snoozed.

Daniel stood still, the feeling of death heavy on him.

Then, a man—not tall, not short—exited the hotel, looking over his shoulder. He eased to the side as another man came out. Daniel recognized him.

The distance between the men grew as they continued walking, watching each other as they prepared to square off in the street.

Daniel knew a gunfight shaping up when he saw one. He also had the distinct feeling that one of these men was the one he was tracking.

But he had no way of knowing which one. After the trail went cold around Dickens, Daniel had gone back to Fort Smith and questioned John Bellanger's neighbors. He scraped together a vague description of a man only seen in the shadows lurking the night John Bellanger's wife was murdered.

He got a better description of the man's horse—a striking albino with blue eyes.

Daniel had never seen one himself, but asking enough questions at blacksmiths led Daniel back into Skullyville in Indian Territory. He found an albino there, sold to the livery two days after Mrs. Bellanger's death. The livery worker gave him a description of the man, and that description could fit either man now squaring off in the street before him.

One of these men had brought Daniel to Eagletown—Stuart Adams, who was part Indian, though his skin didn't betray it. A mean cuss, he was wanted for shooting up a town and attempted murder back in Arkansas. He was riding an albino when he fled the state.

The two men squared off, and the other man, unknown to Daniel drew the tail of his coat around and held it behind his back with his left hand while his right hand casually dangled over his tied down six-shooter. Daniel could tell by his stance the man was an expert killer.

Daniel wasn't the only one taking note of the action in the street.

The men loading the freight wagon dropped the box they were hefting and crawled underneath the wagon, watching. The two men playing checkers on the pickle barrel jumped up, toppling their board as they bumped into each other to get inside the General Store. They slammed the door shut and peered through the curtained window.

The commotion woke the man at the post office. He dashed into the building and seconds later, started clicking away at the telegraph sounder. News of the gunfight would spread through the territory before it even happened.

Daniel took a step into the road. A gunfight in the middle of a public street was a dangerous prospect and he had a duty to stop it.

Before he could take another step, a man burst out of the hotel and rumbled onto the wide porch. The man was intense-looking, a hawk nose and graying temples. He halted at the top of the steps, a tablet and pencil in hand as he watched.

Stuart Adams twitched. Daniel drew his six-gun and fired two shots into the air. He leveled his gun on the man. Adams was in a low crouch, his pistol already half-drawn but not clear of the leather holster.

"Don't," Daniel hissed, teeth gritted. Adams remained frozen.

Daniel cast a threatening glance at the other man. The man's gun was out, cocked, and aimed at Adams' heart.

Daniel growled, "Leather it."

The man looked over at him, deep brown eyes cool and defiant. His gaze lowered to Daniel's marshal badge.

He slowly uncocked the hammer and re-holstered his gun, dropping his coat tail as he shifted to stand straight.

From the corner of his eye, Daniel saw Adams yank his gun the rest of the way out.

Daniel fired.

As soon as he squeezed the trigger, he knew Adams wasn't the woman killer.

Daniel only had another unwanted notch on his gun.

Walking through the sickly, acrid smell of gun smoke hanging thick in the still air, Daniel went to stand over the dead man. Adams was the third outlaw he'd killed in his duty as a U.S. marshal.

The hawk-nosed man stood beside Daniel, pencil scribbling, an action that reminded him of Matthew.

"You're an Indian?"

Daniel shifted to look over at the reporter, taking in his odd opening question. "I'm a United States Marshal, working out of Fort Smith. And yeah. I'm Choctaw."

"And a killer. Figures."

Daniel locked his jaw, absorbing the disdain—no, outright hate—from the man who gripped his pencil so hard his knuckles were white.

Daniel glanced over at the men who peeked out from beneath the freight wagon. He nodded to them. "Fetch the undertaker."

Daniel snapped open the cylinder on his six-gun and emptied the spent cartridges as he spoke to the reporter. "Say your peace, Mister."

The reporter nudged the limp arm of the dead man. "I'm Earl Reynolds, reporter for the Associated Press, doing a series on the violence perpetrated by Indians in this territory. That Indian started the fight in the hotel restaurant. Loud-mouthed heathen. He was out to kill someone today. Looks like you were set on the same."

Daniel slowly slid replacement cartridges into the cylinder. He snapped it closed, holstered his gun, and turned away from the reporter.

A steel-like hand gripped his arm and whipped him around. Reynold's hot breath steamed in Daniel's face.

"I don't care how they dress you people up or that they pinned a badge on you. I've been a reporter for 30 years and I've not found cause to write a good story on Indians yet. My articles are going to be the final nail in the coffin for you people."

Daniel wrapped his fingers around the man's wrist and squeezed. The reporter stiffened, then released Daniel's arm. Daniel shoved the man's hand away from him.

"You've had your say, mister. Now you listen to me. There's good and bad in all races of men. If you haven't met a good Indian and wouldn't consider me one—and I can't say I blame you right now—you go on over to Dickens and find Matthew Teller. You'll never meet a finer man of any race."

"Matthew Teller." Reynolds might as well have spit. "I've heard of him. So-called newspaperman. Troublemaker to the core."

Daniel shifted his jaw, holding back the sensation to grin. The man wasn't entirely wrong.

"You know, the Pharisees said the same thing about Jesus."

One of the checker players came out of the General Store, carrying a blanket. He handed it to Daniel, who took it and draped it over the man he killed.

Dead Man Dan was living up to the reputation he hadn't set out to earn. He'd swap his for Matthew's anytime.

"Sorry to interrupt your checker game, but I need you to send this to Chief Jefferson Gardner."

Matthew had entered the telegraph office and stood over Peter's shoulder. He observed the one-sided game he had going. Peter lifted one finger to hold Matthew off while he clicked off a message on the sounder.

Cousin has urgent message to send. Back soon.

Peter and D, the operator at station TN, often had a checker game going during their shifts. Matthew didn't mind as long as it didn't interfere with paying messages going across the wire.

Matthew dropped the message on the checkerboard and turned to leave. Peter, not looking up, asked, "Why don't you just telephone Chief Gardner that you're coming to see him?"

"I don't have a telephone and neither does he."

"Maxwell does."

Matthew back stepped. "What are you talking about?"

"For those of us who didn't sit head down and grumpy at our desks all day, didn't miss overhead wires getting strung all over town this morning."

Matthew put his hands on the window shelf of the telegraph

office, straining to see out. He caught a glimpse of wire angling in the direction of the *Dickens Herald.*

Peter clicked off another message to D, resuming their checker game. "If I hadn't been late this morning—for which I received a proper balling out—I wouldn't have seen those linemen setting up for work. I asked one of them what the lines were for, and he said that Christopher Maxwell was putting in a telephone company for Dickens. Guess he won't have any trouble getting elected as mayor now."

Matthew felt the blood drain from his face. Even in the rush of preparation for Ruth Ann's wedding, surely he couldn't have missed such a monumental move on Christopher Maxwell's part. How could the man have kept a whole telephone company secret?

Not wanting to show how off-balance the news set him, Matthew drew on what he hoped was a calm expression and turned back to Peter. He tapped the table beside the checkerboard. "Next time, alert me of that kind of news as soon as it comes in."

There wasn't the usual gleam of mischief in Peter's eyes. He looked like he'd been up all night, something else to worry Matthew's mind.

As Matthew left the lean-to, Peter quipped, "That'll be 23 cents for the chief's telegram."

"Put it on my tab."

Matthew headed back to his desk, mind swirling. He planned to meet with Chief Jefferson Gardner as his next step to stop the annexation of Dickens. There wasn't a lot he could do on the legal front until Benjamin returned from his honeymoon, but he wanted to make sure their guns were loaded when the time came.

Matthew was almost at his desk before he realized Hannah was waving at him from the typesetting cabinet. He angled over to her, weaving around Caleb Gentry as the operator stacked newspapers.

"I guess I'm the one hard of hearing these days." Matthew regretted his offhanded comment, but Hannah just smiled.

"I didn't want to shout for everyone on the street to hear."

Matthew returned her smile. She had a sense of humor that she kept reserved around him. He wished he could see more of it.

She motioned at the article she was setting type for. "I wanted to ask if you meant Jenkins instead of Jones here."

Matthew pulled a pencil from his front shirt pocket and scratch out *Jones* and wrote *Jenkins* above the two instances about the man accused of swiping a flock of hens from his neighbor.

This close to her, Matthew noticed that Hannah smelled of lilac and clay. It was a strange but not unpleasant blend with the newspaper's ink and paper that permeated the shop. He recalled that Hannah made pottery in the shed behind the church. She had gifted several pieces to congregates.

Matthew straightened. "Good catch. But how did you know the suspect's name was Jenkins and not Jones?"

Hannah's lips formed a puzzled *o*, then understanding lit her startling lake-blue eyes. "You wrote about him a year and a half ago when he was accused of stealing milk from his neighbor's cow. I remember it, because the article was so bland yet humorous."

"That's remarkable," Matthew said. That word jumped to mind often when it came to Hannah. "I don't even remember that story. So, you've found time to read our archives that far back?"

"I've read all the back issues of the *Choctaw Tribune* in the storeroom."

"*All* of them?" *Remarkable.*

Hannah shifted on her stool, turning her attention to resetting *Jones* with *Jenkins*. Her cheeks held a pink hue.

"I enjoy reading, Mr. Teller."

Matthew didn't move. He waited until Hannah looked up again, questioning, before he asked, "You can recall more details from the articles?"

"I can quote entire passages if you'd like."

"That's….remarkable."

Hannah smiled and turned back to her work. Matthew didn't want the conversation to end. He gave a little wave, close to her face because of their proximity. Hannah drew back and Matthew quickly dropped his hand.

"Sorry. I just wanted to tell you how I appreciate your hard work here. Especially the past few weeks with all the wedding hoopla, and Ruth Ann moving to McAlester. I don't know what I would've done without you."

Hannah smiled again, but it was weak and there was something beneath it that Matthew couldn't make out. She went back to setting type as though not wanting to see anything else he said. She looked flushed and uncomfortable.

Matthew left her to her work and went back to his desk. Sitting, he leaned down to unlock the bottom drawer of his desk. He retrieved his fountain pen from it to write a formal letter to give Chief Gardener when he met with him.

Ruth Ann had gifted Matthew the stylish pen for Christmas a few years back, and later she had his name engraved on it. Matthew kept the pen locked in his drawer so no one could borrow and not return it.

He set to work on the letter, outlining the dangers of Maxwell's proposed annexation, and the leverage the man had with a newspaper and a bid for mayor. Now with the telephone company, the man's influence was nearly boundless.

Matthew planned to be among the telephone company's first customers.

CHAPTER 25

*A*fter his experience at the telephone company, Matthew had gone straight to Mr. Bates General Store, which was still a thriving business despite the competition from two new stores. Mr. Bates was among the first telephone subscribers. He gave Matthew the price he was charged, setting Matthew's mind at ease that the exorbitant rates were normal and not specially reserved for him.

Adding a telephone to the newspaper and home was a drain on the family, and Matthew was still contemplating Leonard Coxwell's invitation to D.C. This investigation into Maxwell was costly, but Matthew's path was set. He wouldn't deviate from it until he reached the end, wherever that was.

The next day, he paid a visit to Chief Jefferson Gardner. That netted him little. As the new chief of the Choctaw Nation, Jefferson Gardner had taken a staunch stand against the Dawes commission, refusing to meet with Senator Dawes or his representatives. Gardner believed the best way to get rid of the commission that was seeking to dissolve the Choctaw Nation was to ignore them.

Gardner wasn't alarmed by Maxwell's filing to annex the townsite of Dickens. He was confident any shenanigans Dawes or Maxwell or any of the like tried to pull would fail.

Matthew left the chief's house worried.

He went straight to the train depot in Dickens and bought a ticket for Washington, D.C. The very last thing he had time for was traveling to the nation's capital. His workload was piling up and energy seeped from his body at a rate that wasn't being replenished in turn.

But one of the biggest pieces to this puzzle regarding Maxwell resided in D.C.

Thaddeus Warren.

By Thursday morning, Matthew was exhausted. It had been less than a week since Ruth Ann's wedding and he had torn full force into continuing his investigation into Maxwell's dealings while running the daily editions. Matthew had the added task of overseeing the installation of telephones in the *Choctaw Tribune* office and at home.

As he leaned back in his desk chair and stared at the candlestick phone with its receiver in a hook, worn out, he couldn't help feeling ridiculously pleased. The *Choctaw Tribune* was as modern as any newspaper in the east, keeping pace with the *Dickens Herald*, and solidifying itself as a prominent newspaper in Indian Territory.

It was early and only he and Peter were in the shop, Peter already at the telegraph wire. Next to arrive was Hannah Stillwater, a full ten minutes early. Matthew stood as she entered. He'd have time to talk to her about his personal research into this newfangled invention.

Her alert eyes landed on him, and he waved her over. She came toward his desk as Matthew spread his hands wide over it.

"What do you think of my desk?"

Hannah gave it a brief survey. "It looks as though it belongs to either a professor or a mad man."

Matthew chuckled and picked up the candlestick telephone, giving it a little shake and rattling the receiver on the hook. She raised her eyebrows.

"I hope you aren't counting on me answering the telephone, Mr. Teller." Her amused smile let him know she was teasing.

Matthew set the telephone down and picked up a magazine he'd bought from Mr. Bates that contained an article on the history of the telephone. He held it up beside his face so she could see it and his lips at the same time. He had the magazine open to the article, which contained a black-and-white photograph of a man holding a telephone.

"Alexander Graham Bell invented the telephone, but did you know it was because of deaf people that he made the discovery?" Matthew asked. "He invented a machine called a phonograph to allow his deaf students to visualize sound vibrations translated into mechanical motion. His experiments gave him the idea for the electric telephone. I thought you might enjoy the article."

Hannah didn't look at it. "I might. I was one of Mr. Bell's students."

Matthew lowered the magazine. "Then you helped invent the telephone, Miss Stillwater."

She smiled, looking genuinely amused. "You draw interesting conclusions in your search for the truth, Mr. Teller. Which reminds me, I've wanted to ask how your investigation is going?"

Matthew tapped the candlestick telephone. "This is part of it. So is my trip to D.C. next week. I wish you could come along to help with research, but at least I know the *Choctaw Tribune* will be in good hands with you...with all the staff here."

Hannah's smile slipped and she excused herself with a nod as she went to the typesetting cabinet.

Matthew spent the morning writing articles for the daily edition, lost in the stories until the bell jingled over the front door. He glanced up to see his mother and Nita bringing lunch. Della had promised a hot casserole and Matthew shoved papers aside to make room.

As he did, he caught a glimpse of a furry tail on the other side of the desk. Who did that dog belong to? He was a pretty fellow, one blue eye, one brown eye, luscious full coat of blue, brown, and white hairs. Shedding *everywhere*.

He frowned at his niece. "Dogs are not allowed inside, Nita. Take him out."

Nita glanced over her shoulder, eyes wide. She obviously hadn't known the dog was behind her. Matthew softened his voice. "Take him outside for us, please?"

Peter came from the lean-to and gave the dog a scratch behind the ears.

"What you got against dogs, Matt? Get your ear chewed on as a baby or something?"

Nita lured the dog to the door with a soda cracker while Matthew helped his mother unpack the picnic basket.

"I don't have anything against dogs. They just don't belong indoors."

Turning back to his desk, Matthew noticed Hannah still working away, her back to the rest of the room as she set type. She didn't know everyone was breaking for the noon meal.

Matthew swung his leg over the low wall surrounding his desk and edged close to the wall as he approached the typesetting desk.

Hannah looked up and then behind her to see the gathering at his desk as Della dished up plates. Hannah stood. "Oh, time for the noon meal already?"

"I don't believe I saw you take one break today. You never do. You're obliged to a break in the mornings, you know."

Hannah reached for her food basket on top of the typesetting cabinet. "Thank you, I just prefer not to disrupt the morning with a break. I didn't realize it was so late."

"Let's see what we can do about that."

Matthew called Peter over and had him heft one side of the typesetting cabinet. Slowly, they turned it around without dumping all the tiny type pieces. Matthew lifted the tall stool and placed it to where it faced the print shop and the front door. He nodded at Hannah with satisfaction.

"This will make it easier for us to communicate."

She looked at him a long moment, then smiled. "I suppose it will, Mr. Teller."

Hannah joined them at his desk with her basket, but Matthew's attention was drawn to his niece. Nita stood by the desk—sans the dog—not meeting his eyes. He'd neglected her this week in his mighty push to restart his investigation into Maxwell.

He didn't have much time remaining of her living in Dickens. Benjamin had left papers with his assistant to file for adoption of Nita right along with the marriage certificate. The proceedings were underway.

Matthew seated himself at his desk and beckoned Nita over. He hefted her onto his lap while Della served up plates of food.

"Nita, why don't you spend the afternoon here with me in the newspaper shop?" Matthew asked. "I'll show you how to call Pokni on the telephone when she goes home."

Della sent him a scalding look. Matthew winked at her. His mother hadn't touched the telephone at home since he'd had it installed.

Peter took his plate after planting a kiss on Della's cheek. "I don't care what Mr. Grouchy says. I'm taking my leftovers to Story. He looks hungry."

Matthew followed his gaze to the window, where the poor dog watched them. He did look starved for food and attention.

"Story?"

"That's what I'm going to call that dog. Matthew Teller never can turn away a good story."

Della chuckled and Matthew shook his head. "As long as that good story stays outside, we can be friends."

After lunch and Della returned home, Matthew toured Nita around the shop. She'd only made brief visits before and never ventured into the far corners alone. They made the telephone call from his desk to the receiver at the box house. Della answered on the sixth ring and shouted a greeting to her granddaughter in Choctaw.

Nita settled in the lean-to with Peter when he promised to let her play checkers over the telegraph wire with D.

Matthew went to the typesetting cabinet. Hannah glanced up without him having to wave. He had something important to ask her, something he thought of after she informed him she'd read and retained most of the content in the *Choctaw Tribune* archives.

She wouldn't have any reason to say yes, and he would make it clear the dangers involved, and hope that wouldn't frighten her off. The *Choctaw Tribune* didn't have a clean track record when it came to the safety of employees.

"There's something I want to ask you about, Miss Stillwater."

Hannah folded her hands over the composing stick she was working on, giving him her full attention. He almost forgot his question.

"I, um, I know how observant you are, which is why I thought of this as part of my investigation. I'm returning to Hot Springs to search the back issues of the Sun again. I had a kid look through them, but he might have missed something important."

Hannah nodded. "I can help with that."

"There's one more thing. I need to ask if you're willing to go with me to a gambling hall."

Hannah crooked an eyebrow at him. "My life has enough gambling in it, wouldn't you say, Mr. Teller?"

"Well, what I mean is, Maxwell has a strong connection with

the Palace Casino. They know me there, but if we went in together, they might not notice, at least until you got to eavesdrop on a few conversations before I'm tossed out. I want to find out what goes on there. I have my suspicions that it's part of a syndicate."

Hannah glanced down at her plain red gingham dress. "I suppose I'd better wear my Sunday best."

Matthew fidgeted with the articles stacked on her cabinet. He mumbled, "That's not all you'll need."

"I'm sorry, I didn't get that."

Matthew snapped his head up. "Sorry. There are some things I wish I didn't have to say. But you've been around here long enough to know the *Choctaw Tribune* gets into more scrapes than not. You may have heard about the time I was shot investigating a story."

Hannah jerked back as though she had been shot, hand going to her throat. "You...you were shot? Um, well, no, I didn't *hear* about that one." She laughed lightly, dropping her hand, but her eyes remained fixed on him.

Matthew shrugged as though the bullet that struck next to his heart hadn't done the physical or emotional damage it did. He should tell her about Mrs. Bellanger's murder after she advised Matthew to visit the Palace, but he couldn't get it out.

"I recovered. But the danger never went away. A few months ago, I was threatened again. I haven't told anyone but Benjamin, but if you're going to get in the middle of my investigation into Maxwell, you have a right to know. I didn't get a look at that man's face, but he did say that I 'ask unhealthy questions.' It was an interesting turn of phrase, so if you ever see anyone using that, let me know."

"I certainly will."

"Are you sure you want to get involved in this? It's likely to get uglier by the day."

"I have a passion for truth myself, Mr. Teller. And passion never counts the cost."

Matthew couldn't help but hope Hannah Stillwater remained at the *Choctaw Tribune* as long as they were in business.

CHAPTER 26

"I haven't heard you say one word since we left Dickens."

Matthew shook himself and turned to look at Hannah perched on the passenger seat across from him. She had a solemn look but a teasing glint in her eyes and he realized the joke she had just made.

"My mind is on…family."

The twinkle went out from her eyes and she glanced out the window then back at him. "I don't mean to pry."

Matthew shrugged. "It's not prying. What my family went through this past year was printed in our own newspaper, stories you read. Not all the personal details were in there, but I'm sure you could read between the lines about my brother Philip, who is in prison."

Hannah nodded. "Nita's father."

She stated it so matter of fact and gentle. She added, "Family is hard, isn't it? But God knows."

Matthew turned to face Hannah, wanting to ask more about her family. But he couldn't expect that if he wasn't willing to share about his own.

"My daddy used to say that when we encountered life's question marks. 'God knows.'" He wished he didn't have to say the next part. "I had to forgive Philip for his part in my daddy's death."

Hannah bit her lower lip. "That must have been tremendously hard to go through. The newspaper article about his trial wasn't very detailed. And I'm sure what I read in the *Dickens Herald* wasn't entirely accurate."

Matthew smirked. "You read our rival's newspaper?"

Hannah paled but then relaxed when she saw he was teasing. "I assumed if the *Choctaw Tribune* publisher himself reads the *Herald* every day it would be fine for me to. It's said that you should keep your friends close, and your enemies, closer."

"You remind me of Annie sometimes."

"Annie?"

"Ruth Ann. My sister."

"Oh!"

Matthew was surprised by her surprise. "You've seen me say her nickname before, haven't you?"

Hannah offered a strained laugh. "Yes, but I didn't realize you were talking about your sister. I wondered who Annie was. Mystery solved. Do you have other siblings I should know about?"

Matthew shook his head. "Just my younger sister and older brother. Me in the middle." He leaned forward, propping his elbows on his knees. "What do you think, Miss Stillwater: Is it easier to forgive a brother or an enemy?"

She opened her mouth to answer and then closed it, eyes showing her concentration. Then she gave a sad smile. "God knows."

Apparently ready to change the subject, Hannah asked, "You said you were known in Hot Springs, Mr. Teller. Do you visit there often?"

Might as well get it over with. "I was sent there on assignment for my first front page story when I worked at the *Dickens Herald*. I nearly got shot."

Hannah pursed her lips. "I didn't quite get that. That was the time you were shot?"

Matthew grimaced. He could hardly keep the dangerous scrapes he'd been in through the newspaper business straight, much less keep straight what stories he had or hadn't told Hannah.

"It was right after suppertime."

Matthew looked at the ceiling of the passenger car, keeping his face forward so she could read his lips. He felt himself slipping back in time.

"The editor of the Sun, Charles Hornet, was showing a young visiting reporter around town when the two men came on them. Kingsbury and Westbrook, owners of the Arlington Hotel. They were infuriated with Hornet's efforts to shut down illegal gambling operations in Hot Springs, including theirs in the Arlington. Westbrook attacked Hornet with a cane and when the young reporter tried to stop it, Kingsbury drew a gun and would have shot him. Hornet shot the man in the leg and drew the full fury. The man gunned him down for writing and publishing truth in his newspaper."

"How do you know so many of the details?"

Matthew brought his gaze down to meet Hannah's. "I was that young reporter with Hornet on the last evening of his life."

Hannah didn't look as shocked as he expected. Perhaps he shocked her enough in the short time they had known one another.

"So you were shot at a different time?"

"Yes, later when I had my own newspaper. But what happened to Charles Hornet gave me fair warning of what I was getting into. Didn't feel I had much of a choice though. I understood that after he told me there's nothing more powerful than the press except God Almighty. The *Choctaw Tribune* might be the death of me, but it's what God has called me to do, and I'll do it to my last breath."

"You have a magnificent calling, Mr. Teller."

Matthew raised his eyebrows. "I've never thought of it as magnificent. Magnificently dangerous, magnificently thrilling, magnificent…maybe." He paused, then asked, "What is your magnificent calling, Miss Stillwater?"

She smiled. "Perhaps I will discover it while working at the *Choctaw Tribune*."

What else could he expect from a loyal employee?

After the litany of changing multiple trains, they finally arrived in Hot Springs. The train ride drained Matthew's physical energy, but he ignored the fatigue and ducked into the depot to check the telegraph wire in case there was a message from Peter back home.

Nothing. No news was good news at this point.

Matthew exited to find where Hannah waited for him on a narrow bench near the street side of the depot as she watched the world before her.

He was suddenly acutely aware of every sound—horse harnesses jingling as a freight wagon passed; shouts of a newspaper boy hawking that day's edition; women laughing as they came out of a dress shop.

Hannah Stillwater heard none of that, yet he wondered how much more she saw than he did. He made sure he crossed her eye line before getting too close.

"Ready?" He was asking so much of her in that question. He felt unsteady on his feet.

Hannah rose, swung her medium-sized bag over her shoulder, and observed him. "Mr. Teller, why don't you go to the newspaper shop first and speak with the new editor? Drink a tall glass of water. I'll stroll around town and make observations before we go to the Palace."

She did see so much more than him. He agreed.

Once she disappeared down the street, he set out for the *Hot Springs Daily Tribune*.

Matthew entered the shop he hadn't been in since early '92. He introduced himself to a secretary at the front desk of the newspaper and requested to see the newspaper's current editor. The white lettering on the picture windows outside had stated his name was G.P. Rankin.

The secretary checked the back office then returned to escort Matthew to the room that had once housed Charles Hornet and the organization system that only he understood.

Upon entering the room, Matthew saw that not much had changed. A fiery looking middle-aged man sat behind Hornet's old desk with its teetering stacks of newspapers and notes.

G.P. Rankin came around the desk and pumped Matthew's hand. "So, you're Matthew Teller, the young reporter from Indian Territory that tried to save Charles Hornet's life."

That fight and shoot-out seemed ages ago. "I'm doing my own investigation into the same matter that got him killed."

The man whistled low and motioned to a chair stacked with books. "Throw those on the floor and have a seat. You worked for the *Dickens Herald* publisher, Christopher Maxwell, didn't you?"

Matthew took the seat. "I was on assignment for Maxwell that day. That article became the first front page story of my own newspaper."

The secretary offered to bring him a lemonade. Matthew accepted.

The middle-aged man shifted a stack of newspapers from the floor to his desk and thumbed through the top layers. "After that kid you sent went through these, I made some discoveries I think you'll find real interesting. I didn't have proof at the time—still don't—so I didn't use Maxwell's name in the story, but you might have better luck putting the pieces together. I suspect there is more going on here than either you or I want to know."

He found the paper he was looking for and folded it open to a section that he handed to Matthew. Matthew took it and skimmed it. It was about gambling on the Red River and mentioned a front man suspected of connections to the Palace and a gambling system set up in Indian Territory where neither white law nor Indian law had dominance.

Matthew and Rankin talked for an hour, comparing notes. In the end, Matthew didn't have the proof he needed but was convinced that Christopher Maxwell had run a gambling scheme throughout Indian Territory for years. But Rankin was right. There was another element to it. Matthew couldn't put his finger on it, but it was somehow related to the man who threatened him in Fort Smith. Something bigger than illegal gambling.

A soft tap at G.P. Rankin's door halted their conversation as the secretary cracked the door open. "Mr. Rankin, there is a young lady out here who says she is with the *Choctaw Tribune* as well."

Matthew nodded. "My assistant."

Rankin beckoned at his secretary and said to Matthew, "I hope she's better than that boy you sent before."

"She is."

Hannah entered, and the men stood. Her cheeks were flaming red, and she didn't look at Matthew. Matthew reached out to Hannah, intending to guide her into the chair he vacated.

"Miss Stillwater, what's wrong?" He waved to get her to look up.

Hannah jerked and cleared her throat. "I'm sorry, Mr. Teller, what did you say?"

"Are you all right?"

She edged closer to the wall, away from him. "I...well, you see, I went ahead and spent time in the Palace. While there, I saw a conversation that indicated gambling is not the only operation it houses."

G.P. Rankin cocked his head at her. "*Saw* a conversation?"

Matthew stared at her. His temper flared hot. "You went to the Palace without me?"

She smiled weakly. "I knew the dangers, Mr. Teller. I just ignored them as you always do." She turned to Rankin and offered her hand to shake. "Hannah Stillwater, sir, and I apologize if I've missed anything you've said. I'm deaf but read lips."

Rankin whistled low. "That's a handy asset for a newspaper!"

He glanced at Matthew, but made sure Hannah could see his face clearly. "I think I can explain the lady's discomfort. In addition to illegal gambling, the Palace runs a high-end brothel within its fine establishment."

Matthew didn't move. He'd hoped to uncover evidence of a syndicate or private gambling among state officials, or whiskey runners. Anything that would indicate a larger network that might have ties to Indian Territory and Maxwell.

He hadn't intended for Hannah to enter that devil's den alone.

Matthew retrieved his hat and coat from beside the door. "Thanks for your help, Mr. Rankin. I'll be in touch."

CHAPTER 27

All the lights were extinguished in the *Choctaw Tribune* save for the kerosene lamp on Matthew's desk. Everyone had long since gone home, leaving him working late that Saturday night. Not everything was in order for him to leave for D.C. In fact, things were a mess. This was the first week he'd run the newspaper without Ruth Ann since those early days. But he had confidence in Caleb Gentry to keep things running while he was gone. And Hannah Stillwater.

How quiet she'd been on the train ride back from Hot Springs the day before. Matthew hadn't managed to engage her in conversation. He had wanted to reprimand her for going alone to the Palace. Yet how could he? She wasn't a child. She was a capable young woman capable of making her own decisions.

She'd chosen to put herself in that situation for the truth. For justice. For all the things he fought for. He'd inspired her to do what she did.

He was more angry with himself than her.

She needed to know that. But the evening was mostly gone and she'd likely be at her room already, retired for the night.

Wouldn't she?

Matthew pushed away from his desk and went through the back storeroom to the door that led to his writing area in the alley there. With all the growth in town, he no longer had a clear view across the pasture to the church. It was a short walk to the end of the alley to see around the buildings and up the knoll where the church rested. It was dark but light shone from the window of the storeroom behind it. Was Hannah in there, working on pottery like she often did in the evenings?

Matthew could imagine the coolness of clay and water, the satisfaction of molding something into a new creation. Hands and mind occupied, the art of making pottery had eased his mind in his youth.

On the cusp of leaving for D.C. on tomorrow's train, his mind could use some easing.

Back inside the *Choctaw Tribune*, he blew out the kerosene lantern and locked up. He started to turn toward the church but pivoted and headed home instead.

He tripped.

Matthew caught himself on the center post holding up the roof of the porch in front of the shop and found the source of the yelp.

There was that stray dog who had made his way into the *Tribune* with Nita. Matthew squatted to get nearly eye level with the handsome, forgiving fellow as he stretched and looked up at Matthew.

"Sorry about that. You should go along home now."

The tri-colored dog thumped his tail on the boardwalk, eyes shining from the gas lamps in the street in a way that told Matthew he'd claimed this spot as his home.

The dog rolled over on his side, front paws drawn up under his snout. Correction. *Her* snout. She'd had puppies.

Matthew gave the obligatory belly rub.

"Don't start something you can't finish," his daddy had teased him

when he did the same with one of the ranch dogs at Uncle Preston's.

That saying stuck in Matthew's gut now.

"All right, Story girl, I've got something I have to finish. Don't distract me."

It was no use. When Matthew headed down the street to the box house, the dog padded after him. Matthew slipped inside so fast he startled his mother and Nita in the living room. Della *tsked* and nodded toward the kitchen. From the front door, Matthew could see a plate on the stove. The supper he'd missed.

"Thank you, Mama, but I have one more errand to run…"

There was no getting around her look. Matthew grabbed the plate from the cold stove and ate it by huge mouthfuls. He still needed to pack for his trip. But not until he'd taken care of things in Dickens first.

When he was almost done eating, he returned to the living room and spoke to Nita, who played with her Noah's Ark on the floor.

"Nita, would you like to go with me?"

Nita was on her feet immediately.

Della raised an eyebrow. It was too late to take the little one out romping through town. Not to mention many of Matthew's errands involved danger.

This wasn't one of them. He did need a chaperone, though. He set his empty plate on the stove.

"We won't be gone long, Mama. Just up to the church for a minute."

Nita looked to her grandmother for permission and Della gave it with a nod. "Not long till your bedtime, Little Bear."

Nita grasped Matthew's hand. He took her straw boater hat from beside the door and plopped it on her head before taking up his own hat. They exited, hand-in-hand.

The dog was waiting on the porch, to Nita's delight. She

scratched her behind the ear, ensuring a loyal companion for the evening.

They headed up Main Street, the dog trotting next to Nita.

The door to the storeroom behind the church was propped open, letting in the evening air. Matthew started to knock on the door frame. He checked himself.

From the doorway, he couldn't see Hannah, so he stepped inside, lifting Nita over the threshold by one arm. She giggled.

Matthew started to close the door to keep the dog out, but she'd slipped into the space beside Nita. Oh well. This was a storeroom, which was like a barn. Not actually "indoors."

He could hear sounds of movement in the back, somewhere beyond the haphazard stacks of boxes, an old desk, and well used chairs and sawhorses that they set up for church picnics. He followed the path a light cast from the direction of the sounds.

When they rounded one of the extra high stacks of boxes, Matthew spotted Hannah seated at a small table. It and she were splattered with wet clay, a bucket of water and a bucket of dry clay nestled beside her. She was smiling with such purity, he knew the pottery had her in better spirits after the trip.

Her face was angled away and Matthew didn't want to startle her. He gave a wave.

"Miss Stillwater?"

When she didn't look their way, Nita shouted, "Hannah!"

Matthew held back a grimace. He'd watched people speaking loud and slow for Hannah, as though it would help her hear better. It seemed something she was used to.

Story solved the problem. She trotted over to Hannah and sat by her feet. She pawed Hannah's dress.

Hannah smiled and scratched the dog behind the ears.

Matthew wondered if he'd seen what he'd just seen.

Hannah looked up. Her smile disappeared and she quickly stood. "Mr. Teller." Her gaze dropped to Nita and she visibly relaxed. "Halito, Nita."

Nita edged forward, eyeing the pottery piece Hannah was working on. "Why did you call me that?"

"Nita? It's your name."

"Before that."

"Oh." Hannah glanced at Matthew, then knelt on the floor in front of Nita. "'Halito' is a Choctaw greeting. You can say it to people if you'd like. It's good to speak the language of your people."

"Oh." Nita ran a hand along the edge of the table, just enough to get wet clay on her fingertips. "I've heard that word before. How did you learn it since you can't hear?"

Hannah chuckled softly. "That's a long story, little one. I think you'd have far more fun molding clay than listening to it. Would you like to try?"

Nita nodded vigorously and Hannah hefted her onto the low stool by the table. Hannah draped her large apron around Nita and scooted the table closer. Then she straightened to face Matthew.

"Shall we talk about what happened in Hot Springs, Mr. Teller?"

Matthew found his voice. "Yes, well, first though, I can't believe what that dog did."

She glanced down at Story, who was giving Hannah her full attention. "Oh, yes, your cousin mentioned you don't allow dogs inside. I guess she wandered in with Nita..."

Matthew held up a hand then pointed at the dog. "No, I mean, yes she did, but when Nita said your name, the dog went right over to you and got your attention. It's like she wanted to let you know we were here, and it's got me thinking. What if we could train her to do that every time someone says your name? That would make it easier to communicate in the shop."

Hannah's smile returned, teasing. "That, sir, would require you to let her into the shop in the first place."

She had him there. "I guess we could make this one exception."

Hannah laughed and turned to move a finished piece from the table to a back shelf. A row of pottery was shelved there in various states of completion.

Hannah turned back to him, solemn. "Now, about the Palace."

She glanced at Nita. The little girl had her tongue stuck in her cheek, concentrating on making a tall flute on a square block of clay.

Hannah angled her head close to the sawhorses and Matthew joined her there. His face was shadowed and she would have difficulty reading his lips, but Hannah seemed to prefer that to Nita hearing them.

"First, I do apologize for going alone to the Palace. I knew you'd object, but I didn't see us being able to accomplish what we needed to with you getting thrown out every time you show your face there. I, on the other hand, had quite an advantage. What I learned, though, was simply too…indecent to speak of in public."

Matthew pinched his lips.

"But I think you need to know what I saw," Hannah continued. "First, I will show you how I saw it and why I wouldn't have had any success with you around."

Hannah crossed the room to retrieve the bag she'd toted with them to Hot Springs. She pulled out a stereoscope loaded with a photo for viewing. She handed it to Matthew. He was sure she was holding back a sly smile.

"Should I look at the photograph?"

"Be my guest."

Matthew placed the photograph viewer to his eyes and took a step back. Tiny holes in the photograph showed Hannah's face with startling clarity.

"When you asked me about us spying in the Palace, I knew I'd need something to help me watch conversations without drawing suspicion. So I modified my stereoscope to use as a spyglass, if you will."

"Ingenious. Remind me to never fire you."

Hannah laughed softly. "That would be delightful."

She went on, "When I entered the Palace, I spoke with the clerk at the desk and asked if a Miss Willoughby had left a message for me. When he replied no, of course, I told him I would wait, and he directed me to a settee in the lobby. I could clearly see inside the casino—well, clearly except for the cigar smoke—and busied myself with the stereoscope. I had modified three photographs to change out while I watched for anything interesting. That did finally come."

Hannah paused and the victory of her clever idea faded from her expression. "A young woman came out of the casino on a man's arm. I recognized him from my observations. He appeared to be a manager. They reached the staircase and she halted, turned to him. Her face was directly in line with me. She was flushed and asked if she could go back to the casino. I don't know what the man said—his back was to me—but she began pleading. She said, 'That man...I can't. Please.'"

Matthew tightened his grip on the stereoscope.

"The manager jerked her by the arm and said something. She grew so pale, Mr. Teller. I thought she was going to faint. She said, 'No. She's too young. You can't take her, too.'"

Matthew heard a crack and looked down to see he'd broken the arm on the stereoscope.

Hannah gently took the pieces from his hands. "I can repair this, Mr. Teller. But I cannot imagine what it would take to repair a young woman like her. She is not allowed to decide her own fate each day."

Matthew felt that even the sound of his voice would violate the moment. He mouthed, "You believe the girls at the Palace are forced there against their will?"

"I do."

The past three years were beginning to make sense—Mayor Warren's tight hold on what was printed in the *Choctaw Tribune*; Jake Banny's hotel with its numerous rooms not available for rent; Christopher Maxwell's ties to the Palace and the tight control he wanted of the story after it was wrecked.

Slavery.

Matthew had thought their crimes centered on whiskey running and gambling. This went beyond that. Far beyond.

Matthew rubbed his face then steepled his fingers over his lips. His eyes went to Nita, who had mashed the clay into a ball and was starting a new creation.

"Mr. Teller, may I share with you the thought that has haunted me since then?"

Matthew breathed through his nose and nodded.

"I can't help but wonder that if it hadn't been for what my parents put me through with my education, I might have been caught in a situation like that. A deaf girl is vulnerable in this world with limited options. On that note, I want to…thank you again for hiring me to work at the *Choctaw Tribune*." Her voice broke.

Matthew dropped his hands. "There is no way I could ever thank you enough for working with me, Miss Stillwater. What you uncovered gives me all the reassurance I need to not stop until I get Maxwell."

CHAPTER 28

The train ride to Washington, D.C. was as boring with a traveling companion as not. Both Matthew and Leonard Coxwell spent the trip reading or writing. Coxwell did much of his activities in the smoking car. Matthew did most of his on his bunk in the Pullman sleeper.

At least Matthew could finally rest without interruption. Though he didn't, not really. He had a suitcase full of back issues of newspapers he'd fallen far behind on reading.

By the time they arrived at the Baltimore and Potomac Railroad Station in Washington, D.C., Matthew still hadn't learned exactly what Leonard Coxwell's business was.

They rented a cab that took them to the Willard Hotel, a place familiar to Coxwell who offered to share his room since the hotel was booked to capacity. Matthew appreciated the accommodations, both the grandeur of the hotel and because several Washington politicians boarded there.

It was a good thing Ruth Ann hadn't known he was making this trip. She would've given him a laundry list of sites to see and people to give her regards to. He had to admit meeting the president and first lady would have been fine, but he was just there for a quick three days.

And Matthew only had one man in mind that he had to see in the nation's capital.

Matthew took his camera when he left the Willard Hotel the first morning. He didn't take many pictures as he walked to the trolley stop and caught it toward the Capitol building. Ruth Ann had gotten gobs of good photographs of the nation's capital, and he didn't want to waste film on the same places. He did stop in front of the neoclassical U.S. Capitol building and asked someone to take his photograph in front of it. He wanted to give it to Nita.

Inside, he made it to his appointment with a clerk from Benjamin's references. The clerk took him down a narrow spiral staircase to the basement of the U.S. Capitol building and left him there to "knock himself silly" in the boxes and boxes of archives that pertained to Indian affairs.

Matthew didn't know what he could find that would give him footing for declaring the townsite of Dickens illegal, but the pleasure of being surrounded by stacks of records going back to before the removal from his people's homelands was monumental.

He wanted to dive into the older records but recent discussion in congressional sessions needed his attention. He read through hearings pertaining to Choctaws until he was cross-eyed. Then he came across a proposal that made him sit up in the hardbacked chair.

TOWN SITE ACT

Congress should pass a town site act for The Five Tribes, forcing their consent, if necessary, to the end that valuable accrued property rights shall be protected. Millions of dollars are now invested by citizens of the United States in the several towns of Indian territory with no legal or proper protection. Trade and the interests of commerce necessitated the building of stores, warehouses, hotels, and dwellings, and these outlays would thus be protected.

Matthew positioned his notebook next to the document and began copying it.

Railroads are chartered through The Five Tribes, and cities, towns, and villages grow up along them in aid of their operation. Congress should incorporate these towns and provide for a legal method of registering and passing title to these various properties or adjuncts of railroad trade and commerce...

The Indian occupancy claimant to the land on which the town is, or the nation claiming the land, could be paid, say $10 or more per acre for it, and the town site then be parceled out to lot holders, the remaining lot to be sold for the benefit of the town.

Matthew broke the tip of his pencil. He quickly sharpened it and continued.

The commission in charge of the allotment in each of The Five Tribes could take charge of the town site allotment as well. In any view of Five Tribe affairs, town sites are the serious problems. They should be settled first, and at once, by Congress exercising its right of eminent domain in aid of internal commerce. Much of the discontent among the whites of The Five Civilized Tribes would cease could title be acquired to town lots. The Five Tribes will probably never pass an incorporative law by which white or colored, so-called intruders, can get title to lots. Congress will have to do this. The passage of a general town site act of 320 or 640 acres each by Congress will be first in order. Then the question of allotment of the remaining lands can come up. Whatever is to be done as to town sites should be done quickly, as delay only thickens the danger and makes the work more difficult.

The proper settlement of the land question in The Five Civilized Tribes of Indian territory presents one of the most serious problems the United States has as yet had to deal with in connection with the Indians. They are not on reservations, but on lands patented to each nation.

Senator Dawes was setting individual land allotments—and the end of the Choctaw Nation—into motion.

No wonder Maxwell had put forth his brazen proposal to have Dickens annexed and removed from the Choctaw Nation.

Was there really anything Matthew could do to stop any of this?

Shoving the congressional records aside, he dug through the older boxes and found decades-old ledger books from Mississippi that held the records of a store at a place called Robuck Landing—a simple accounting of the goods people bought and sold there. Then he stumbled on a letter from the time of Removal in the 1830s—a letter from one of the chiefs of the Choctaw Nation.

To the American People:

It is with considerable diffidence that I attempt to address the American people, knowing and feeling sensibly my incompetency; and believing that your highly and well improved minds would not be well entertained by the address of a Choctaw. But having determined to emigrate west of the Mississippi river this fall, I have thought proper in bidding you farewell to make a few remarks expressive of my views, and the feelings that actuate me on the subject of our removal.

...We were hedged in by two evils, and we chose that which we thought the least...We as Choctaws rather chose to suffer and be free, than live under the degrading influence of laws, which our voice could not be heard in their formation.

...I could cheerfully hope, that those of another age and generation may not feel the effects of those oppressive measures that have been so illiberally dealt out to us; and that peace and happiness may be their reward. Amid the gloom and horrors of the present separation, we are cheered with a hope that ere long we shall reach our destined land, and that nothing short of the basest acts of treachery will ever be able to wrest it from us, and that we may live free...

...I will not conceal from you my fears, that the present grounds may be removed. I have my foreboding; who of us can tell after witnessing what has already been done, what the next force may be.

I ask you in the name of justice, for repose for myself and for my injured people. Let us alone — we will not harm you, we want rest. We hope, in the name of justice, that another outrage may never be committed against us...

Taking an example from the American government, and knowing the happiness which its citizens enjoy under the influence of mild republican institutions, it is the intention of our countrymen to form a government assimilated to that of our white brethren in the United States, as nearly as their condition will permit.

We know that in order to protect the rights and secure the liberties of the people, no government approximates so nearly to perfection as the one to which we have alluded. As east of the Mississippi we have been friends, so west we will cherish the same feelings with additional fervour; and although we may be removed to the desert, still we shall look with fond regard, upon those who have promised us their protection. Let that feeling be reciprocated.

Friends, my attachment to my native land was strong — that cord is now broken; and we must go forth as wanderers in a strange land! I must go — let me entreat you to regard us with feelings of kindness, and

*when the hand of oppression is stretched against us, let me hope that
every part of the United States, filling the mountains and valleys, will
echo and say stop, you have no power, we are the sovereign people, and
our friends shall no more be disturbed. We ask you for nothing that is
incompatible with your other duties.*

*Here is the land of our progenitors, and here are their bones; they left
them as a sacred deposit, and we have been compelled to venerate its
trust; it is dear to us, yet we cannot stay, my people are dear to me, with
them I must go. Could I stay and forget them and leave them to struggle
alone, unaided, unfriended, and forgotten by our great father? I should
then be unworthy the name of a Choctaw, and be a disgrace to my
blood. I must go with them; my destiny is cast among the Choctaw
people. If they suffer, so will I; if they prosper, then I will rejoice. Let me
again ask you to regard us with feelings of kindness.*

George W. Harkins
February 25, 1832

Matthew swiped a sleeve under his nose as he copied the
letter word for word. He saw where it had been printed in several
newspapers back in its day. It was time for it to make the rounds
again.

Chief Harkins words were prophetic. The Choctaw people
faced destruction in Matthew's generation.

*... my destiny is cast among the Choctaw people. If they suffer, so
will I...*

Matthew could almost sign his own name to the letter.

When he emerged from the historical cave hours later, he
knew parts of his people he had never known before.

Coming to D.C. was the right choice, but he wished he had
started with his primary task first. As it was, the injustices of his
life and for his people were foremost on his mind when he
retired that night.

Why did he have to visit Thaddeus Warren tomorrow and forgive him for his part in those injustices?

~

Matthew stood outside the prison gates, staring at the cold, hard place. One of his worst enemies was inside. Matthew didn't feel any gratification at that fact. Maybe that was enough to prove he wasn't on this journey for revenge. Pastor Rand was right, though. There was only one way to know for sure.

It was a cloudy morning, a nip in the air as rain threatened from the slate gray sky. Matthew tucked his hands in his pockets and glanced around. His acquaintance who was meeting him there was running late, but Matthew didn't mind. In all honesty, he'd gotten there early, wanting time to stand a while and absorb the place before he physically entered it.

Ruth Ann was opposite him in that way. She preferred to push right into wherever she was going. But she had learned patience well in the past few years with their trials at the *Choctaw Tribune*. If anything, Matthew had less.

Perhaps it was the three years solid he spent fighting injustices without a breather. When could he take a breather? Only after he stopped Maxwell's attempted takeover of Dickens to openly run illegal gambling and prostitution there.

A cab rolled to stop in front of the prison and Matthew waited as a man disembarked and paid the driver. The portly man turned, more gray hair around his temples, but otherwise looking unchanged from the sharp-minded reporter Matthew had met three years ago in Dickens.

When Matthew decided he would travel to D.C., he had contacted Angus Rice and was pleased to discover he was in D.C. for the summer. They spoke over the telephone—the first long distance call for the *Choctaw Tribune*—and planned to meet. A prison was an odd place for a reunion, but Rice had good connections and offered to use them when Matthew told him about this stop.

Angus Rice spotted Matthew and stuck out his hand in greeting. "Well, if it isn't the young gunslinging newsman from Indian Territory."

Matthew shook the man's hand firmly. "I left my gun at the hotel today. Seemed a good idea considering where we are."

The man slapped Matthew on the shoulder. "At least we've gotten past the days of when you could railroad a man into a gunfight, kill him, and call it self-defense."

"It's been a while since you've been in Indian Territory, hasn't it?"

The man chuckled, keeping his hand on Matthew's shoulder as they approached the guard house.

"Son, you may have to keep that gun loaded, but you keep your pencil sharp, too. I've been impressed with your work the past few years despite the friendly opposition."

He halted before the guardhouse and turned to Matthew. "I was sorry to hear how your print shop burned down, and then how you were ambushed in the mountains. That's dirtier politics than I've seen anywhere."

Matthew felt a rip in his chest, a flash of the memory of a bullet striking it. He'd mentally prepared himself to see and forgive Thaddeus Warren today, but his resolve wavered in the face of that memory.

Angus Rice squeezed his shoulder. "Are you certain you want to do this?"

Matthew gave a tight nod. It was now or never. Besides, he had another reason for seeing Warren.

Rice spoke with the guard and received access to the inside. They entered the prison where the guards checked them over for hidden weapons but no harassment. Rice was known there from interviewing prisoners. He and Matthew were soon waved through and toward a long hallway. The place was rank and dark.

A guard led them into an open room with several tables and prisoners in black and white striped trousers and shirts. White patches were stitched to the arm sleeves with their numbers. The prisoners wore round caps and sat mostly quiet across the table from solemn visitors.

As they settled at an empty table, Rice whispered, "We are Thaddeus Warren's first visitors since he was incarcerated."

The comment was meant to give Matthew a stab of satisfaction. He did feel a stab, but he couldn't say it was from that.

After a few minutes, a hefty white-haired man shuffled to their table. His cheeks sagged and his eyes bulged. It took a few minutes for Matthew to recognize the former mayor of Dickens.

The sentiment was mutual as Warren stared at him. Then his head jerked back. Apparently, he'd only been told he had visitors, and a man incarcerated in a place like this for months should welcome any visitor, even an enemy.

Thaddeus Warren shifted his feet as if to leave.

But he stayed. Angus Rice indicated the chair across from them. "Mr. Warren. Won't you sit down?"

The polite invitation gave the moment a parlor room feel. Matthew had a feeling Rice was well-versed in dealing with uncooperative prisoners. He told Matthew that some prisoners refused to talk but most were eager, hoping that Rice would write a positive story about them and sway public opinion in their favor.

Thaddeus Warren was under no such delusions.

Still, he lowered his creaking frame into the chair and sat staring at Rice, ignoring Matthew. An aura fell over him, like a king pulled from a mud pit to drape on a clean purple robe. He'd always been little more than a walking windbag.

He addressed Rice. "To what do I owe the pleasure?"

Rice nodded toward Matthew. "You'll have to ask Mr. Teller. He's the one who requested this meeting."

Warren refused to look at Matthew.

There was no point in beating around the bush. "Warren..." Matthew's voice came out like a croak and he paused, cleared his throat, and started again.

"Mr. Warren, I've come to talk to you about two things. First, your old compatriot, Christopher Maxwell, has filed to annex the town of Dickens out of the Choctaw Nation."

Matthew waited a second for Warren's delayed reaction. But it never came. The man stared blankly at Rice as though the names "Maxwell" and "Dickens" meant nothing to him.

Matthew reached into his coat pocket and pulled out an affidavit that Benjamin had drafted prior to the wedding. They had wanted it ready to mail off to Thaddeus Warren on the long shot that he would sign it. Benjamin had friends in high places who might work to get Warren's sentence reduced if he cooperated.

Matthew unfolded the affidavit and laid it on the table in front of Warren. The man glanced down at it, blinking several times as though his eyesight was too poor to read it, but he wouldn't admit it. Matthew filled in.

"This states that you, Maxwell, Banny, and Carter illegally formed the town site of Dickens by leasing the property from Sam Mishaya. That was legal, but you formed a town site without permission from the Choctaw Nation, and as white men, you had no authority to even propose it. It includes a confession that you knew of Jake Banny's plan to burn down my shop, and how Christopher Maxwell hired Cub Wassom to shoot me in cold blood, all in an attempt to silence the truth about the businesses you were forming and planned to form in Dickens. You sign this and we can work on shortening the length of your stay here."

Warren finally looked at Matthew. He slapped his hand over the affidavit and crumpled it into a ball. He flung it at Matthew, bouncing it off his chest.

"You sorry Indian."

Matthew scooped the crumbled paper from the floor,

smoothed it on the table, folded it neatly, and put it back into his coat, never taking his eyes off Warren.

"That brings me to the second item. I know you were part of having my newspaper shop burned down and me shot."

Warren was shaking, his face a pasty white. Sweat broke out on his forehead. "I did nothing of the kind."

"I forgive you."

Warren flattened his hands on the table. He pushed hard as if trying to stand, but he couldn't move. Whether his tremendous shaking was from anger or fear or sorrow, Matthew didn't know.

Matthew slowly rose from his chair and tipped his hat at the former mayor of Dickens.

"Goodbye, Warren."

Matthew suspected they both hoped this goodbye was permanent.

Matthew had dinner with Angus Rice in Georgetown. Matthew hadn't seen Leonard Coxwell since that first day at the Willard. So much for learning what Coxwell's business was in D.C. or Indian Territory. Unless he learned something on the train trip home, he was left to wonder if Leonard Coxwell was a friend or foe of the Choctaw people. For Sissy's sake, Matthew hoped it was the former.

Ruth Ann had told Matthew about a quaint bookstore in Georgetown and he asked Rice about it. They spent the rest of the evening there.

Matthew felt tension seep from his body. This was the kind of place he could get lost in, rows and rows of bookshelves that could take him anywhere in the world.

Funny thing, there wasn't really anywhere in the world he wanted to go except Indian Territory.

His people were there. Family. Friends. His newspaper...and Hannah Stillwater.

Matthew went to the clerk at the counter and asked if the store had books on sign language. The lady directed him to the back corner where he had to search several minutes before finding one. He thumbed through the pages and smiled. Just what he was looking for.

Matthew spent time picking out a book for Benjamin, and also one for Ruth Ann. He found a copy of the novel she'd lost in the train wreck—*On the Blue River* by T.A. Paige. Though Matthew detested fiction, Ruth Ann liked this author and Matthew would need something to soothe her temper when she found out he slipped away to D.C. and didn't visit all the sites she would've wanted him to see.

When Matthew arrived back at the Willard Hotel, the room was empty. He couldn't say for sure the other bed had even been slept in.

CHAPTER 29

The three days came and went in a blur. Matthew met with congressmen who were working with Senator Dawes on the allotment of Indian tribal lands and gathered every scrap he could to prevent Maxwell from jumping the gun and forcing the issue of town sites in the Choctaw Nation.

He wasn't surprised at a few of the men who shut down when he mentioned Maxwell's name. The *Dickens Herald* newsman was known in D.C. and had some influence in the halls of congress. How much? That was something Matthew could spend months trying to uncover.

He didn't have the time.

Leonard Coxwell finally appeared late on their last night in D.C. Matthew was packed and ready to go early the next morning.

Matthew spent the first half of the train ride in the rocking passenger car, studying the sign language book. He wanted to have a rudimentary understanding of the language so that he could begin communicating with Hannah in it. He let memories of her occupy his mind and dampen the cold encounter with Warren. He'd done what he set out to do.

So far, Matthew had forgiven Josiah Carter face-to-face and now Thaddeus Warren. That left Jake Banny, who was dead, and Christopher Maxwell. Matthew wasn't sure forgiving that man in person was possible.

It was long past supper, which he'd taken alone in the dining car, and Matthew felt himself nodding off. He stirred and earmarked the page where he stopped in the sign language book, a habit that annoyed Ruth Ann to no end. Tucking it in his bag, he prepared to move to the sleeper car.

Leonard Coxwell, who had been seated across the aisle for a conversation with fellow traveling businessmen, stood. Matthew realized the man was watching him.

Coxwell slid across the aisle and into the vacant bench facing Matthew. "May I speak with you?"

He had a folded newspaper in hand, and he tapped it on his knee. Matthew could see it was a copy of the *Choctaw Tribune*.

"What's on your mind?"

Coxwell glanced down at the newspaper then back at Matthew. One thing about this man, he wasn't afraid to look you in the eye.

"I don't understand your people."

Matthew settled back in his seat. "They are your people now."

He waited for the fact to settle in deep for Leonard Coxwell. The man didn't break off his gaze as he contemplated the simple statement. Being married to a Choctaw woman made Leonard Coxwell an intermarried citizen with the same rights and privileges of anyone who was Choctaw by blood.

It was clear, though, that Leonard Coxwell hadn't considered anything beyond the Choctaws being his wife's people and his license to conduct business freely in the nation.

Coxwell double tapped the newspaper. "Our upbringings were quite different. Eliza and I…our marriage is not going how either of us expected when we made our vows. Now, since her miscarriage…" He shrugged and looked out the window.

A sadness spread through Matthew. He hadn't known about the miscarriage.

"That must've been hard on you both."

"I'm led to believe she is the only one suffering."

Matthew said nothing. The man went on, his voice rising.

"I give her everything—music, art, the finest furnishings, servants—have you seen our home? No, I suppose you haven't. She never wants to entertain people in the home I provide for her. She is ungrateful, and when I want her to express intimacy—"

Matthew stood. "Mr. Coxwell, what is between you and your wife, it's between the two of you. I'm sorry. Goodnight."

Matthew headed for the sleeper car. He had learned more than he cared to know about Leonard Coxwell.

In the late hours of the night, the rocking of the train woke Matthew. No. It was the hand shaking his shoulder that woke him.

Matthew peeled his eyes open to receive the glare of lamplight from the hall. He'd closed the curtain on his bunk to block out the interior lights, but Leonard Coxwell had pulled it back. He looked even more solemn than when Matthew left him in the passenger car hours ago. He'd also looked to have had a few drinks in the smoking car.

Coxwell spoke slow and careful. "Mr. Teller, I received a telegram at the last stop. There's something I need to address in St. Louis, so I will be a few days delayed in returning home. Would you take this to Eliza? It is urgent she have it as soon as possible."

He held up a package and Matthew frowned. Maybe Coxwell was also hoping Matthew would talk to Sissy about her part in wrecking the marriage. He had no intention of getting in the middle of their troubles, but he nodded, taking the package and tugging on the curtain.

"Goodnight again."

Matthew halted on the walkway in front of the three-story mansion on a quiet neighborhood street in Antlers, Choctaw Nation. He was there to drop off a package and excuse himself immediately to see if there was anything newsworthy in town before catching the next southbound Frisco train to Dickens.

He didn't even want to approach the white veranda covered with hanging plants and pristine white furniture.

Might as well get it over with. Matthew climbed the steps and rapped lightly on the door. It remained quiet on the other side, so he knocked again. He remembered Coxwell mentioning they had servants, but none appeared.

Matthew tried to peer through the window to the parlor. The curtains were drawn tight. Sissy might be out shopping, although with how ill she looked at Ruth Ann's wedding, he didn't imagine she would be gone long. Matthew could wait on the veranda, but he would check around back first, just in case.

He found Sissy kneeling in a flower garden that filled the backyard. A gravel path guided visitors through the explosion of summer blooms. Matthew's boots on the gravel alerted Sissy of his presence. She looked up.

Gone was the youthful, jubilant smile that once greeted the Teller siblings when they visited the Barnes' family. Normally attentive to her appearance, Sissy's hair was stringy and falling loose over her sagging shoulders. She grabbed a kerchief discarded on the path and wrapped it around her head, trying to capture the mess. She failed.

The soil from her hands smeared across her forehead and she

sighed, dropping her hands and the cloth. "I didn't realize the train had arrived."

Matthew knelt across from her, a flowerbed between them as he held up the package. "Your husband asked me to drop this off. I knocked at the front, but no one answered."

She went back to weeding the bed. "He sent a telegram, said he was staying in St. Louis a few days, so I gave the servants time off." She shrugged as if that filled in for everything she couldn't say. "Just leave the bottle on the back porch. I'll put it away later."

Matthew instinctively tightened his hand on the package and realized there was a lot of cushioning. Surely he hadn't inadvertently transported illegal alcohol into the Choctaw Nation?

Sissy glanced up and a girlish smile touched her lips. "Don't worry, you're not a whiskey runner. It's just some medicine Leonard got from a fancy doctor in D.C. He wants it to cure whatever it is that ails me."

"I'll leave it on the porch for you." Matthew started to rise, but Sissy beckoned him to stay. She looked into his eyes and asked, "Were you and Leonard together the whole time?"

Matthew lowered back into a squat and shook his head. "We weren't really together at all. I had a lot of business to take care of."

Her intense eyes drilled into him, and Matthew's stomach soured. He hadn't given enough thought to Leonard Coxwell's undisturbed bed until now.

Sissy didn't break off her stare and Matthew knew his own expression was telling. He needed to say something. But what?

"Maybe you should speak with your folks."

Sissy paled and shook her head, black strands of hair whipping her face. "I don't want my family to know. Please. Don't make anyone suspicious. I'm sure there's nothing to be suspicious of."

Matthew slowly rose. "I'll leave the package on the porch."

As he emerged onto the sidewalk, Matthew felt an itch on the back of his neck. He glanced over his shoulder, sure someone was watching him.

But the light traffic on the street paid him no mind and he strode toward the depot. It was still a few hours until the next train, but he had lost all desire to talk to anyone about anything. He was done for the day.

CHAPTER 30

Matthew was in better spirits by the time the train chugged into the Dickens depot. He'd spent the remainder of his trip going through the sign language book, picking out the phrase he wanted to greet Hannah with. He ignored the frowns fellow passengers gave him as he made broad hand motions while holding the book open with one elbow.

The train jerked to a halt and Matthew was the first off instead of the last. He'd just reached the edge of the wooden platform when a long-haired tail appeared over the side. Story propped her paws on the end of the platform, tail wagging vigorously as if she'd known he was coming today and waited right there to welcome him home.

He was really beginning to like this stray.

Matthew shifted his baggage to one hand and one arm so he could scratch her head. She licked his hand and followed as he headed for the house. It was empty, indicating his mother was out shopping with Nita.

Matthew left his bags in the living room and bounced down the porch steps. He'd never been quite so anxious to reach the *Choctaw Tribune*.

The dog followed him and when Matthew opened the door to the newspaper office, he used his boot to hold her back a moment. He glanced inside and saw Hannah at the typesetting cabinet with Nita on her lap, letting her set type. Caleb Gentry was at the press as usual and gave Matthew a curt nod.

Matthew returned it then glanced down at the dog as he lowered his boot. He pushed the door wide open and pointed at the typesetting cabinet. "Go to Hannah. *Hannah*."

The dog looked at him, then inside the shop, and back at him. She trotted inside.

Quite a lady, carefully weaving between the press and Matthew's desk to reach the cabinet without knocking anything over, her tail gently swishing. Matthew followed.

Story sat by the cabinet and pawed on Hannah's dress. Hannah looked down. She gasped and set Nita on the floor as she stood. "How did you get in here? You're not supposed to…"

She looked up to see if the door was open and found Matthew in her line of sight.

He could hardly help feeling ridiculously pleased with himself as he signed, *Hello. How are you today?*

Hannah stared at him in a way that took the pleasure right out of the day. She drew back as though he had struck her.

Nita rushed him and hugged his legs, asking, "What did you say to her, Uncle Matthew?"

"Apparently the wrong thing."

Matthew had a sick feeling he'd messed up the signs and said something awful. Or maybe there was a different sign language that Hannah used. He stepped toward the typesetting cabinet, but she took a step back.

"Mr. Teller…I wasn't….we weren't…how was your trip?"

Caleb Gentry halted the press and grabbed a newspaper from the table beside it. "What she's trying to say, Teller, is you've gotten us into more trouble." He slapped the newspaper in Matthew's chest.

Matthew lifted one hand to secure it and Gentry went back to slamming the lever on the press. Matthew couldn't take his gaze off Hannah for several seconds. She was redder than when she'd returned from the Palace.

Nita laid her head against his leg. "I'm sorry, Uncle Matthew."

He didn't know why she was apologizing. She likely didn't either. She just knew he hadn't received the welcome home he'd expected.

Matthew slowly raised the newspaper to take in the familiar typeface of the *Dickens Herald*. The newspaper was unfolded to the Local Happenings section, which amounted to nothing more than a gossip column. It only took seconds for him to understand Hannah's horror at seeing him.

Indian Newspaperman in Questionable Circumstances with Deaf Woman

Lady citizens in Dickens recently sounded the alarm on a compromising situation concerning the Choctaw Tribune newspaper publisher Matthew Teller. Mr. Teller was seen departing by train with his employee, a young female who is deaf. Destination unknown. They did not arrive back until late evening.

The concerned citizens reported several other incidents where the publisher was alone with the young woman in the dark recesses of the Choctaw Tribune *building.*

What sort of story is he writing with this vulnerable young deaf girl?

The article disappeared as Matthew ripped it in half. Nita scrambled away, bumping her head on the cabinet. Matthew halted the tirade threatening to break loose in his soul, tried to satisfy himself with quietly crumpling the torn newspaper in his fists.

Hannah hadn't moved since first seeing him. He couldn't speak to her. Couldn't even move his lips. He did the only thing he could think of.

Taking one of his fists, he moved it in a circular motion across his chest.

I'm sorry.

Though he was tired, Matthew obliged family and friends with stories of his trip to D.C. that evening during dinner at the Teller home with Peter and the Levitts. Hannah was understandably absent. The fact that she needed the job so much had to be the only reason she stayed at the newspaper after the article came out while Matthew was gone. He didn't know how to keep her there and her reputation intact, though.

He didn't have as much to share as Ruth Ann had from her trip to D.C., but he did go into detail about his findings at the archives and how none of Ruth Ann's descriptions were exaggerated.

No one said anything about the *Dickens Herald* article. Matthew didn't say anything about how he was stared at all day in town.

He helped clear away the supper dishes while the small group moved into the living room. Matthew had just picked up two cups for coffee to serve when soft tapping on the back door caught his attention. His mother had already gone into the living room with the coffee pot so he set the cups down on the table and opened the door.

There stood Daniel, looking more solemn than Matthew had ever seen. Matthew beckoned for him to come inside, but Daniel shook his head. His face was dusty from a long, hard ride, hat pulled low to his eyes. He said quietly, "Is Pepper Barnes here?"

Matthew stepped into the cooler air from the heat in the kitchen and closed the door behind him.

"No, he's not."

Daniel's face was shadowed by his hat brim. His voice sounded even darker. "He's back, Matthew. The woman killer. I'm sure it's the same man."

Matthew tightened his fist, still wondering if that man was the same who had put a gun to his head in the basement in Fort Smith.

"What's happened?"

"It's Sissy Barnes. Or Eliza Coxwell, I mean. She was attacked this afternoon. Nearly killed."

Matthew blinked, shock vibrating his body.

"The doctor thinks she'll pull through, but they don't know for sure. Pepper Barnes is on the man's tail, so I'm tracking them both."

Matthew leaned against the outside wall of the house, staring at the barn. Staring at the scene from his life that very day.

"I saw Sissy this morning. Her husband had asked me to drop off a package. She was fine...just fine."

Daniel rubbed his chin. "You say you saw her this morning?"

Matthew nodded absently. Was it the same man who had threatened Matthew and murdered Mrs. Bellanger? Sissy had nothing to do with Matthew's investigation into Maxwell's dealings. Still, these two women being attacked right after Matthew saw them...

He shifted his focus back to Daniel and saw his cousin had arrived at the same thought.

Neither of them had the answer.

CHAPTER 31

Two days later, Daniel rode into Paris, Texas. He had Pepper Barnes and a dead man in tow.

Daniel hadn't caused this man's death. He discovered him in Dead Man's Lake near Antlers. The watering hole had gotten its name for its popularity in turning up dead bodies.

The fact that this man floated up with a bullet in his head with Pepper Barnes in the vicinity was enough for Daniel to bring them both to Paris.

But as they dismounted and Daniel glanced at the tarp covered body, his gut instinct told him this was not the woman killer. Still, he hoped it was.

They went inside the Lamar County Jail and Daniel explained to the deputy what was going on and asked for the appropriate paperwork. He needed to record Pepper's statement that he hadn't killed the man.

Before they'd gotten to the jail, Daniel reminded Pepper to leave out the part saying that when he did find his sister's attacker, he *would* kill him.

It took half an hour to fill out the paperwork and Pepper was antsy long before then. His eyes were bloodshot and rage-filled.

Daniel figured this was as good a way as any to let him cool down before turning him loose.

A shadow fell across the doorway and Daniel looked up instinctively. He'd become much more aware of his surroundings, taking Bass Reeves' words serious. He told Daniel that his badge was a target on his chest and on his back.

But this wasn't that sort of threat. This was Earl Reynolds, the newspaper reporter Daniel had encountered in Eagletown.

Reynolds looked at him a long moment, then went to the deputy. They talked while Daniel signed the last of his paperwork, gathered it with Pepper's testimony that he knew nothing about the man found in Dead Man's Lake, and took the papers to the deputy.

"This should take care of everything, George. You know how to get in touch with me if there are any questions."

Reynolds squared off with Daniel as though they were about to get into a gunfight. "I have a question."

Daniel had been around Matthew enough to know how reporters could get real serious about their stories.

Behind him, Pepper swiped up his hat and stomped out the door. Through the open doorway, Daniel watched him ride away.

Reynolds growled, "If he were an Indian from another tribe, would you have let him off for murder? Or do you only show favoritism to Choctaws?"

Daniel flexed his fingers, keeping them from balling into a fist and smashing it into the man's nose.

"I don't favor anyone."

Reynolds met Daniel's hard stare with his own. "I've been checking you out, Marshal Indian. In your short career, you've already killed three men. You haven't arrested one Indian, not even today when you found one with a dead body, a man who happens to be on the hunt to kill someone. I'm sure whites in Indian Territory would be interested to know they need to keep clear of you."

Daniel took a long breath and turned to the deputy, tapping the top of the papers. "See these get filed proper, will you, George?"

Daniel had only met this deputy one other time. He wished they had some sort of camaraderie to show Reynolds. But George just gathered up the papers and left his desk for the file cabinets on the other wall.

There was nothing more to say. Daniel brushed past Reynolds, bumping his shoulder on the way out and setting the reporter off balance. He shouldn't have, but Daniel did enjoy the brief satisfaction before mounting his horse and pointing its head in the direction of the Red River.

CHAPTER 32

Christopher Maxwell entered his home and felt a chill. Impossible in the hot summer evening.

The cracking, high-pitched voice of his wife squealed from the parlor.

"I told you to get out!"

Christopher closed and locked the front door then strode into the parlor to find it lit by only one of the gas lamps. His wife stood in the middle of the room, a robe thrown over her night-gown, barefoot, hair down over her shoulders. She might look appealing if not for her blood-shot eyes and how she could hardly stand. She had been drinking heavily this evening. Or maybe she'd never stopped from the morning.

Christopher Maxwell glanced at the other occupant in the room, the target of his wife's fury. The man stood casually with one arm propped on the fireplace mantle, other hand on his hip as he nodded at Maxwell. Dorothy turned to see her husband, causing her to stagger to one side.

Christopher Maxwell took off his hat and dropped it into one of the wing-backed chairs.

"Go to your room, Dorothy."

"But he—he just came right in through the window…make him leave, Christopher! Make him leave."

"To your room. Now."

Dorothy sent daggers of fire at him from her eyes, and he straightened. She backed up, stumbling on the chair behind her. She regained her balance and ran from the room, tripping on her robe as she flung herself out and up the stairs.

Christopher Maxwell turned his attention to the man who was causing more problems than he was worth.

"I see you finally got out of jail."

"And I've gotten right back to work."

The man's voice was low, gravelly, and there was a hint of pleasure in it. Christopher only liked playing games when he was the one making the rules. He didn't like this man's game.

"Eliza Coxwell?" Christopher growled.

The man's eyes were hidden by the shadow of his hat, but Christopher still saw the glimmer of evil there.

"So, you've heard. I guess half the territory has. Good timing with your little gossip article. Now it's up to you to make sure people know it was Matthew Teller who visited poor Mrs. Coxwell the morning she was attacked."

Maxwell shifted, not wanting to let this man know he'd caught him by surprise. "How do you know Matthew Teller was with Mrs. Coxwell Saturday morning?"

The man cocked his head, showing his smile. "You're not the only one who knows how to tap a telegraph wire, especially if you're tracking a man traveling back from Washington D.C. I knew Matthew Teller would be stopping by Coxwell's place on his way home. It's also how I knew she'd be alone."

Christopher Maxwell worked his jaw. "She is still alive though. She can identify you."

"Not a chance. Now, I gotta admit I thought she was dead. But with the hood I wore, she can only give a vague description, one vague enough to fit Matthew Teller. If you want me to go into detail, I can."

No wonder Dorothy wanted the man out.

Christopher shoved his hands in his pockets to keep his balance in the presence of this unearthly man. "I just want Matthew Teller out of the way. I don't care how you do it, but I want you to do it quick. The vote for the mayoral election is July Fourth."

The man ran his thumb along the fireplace mantle and then dropped his arm, straightening. "Oh, don't worry. Matthew Teller's credibility as a newspaper reporter, and as a man, is about to end. I have my next target picked out, and trust me, the good people of Dickens will be ready to crucify Matthew Teller after this one."

The man tipped his hat and slipped back out the open window, vanishing as though he never existed. Christopher Maxwell almost wished he didn't.

Whatever the man was planning might not be soon enough for Christopher. His finances were a sham. His primary investors promised to cut the first checks only if he won the bid for mayor. Christopher stood on the verge of losing everything.

He needed to get Matthew Teller distracted from the mayoral election and the gossip article wasn't nearly enough.

Christopher knew something that would be.

CHAPTER 33

*M*atthew got off the Katy train at the McAlester Depot and strode at a brisk pace up the street to Benjamin's office. Benjamin had sent him a telegram that morning.

Please come to my office as soon as you can.

Benjamin was a man of careful thought and planning. If he summoned Matthew with no prior notice, that constituted an emergency. Matthew had already met with Benjamin about the next steps in Maxwell's case, so Matthew suspected his brother-in-law had found something.

Was it for or against their purpose? Urgency typically was not in Matthew's favor.

He mounted the steps of the boardwalk in front of Benjamin's office building and entered. A crackly older woman was at the reception desk. She quickly stood and barred Matthew's entrance through the closed door leading into Benjamin's office.

She hissed, "You might be a relative, but you are going to sit here and wait like everyone else while I make sure Mr. Dunn is ready for you."

A soft chuckle sounded from the other side of the door. "Let Mr. Teller in, please, Mrs. Bridge."

Mrs. Bridge gave Matthew a reprimanding look before she twisted the doorknob and pushed open the door.

"Mr. Dunn will see you now."

Matthew gave her a wide berth as he scooted through the doorway. She closed it with a loud snap behind him.

Benjamin indicated chairs across from his desk as he came around to shake Matthew's hand. "I told Mrs. Bridge I was expecting you today, but her having been secretary for her husband 30 years before he passed, she takes her duties quite seriously."

Matthew took a seat in one of the wing-backs in front of the desk. These chairs and the desk had come from Benjamin's former mentor's office, Judge Eldridge. Some of the furnishings in Ruth Ann and Benjamin's house were from his home in D.C. as well, although Benjamin also bought pieces that were uniquely his and Ruth Ann's to start their new life together.

Matthew settled back while Benjamin poured them each a cup from the pot of coffee on a stand near the window. He was somber and too quiet, so Matthew spoke. "Your telegram sounded urgent."

After spending a week trying to avoid being in Hannah's presence—pretty well impossible since they worked in the same building—Matthew was worn out. He'd wanted to print a rebuttal to Maxwell's gossip story, but responding to mudslinging only added to the mess.

There was nothing Matthew could do but stay away from Hannah until the slander blew over and pray she didn't quit. He spent as much time at home as he could, sorting through his notes and documents from D.C., writing articles at the kitchen table, and corresponding with Benjamin on the case. All while preparing his own heart for Nita's adoption hearing.

Benjamin set the cups on the table between them and took a

seat, not meeting Matthew's eyes. The news was worse than he feared.

"What happened?" Matthew asked.

"More accurately, what *three* things have happened."

"None of them good?"

Benjamin shook his head and picked up his coffee but didn't drink. "The first is about Nita."

Matthew tried to bring up scenarios that could have Benjamin so concerned about his niece, but he couldn't land on anything as terrible as Benjamin looked like the news was. The adoption hearing was in two days. What had come up to derail it?

Benjamin didn't keep him in suspense. "Part of the legal proceedings for adoption is placing notifications in newspapers where the child has lived or may have relatives. A relative responded, objecting to the adoption."

A stone landed in Matthew's heart, and he scooted to the edge of the chair. He felt like he might shoot out of it. "Ruth Ann is as close of a relative as anyone could be. It was her mother's wish…"

Matthew halted. Benjamin's expression clouded over, and he finally met Matthew's eyes.

"It's Nita's mother who objected. She sent a letter to the court at Fort Smith, wanting her daughter back."

Matthew shook his head. "That's impossible. Kat told me she had tuberculosis, that she was on her way to a hospital. It sounded like she never planned on getting out."

Benjamin took a sip of his coffee. "The return address on the letter was the tuberculosis ward in Paris."

"I don't understand. How does she expect to raise a child in a hospital?"

"That's where it gets complicated." Benjamin rubbed his thumb over the coffee mug. "She appointed her mother and sister as legal guardians of her daughter. They are the ones who want her, Matt. I doubt Kat Russell even wrote the letter herself. The signature was shaky and didn't match the rest of the letter."

"None of this sounds right."

"It isn't. And there is more." Benjamin studied his coffee mug. "The Russell family's attorney filed a report about my father's imprisonment for murder, attempting to discredit my suitability as an adoptive father. They also filed an affidavit signed by Kat. It states Philip forced himself on her and the child is the result."

Matthew gritted his teeth, breath heavy through them. "All we have to do is prove Kat was incompetent when she signed the letter and affidavit, right?"

Benjamin shook his head. "We aren't being given time to sort it out. The adoption hearing has changed to a custody hearing. I filed to have the date rescheduled but was denied. There is more going on here than should be."

Panic seized Matthew. All the future plans he had as Nita's maternal uncle flashed in his mind. "They can't have her, Ben. I promised my brother…"

The Teller family had the right to Nita. In Choctaw law, if anyone married into the tribe, had children, and left, the children remained with the tribe.

But that was decades ago. Matthew feared what the law was now, especially with the finest lawyer in the country seated next to him and looking doubtful.

"I promise I will do everything I can to keep Nita here, Matt. But you need to prepare yourself."

Matthew gripped the arms of the chair. There was nothing he could do to prepare himself for losing Nita.

He couldn't imagine anything being worse than the news he'd just gotten, but he had to ask, "You said there were three things."

The long pause before Benjamin's answer told him the last item was just as bad.

Benjamin set aside his coffee mug and leaned forward, mimicking Matthew by propping his elbows on his knees. "It's about Ruth Ann. On our honeymoon, we promised to keep no secrets from one another. She told me what she was afraid to say before the wedding, afraid of what you or I would do."

Matthew could feel his fingernails cutting a hole in the upholstered chair. "Is this about Maxwell?"

"Your reputation as a perceptive reporter is well earned."

"Just tell me."

Benjamin's face darkened, a storm in the horizon of his eyes. "The night Ruth Ann encountered Christopher Maxwell, he grabbed her and held her close."

Matthew shot up from the chair, knocking it over. He paced the floor, trying to restrain himself from shooting out the door and straight back to Dickens to shoot Christopher Maxwell. He needed to hear Benjamin out.

Benjamin remained seated as he watched Matthew pace.

"She told me everything, Matt, I'm confident of that. He more frightened than harmed her. If there was anything more, I would not have called you up here. You would have been visiting me in jail."

Matthew halted by the desk, wanting to blow up at Benjamin's calm demeanor. He expected his brother-in-law to care for and protect his sister the same as he would.

But he couldn't fault Benjamin. He was a levelheaded man who knew when and how to pick and fight his battles. That was why he never lost. Matthew had to trust that, hard as it was.

Benjamin sighed, releasing a day's worth of tension from his body. "I wish Ruth Ann had told me right away. I would have sued Maxwell for harassment. We likely wouldn't have won, but I favor having things in the open rather than letting them fester. Which leads me to our last problem."

Matthew rubbed his forehead. "I thought that was the last problem."

Benjamin pressed his lips tight. Then he said, "There was a photograph taken."

Matthew felt his energy drain. Benjamin went on, "Maxwell

had his cameraman take at least one photograph, maybe more. Ruth Ann knew it was Maxwell's intention to use it to blackmail her or you. That's why she didn't say anything. Don't be hard on her, Matthew. She wanted to get through the wedding."

Matthew slowed his thoughts enough to take in Benjamin's wisdom. If Ruth Ann had told the full story when it happened, it would have ruined her and Benjamin's wedding. It could have even led to bloodshed. Matthew couldn't blame her for waiting until she was married and out of Dickens before confessing the full story.

But now Ruth Ann was safely away from Dickens and there was nothing to keep Matthew from pummeling Maxwell—whether in court, in his newspaper, or with his fists.

Benjamin stood and went around his desk where he took a seat in the large leather chair on wheels. He opened up a folder.

"I've prepared templates for statements I need from you and your family right away. We want written affidavits stating how our family is capable of caring for and raising Nita. We are also getting statements from people who have known Ruth Ann several years and can attest that she is an upstanding citizen."

Benjamin stopped shuffling the papers and stared at them. "I wish I had a better reputation in Indian Territory to offer."

He added two more sheets of paper, closed the folder, and handed it to Matthew. "Fortunately, already having three letters from senators back in D.C. will help my prospects as a father."

Benjamin looked Matthew in the eyes. "We're going to do everything we can to keep Nita with her people. Meanwhile, steer clear of Maxwell. Even in self-defense, a killing wouldn't look good for our case."

～

An agonizing two days later, Matthew stood with his family at the federal court in Fort Smith. For someone who never broke the law, he spent a lot of time in court.

It wasn't a place he liked to be. Not for Philip's trial, and especially not for this as the judge prepared to give his ruling on custody for little Nita.

Matthew had expected a long day with testimonies and witnesses in favor of the Teller clan. They even had a letter from Chief Gardner, but Matthew didn't think the judge looked at any of it.

The biological father was in prison. The biological mother wanted her child back even though she was in the hospital. The maternal grandmother and aunt stood stoic with their well-dressed lawyer who made the case sound simple and sterile.

Benjamin gave a good summary for the Teller family, but Matthew could tell his brother-in-law already knew the outcome. Back in D.C., he only accepted cases he felt he could win. He had made an exception once again for the Teller family.

The judge pronounced his verdict and banged the gavel. Matthew didn't move, couldn't move as Ruth Ann, tears flowing down her face, knelt to try and explain to Nita what had happened.

The sheriff interrupted with taking the little girl's hand and pulling her toward the other family.

Nita screamed and yanked away. She ran straight for Matthew who swept her up in his arms, holding her tight as she wrapped her thin arms around his neck. The sheriff stepped toward him, but Benjamin blocked him and began speaking quietly.

Matthew took the precious few moments to whisper in Nita's ear, "I haven't told you what your name means in Choctaw."

His voice shook. He had never known this brand of pain. "Your father gave you the name *Nita*. It means Bear. God made the bear the strongest in the wilderness and He gave you that kind of strength. The bear is also wise and always knows where home is."

He swallowed down tears. "Never forget who you are, Little Bear. Never forget I love you. *Chi pisa la chike.* I will see you again soon."

Matthew didn't want to let her go, didn't want to release the image of him walking her down the aisle someday as Uncle Preston had done with Ruth Ann.

But he leaned her toward Della, who was crying as she kissed her baby granddaughter all over the face. Ruth Ann pressed a hard kiss to the little girl's forehead just as Benjamin turned, solemn. He reached out to take Nita. She kept one arm hooked around Matthew's neck and he whispered, "God knows."

She looked into his eyes, her own so full of innocence yet understanding. She had lived too much life in her short five years.

Benjamin gently pulled her into his arms and went to Kat's family. The older woman and her daughter shrank back from the tall Indian man who towered over them. He carefully set Nita on her feet and said something that made the woman gasp and look to their lawyer as though for protection.

Benjamin backed away, shoved folders into his briefcase, and said, "I am going to speak with the judge."

Staring at Nita being taken away by the two women, Matthew grabbed his arm. "I want her back, Ben."

Benjamin sighed. So deep. "We cannot always have what we want, brother."

As the women were about to exit, a man stepped inside the door in front of them and took off his hat. The older woman smiled at him and gave a rigorous nod to his question, pointing at the little girl. The man shook their lawyer's hand, grinning, and Matthew was sure he heard something about payment.

The man was Christopher Maxwell.

The women departed with Nita and their lawyer. Maxwell turned his grin toward Matthew.

Before anyone knew what was happening, including Matthew, Maxwell was laid flat on his back with Matthew standing over him, knuckles throbbing.

Matthew surged forward again but was arrested by powerful arms around him. Benjamin held him fast while the sheriff helped Maxwell to his feet and asked him something. Maxwell shook his head, spit blood. And grinned again.

CHAPTER 34

In the Teller home that evening, Matthew and Della sat quietly in the parlor. Neither had spoken for two hours. They didn't talk about having supper, didn't talk about the heartache they'd endured.

Nothing.

Della sat in her rocker, her hands still. Matthew had a stack of newspapers he subscribed to spilled all over the coffee table he'd used as his desk that week.

Also on the chest table was Nita's wooden Ark. This was the last thing she played with, leaving it on the chest that morning before they left for Fort Smith. Her little sewing basket rested next to Della's.

Nobody died.

Matthew kept telling himself that, but it wasn't a comfort. The absence of Nita was like a death in the family.

The rocking chair creaked as Della started it in motion.

"I am moving back to my brother's ranch."

Matthew's whole body shook. He looked at his mother and knew she had given this a great deal of thought and her mind was set. He stared at her, not knowing what to say.

She met his eyes. "It is time for me to care for my mother."

Fear stabbed Matthew's heart. "What's wrong with Pokni?"

Della smiled soft, sad. "We all grow old, son. This is a new season in life, and God has shown me that my place is caring for her now."

Matthew leaned back on the sofa, not wanting to think about what this meant. He directed his thoughts to wondering if his mother would want to take the sofa with her.

It was special to her, but where would she put it? Where would she live at Preston's ranch? The house was large and there were empty rooms, but Melinda was the woman of the house. How would Della find her place in the kitchen?

A tapping on the front door was a merciful distraction. Matthew went to open the door. He was so worn out, he didn't know what to make of Hannah Stillwater standing on the porch, the tricolored dog sitting beside her. She held a dish covered with a towel.

She spoke quickly. "Mr. Teller, I heard the results of the hearing, and I am so sorry. I wanted to bring you and your mother some dinner in case you haven't eaten."

She offered him the dish, but he beckoned her inside. "That's kind of you. Please come in."

Hannah didn't move. She glanced past him to see Della in the rocking chair. "I don't want to intrude."

Matthew took the dish and she nodded. "I'll see you at the shop tomorrow."

She turned and headed down the porch steps. Matthew opened his mouth to say something else, anything to keep her from leaving. But she couldn't hear him.

Matthew closed the door and took the dish of food to the kitchen where he left it on the cold stove. He came back to sit on the sofa again and found his mother watching him.

"She is a good woman."

Matthew stared at the mantle and the family photograph that

had sat there since they moved into the box house. The photograph he'd used to introduce Nita to her father's family.

The rocking chair creaked as Della stood and came to sit on the sofa beside Matthew. She rubbed the back of his neck, patting his knee firmly with her other hand.

"God directs our steps, but we got to pick up our feet."

Matthew shifted his gaze from the photograph to his mother's worn face. She'd been through so much since they'd moved into Dickens and before that, with what happened to his father and brother. Her going to Uncle Preston's would let her have a rest from it all.

Her fingers massaged his tight neck muscles, but he couldn't relax. "Where am I supposed to be picking my feet up to go?"

"To see Hannah Stillwater."

Matthew jerked again, as startled as when she announced she was moving back to the ranch. He stared at her, the gleam unmistakable in her eyes.

"Mama…"

She moved her hand from the back of his neck to brush away the hair falling across his forehead. He needed a haircut. As usual.

"Son, you have been the man of the family for me and your sister. You have done well. But your sister is married now and I'm moving to the care of my brother. This is a new season for us all. You open your eyes to that."

Matthew took his mother's hand in his and pressed his lips to the back of it. He released her hand with a deep sigh and leaned forward to pick up Nita's Ark.

Maybe God did have more for him to live in life beyond the boundaries of the *Choctaw Tribune*. Maybe he would ask Hannah about meeting her parents when the time was right.

If she would consider having him.

~

Friday was miserable. Matthew was behind on all his work despite it not being as much as it should. Ruth Ann insisted on taking care of hiring and training employees for the new office in McAlester.

So much was out of Matthew's hands these days. He avoided looking at the typesetting cabinet all day. Not even the sight of Story there lifted his mood.

Nita was gone. Ruth Ann was gone. His mother was leaving.

Hannah Stillwater was staying.

She was quiet, but Matthew didn't feel there was hostility between them despite the sordid article damaging both their reputations. What would she think if he talked to her about… Should he come right out and express his desire to court her? How did someone go about that sort of thing? It should be easy, with her only a dozen steps from his desk.

But he couldn't grapple with it and his investigation. Something had to give.

Matthew hardly stirred when Peter dropped a fresh copy of the *Dickens Herald* on his desk, open to the gossip column. Matthew wasn't surprised to see what Maxwell wrote about the incident in Fort Smith.

He called Matthew a "violent and unpredictable man" and what a good thing it was that the little girl was with her real family. He also included about the affidavit stating Philip had taken advantage of Kat Russell, the innocent young white woman. Maxwell openly took credit for orchestrating the child's safe return to her family.

The daily edition of the *Choctaw Tribune* didn't go out on Friday.

On Saturday, Uncle Preston and part of his crew came in to help move Della and her sewing room to the ranch. They left all the other furnishings in the house with Matthew, including the sofa. Della would take a room adjoining Pokni's so Della would be close if her mother needed her.

Della stayed one last night in the box house to attend church the next morning.

Church came and went and Della departed with Uncle Preston and all his family. Everyone except Matthew.

Matthew returned to the box house alone. It was still and quiet. The sewing room had a lonely echo to it. Maybe he would turn it into an office, a place he could work evenings.

Work. Day and night.

It seemed the only thing left in his life. Circumstances and Christopher Maxwell had taken the rest.

CHAPTER 35

The Fourth of July was Glenrose Jessop's favorite holiday. At least, this year it was. Dickens was putting on a big to-do and she was going to enjoy every bit of it that she could, even if it was sponsored by that nasty publisher of the *Dickens Herald*. He'd won his bid for mayor, and that couldn't be good from what Peter had told her.

But politics aside, it was finally time to celebrate Independence Day after working at the hotel restaurant all day. She had a fella who promised to celebrate it with her and her family. After working the morning and afternoon shifts, she had just enough time to go home and freshen up before Peter arrived from his family's ranch for the evening. The town promised a fireworks show like the territory had never seen.

Glenrose stepped into the heavy air behind the hotel. In late afternoon, the sun was dropping its heat but little of its light in the alley behind the tall hotel building. The way the street in front turned a corner, the end was cut off from view, and the other was a dead end, leaving no way for much breeze or light to get through.

Crates of supplies and broken furniture that needed repair

cluttered the backside of the hotel. Glenrose found the usual path through it. The hotel owner preferred the employees to leave out the back so as not to disrupt the flow of traffic in the hotel lobby. That was fine with Glenrose. Still in her service uniform, people always stopped her to ask for something.

She sidestepped a broken bed frame, a cast off from one of the hotel rooms. She didn't touch the frame, but it still rattled. She paused, listening. No one else was getting off work at the same time as she was.

"Who's there?"

She turned toward the bed frame to see a man coming from the shadows of it. He put a hand over her scream and pressed her back into the darkness.

CHAPTER 36

*M*atthew pushed open the front door of the box house and inhaled. Ham was frying on the stove in the kitchen, along with potatoes. He closed the door and hung his hat beside it. In the kitchen, he could see Daniel stabbing a chunk of ham and turning it in the pan.

The stove hadn't been in service for days. Not since Della left. "Sorry I'm late."

Daniel grinned. "When are you not?" He flipped the potato skins. "I'm not as good a cook as Aunt Della, but it'll be palatable since these steaks are from the left side of the hog. Plus, Melinda taught me a few cooking tricks. Daisy wasn't much of a cook."

A shadow crossed Daniel's face and Matthew patted him on the shoulder, then headed to the washstand.

"Thanks for getting it started. Had to put out a special edition with the election results. At least I had the pleasure of beating Maxwell to print. I'll take any victory these days."

"I feel you, brother."

Matthew set out plates and forks. Most of his family would stay on the ranch for the Fourth of July, even Benjamin and Ruth Ann. Matthew wanted to go there, but…work. Always work. He would have made a better effort if Hannah had accepted his invitation to go out there, too. She hadn't.

"I don't suppose two bachelors like us are on a strict timeline," Daniel said as he tossed hot pads on the table and set the skillets on them. "I'm going to enjoy my holiday, stay up till 9 o'clock if I want to."

They chuckled and sat down to eat, the sounds of kids hollering and shooting off firecrackers in the streets of Dickens in the background.

Daniel and Matthew talked about the latest happenings in the Choctaw Nation, the D.C. trip, the Dawes commission, all while avoiding talk of anything that hurt too much.

They cleared away the supper dishes then Daniel opened the oven and pulled out a cherry pie.

Matthew whistled. "Pretty impressive for a bachelor."

Daniel put it on the table with a flourish as though he had won the blue ribbon at the county fair. "My own secret recipe. I call it the *Amarillo Fuller Special.*"

Matthew chuckled. Amarillo sold baked goods out of their home for extra income. She was a good baker, so Matthew was happy to see Daniel cut the pie into four generous slices.

A loud knock sounded at the back door. Daniel dropped the pie knife, his hand instantly going to his side as though to draw his gun. But he wasn't wearing it.

He smiled sheepishly at Matthew. "When you fall into a rut of killing men, it makes you a little jumpy."

Matthew went to the door. "It doesn't hurt to be a little jumpy when you live in this territory."

He opened the door to the evening dusk to find Lance Fuller there. Matthew motioned him inside. "You're just in time for a healthy slice of your wife's cherry pie."

Lance Fuller stepped in, and Matthew detected the cloud of worry in his sky-blue eyes. Lance glanced around. "Is Glenrose here? She hasn't come home from work. I thought maybe Peter would know where she is."

"He was supposed to be here for supper, but I guess he got hung up at the ranch. Is she long overdue?"

"About an hour. I've told her never to be out after dark in this town. Isn't safe for a young woman."

Matthew's mind flashed to the woman killer. "No, it's not."

Daniel buckled on his gun belt. "We best go check the hotel."

The sound of a horse clattering into the backyard made Matthew open the back door again while Lance and Daniel headed for the front.

Peter skidded his horse to a halt and dismounted. He glanced up in the light of the doorway and grinned at Matthew's disapproving frown.

"It's all right, I walked him to cool him off, just galloped into the yard to get your attention. Wanted to let you know I am going over to Lance's. "

"To see Glenrose?"

Peter's grin didn't fade until he realized Matthew wasn't teasing.

Matthew said, "Lance just came, looking for her. We're going to check the hotel. You coming?"

Peter quickly tied his horse to the post and followed Matthew through the house and out the front door. Daniel and Lance were already in the street at a quick clip. Why it took four men to find one young girl in a relatively small town, Matthew wasn't sure. None of them questioned it.

They hit the cross street and continued up two blocks to the newest section of town that boasted the Enterprise Hotel where Glenrose worked.

They entered the front lobby and split up. Lance paused to talk to the clerk while Daniel questioned one of the waitresses handling the dining room. It was mostly empty as people went out to find their places for the fireworks show. Matthew zeroed in on the young hotel manager, Blane Johnson, who was seated at one of the back tables, talking with a stranger.

Peter followed Matthew over to them. Matthew didn't wait for them to look up before asking, "Has Glenrose Jessop left for the day?"

Blane Johnson looked up in surprise, glancing between the two. The Enterprise was one of the *Choctaw Tribune's* largest advertisers. Matthew should have been more polite, but his stomach was churning.

Johnson glanced at the clock on the wall. "Let's see, her shift ended over an hour ago. I suppose you could check with the cook and see when she actually left. We've been quite busy today with all the festivities. Fireworks will start soon, you know."

Something was wrong.

The stranger spoke to Matthew. "Excuse me, are you Matthew Teller?"

"Excuse me, I'm in a hurry."

Matthew went to the kitchen door, meeting Lance and Daniel there.

Daniel spoke. "The waitress said Glenrose left a little while ago."

Lance added, "The clerk told me employees always come and go through the back door."

Peter was already through the kitchen door. Matthew and the others followed, skirting the cook who scolded them for weaving between the food prep table and the stove to reach the back door.

Peter flung it open, calling, "Glenrose!"

Lance was behind him, and the four men paused, letting their eyes adjust to the dusk of evening illuminated by slivers of light coming from the hotel. Peter started down the narrow space in the alley, leading to the corner and the exit to the street. He stopped cold and made a guttural sound that raised the hair on Matthew's neck.

Matthew rushed forward behind Peter who collapsed on his knees beside a very still Glenrose Jessop.

Matthew grabbed Peter's shoulders and yanked him back as Lance fought his way forward, screaming something incomprehensible. Matthew locked his arms around his cousin's flailing arms.

"Let me go! I'll tear him to pieces! I'll kill whoever…"

The cook and waitress came out the back door along with the hotel manager and two guests, including the stranger who had tried to gain Matthew's attention. They hurried forward but Daniel waved them back while Lance removed his coat and laid it over his little sister. The cook and waitress knelt over the young girl.

Matthew held tight to Peter, his cousin's hot blood pumping through his body, threatening to rip them both apart. He whispered in Peter's ear, "Let the women take care of her. She'd want it that way."

Peter stilled. He heaved in a huge breath and Matthew loosened his grip enough for his cousin to vomit on the ground. He held tight as Peter went down to rest on his elbows.

Matthew glanced up as Lance sat beside him, staring at the restaurant wall. "She is still breathing. Barely, but… breathing."

Daniel sent one of the guests off to fetch the doctor then came over to Matthew.

"Whoever did this has to be close. I'm assembling a posse. You take care of getting the word out by telegraph?"

Matthew nodded.

The waitress called for Daniel. She held something up, and the stranger took a step closer, brows furrowed.

Daniel barked, "Stand back, Reynolds."

Daniel took the small object and held it up to the light. That was when Matthew saw it was a pen. A very familiar pen.

The first explosion from the fireworks show on the outskirts of town shattered the night even more.

Matthew rose and walked over to take the pen from Daniel. It was etched with the words, *Matthew Teller.*

The man, whom Daniel called Reynolds, looked sideways at Matthew and spoke, malice dripping from his voice. "Excuse me again, but aren't you Matthew Teller?"

Daniel cleared his throat loudly. "You must've dropped it when you leaned over Glenrose, Matt."

Matthew had no intention of saying that he hadn't leaned over the girl, nor did he carry that pen on him. He always left it locked in his desk at the *Choctaw Tribune.*

CHAPTER 37

$\mathcal{I}$t was a quiet night. They all were for Hannah, but she enjoyed this one a bit more as she watched the fireworks display from her second-floor window at the Monarch Hotel. The name was sweet, but the accommodations didn't compare to its competitor, the Enterprise Hotel. It did match Hannah's need for her budget, though.

She had sent a sum of money home this past week despite her folks' insistence that she not. After months of unsteady work, it was an incredible feeling to finally contribute to her family again after burdening them for so many years.

The grand finale of the fireworks show lit up her room and her face. What brilliant flashes of color! If only she could capture it in words. She hurried to the writing desk in her room to try.

Twenty minutes later, Hannah sat back in her chair, moderately satisfied with the scene she was writing in her next novel. Her draft was due in the fall, but with all the work at the *Choctaw Tribune*, she'd neglected it. One thing about Matthew Teller and the Tribune though—she never lacked conflict inspiration for her story.

Matthew Teller was passionate almost to a fault. But she

didn't fault him in his relentless digging down to the bedrock of truth.

Still, in all he had going, he had thought to learn sign language for her. It was a sweet gesture, one she wished she could freely appreciate. She rarely used sign language these days since there was no one to communicate with, but it was much easier than reading lips. Especially in the dark, which was why she preferred staying in during the celebration this evening.

This was a good chance to catch up with her own life, so she tidied her room, sorted her washing, and picked up a short stack of mail from the week. She flipped through it. A check-in letter from her publisher, Apple House Publishing in Connecticut. A letter from her siblings on the Blue River with postscripts from her parents. She'd read it when it came in at the *Choctaw Tribune* office. An issue of Ladies Home Journal. At the bottom of the pile was an envelope she hadn't paid much attention to. It looked like a solicitor's, her name and address written in block letters and no return address.

Using her silver letter opener, she slit the envelope and withdrew the single sheet of a handwritten letter. She dropped the letter opener to the floor.

This letter was from someone she knew. Handwriting she knew. She well knew the face of the man who wrote it. His mustache made reading his lips more difficult, but she learned words from him none of the other teachers used.

Jackson Thomas.

The letter was addressed in his cold demeanor.

To Hannah Stillwater:

I have learned of your latest disgraces in public society. As an inferior human being, the position you are attempting to take among civilized people is pathetic. And now, your latest escapade as a mistress to an Indian. Positively disgusting.

Hannah wanted to stop reading. Even now, she could visualize the whites of Jackson Thomas' angry eyes as they'd been the last day she had seen him, the day he was fired from her school. Thomas was beyond infuriated. His position at the school was his life, his sole identity. When that was stripped away, Hannah knew she had made an enemy.

She had hoped—prayed—that he had finally lost track of her movements. Apparently he had until now, thanks to Matthew Teller.

The letter went on in detail of how inadequate she was, how she belonged on the fringes of society, how she could never dare to marry, on and on. All the things he abused her with through school, what had made her run away to home. But her father wouldn't let her quit.

"You are Chickasaw. Unconquerable."

She felt conquered back then. The feeling threatened to rise in her again. She wanted to run away to home before Jackson Thomas came to Dickens. Or sent a letter to Matthew Teller, accusing her of being a liar and a thief.

Hannah pressed her fingers to her lips. What if he already had? What if Matthew Teller was reading his mail now and preparing to fire her? He had enough trouble without being suspicious of her.

Hannah could bear many things. But the thought of losing Matthew Teller's respect was something she couldn't face. Now that Thomas had found her, it was inevitable. Even if Matthew Teller said he believed her, there would always be doubt between them.

She couldn't face that. Not after what she'd been through before.

CHAPTER 38

*I*t wasn't hard to round up a posse after news spread through town like wildfire of the horrendous attack on the local girl.

While Glenrose was taken to the doctor's office, Matthew used the telephone at the *Choctaw Tribune* to call everyone he knew who had a phone. Caleb Gentry showed up and woke several telegraph operators who slept near their sounders.

Only one person was missing from the fray.

Hannah Stillwater.

So far, all the women who had been attacked were women Matthew knew. That was too much of a coincidence.

Matthew shot out of the office and ran for the Monarch Hotel.

This hotel was at the far end of town, a shabbier establishment than the Enterprise. Matthew should have been paying Hannah more.

He bounded up the stairs and down the hall to room 215. He knew Hannah's room number for having mail forwarded to her. He halted in front of it now, taking quick note of the light under the door. She was still awake. But was she safe?

Matthew knelt by the door and tried to look through the keyhole. He was no peeping Tom, but this could be life or death.

Blackness. The key was in the lock.

How could he make sure she wasn't hurt?

There was only one way he could think of. He withdrew his pocketknife. He wasn't good at picking locks like his brother, but he had to try.

Shifting, he felt of his tablet that was almost always in his inner coat pocket. There was something else he could try.

He pulled out the tablet and ripped a page from it. He carefully slid the page under the door beneath the knob and, with his pocketknife, slowly nudged the key out. It landed with a clink on the paper. The gap at the bottom of the door was just enough for him to slide the paper back out, the key on it. He quickly stood, inserted the key, and cracked open the door.

Hannah was at a writing desk by the single window in the room, back to him and shoulders hunched as she read a letter. She had no idea Matthew stood in the doorway. He could be the attacker and she'd be completely unaware.

He had to let her know of the danger in the town at that very moment without terrifying her by the fact that *he* had broken into her room. He hoped she trusted him like he thought she did.

Matthew wadded up the paper, took aim, and tossed it at her head. It bounced against her neck, and she reached up a hand to rub it, glancing around. She spotted Matthew in the doorway and sprang out of her chair, sending it crashing to its back.

"Mr. Teller!"

Matthew quickly stepped back outside the door, his face in the darker hallway where he knew she couldn't read his lips. He quickly signed, *we* and *talk.*

Matthew pulled the door half closed in front of him and waited for her to properly receive him.

Footsteps told him she was coming to the door. He wondered if she had a gun. He certainly deserved to be shot.

The door swayed and Hannah peered around it, using it as a shield between them. "Mr. Teller, what on earth are you doing?"

Now that she was closer, Matthew figured she wouldn't have trouble reading his lips with the lamp on the wall one door down. "Glenrose Jessop was attacked. She's alive, but hurt. Very badly. The doctor isn't sure she will make it."

Hannah covered her mouth, eyes wide. Matthew went on.

"I had to make sure you were all right, Hannah."

It wasn't an accident that he called her by her first name, and the way her eyes flickered showed she realized that. She lowered her hand and grasped the edge of the door.

"That was kind of you."

Matthew should go. He had checked on her, warned her of the danger. That was what he'd come to do. But he couldn't leave.

His sister was gone. His mother. He'd lost Nita.

His heart was almost spent. If he didn't speak now, he never would.

He propped one hand on the doorframe, leaning against it for support. "Hannah Stillwater. I've wanted to ask you something important. This isn't the right time, but I'm going to ask anyway."

She didn't move, didn't take her eyes off his face. Matthew wished he could finger spell everything that was in his heart.

"Will you permit me to court you?"

Hannah stared at him, dropping her hand to show her mouth agape.

"Mr. Teller. You…you are very kind. A good, good man. But I couldn't…you don't know…"

Matthew's arm shook from his weight leaned on it. His body was giving out on him. "If it's about you being deaf, like that somehow makes you less than…" He didn't know how to stop, didn't know how to go on.

Hannah smiled, tired. Teasing almost. "You are going very fast, Mr. Teller. Are you certain you're going in the right direction?"

Matthew gave in to his elbow pain and leaned into the doorway. "Wherever I go, Hannah Stillwater, however slow or however fast, I want you with me."

She let out a breath that sounded like a strangled cry. He'd frightened her, just like he had Nita. He was going to lose her. Just like he had Nita.

"Hannah, I'm sorry. I am sorry I didn't protect your reputation like I should have. I'm sorry for the messes I've dragged you into. I'm sorry..."

"Slow down, Mr. Teller. Slow down, please."

"I'm sorry I blundered into all of this. After...after what happened tonight, I should never have asked you. I..."

"Stop." Hannah was crying. "Please. It isn't your fault, but I can't bear this." She looked into his eyes. "Please. You must understand that it can never be. Goodnight, Mr. Teller."

She started to close the door, but Matthew pressed against it with his shoulder. She looked up at him, her eyes showing fear, but she wasn't afraid of him. She was afraid of what she was feeling, the same as he was.

"Please, Mr. Teller." Hannah's chin quivered, tears spilling out. She tried to close the door again, pushing hard against him. "Please."

Matthew reached out a hand and tipped her chin so she could read his lips. "Hannah. Please."

She stared at him, then spun away, pressing her back against the door, pushing it against him.

Matthew eased back, allowing the door to close.

Dawn took a long time to come. But the longest night of Matthew's life eventually ended when orange and pink streaks of light came through the window of the Monarch Hotel lobby. He'd spent part of the night with the posse, going door to door of every residence and business while another search party checked the outlying areas and homes around Dickens. There were no leads to the man who had half bashed in Glenrose Jessop's skull.

No clues—except Matthew's pen found beside her.

He had spent the other half of the night on the sofa in the hotel lobby, unwilling to leave Hannah unguarded. Unwilling to leave Hannah at all.

Matthew rose from the lobby sofa, wiping his eyes and trying to rub the headache away. He would try again, try to talk to her. But he had to give it time. He would find ways as they worked side-by-side in the *Choctaw Tribune* to guide her into understanding all she meant to him. How she had quietly grown to be a part of his life to the point he couldn't imagine life without her.

Matthew left the hotel and went straight to the *Choctaw Tribune* office. There was no point in going home, no one there worrying over where he'd been all night. He'd sent word out to Uncle Preston's with the news, wanting them to be on the lookout for the attacker. Matthew had wanted to send Peter, but his cousin was staying close to Glenrose at the doctor's office.

Matthew halted when he saw a rolled newspaper laid neatly on the door jam. He picked it up, but he didn't need to unroll it to know it was the Dickens Herald, delivered earlier than usual.

He yanked the string and unfolded to see the front-page headline in two-inch type.

Prominent Businessman Wins Bid For Mayor; Assures Coming Improvements To Dickens

That pompous announcement was quickly overshadowed by a note delivered to Matthew by one of his paperboys.

Hannah Stillwater's resignation.

ccusations Mount Against Choctaw Newsman

July 6, 1895

By Earl Reynolds

On the evening of the Fourth, an indescribable act of horror took place. A local white girl was violently assaulted and left for dead in the alley behind the Enterprise Hotel. She is the third in what law-enforcement claim is a connected string of violence targeting women. The first victim was the wife of John Bellanger of Fort Smith, Arkansas. The second was Mrs. Coxwell, who survived the attack. The third is but a child who worked at the hotel.

There are no leads on the attacker, save for the fact that a fountain pen was found by the girl's body in the alley. It belongs to Matthew Teller of Dickens.

It's been discovered that Matthew Teller, prominently known as the publisher of the Choctaw Tribune, *has a violent past. He killed the former sheriff of Dickens during a personal dispute. Among his numerous altercations is his most recent with the* Dickens Herald *publisher, whom he assaulted inside the courthouse at Fort Smith.*

Furthermore, it is rumored he stayed the night of the Fourth inside the hotel room of his female employee, a deaf woman.
It would serve the good people of Dickens to track the movements of this Choctaw Indian.

Matthew tapped his pencil on the pad, sliding it through his fingers, and turning it the other way to do it again. The sounder was clicking, but it was just other operators chatting on the wires.

The first telegram he had received that morning was from D, who thought Peter would be on. The man asked what on earth was going on for the *Dickens Herald* to run such a dastardly article about Matthew.

Matthew opened the sounder and responded that Peter wouldn't be on the wire that day.

He didn't know when Peter would be back. The last he'd seen of his cousin was Peter boarding the train taking Glenrose Jessop to the hospital in Paris.

Between his absence, Hannah's immediate departure, and Ruth Ann away in McAlester, Matthew was more shorthanded than he'd been since he started the newspaper.

He had his tablet in the telegraph office to work on articles for the day, but it was hard to focus with the telegraph's constant clatter. Not to mention the *Dickens Herald* article in his view, was still smoldering in the otherwise cold stove. Matthew was still smoldering about it as well.

The fact that Earl Reynolds had connected with Christopher Maxwell, and that Maxwell had printed the erroneous article surprised even Matthew. Maxwell played dirty, but this was intense. Matthew had never been accused of being a violent criminal. It felt like a noose tightening around his neck.

But Matthew had to stay focused on his work. Maxwell had started a story war by printing Reynolds' article and Matthew intended to respond. To do that, he had spent the hours before dawn posting flyers around town for openings at the *Choctaw Tribune*. He hardly expected anyone local to respond after the article, so he also sent out telegrams to newspapers to run the ad, the same one that had drawn Hannah to him.

He couldn't dwell on her, either. He'd already tried to chase her down when the resignation note arrived on his desk, but she'd long since boarded the Frisco to parts unknown.

Matthew had once asked Hannah where she was from and she laughed, saying, "I'm from many places, Mr. Teller." There was so much she hadn't wanted him to know.

But he had to know.

The bell jingled over the door of the *Choctaw Tribune* and Matthew glanced up. He'd positioned his chair in the lean-to so he could see the front door.

A young man entered, hat in hand, glancing around furtively. Matthew stood and called out, "Can I help you?"

The man jerked around and hurried toward him. "I heard you're hiring. Can I have the job?"

"Do you know how to run a printing press?"

"No, sir."

"Run a telegraph wire?"

"No, sir."

"Set type?"

The man's eyes blazed with panic. "No, sir, but I'm a quick learner, and if you don't give me a job, I'm going to hit you."

Matthew cocked one eyebrow. The young man gulped. "My wife told me not to come home until I had a job. I've been away two days, hunting for work, and I can't stand it anymore."

Matthew took up his tablet. "What's your name?"

"Hugh Eberlin."

"Hugh, here's the first thing you need to learn quick: don't threaten your boss on your first day of work."

The young man's features melted with relief. "I won't let you down, sir."

Matthew extended his hand. "Welcome to the *Choctaw Tribune*."

Matthew got the young man started with Gentry showing him how to run the printing press. That was easier than setting type, something Gentry could do if he had to. They needed a full-time typesetter. Make that two. Matthew needed two men to replace the work Hannah had done.

It was almost closing time when a shadow fell over Matthew's desk. He looked up to see a man standing in the doorway of the lean-to, blocking the sun from entering through the picture windows. Matthew hadn't heard the bell over the door. The telegraph sounder must have disguised it, though that hadn't happened before.

Matthew slowly stood as the man took a step inside, his hat still on and shadowing his eyes. Matthew could only see his smile.

"I understand you're hiring. I can run a telegraph."

Matthew couldn't place the uneasiness he felt in the pit of his stomach, as though he'd swallowed a chunk of coal. There was something not right about this man.

"Where have you worked before?"

"Stations out west."

The answer was too vague. "What did you say your name is?"

"I didn't. But it's Clyde. You're Matthew Teller, aren't you?"

"That's right. The one the *Dickens Herald* ran a story about today."

Why Matthew added that, he didn't know. He gauged the man's reaction.

Clyde, who hadn't offered a last name, continued to smile. "I have no qualms about associating with a man of ill repute. As long as he pays in cold cash."

Matthew didn't want to hire this man. But if they weren't going to fall behind on the daily, he had to get out of this telegraph office and back to his desk.

"Let's see what you can do. But the position may only be temporary, until my cousin returns."

The man nodded, his hat still shadowing his eyes. "Temporary is all I need."

CHAPTER 40

*D*aniel had never been to the hospital in Paris. The building was three stories high with windows on every floor on every side. At least there was plenty of light to shine on the ill people there—including Glenrose Jessop and his young brother-in-law.

Inside, Daniel got directions to the ward where the young girl was. Curtain partitions separated the beds. Daniel went down the quiet rows where most of the patients were unconscious, in as critical condition as the one at the end. Glenrose was laid on a bed set in the corner where two windows allowed light on her pale face.

Daniel wasn't sure if the girl looked better or worse than when he had seen her in the alley. Then, blood and dirt covered her face and clothing but there was still a flush of life to her. Here, against the sterile walls of the hospital, her cheeks were sunken, her lips pale. Except the thick bandage around her skull, she looked as though she were laid out for burial. Nothing at all like the bright young girl he'd teased about serving ham from the left side of the hog.

Peter sat by the bed, his back to the wall, a book open in his lap, but he was just staring at the pages. He glanced up as Daniel approached, but otherwise didn't move.

Daniel squatted on the other side of Glenrose Jessop's bed. He spoke to Peter. "How you faring?"

Peter stared at him. His lips moved and then words finally came out. "I didn't really understand what it was like for you. Until now."

Peter was talking about Daniel's vigilance over his wife, Daisy, and the baby. After their deaths, Peter had hardly spoken to Daniel. None of the family did, except Melinda, William's wife. She told him the family needed time, that they all felt lost, especially Preston. Daniel had packed his bags and left the ranch he once thought he would grow old on.

Daniel reached out and touched Glenrose's cold hand. "It's hard. But you'll make it."

"I wouldn't want to live if she doesn't."

He does understand. "I came to check on you, and to see if she could answer questions. Has she said anything at all about who attacked her?"

Peter shook his head. "She hasn't opened her eyes or her mouth one time."

"Got any ideas who would want to hurt her like this?"

Peter's eyes darkened. "That's all I've thought about since being here." He snapped the book shut. "You better find him before I do."

Peter took Glenrose's other hand between his own and rubbed it. "You know, she did the funniest thing a couple of months ago. She brought me and my horse in the parlor of their house."

Daniel would have chuckled if not for the feeling of death around them. "Why would she do a thing like that?"

Peter's eyes flickered up to meet Daniel's, then away. "I was sort of on the run from some fellows that wanted my scalp."

Daniel cocked his head. He'd known Peter was veering off

since Daisy's death, cutting loose more than he should. But he didn't know it was anything serious. "Who were they? Why were they after you?"

Peter kept his gaze on Glenrose. "I stumbled onto them down by the Red River. Well, I was kind of there on purpose to meet them. I'd heard they had a little fun going on at the expense of some local Indians. They were running rigged gambling on all kinds of things. I thought I'd get a little revenge and pulled my 33-feet trick on them."

"You didn't."

"How was I supposed to know they took gambling so serious? Well, I didn't want to lead them back to the ranch, so I rode for Dickens. I hoped Lance would help me out. He doesn't exactly have a squeaky-clean past, you know."

"I know." Daniel looked at everyone differently now that he was a lawman.

"When I got to the house, Glenrose met me on the porch, and I told her bad men were after me. She pulled me and the horse right into the parlor." Peter's eyes watered. "I told her I would marry her someday."

His hands tightened around hers and a tear spilled out.

Daniel looked between them. Young love was fragile enough. Something like this could seal or destroy it. If Glenrose survived.

This was one of the best seasons to be on the ranch. Gone were the cold muddy days of winter and the jungle grasses of spring. There were trees and a breeze from the large lake to keep things cool enough to enjoy a glass of lemonade down on the dock after the day's work was through.

This was the thought Daniel held as he rode up to the main house on his father-in-law's ranch. Ruth Ann's wedding was the first time he'd been there since Daisy's passing. This would be the first time of speaking to his father-in-law since that day.

Melinda was on the front porch in the shade from the sun directly overhead, splitting peas with three of her little ones playing quietly with wooden animals at her feet. She had seen Daniel coming up and kept at her work as he dismounted. She was a woman who never stopped working, something that had intimidated Daisy as a young wife and mother. She wanted to follow her sister-in-law's example, wanted to always be working and busy taking care of her husband and baby.

But her health didn't hold out long enough for her to prove herself. Not that Melinda ever challenged her to. That was just who she was, and Daisy wanted to measure up.

Daniel tied his horse to the hitching post. "Afternoon, Melinda. Preston about?"

After the baby was born, Daniel was almost comfortable enough to call Preston "Daddy," the way Daisy did. He never would now.

Melinda had snapped half a dozen peas while he talked. "Good to see you, Daniel. He's down at the barn, mending harnesses."

Daniel nodded his thanks and started to turn away. Melinda said after him, "You're always welcome around here, Daniel. You're a part of this family."

Daniel nodded again, but they both knew the words needed to come from Preston to be true.

Daniel strolled down to the barn, the six-shooter on his hip, an unfamiliar weight in this place.

He was a different man than when he first came to the ranch. He wasn't sure if that was a good thing. The echo of the reporter's words about him favoring his own people as a lawman hadn't bothered him...until he tried to cover for the mysterious appearance of Matthew's pen found next to Glenrose. Aside from the fact that Matthew could stand on his own two feet, it caused

Daniel to wonder what he'd do if he did ever have to track down someone he respected and admired.

Maybe that was why he was at the ranch. He needed conversation with someone wiser than him.

The barn doors were wide open at each end, letting the breeze through from the lake. Daniel stepped inside the dim interior. He glanced around to see Preston in one corner, a jumble of leather harness and metal buckles on a table where he worked. Daniel approached, wondering if his father-in-law was getting hard of hearing. But he sensed Preston knew he was there, had known from the moment Daniel rode up into the yard.

Daniel hesitated. Maybe this wasn't the right thing after all. He was the last person Preston cared to see. Daniel turned away.

"You've come this far. Might as well have a seat."

Daniel stood in the doorway, feeling the urge to escape, to run from the pain again. But not this time.

He turned back and pulled up a tall stool next to the table. He looked over the leather harness, wondering how he could help with the repair. But he had no idea. He had grown up an orphan in a boarding school and was just learning the basics of ranching when Daisy became ill.

"I came for your advice about something."

The harness jingled as Preston shifted it around to the other side, a sharp razor in one hand where he cut a piece of worn buckle off. "I'm right here where I've always been."

Daniel closed his eyes against the wash of grief that choked him. Preston was right. He'd never turned Daniel away. It was Daniel who left this family.

"I'm sorry I didn't save her."

He swallowed and opened his eyes to find Preston staring straight at him.

"The word you're looking for, son, is *couldn't*. It's not that you didn't save her. You couldn't. I couldn't." Preston worked a new buckle under the leather. "I prayed hard that night. Hard. I said, 'Take me, God. Not them. Take me instead.'"

A shrill of laughter sounded from the barnyard. Daniel glanced back through the open doors to see William had ridden up and was chasing his three children around in the yard as Melinda scolded them from the porch. William rushed up the steps and swung her around, kissing her as she protested.

Daniel smiled, the sad kind that was the only one he had lately. He had imagined himself on the ranch, a mess of kids and a beautiful Choctaw bride waiting for him at the end of each day. That was gone, lost forever.

Daniel looked Preston in the eyes. "How did you do it? How did you bear the loss of stillborn babies and your wife too young?"

Preston's hands went slack. "I'm still bearing it. Not a day goes by I don't miss loving on her. But God gave me purpose in this life. I got to keep living it as long as he gives me strength to do it."

Daniel reached down to finger the marshal's badge pinned on his vest beneath his coat. Right over his heart. "I reckon that's what I've been trying to do, but I'm not doing well with it. I keep taking life, not giving it like you have."

"You doing good work as a lawman. No shame in that."

Daniel lifted his eyes to meet Preston's again. "Maybe. But right now, I'm questioning my integrity. There are some men I'd die for. Lie for, even. On the other hand, I do want to kill a man for the first time in my life. I don't know what to do with that feeling."

Preston motioned for Daniel to take hold of the leather harness. Together they pulled the new buckle tight. "Before you lie or kill, take a look at your badge first. Then do what you got to do. I know this, there's been more than one time in my life when I felt a man needed killing."

Daniel loosened his grip on the leather, startled. "Did you do it?"

It was a ridiculous question. Daisy's gentle father would never set out to murder anyone.

Preston chuckled. "I thought about it. But in the end, God always give me the grace to forgive. Those kinds of men always get it in the end. One way or another, and without us blacking our souls with hatred and blood."

The words hit Daniel in the heart with the arrow of truth he needed. He'd done right to come back to the ranch today. Maybe it was a habit he should develop.

After a few quiet moments, Preston said, "I can tell you something true. Your wound will heal."

"It'll leave a scar though, won't it?"

"Scars come with living, son."

He and Preston talked a while longer, discussing Peter's pain over Glenrose and the three men Daniel had killed in the line of duty. They also talked about Nita, and Matthew's new situation of living alone in town. Preston said Della was doing well but that Matthew was too busy in town to come out to the ranch and Preston indicated he was going to talk to his nephew about that.

It was good that Matthew and Ruth Ann had had this man in their lives as a father.

When Daniel rose to leave, Preston stood and clasped Daniel on the shoulder, looking him square in the eyes. "You just remember, you're still my son."

Daniel embraced him.

CHAPTER 41

Matthew hammered on the typewriter, pounding out a front-page story for the *Choctaw Tribune* in response to Maxwell's response to Matthew's response to Reynold's article.

Talk around town was heating up about the two newspapers directly attacking one another like never before. They moved past the realm of rivalry and into what amounted to a gunfight in the streets.

Matthew might have lost his heart. He wasn't going to lose his head in this fight.

Don't start something you can't finish.

Matthew had neglected using the typewriter of late, but now he was faster at spilling out his thoughts on it than with a pencil. Whether that was a good thing or not, he wasn't going to stop and think about.

All of Matthew's anger, frustration, and pain over his loss of Nita, Hannah, and his reputation flared in every sentence. Maxwell was not going to win this war. He was not going to seal his takeover of Dickens. He was not going to do more to destroy the sovereignty of the Choctaw Nation. Matthew would tear the town down with his own two hands before he let that happen.

Matthew reached the end of the line and slapped his palm against the carriage-return lever, shoving it to the other end, and started pounding again. The typewriter clacking also helped drown out the noise in the shop—Caleb Gentry and Hugh Eberlin worked at the typesetting cabinet and printer as fast as they could. Matthew couldn't push them too hard or they'd quit, but he cut no one slack.

The only one he really wanted to keep an eye on though, was the one constantly out of his sight. Clyde—the new man operating the telegraph. Peter needed to get home soon. But after a week in the hospital, there was still no change in Glenrose Jessop's condition and his cousin wasn't going to leave her side.

The bell rang over the door of the shop. Matthew refused to look up. Gentry didn't do well with customer interactions, but Matthew kept at the keys, aware of footsteps approaching his desk.

He started to slap the carriage-return lever again, but the double barrels of a shotgun pointing between his eyes halted him.

Matthew slid his line of sight past the barrels to the cocked hammers, then to the shaking hand holding the shotgun, up the brown sleeve of the jacket and into the face of the man staring down at him.

John Bellanger.

Matthew didn't move, one hand poised over the typewriter keys, the other palm out to halt Gentry and Eberlin from where they had both started forward.

"Something I can do for you, Bellanger?"

John Bellanger spoke in a gravelly voice. "If I find out it was you, that it was you all along, that you killed my wife, there won't be enough left of you to bury."

The *Dickens Herald* had a long reach, but Matthew wondered if a copy had landed on John Bellanger's porch intentionally.

There was little point in responding to the accusation, but Matthew said it anyway.

"I didn't kill your wife."

The muzzle of the shotgun pressed closer, the haze of the cold steel touching Matthew's nose. Bellanger's hands shook violently then he lifted the shotgun, uncocking the hammers. "You remember what I said, Indian."

Bellanger glanced around at the others in the shop, frozen and breathless. He kept his gun across his chest as he backed toward the door, bumping into it. He glanced quickly to his right and Matthew noted a shadow in the lean-to doorway. Clyde was observing the exchange.

Bellanger fumbled with the door, jerked it open, and ran out. Through the picture windows, Matthew watched him run up the street, mount a horse tied to a hitching rail across the way, and ride out of town.

A little gasp sounded at the back of the shop. Beulah had her hands pressed against her cheeks and she let out a long breath, eyes closed. Caleb Gentry and Hugh glanced at Matthew, both poised as if wondering if they should pursue the man.

Matthew shook his head. "Everyone, back to work."

He shoved the carriage-return lever, nearly dislodging the carriage. A shadow fell across his desk, and he looked up at Clyde standing over him. He still couldn't see the man's eyes. That man wore his hat all day, even inside the shop. But his smile was there.

"Looks like you have more enemies than you know what to do with, Teller."

"When I said everyone back to work, I meant *everyone*."

Clyde, still smiling, tipped his hat and returned to the lean-to. Matthew hit a few keys on the typewriter, then halted. He couldn't go on like this. But he had to.

Don't start something you can't finish.

〜

Matthew sat in the living room of the box house, newspapers and notes spread across the coffee table, the sofa, the floor. His mother would have whacked him with a wooden spoon for making such a mess in the living room, where she always kept it ready for hospitality.

But Matthew expected no visitors. No one was coming to see just him, and he had work to do that required a lot of space.

Benjamin said they didn't have what they needed to stop Maxwell. He was operating in Indian Territory legally. He had influential congressmen in D.C. who were favoring his proposal to protect the interest of white business owners in the Choctaw Nation. He ran a highly-read newspaper that was tearing Matthew and the *Choctaw Tribune* apart with its slander.

Benjamin advised Matthew to let up for awhile.

He couldn't.

So, he spread papers across the floor in the empty sewing room and table. The mess spilled out to where he was now, seated on the sofa and rubbing his chin as he read through his notes with fresh eyes.

Hot Springs. D.C. Fort Smith. St. Louis. McAlester. Dickens. Whiskey running, illegal gambling, girls forced into a place they didn't want to be.

Maxwell, Warren, Banny, Carter. The woman killer.

It all tied together and was right in front of him if only he knew the details to write the story.

Matthew leaned back and rubbed his eyes.

He couldn't think anymore.

Stop striving. The words echoed in his heart like a thunderclap. Not a voice from heaven, but it almost felt like it.

But if he stopped, if he didn't do it all, how would it all get done?

Scratching at the front door drew his attention. They hardly had raccoons and skunks in town with how the population had grown. Still, Matthew chalked it up to that.

But the scratching persisted, along with a low whine. The sound pierced his heart. He stood and went to the door. Opening it, he found what he expected.

Story stood on the porch, her head low, eyes angled up at him, tail low with hesitant wagging. Matthew reached down and gave her a scratch behind the ear. She leaned into it with a sigh of contentment, licking her lips. Matthew straightened, stepped back, and whistled low. She hopped over the threshold and turned in a circle, eyes never leaving him. She had focus.

Matthew closed the door and went to the wingback chair that Ruth Ann used to sit in for reading and sewing. She liked how it was positioned by the window where she could see the train depot and all the comings and goings of the growing town of Dickens.

Matthew settled in it and let the dog lay her head on his lap as he cradled her behind the ears.

"You miss Hannah, don't you?"

Story pricked her ears at the familiar name.

Matthew looked around at the empty house. Ruth Ann wasn't coming back. Nor his mother. They were where they belonged now.

Matthew was alone.

He put his fist over the hollow spot in his chest and closed his eyes, savoring the warmth of the furry head over his knees.

"God, it hurts."

He opened his eyes and looked at the mess of papers scattered around the house. He couldn't live like this, his life nothing but work, day and night. He couldn't keep waiting for Hannah to return.

He had to find her.

Pushing a newspaper off the coffee table, Matthew laid out a fresh sheet of paper and wrote down every detail he could recall from his conversations with Hannah that might indicate her home roots.

After some scribbling, he halted, a fuzzy image in his mind. It was Hannah, seated at the typesetting cabinet, eating her lunch, and reading a letter that had arrived for her at the *Choctaw Tribune* the week before she left. She alternated between taking a small bite of her sandwich, reading a few lines, smiling, and taking another bite.

In under a minute, Matthew was lighting the lamp on the wall by the typesetting cabinet. He rummaged through the waste basket by Hannah's desk. Beneath his poorly scribbled articles that she'd set type on was an envelope.

The return address read:

Ned & Hattie Stillwater
Tishomingo (on the Blue River)

He had a destination.

CHAPTER 42

It was Saturday and while everyone at the paper had the day off, Matthew headed west. It took some train switching but he finally arrived in Tishomingo. It didn't take much checking to discover the Stillwater homestead was ten miles east, near the town of Milburn. Matthew had made that trek before to interview the Chickasaw governor at his White House there.

He was in Chickasaw country.

Matthew rented a horse from the livery and set out at a fast clip. He couldn't know for sure that Hannah had returned to her family's farm. But he knew for sure.

The rumble of the Blue River told him he'd arrived before he saw it. The fresh scent of clean water and wild sage greeted him as the cedars and dogwoods along the road gave way to weeping willows at the river's edge. Matthew halted the horse and listened.

The Blue River was singing its song—splashes of water that gushed over white granite falls; a trickle of a tiny tributary meandering through rocks near the bank; the flick of a bass' mouth in the deeper pools.

A blue paradise.

The Blue River cut through the middle of the Stillwater homestead on its way to the Red River. A double log house stood on the other bank, fireplace at one end with a chinked and daubed chimney and a lean-to kitchen off the back.

One room, many heads sleeping inside in the winter. Based on the long table outside in the yard, Matthew knew most of the family slept outside on the hot summer nights.

Right by the coolness of the Blue River.

Matthew nudged his horse into the low water to cross as he observed the emptiness of the place, save the chickens that scattered as he reached the yard and the pigs in a small corral near the barn.

The family was away.

Matthew started to dismount in front of the cabin. He halted when an Indian man came around the corner, a rifle resting in his crossed arms.

Matthew straightened in the saddle again. "I'm Matthew Teller of the *Choctaw Tribune* in Dickens."

If Hannah Stillwater was there, the man would know who he was and maybe even why he was there.

The man's expression didn't change, and he didn't loosen his grip on the rifle. This man might also recognize Matthew's name as the one in Reynold's article, accusing him of being a woman killer.

When the man didn't say anything, Matthew switched to Chickasaw. "I am looking for Hannah Stillwater. I understand this is her family's home."

The man pointed with his chin to the chopping block. He spoke in English. "Lot of work to do."

Matthew dismounted and tied the horse to the post near the cabin. The man kept the rifle in his crossed arms as he took a position near the chopping block.

Matthew draped his suit coat over the split rail fence next to the chopping block that kept the horses corralled. He grabbed the ax handle and dislodged the head from the block before picking up the first round of wood. He settled it upright on the block and took a hard swing. The round split in two.

While he was bending to pick up one of the split pieces to half it, he asked, "Are you Hannah Stillwater's father?"

"I am Ned Stillwater."

Matthew came down on the half to quarter it. "I've come to ask her about returning to the *Choctaw Tribune*."

Matthew split the other half and picked up a new round. He paused to meet the man's eyes.

Ned Stillwater said, "I raised her to be independent."

Matthew went back to chopping. "You know about our last conversation?"

Ned Stillwater leaned back against the split rail fence. He hadn't set aside the rifle.

"She is hurt."

Matthew came down on another half round. The ax glanced off the side and the blade swung past the block. It missed Matthew's leg by a pencil tip.

He halted, breathing hard.

Ned Stillwater continued. "Her mother is Chickasaw. Me, half white, half Comanche. Being half of somethin' amounts to being whole of nothin'. I wanted Hannah to be whole. She done good on her own. Until now."

Matthew slammed the ax blade through the split this time. "My fault, I guess."

"Yeah."

Like the man said, there was a lot of work to do.

Matthew took up another round, and another, and another. He split wood until his shirt was soaked with sweat and he couldn't see straight. He sank the blade into the block and swiped his shirt sleeve across his forehead.

"The river's cold."

Matthew headed for the bank and splashed the icy water from the Blue River on his face, neck, over his head. He wanted to plunge in but settled on returning to Hannah's father, water dripping from the longer strands of his hair.

Ned Stillwater observed him a long moment. "Her mother never wanted her to leave the homestead, you know."

Matthew hadn't. He knew so little about Hannah Stillwater.

He began scooping up the split logs and stacking them on the woodpile. When he finished, Ned Stillwater jerked his head toward the house. "Got something to show you."

Inside, the interior was lit by sunlight coming from the windows. Ned placed his rifle in the rack over the fireplace and went to a small bookshelf built against the wall near the door. It was an odd sight on a rural homestead—to have shelves dedicated to books.

Ned pulled three books off the shelf and handed them to Matthew. Matthew turned them over, flipping through to see the titles. He halted at the last one.

On the Blue River by T.A. Paige.

"My Hannah wrote those novels."

Matthew fumbled the books, nearly dropping them. He stared at Ned Stillwater to see the truth in his eyes.

Matthew recalled the conversation at the dinner table when Hannah first arrived in Dickens. While Ruth Ann praised works of fiction, Matthew had blatantly criticized them. What horrible things had he said? Without knowing it he had, in a few words, crushed a part of Hannah's heart that she poured into these novels.

Matthew ran his thumb over the embossed title of the book, wondering how he could ever make it up to her.

On the Blue River.

No wonder she never told him where she was from. Any detail would give away her identity as an author in a publishing world that favored a men-only policy.

That wasn't the reason, though, why she'd run from Dickens. From the *Choctaw Tribune*. From him.

Matthew offered the books to Ned Stillwater. The man pushed them back into Matthew's chest. "Read them."

"I will."

Ned Stillwater regarded him closely. Matthew felt him reading his soul and learning all he believed, hoped, dreamed, feared.

After the silence, the father said, "I was proud when she wrote that she was at a newspaper office owned by an Indian. I read your paper. You do good work. Until you rode up, though, I did not know why she left."

Matthew bowed his head and cracked open the cover for *On the Blue River*. In familiar script he knew was Hannah's she'd written, *To my beloved family*. Ned Stillwater was willing to give this to him.

"Your heart beats for her."

Matthew nodded. "I am hoping for your permission to court her."

"You do not know what you ask."

"I know Hannah faces challenges because of who she is. But my daddy taught me to not start things I can't finish."

The sound of a wagon approaching the river echoed outside.

Ned Stillwater looked Matthew in the eyes. "I thought only a man who pitied her would want to marry her. Or one who would only take advantage of her. I raised her to stand on her own two feet. Do not hurt her."

Matthew shook his head.

Ned Stillwater looked out the open doorway. "I protected her. But I did not take care of the little girl inside her. You will do that?"

Matthew nodded. He took a step forward to look out the door. A small wagon was crossing the river. A Chickasaw woman with Hannah's eyes and nose drove the wagon. In the back was a bundle of kids. And Hannah.

Matthew stepped out on the porch. Her mother pulled the wagon to a sharp stop. The kids piled out, and Hannah jumped off last. She turned and froze.

He didn't know whether he should sign to her or speak. He didn't get a chance to do either. Hannah raised her skirts and ran for the riverbank, disappearing into the weeping willows.

Matthew started forward, but her mother was in front of him in a flash, blocking his way.

"You will not go to her."

Matthew locked his jaw. He'd come a long way—in heart and body—to find Hannah and he couldn't walk away. But he couldn't walk through her mother, either. Apparently Hannah had talked more about her wishes to her than to her father.

"I will come back."

Matthew mounted and set his horse on a walk toward the river.

Like the man said, there was a lot of work to do.

Matthew had never known life to be like this. He always had the next task, the next search for truth and justice. The next job to do. Why did none of that seem to matter now?

Matthew paced the cramped room in a small hotel in Tishomingo. Tomorrow was Sunday and he needed to return for church, or his family would worry. Yet he wasn't sure anyone would worry and that didn't seem to matter either, at least not enough to cut through the fog of his mind. He had to go home, yet he couldn't leave without Hannah.

Matthew set himself down on the edge of the bed once again. He knew he wouldn't sleep. He reached for one of Hannah's novels. *On the Blue River.* By T.A. Paige.

A name that most would assume was male, which was what Hannah intended. Writing was a man's world. At least Hannah knew he didn't feel that way, thanks to Ruth Ann. His sister had broken so many barriers through the *Choctaw Tribune*. Hannah could do the same. She could write articles using her real name. He'd publish them every day.

He'd publish her works of fiction if she wanted.

If only she would trust him. Yet why should she? They had known one another a few months and the charges against Matthew...how did Reynolds put it? *Accusations Mount Against Choctaw Newsman.*

Maxwell was costing Matthew everything, even Hannah.

Matthew opened the novel and traced the drawing of the Blue River adjacent to the title page. The black and white image didn't do the blue paradise justice. Hannah's words would, he was sure.

He read his way through the long night.

Matthew checked out of the hotel at dawn the next morning and rented the horse again. He took the road toward the Blue River but only made it a few miles when a wagon met him and waved him down. The driver, looking much like a relative of Ned Stillwater's, handed Matthew a note before slapping the reins over the backs of his team.

The note was short.

She will come to you at the Choctaw Tribune *if she chooses. If she does, ask her about Zachary Hail.*

When the afternoon train rolled into Dickens, Matthew went to the box house and found Story waiting on the front porch. He had left out a bowl of food and water for her. He did have himself a dog.

He went to the church where there were leftovers from the picnic lunch and most everyone still socializing. His mother was waiting for him. They didn't talk much. Matthew could tell she knew why. Hannah wasn't there.

Matthew left before the family, half asleep on his feet. Back at the house, he had just pulled his boots off and stretched out on the sofa when a knock came at the door before it opened.

"Hello the house?" Uncle Preston.

Matthew waved a hand above the back of the sofa and Uncle Preston came around to seat himself in the wingback chair with a chuckle.

"Boy, you wearing yourself out. You gotta get the right pacing in life. That's a key to living. Man tries to get there all at once is just killing himself for no good reason."

Matthew had his reasons, but he didn't want to go into them. He wasn't sure they were good, anyway. He sat up and rubbed rough hands over his face. Uncle Preston reached a long arm across the space to grasp Matthew's wrist and turn his palm up. Cuts and bruises showed.

"You done some heavy work."

Matthew shrugged. Uncle Preston leaned back. "Son, you're trying awful hard, but you're just wearing your heart out. The destination is miles away, yet you're trying to reach it all right now."

"Pacing?"

"Pacing."

After Uncle Preston left, Matthew found himself staying up late with the papers as he continued to try and pull pieces together.

But his heart wasn't in it. His heart was back at the Blue River.

She will come to you... Those same words Matthew had whispered to Benjamin at the wedding. He now understood how hard that was.

Matthew was the most patient and stubborn in his family. But even if Hannah came back to Dickens tomorrow, it would still be the longest wait of his life.

CHAPTER 43

*P*eter never realized a hospital could be a home. But he was beginning to wonder if this one would be his forever.

At least they were now in a room with only one other patient, a curtain separating Glenrose's bed.

He turned the page on the book he was reading aloud to her. Even though the doctor said she couldn't hear anything, Peter had read three books to her since they got there. He wasn't going to quit now, not after her four-hour surgery that left her even more pasty white. The doctors had gone in for a final surgery, only giving her a slim chance of pulling through. But she had, and Peter was determined to pull her the rest of the way through, if willpower alone could do it. And prayer.

He begged and pleaded with God. Confessed every sin he could think of since he was five years old. He bargained and made promises. Anything for God to save her.

There was no change.

Lance and Amarillo had both been there through the surgery and in the hours following the recovery. Stephen Austin was back home, taking care of the kids until Lance and Amarillo returned. Once they did, Stephen Austin came back to the hospital and stayed at Glenrose's other side.

Peter found himself talking with the young man more than they ever had. The same age, they came from completely different backgrounds. Stephen Austin's father was one of the outlaws involved in the killing of Peter's uncle—Jim Teller, Matthew and Ruth Ann's father.

Peter didn't hold that against the Jessops, certainly not Glenrose. Stephen Austin had an angry side to him, though Peter found it wasn't as dominant as when the family had first moved into town. Stephen Austin was trying to become a good Christian man.

Peter once had that aspiration. Now he wasn't sure. Things changed when his sister Daisy died.

What kind of man would he become if Glenrose didn't make it?

He prayed he didn't have to find out.

Peter read awhile more, then stretched. Stephen Austin had fallen asleep in his chair. Peter woke him to stay vigilant in case Glenrose stirred while he took a walk outside.

The fresh air reminded Peter that a world existed beyond the hospital. He knew Matt needed him at the Choctaw Tribune, but at least he had hired on a couple of new employees. They would manage fine without Peter.

Life was more than work, he'd learned.

Peter picked out two new books from the library down the street. When he first went there, he grabbed whatever was on the closest shelf and rushed back to the hospital. The past few visits, though, he had taken more time to select books Glenrose would enjoy.

He was striding up the steps to the hospital again when a familiar voice called out, "You're becoming quite the bookworm."

Peter looked over his shoulder to see Daniel mounting the hospital steps. Peter said, "I've read more books in the past week than I have in my whole life put together."

Daniel came beside him. "I'm sure she appreciates it. You've been reading the Bible to her too, haven't you? I know she'd like that."

Peter looked down at the books in his hands. "I don't suppose I have."

Daniel shifted and motioned to one side of the wide hospital porch, out of the foot traffic. "Want to talk about it?"

Peter met Daniel's eyes. He didn't know if he could ever become a real man like his father, brothers, and Matthew. And Daniel.

"Did you feel like you might lose your faith when Daisy passed?"

Daniel glanced off at the busy street where hacks and foot traffic showed how the world was going on about its business without them.

"To be honest, I did lose my faith when she passed. And that was a good thing."

Peter raised his eyebrows. "How you figure?"

"A faith that can be lost isn't a faith worth having. It's all well and good to praise God when the skies are blue and the sun is shining. But it's when the roof caves in and the bottom falls out that you really get a notion of just who God is. That's when real faith begins. At least, that's how it was for me."

Peter sniffed back tears. "Daniel, I don't reckon I've ever said this, but you're one of the best men I know."

Daniel smiled, sad. "There's a few to put in line ahead of me."

Peter started to ask if there was any news on finding the attacker, but the hospital door banged open and Stephen Austin leaped onto the porch.

He stopped hard when he saw Peter and Daniel standing to

the side. His eyes were wild, and Peter felt the bottom of his world falling out.

Stephen Austin shouted, "She's awake! She opened her eyes!"

251

CHAPTER 44

Matthew flipped another page on his tablet, trying not to break the flow of writing he was finally in. It had been two days since he'd gotten the wire from Daniel, saying that Glenrose finally regained consciousness.

But she couldn't speak, hadn't said a word now in two days. Peter and Stephen Austin were with her around the clock and Matthew knew they would alert him of her progress and if she managed to give any kind of description of her attacker.

Maxwell hadn't given up the story war, fueled by the latest news. He wrote a front-page story, painting a grim picture of a young girl who would be nothing more than an invalid and a burden on her family for the rest of her life. He ended with writing that she hadn't said one word about the publisher of the *Choctaw Tribune* not being the attacker.

Matthew needed Ruth Ann there more now than ever, but she was consumed with being a new wife and publisher at their second office in McAlester. She'd been down to visit every week, going out to the ranch to see their mother. She did better at keeping up with Della than Matthew did, adding that shame to his life.

Though Della was surrounded by family at Uncle Preston's, it was still her three children's responsibility to see after her. Nieces and nephews were not substitutes for the children she had borne from her own body.

Matthew flipped to a fresh page as he continued writing an article in response to Maxwell's response to Matthew's front-page story when he broke the news about Glenrose.

He shifted on the crate, his back beginning a new ache, protesting at how he was hunched over, writing with the tablet in his lap. He ignored the pain. He rarely used this outside area for writing anymore, but he needed a new view.

Some view.

The street behind the *Choctaw Tribune* blocked what used to be his view of the field and church in the distance. This was now an alleyway where junk accumulated from the businesses and stores that backed up to his shop. This town had gotten too big.

Matthew sensed its hold in the Choctaw Nation.

Story lay by his feet, his constant companion since he returned from the Blue River. The dog rested her head on the top of his boot, content just to be near him. Matthew didn't know why he'd been such an ardent proponent of keeping dogs outside. She slept on the sofa with him.

There was no point in staying in his lean-to bedroom at the house. Anything personal in his life was pointless. All that mattered was his work. A part of that was fighting to save his reputation from Maxwell's vile attacks.

At least Earl Reynolds had left town, though Matthew suspected he would be back. A man like that had a taste for blood and he wouldn't stop until he got some of Matthew's.

Matthew was almost finished with the article when Story lifted her head. She let out a low *woof* and scrambled to her feet. She took off for the corner of the *Choctaw Tribune* building and Matthew stood to find what had gotten her attention. He followed her around the building and halted. In the space between the two buildings, he could see the street and the light traffic on it.

Specifically, he could see the boardwalk and the young woman who knelt on it, smiling as Story licked her face. She caressed the dog's head, causing Story's tail to wag with unabated joy.

Pretty much like the thumping of Matthew's heart.

Hannah Stillwater looked up. Story gave her one last lick on the chin before Hannah rose, eyes soft and cautious.

Matthew closed the distance between them, but said nothing. He had to wait for her.

Hannah kept one hand on Story's head as the dog leaned against her. She kept her eyes on Matthew's face. "Please don't misunderstand, Mr. Teller. I know what this fight means, and I shouldn't have abandoned it. If you're willing, I would like to return to work at the Choctaw Tribune. I also have a story that might help you oppose the annexation of Dickens."

Everything she said was important, but Matthew was still at the beginning of her speech. *Don't misunderstand.*

Matthew would wait. "You're welcome to return to work. I… we do need help."

They entered through the front door of the *Choctaw Tribune* together. Hannah started to shoo Story back. The dog looked at her, confused.

Matthew touched Hannah's arm to get her attention before saying, "I've kinda been letting her come inside."

Hannah's half-smile told him she wanted to tease him about it. But they weren't ready for that.

Matthew introduced Hugh Eberlin to Hannah while Beulah came over and gave her a hug, welcoming her back.

Clyde stepped to the door of the lean-to even though the

sounder was going off. Clyde gave Hannah an appraising look and Matthew stepped between them. Clyde grinned and held his palms up while backtracking into the lean-to.

If one of his other employees knew how to run a telegraph, Matthew would send the man packing.

Matthew directed Hannah to the dark room. He left the door open and lit the lamp he used after developing photographs to examine how they turned out. He faced her, making sure that his face was lit by the light.

"Hugh learned typesetting quick, although he still struggles with the Choctaw version. I'd like you to set those articles and also be available to develop photographs. I want to use photography more to give us an edge in the story war we have going with Maxwell. If you're up for learning, that is."

"Life is a constant learning experience. But I do know how to develop photographs."

Remarkable. "Good. And since it's dark in here most of the time, I'll use sign language when I can."

Matthew hesitated. He didn't know how she would react if he directed the conversation to them. But he had to try.

"I want to apologize for what I said about novels a few months ago. I'm sure it must have hurt. I always believed novels were a waste of good words. I hadn't read yours."

Hannah looked down at the developed photographs on the table, then back at him. It must have been hard to always have to watch for words, not able to look away when you bared your soul.

"You know something true, Mr. Teller? I've given away so many feelings in my stories, I question if I have genuine ones left. Hurt. Fear. I deposited them into stories so I didn't have to live with them and my deafness, too. So please know—if my actions are hard to understand, it's my fault, not yours."

Matthew spoke two words. "Zachary Hail."

Hannah didn't flinch. "Yes. He courted me for a year and a

half. My deafness did not intimidate him. Society, however, eventually did. As did my gift of writing. He wanted me to quit."

She looked beyond Matthew, into the newspaper office. His life.

"You are a good, good man, Matthew Teller. A strong man. When everything, everybody, is against you, you stand and do what is right. But you have never faced the brute force of a society who wishes there were not people like me. Only when that time comes, can you truly understand and commit to what is in your heart right now."

Matthew swallowed all his hopes and dreams, pressing them down to a place in his heart where they hopefully wouldn't slip away when he wasn't looking.

"I guess we get to work then."

CHAPTER 45

The town of Antlers went about its daily business outside the drawn curtains of Sissy's home. She stood near one of the windows, at just an angle to see the street filled with traffic.

She'd grown up on a large ranch with her family and wasn't accustomed to town living. She wasn't accustomed to being in a loveless home.

A vaguely familiar form materialized out of the traffic, the young woman's skirts catching dust as she made her way to the Coxwell's picket fence.

To Sissy's dismay, a toddler rested on Amarillo Fuller's hip. Sissy hadn't thought of her bringing the child, but it made sense for a mother to have her child with her.

Even when Amarillo approached the front door, Sissy didn't move. The knock came and still she stood. She had sent her servant away for the afternoon and there was no one to answer the door.

On the third knock, Sissy shifted her feet, not wanting the young woman to leave. She had to answer the door. That was all.

At the sound of the door opening, Amarillo turned back toward it. She wasn't smiling.

She knew why Sissy had sent her the letter and train ticket. The two women hardly knew one another, but through their mutual friends, Sissy was willing to trust this young woman with what was about to become the greatest secret of her life.

Without a word, Sissy beckoned Amarillo and the child inside. While Amarillo didn't have a drop of Indian blood in her veins, the child's dark skin and crop of black hair gave away his father's heritage.

Sissy nodded her head toward the parlor, unable to speak. She needed to save her words, words she couldn't speak to anyone in her family or those who knew her family. They were a prominent Choctaw lot.

Sissy followed Amarillo into the parlor. Amarillo was stiff and Sissy indicated she sit on the golden brocade sofa where she would have room with her child. Sissy took one of the matching wing-back chairs.

They sat and stared at one another a while. Amarillo shifted her son from her lap and seated him on the sofa next to her. He wore a darling suit of blue and seemed a content child. He sat beside his mother and quietly played with two wooden horses that had come out of his pockets.

Suddenly, Sissy's request seemed impossible. But she pressed in. "I know you're wondering why I asked you to come."

Amarillo didn't move, didn't seem uncomfortable with the awkward situation of sitting in a fancy parlor without even being offered tea. This wasn't that sort of social call, and she knew it.

Sissy met Amarillo's eyes. "You know what happened to me."

Amarillo nodded. Sissy swallowed, wishing the young woman would say something. She wasn't going to make this easy.

Sissy shifted in the chair, trying to find a position that didn't strike pain in her bruised body. "I asked you to come here because I didn't want anyone in Dickens to recognize me. I don't want anyone to know."

She stared into Amarillo's blue eyes and received another nod. Sissy plunged on. "I'm with child and I don't want to be."

Amarillo broke the gaze, looking down at her son and taking a moment to straighten his collar. He bumped the noses of the wooden horses together and giggled.

Amarillo said quietly, "I know what you're meaning."

Sissy felt jolted to her core. She wanted to blame the stark Texas drawl of Amarillo's level tone, but it was more than that. In an instant, their pasts collided, and they shared an understanding few women could.

Amarillo looked up. "The difference between what happened to me and you, mostly, is that you've got a husband. It won't be a big public thing."

Sissy gripped her hands together in her lap, the coldness of a stone pressing against her heart as it had since her marriage began. She let the truth spill out.

"I don't want this baby no matter which is the father."

Amarillo raised her eyebrows, cocking her head to study Sissy.

"You ain't told your husband, have you?"

Sissy held her ground, her chin lifted. She wasn't going to defend her position to this stranger. "Do you know how to do it, or where I can go? You must have thought about it when…"

Sissy kept her chin up to prevent looking at the toddler who swung his legs as the horses galloped across his lap. Amarillo pulled the little boy onto her own lap again.

"Yeah. I thought about it. Had what I needed to do it, too."

Sissy's stomach turned and she didn't know if it was the morning sickness come to visit in the afternoon, or if it was a twisted joy inside her.

"I'll pay for whatever I'll need."

Amarillo shifted her son to cradle him. He objected and

wiggled, wanting his legs to hang over the sofa's edge. Amarillo slipped her arms under his and held him close.

"You got to know, I was raised ignorant of a lot of things, especially with my ma dying too young. It took me a long time to realize what was happening inside me. By the time I did, I was pretty far along. The old woman down by the Red River told me it was too late, that I'd kill myself in the process. I didn't care. I would just as soon die too."

Sissy closed her eyes. They understood one another.

When she opened her eyes again, Amarillo was watching her.

"I went into the field behind the house where my siblings wouldn't find me for a while. I knelt down on the ground and prayed. Didn't figure God would want nothing to do with me, but I didn't want to go without talking to Him first. Then I put the cup to my lips. That's when I felt it. Felt him."

Amarillo fingered her little boy's booted feet. He pushed against her hands as though they were playing a game. "I felt him kick. That's when I knew he wanted to live. And then…I knew I had to let us both live."

Sissy couldn't move. At least she thought she couldn't until she realized the warmth rising in her midsection was from the palm of her hand pressed against it. Her body trembled and a flash of the man's eyes glared in her vision.

She scrambled for the ashcan near the fireplace. She dry heaved, not having eaten all day.

A hand pressed against her back then moved up to massage her neck, gently.

"I'll help you, Mrs. Coxwell, to see your baby born safe and sound. Whoever the father is or whether you stay with your husband don't matter. I'll help you."

Sissy shifted to her side, head in her hands. Amarillo cradled her as tenderly as she'd cradled the child and held her while Sissy cried the tears of her ruined life.

CHAPTER 46

This was an easy article to set the type in Choctaw. Hannah worked her fingers rapidly, hardly looking at the article. She had every word imprinted in her memory. She had written it.

Once she went over the details of the information for Matthew Teller, he had asked her to write the article in an unbiased manner, focusing heavily on the facts of the case: A township in the Chickasaw Nation had been revoked because it was built by white businessmen prior to the railroads coming. The men lost their physical properties and investments in the town.

One hangup Matthew Teller had with the townsite of Dickens was that one of the founders, Thaddeus Warren, claimed intermarried citizenship. All of that was muddy and Matthew thought it would unravel in the case he was building with his brother-in-law.

As Hannah neared the end of the article, her thoughts were of Matthew Teller and his dogged determination for the truth. She hoped and prayed this truth she was setting in type wouldn't contribute to getting him killed someday. In her time at the Blue

River, her thoughts were of him. And then there he was. And she was so afraid.

She was still afraid.

Matthew Teller wasn't intimidated by her gift of writing. He read her books. Asked her to write more. So unlike Zachary.

That frightened her.

She couldn't risk her heart again. Life had dealt her enough pain.

When Matthew Teller expressed his desire to court her, Hannah had done the very thing her father told her never to do.

Don't come running home when things don't go your way. Stand your ground.

Somehow, Matthew Teller had turned her into a coward.

She knew why. She was growing dependent on him. Something else her father taught her to never do.

Hannah rose from the cabinet with the full composing stick, preparing to finish the chase for the article.

Clyde stood by the printing press, chatting with Hugh. He should be in the telegraph office, but Hannah noticed he did things the way he wanted, especially in Matthew's absence, like now.

Clyde was facing her as he talked to Hugh, who continued working. "He's good enough as far as bosses go and the pay's all right, sure. All I'm saying is, he asks an unhealthy amount of questions."

Hannah froze, uncertain if she'd read Clyde's words correctly. His lips were always curled in a semi-smile, which made it harder. But she was almost certain those were the same words Matthew Teller had shared with her. Words spoken by the man in Fort Smith who had threatened to kill him.

Clyde shifted and caught Hannah watching him. The composing stick in her hand shook and she laid it back on her desk.

Clyde smiled and tipped his ever-present hat that shadowed

his eyes. She returned a brief nod of acknowledgment while squeezing between the cabinet and the wall not meant for a walkway. She tried to not rush through the door of the dark room as she entered, moving to the side where she would be out of sight. She took a calming breath, but it didn't help.

If Clyde was that man from Fort Smith, then he could be tied to the death of Mr. Bellanger's wife, and the attacks on Sissy Coxwell and Glenrose Jessop.

What should she do? Matthew Teller was out of the shop. The Levitts were gone for the day. Only Hugh and Clyde were there, and Hannah hardly knew the new young man.

Even if Matthew Teller was there, there was nothing they could do to prove guilt against this man. Only a few people could possibly identify him—Sissy Coxwell and Glenrose Jessop. But how would they know without seeing him?

Hannah's eyes landed on Matthew's pocket Kodak resting at the end of the table of developed photographs. Hannah picked it up, blocking her actions from the doorway in case Clyde was watching. She moved further back in the room where it was nearly completely dark, the lamp out. She glanced over her shoulder to see Clyde leaned against the press, arms folded. He faced the dark room door, but had his head turned, still chatting with Hugh who seemed to be ignoring the man.

Hannah positioned her finger over the shutter of the camera, held it at her midsection, and carefully turned. She pressed the button.

Was the click of the camera louder than the press?

She quickly set the camera aside. Clyde glanced her way as she started to close the door to the dark room.

She turned the sign that Matthew Teller had tacked on the door saying, *"Do Not Enter."*

Hannah closed the door and hurried back to the camera. She let her sharp eyes adjust to the darkness. She didn't like being in the dark, but that was something she had learned to overcome at a young age. It served her now.

She carefully opened the camera and withdrew the film roll. She began mixing the chemicals and poured them into the tray.

A shaft of light fell over the chemical tray and Hannah pulled back. The door was open.

Clyde stood there; his curled smile gone. He stepped inside the room, clearing the doorway enough for her to see the press was vacant. Where was Hugh?

Clyde began speaking as he closed the door, but Hannah couldn't see his lips clearly in the dark.

She found her voice and shouted, "You leave this instant!"

He didn't stop advancing into the room. He lit the lamp and retrieved the roll of film on the table. His lips curled up. "Like to take photographs, do you, missy?"

Still watching her, he held the film roll over the lamp's flame. It twisted in the heat. "I did want to get more out of this job than the money. Looks like I will."

Hannah spun away when he reached for her. She lunged for the door. Arms stronger than her wrapped around her middle and yanked around, slamming her into the wall of the small room.

Pain shot through Hannah's shoulder, but she clawed at his arms. Screamed. He covered her mouth and kept her pressed against the wall, lips near her ear. For the first time in her life, Hannah was grateful she couldn't hear.

CHAPTER 47

$\mathcal{M}$atthew walked into an empty *Choctaw Tribune* building. Hugh was gone from the press, Hannah nowhere in sight, and the sounder was clacking away unmanned in the telegraph office.

He started to head in there, annoyed that Clyde wasn't at his post. But Story, who had been under his fingertips, bolted toward the dark room door, barking. It wasn't her happy bark.

Matthew noted the sign was on the door to indicate that photography development was in progress. He hadn't given Hannah anything to develop yet.

Matthew should have left Story there with her so that the dog could alert Hannah of his knocking.

He had a sickening feeling he should have left the dog there.

When he reached the door, Matthew didn't hesitate. He twisted the knob, pushed the door open, and froze.

Clyde turned up the lamp on the table, illuminating his smile but obscuring his eyes. "Thought you could read better than that, Teller."

Matthew's gaze landed on Hannah. Story had shot straight into the room as soon as he opened the door and stood licking

Hannah's hand. She was leaning against the wall, her lake blue eyes wide.

He balled his right hand into a fist but held himself in check, trying not to think of the sweet pain in his knuckles after belting Maxwell at the courthouse.

Matthew loosened his hands and signed to Hannah, *Are you hurt?*

Hannah didn't move, looking pale in the light as Clyde glanced at her. He looked back at Matthew, smirking.

"I don't know what you're trying to do with that monkey language, but I'll tell you what happened. She asked me to help with developing a roll of film." He glanced at the chemical tray. Crumpled film floated in it. "Looks like you ruined it, boy."

There was something in the way he said *boy* that sent a chill down Matthew. Something old and familiar.

"You're fired."

"Suits me. This place gives me a headache."

Clyde half-turned and tipped his hat at Hannah. "Was a pleasure working with you, darling. You do really, really good work."

Hannah rushed in front of Matthew, putting both hands out to stop him from attacking Clyde. Story growled and Clyde laughed as he left.

Matthew stayed stiff and still until the bell jingled over the door with the man's departure.

He looked down at Hannah, her open palms inches from his chest. Her hands were shaking.

She had that same look Ruth Ann did after Maxwell accosted her. "No secrets, Hannah. Just tell me what happened."

Hannah lowered her hand as her eye released a tear. Up close and in the light of the lamp, he realized how red and terrified her eyes were. She swallowed and spoke rapidly.

"I was finishing type on the townsite article. Clyde was speaking to Hugh. Matthew, I'm almost certain he said that you 'ask an unhealthy amount of questions.'"

The chill Matthew felt earlier returned.

Clyde. He knew there was something familiar about that man.

Matthew searched Hannah's face, prompting her to go on. Maybe use his first name again.

She broke eye contact. "I got the camera and took a discreet photograph of him and started to develop it. But he came in and… stopped me."

She stared at the tray with the ruined film roll. Matthew wanted to lift her face to look at him, but he settled with a little wave in her line of sight. She yielded to it and looked up.

"Did he hurt you? Please, Hannah."

Another tear escaped and she quickly wiped it away. "When he heard Story barking, he let me go. He told me to say nothing or he would kill you."

Matthew gritted his teeth. "You need to go back home."

"I won't run again, Mr. Teller. That much I know."

The bell jingled and a few seconds later, Hugh was back at the press. He glanced through the open door to the dark room. "Oh, Mr. Teller. Sorry I stepped out a minute. Clyde asked me to get us sandwiches. He couldn't leave the telegraph, you know."

Matthew worked his jaw as he exited the dark room. "You can have both sandwiches."

Christopher Maxwell was tired of these clandestine meetings. He missed the days when he, Warren, Banny, and Carter could meet in the *Dickens Herald* office or the back rooms of the hotel to discuss their business dealings headquartered in the newly founded Dickens. Everything would have gone according to plan if it hadn't been for Matthew Teller.

Christopher was ready to shoot that Indian himself.

But Christopher was in too deep with this man who stood before him, staying near the half open window, smiling as though everything was going according to plan.

It wasn't.

Christopher squeezed his fingers around his empty shot glass. Being mayor-elect still didn't get rid of Matthew Teller.

"You said this would be over by now. That you had him where you wanted."

The man leaned against the window frame, crossing his arms and letting his jacket hang open to show off his low slung six-shooter. "Crucifixion is a slow death."

Christopher scoffed. "You said you attacked that deaf girl

because she seemed to recognize you. Does Teller know who you really are?"

"Nope."

Christopher snatched the whiskey bottle by its long neck and poured another glass, sloshing some over his hand. His vision was blurry, but the man's words came through clear.

"We just keep moving and stay buttoned up, everything will be all right. Trust me."

That was the problem. Christopher didn't trust this man no more that he had trusted the man's brother. But like then, he was stuck with him.

"Just get it done. Quick. Forget this crucifixion game."

"Not a chance. I'm enjoying it far too much."

The sound of the window closing ended the conversation. Christopher shifted the shot glass to his other hand and shook the whiskey droplets off. A stinging voice hit him from the parlor entrance.

"You shouldn't drink alone, dear."

Christopher jerked his head around to see his wife sauntering into the room. She had been drinking alone, that was obvious, but she still managed the mocking words he used when she was sobbing in the bedroom one night.

He grabbed the bottle and poured a shot for her. "Then join me, *dear*."

Dorothy crossed her arms, tight, as though trying to muster the willpower not to take the glass from him. He chuckled and downed his.

She hissed, "When are we going to go back east where we can live a civilized life?"

Christopher laughed. Loud. "As though you could live a civilized life in your condition."

Dorothy's expression melted and she rushed toward him, her eyes red and desperate. She gripped the lapels of his jacket and stared up at him, eyes pleading.

"Please, Christopher. We can go away somewhere, somewhere and can start over. You're a smart man and I'm young. Let's go away from all of this. We can be happy somewhere, just you and me—"

Christopher brought up one arm to dislodge her hands. He shoved her away.

She stumbled and landed on the sofa, her loose hair thrown back to show her once beautiful face. He thought he had a real prize when he deceitfully wooed this beautiful young woman into marrying him. It wasn't the only mistake he made in his life, but one of the biggest.

"You, me, happy? You never gave me children. An heir. That's all you were good for, and you failed."

Her face blanched. He had brought up the topic of children two years ago. That was when she started drinking alone.

Dorothy's demeanor changed as quickly as it had before. She shot up from the sofa and rushed him again, this time her fists out. She pounded his chest.

"I hate you! I wish they would hang you, then I could get a real man for myself. A man like Matthew Teller!"

Christopher threw his shot glass to the floor and grabbed her wrists in a death grip. He twisted them and she screamed.

He pressed close and waited until he felt in control of his voice before speaking. "You ever say that again, I'll kill you."

He squeezed tighter and she whimpered. He let her collapse at his feet. He paused, then lifted her roughly. "Maybe it is time we got to know one another again."

CHAPTER 49

St. Louis was busier than ever these days, reminding Matthew of how quickly a city could grow. Like Dickens.

He knew the way to the Carter home and hurried from the train station to that neighborhood, the telegram from Josiah Carter tucked in his pocket.

Since he was operating the telegraph himself, Matthew had received the message personally: *Have information for you. Come to my home. Friday. 2 PM. Josiah Carter.*

Matthew managed to hire a temporary telegraph operator, someone who was retired but looking for a bit of work. Matthew left the shop under Gentry's supervision.

Now he took the short walkway to Carter's home, up the steps, hand raised to knock on the door. He halted. The door was ajar.

He knocked anyway. The door creaked open at his touch. He listened. No sound came from inside.

Matthew leaned in and called, "Hello? Anyone home?"

He took a step inside and noted drops of blood on the floor. A trail led up the stairs.

Matthew shifted his coat back and withdrew the small pistol he kept holstered beneath it. He carefully mounted the stairs. One creaked and he winced but continued up.

At the top of the stairs, he glanced up and down the hallway. One door was cracked open. The blood trail led to it.

He crept toward the door, crouched. Staying to the side, he touched the door and it moved.

A gunshot exploded from inside the room and a bullet pierced the door above Matthew's head. He pressed against the wall, cocking the hammer on his pistol.

A woman screamed, "I said if you come back, I'd shoot you dead!"

Viona.

Matthew shouted, "Viona! It's Matthew Teller!"

The screaming stopped and Matthew took a breath to steady himself. "It's Matthew Teller from Dickens. Put your gun down."

"Matt Teller? What on God's green earth are you doing here?"

"I'll explain if you promise to stop shooting at me."

Viona's laugh sounded and he heard her say softly, "It's all right, babies, it's a friend."

Matthew uncocked and re-holstered his gun, cautiously pushing the door all the way open. The bullet had blown out a good chunk of the top half.

He spotted Viona barricaded with tea tables and two chairs in the far corner of the bedroom. She had one arm around her babies, and the other hand held a pistol resting now on the seat of one of the chairs. Her hair was ruffled, her dress torn.

Matthew straightened, staring at the wrecked room. Viona laughed again, tears in her voice.

"You should've seen the other fellow."

Viona started to stand but collapsed. Matthew rushed forward, eliciting screams from the children. He helped Viona into one of the chairs, her babies clinging to her skirts and crying.

Matthew knelt in front of her. "Who was the man, what did he look like?"

Viona shook her head. "You talk first. Give me a chance to catch my breath."

Matthew quickly told her about the telegraph he received from her husband. Viona cocked her head, her hair updo undone, falling over her shoulder.

"Joe didn't say nothing to me about meeting you here today. In fact, he told me he had a long business meeting downtown. Said he'd be late for supper."

Matthew's heart thudded.

Heavy footsteps sounded on the stairs along with a frantic voice calling, "Viona! Where are you, love?"

Viona shouted, "Up in the babies' bedroom."

To Matthew, she said, "I telephoned him right after I ran that skunk out of here."

Matthew quickly stood and backed away from the woman. This looked bad enough as it was.

Josiah Carter burst into the room, two uniformed policemen behind him. He rushed to his family and gathered them in his arms. Matthew noted the policemen zeroing in on him.

He lifted his hands to show they were empty. "I'm a friend of the family."

Josiah Carter stood, pulling Viona up in a tight grip beside him, his two babies curled in his other arm. He stared at Matthew.

"What are you doing here, Teller?"

This wasn't good. "I got a telegraph from you yesterday saying to meet you at your home today at 2 PM."

One of the policemen glanced at Carter. "That true, sir?"

Carter shook his head, deep confusion in his eyes. The policeman turned to Matthew with a hard stare. "You best come with us to the station."

Matthew instinctively took a step back. Another mistake. The officer whipped out his billy-club and slapped his palm with it.

Before anyone made another move, Viona pulled away from her husband and planted herself in front of the policemen, hands on her hips, her Irish brogue leaping to the forefront. "This here man said he's a friend and you better believe he is. This ain't the man that attacked me."

The officer glanced hesitantly between Carter, Viona, and Matthew. He settled on Viona. "Are you certain of that, ma'am? When your husband called the station, he said a man wearing a hood had attacked his wife. How can you be certain this isn't the man, come back and acting innocent?"

Viona huffed. "Don't you think I can tell two men apart? Asides that, I shot the devil. Nicked him in the arm. See the blood?"

She pointed at the blood outside the door. The policeman gave Matthew another long look then sheathed his club.

"I still need your name, where you came from, and why you're in the Carter home uninvited."

There was little point in Matthew repeating about the telegraph. If Carter didn't send it, only the man who had sent it knew why Matthew was there.

CHAPTER 50

"I really shouldn't show you this, but I just can't trust the Indian law-enforcement in this territory." Christopher Maxwell handed a letter to Earl Reynolds, his tone sincere and regretful.

Christopher's man had botched yet another attack and Christopher was doing what he could to salvage the mess and use it in his favor. He had little choice but to play the game the man's way now, getting them both in deeper than Christopher wanted.

He gestured to the fake letter he'd written himself as he sat at his desk in the *Dickens Herald* across from Reynolds. "Something's not right here."

He watched as Reynolds quickly read the letter, signed with the name "Josiah Carter." It was addressed to his friend Christopher Maxwell, telling how Matthew Teller was found after an attack on his wife. That Carter had always suspected Teller was capable of foul play.

Reynolds could easily uncover the facts of the case with a wire to the St. Louis police. But Christopher was gambling on the high emotions and prejudice of the man. His gamble paid off.

Reynolds looked up, eyes ablaze. "Why hasn't Matthew Teller been arrested?"

Christopher shrugged. "The police in St. Louis released him because Carter wouldn't press charges."

He motioned out the front window of his office. "You have to understand—this is Teller's town, his peoples' territory. And Teller still has an ax to grind with Carter. He accused Carter of trying to ruin his newspaper. Teller's a vengeful young man."

He cocked one brow at Reynolds. "As newsmen, we both know that everyone has a dark side."

Christopher was pleased when Reynolds included that turn of phrase in the article he submitted for the *Dickens Herald* to publish. Reynolds' article proclaimed that Matthew Teller had allegedly committed another atrocity, and no one would do anything about it. He added a nice touch of mentioning U.S. Marshal Daniel Garvin, who favored letting Indian prisoners off the hook for murder.

The folded newspaper landed *splat* in the middle of Daniel's chicken fried steak and mashed potatoes. The *everyone has a dark side* article was something he was already privy to. He didn't appreciate the article in the middle of his dinner at the Enterprise Hotel.

His eyes trailed up to the man standing over him with a wide grin, showing off white teeth against his black skin. "I hear that Teller character is your cousin."

Daniel plucked the newspaper out of his plate and tossed it to the center of the table. "Could be."

"Sounds like a mighty mean Indian."

Daniel shot to his feet to find the man a head shorter than him. He was the confident sort, bested Daniel by a decade, and sported matching six-shooters.

The fellow held his hands up in surrender. "Well now, Dead Man Dan, don't go drawing down on one of your own."

He used one finger to lift his coat back enough to reveal a United States Marshal badge pinned to his vest.

"Grinning Green, at your service. Bass sent me."

Daniel knew Aaron Green by reputation, and that he'd had

been out of commission the past several months, recovering from gunshot wounds received while taking on a band of five outlaws. He brought them all in, dead and half dead.

Daniel held in his sigh and pointed with his chin at the empty chair at his table.

"Marshal Reeves figures I need a nanny, that it?"

"Could be."

Daniel took his seat and stirred his mashed potatoes over the chicken fried steak. Marshal Green lifted the empty chair and swung it around backwards before throwing his short leg over to straddle it. His feet barely touched the floor.

"I reckon Judge Parker don't care to have one of his marshals smeared like that. Asides, I know something that's been going on in this territory that might have something to do with your cousin and the woman killer."

Daniel stilled. The man couldn't possibly understand how desperate Daniel was to find the killer. One, to stop the violence. Two, to save his cousin. Matthew had always been there for Daniel when he needed him.

There was that time on the Red River when he was a young, expectant father caught in quicksand with the river rising to claim his life. Matthew had kept him calm until Preston came along with the solution to get Daniel out.

That incident paled in comparison to the day of Daisy and their little boy's funeral.

Their bodies were laid out on the bed in the cabin. Daniel couldn't bear to be away from her and had slept on the floor. When the time came, Preston and his three sons arrived at the cabin and carried his wife out. Melinda carried the baby.

Daniel was curled on the floor, shaking. Matthew came in and lifted Daniel to his feet, throwing one arm around his stronger shoulders and helping him out to the graves of his little family.

Daniel met Marshal Green's steady gaze. "Matthew Teller wouldn't hurt anyone."

"I heard tell what he did to that other newspaper publisher at the courthouse. Laid him out flat."

"He deserved it."

Green shrugged. "Likely so. Anyhow, I don't believe Matthew Teller's guilty of hurtin' women. Bass said he's a good man. That's enough for me. So I'll help you prove it by finding the real killer. After I have myself one of those steaks." Marshal Green grinned.

Daniel reached across his plate and offered his hand to shake. "We might make a passable team."

Marshal Green shook his hand hard, sending Daniel's elbow into his steak dinner.

"Dead Man Dan and Grinning Green. I like the sound of that."

Daniel and Marshal Green headed to the *Choctaw Tribune* office, shoulder to shoulder. Well, with Green well below Daniel's shoulder. But he had no trouble keeping up, taking two quick steps to Daniel's one stride. Daniel found himself having to pick up his pace.

Daniel had traveled to Dickens to talk with Hannah Stillwater about what had happened with the man called Clyde. If this man was the one who threatened Matthew, it put him in the right location where the string of violence started. Daniel might have found his man.

They entered the shop to find it empty except for Henry Levitt at the back of the shop with his woodworking. He glanced up and nodded at the odd pair of marshals before continuing his work.

Daniel was surprised to see Hannah Stillwater seated at Matthew's desk, typing on his Remington. The only ones Daniel ever saw at that desk were Matthew or Ruth Ann. Somehow, though, this woman fit there as well as them.

And man, was she pretty. Had Matthew noticed? He didn't

seem to have at Ruth Ann's wedding, which was the only time Daniel had seen Hannah Stillwater—at a distance.

He didn't know how to talk to her, though. Matthew said she read lips, but she hadn't looked their way yet. The dog laying on the floor next to her sat up as Daniel approached.

"Miss Hannah Stillwater?"

The dog pawed at her dress. She glanced down then up to see Daniel and Green. She quickly stood.

"Marshal Garvin, isn't it? I'm afraid Mr. Teller isn't here this evening. We were just about to close up shop."

"I've actually come to see you, Miss Stillwater. We need to talk to you about what happened with Clyde. This is…" Daniel turned to nod at the man beside him. "…U.S. Marshal Green."

"Pardon, I didn't catch that," Hannah said.

Daniel quickly faced her again, embarrassed. "Sorry. This is Marshal Aaron Green out of Fort Smith. He's tagging along on my investigation."

Green harrumphed and reached out to shake Hannah's hand. "You sayin' you can read this fool's lips the way he talks?"

Hannah smiled congenially. "I can even read yours."

Green threw his head back with a raucous laugh. "Well, I'll be dipped!"

Hannah turned her attention back to Daniel. "Before we get into questions, how is Glenrose? I understand your brother-in-law has been staying close to her."

Daniel grimaced. "She regained consciousness but hasn't been able to speak. Don't know if she'll ever be able to give us a description of the man who attacked her."

A thought shot like a lightning bolt through his mind and he stared at Hannah. She looked taken aback. "Is something wrong, Marshal Garvin?"

"How would you feel about taking a train ride down to Paris this evening?"

Right at dusk, Daniel, Hannah Stillwater, Marshal Green, and Peter gathered around Glenrose Jessop's bed. The young girl was propped up on pillows to sip the soup Peter was feeding her. She didn't look a great deal better than the last time Daniel had seen her, but at least she was sitting up.

Peter warned them not to tire her out with a bunch of questions. Daniel promised to keep it brief. He sat on the edge of a chair next to her bed.

"Miss Glenrose, I know you're not much up for talking about what happened. But I need to know a few things in order to find the man that did this. Now, you know this lady here, Hannah Stillwater. She works at the *Choctaw Tribune*. She can tell me what you're saying if you just move your lips."

Daniel gestured toward Hannah, realizing too late he'd kept his back to her. He turned enough to speak to Glenrose with Hannah able to see his lips.

"Just mouth your answers and she'll tell me what you said. Now, can you tell me what the man looked like?"

Glenrose continued staring at the far wall of the hospital, eyes glassy. Daniel wondered if she'd comprehended anything he said.

Hannah touched his shoulder. "May I try, Marshal Garvin?"

He nodded and vacated the chair, letting her take a seat. She leaned forward and gently took Glenrose's hand. "Let's just start with the eyes, Glenrose. One word. What color were they?"

Daniel watched their hands and was sure he saw Glenrose tighten hers around Hannah's. Her eyes still didn't move, but her lips did. It was so faint, Daniel had no idea if she'd actually formed a word or not. But Hannah glanced up at him quickly.

"Brown."

Instead of asking Glenrose another question, Daniel directed it at Hannah. "What color are Clyde's eyes?"

"Brown."

Though he wanted to narrow in on that man, three fourths of the men in Indian Territory had brown eyes, him included. And Matthew Teller.

Daniel motioned for Hannah to continue. Word by word, she drew a little bit more out of the girl: The man had worn a hood with a cord securing it, same as Sissy Coxwell and Viona Carter described. His height and weight could match Clyde as well. And Matthew.

Marshal Green, who had stayed back to not overcrowd the girl, stepped to the foot of the bed, and leaned his small hands on the railing. He pushed his hat up so Glenrose would be able to see his face easily. "Darling, I'm Marshal Green. I got one question for you. Was it Matthew Teller that attacked you?"

Peter sputtered, but Daniel held up a hand to quiet him. Glenrose blinked and for the first time, Daniel saw her eyes trying to focus. There was a shadow over them, and his heart skipped a beat. Her lips moved with a few words.

Hannah turned to look at Daniel. "She said 'No, it wasn't him.' What did you ask her?"

While Daniel was relieved that the girl was able to articulate it wasn't Matthew, so had the other women. At least Green was able to see that for himself.

Daniel answered Hannah, "We'll talk about it on the train. We best get you back to Dickens now before it gets late."

Daniel intended to keep riding the train all the way to Fort Smith that night. He had to check through all the criminal records and Wanted posters at the United States Marshals office. There had to be something about Clyde in them.

If only he had that photograph Hannah had taken, rather than just the man's description. But he was going to run him to ground regardless. He was getting close to the killer. He could feel it.

Before they left, Daniel pulled Peter aside and had him tell Marshal Green about the gamblers at the Red River. Green knew more about the criminals in Indian Territory than he did, and Daniel wanted to see if he could pick up anything helpful from Peter's story.

Peter was hesitant but spilled the whole thing. Green didn't indicate it was anything new, and Peter headed back to Glenrose.

He halted and turned back. "Something I didn't mention to anyone, didn't think about it much, but maybe it's something. When I first got there and was talking to those men, they asked if I knew any pretty young girls looking for high-paying work. That was another reason I didn't mind skinning their hides in that bet."

CHAPTER 52

M atthew blew out the lamp at his desk, the only light in the *Choctaw Tribune* office. He hadn't bothered lighting the large chandelier when he came to the office after hours. Hannah had locked up as he asked her to and stowed Story at the box house, but he was disturbed by her note on his desk, saying she'd gone down to Paris with Marshal Green to see Glenrose Jessop. He didn't like the thought of her out roaming around. But then Glenrose had been attacked right there in Dickens. He knew Daniel would look after Hannah.

He'd come straight to the shop when he arrived back in town after his trip to see Chief Gardner. The chief had sent a wire earlier that day, asking Matthew to visit. Matthew was leery of being lured into another trap, but this really had come from the chief.

Chief Gardner wasn't happy with the article in the *Dickens Herald* and warned Matthew that whatever had started the vicious story war between him and Maxwell, that Matthew needed to stop it. The Choctaw people didn't need the bad press about violence and corruption in their nation.

At least Matthew could show him a letter he'd received

284

from Carter, confirming that Carter hadn't sent Maxwell information about the attack. Maxwell had known what he was doing when he baited Earl Reynolds with a fake letter from Carter.

A lie can make it halfway around the world while the truth is still putting on its boots, so the saying went among reporters.

Matthew thought he had to write his response to Reynolds' article when he returned, only to find a typed outline draft on his desk with Hannah's note. She'd written such a detailed outline based on Carter's letter he showed her, that he could well use it as the article instead of writing a new one. She'd wisely tamed it down to a professional tone. That should help satisfy the chief for now.

He'd heard Earl Reynolds was still in Dickens, staying at the Enterprise Hotel. Matthew intended to show him the real letter from Carter, along with a copy of the police report, first thing in the morning. Matthew doubted those would convince the aggressive reporter of Maxwell's duplicity, but maybe he would think at least once before writing garbage.

It was well past dark when Matthew stepped onto the boardwalk. There was no one about the streets of Dickens this time of night, so he'd have a quiet walk home. Or so he hoped. He sensed a presence nearby.

Matthew turned the key in the lock and spun around to catch whoever was sneaking up on him, half expecting John Bellanger or even Clyde with a gun leveled on him. It was neither.

It was Dorothy Maxwell.

Matthew frowned as the woman put a hand on the supporting post of the porch as she stepped onto the boardwalk from the dirt street. She stumbled.

Matthew reached out to break her fall, grabbing her arm and holding her upright. He could smell alcohol spilled on her baby blue silk dress with its plunging neckline.

"Mrs. Maxwell. You should be home."

She coughed out a dry, humorless laugh. "That is the last place in the world I want to be ever."

Matthew guided her toward the street. "You'd better go along now."

"Matthew."

The intimacy in her voice caused him to release her arm like it was on fire. She faced him, eyes dripping from tears or the alcohol. Her words came out slow and helpless.

"Matthew. You don't…know what it's like. That man abuses me…every day. That's why I drink, to escape the pain and humiliation of being Mrs. Christopher Maxwell."

Matthew's instinct told him to get away from this woman. Now.

"Mrs. Maxwell, if you're having trouble with your husband, you need to go to the U.S. Marshals. At least talk to Pastor Rand. He can help you. Have a good evening."

Matthew tipped his hat and started for the street. Dorothy Maxwell fell toward him, grabbing onto his coat.

"I don't want a marshal or a preacher. I want you! Please, Matthew, help me. I can tell you everything, every illegal thing that Chris has done in Indian Territory. If you only knew the filthy operation he runs. Please. Take me away please, get me away from him!"

Matthew tried to pull back even as the gears in his mind turned. Dorothy Maxwell would know a great deal, if not all, of Maxwell's secrets. All the secrets Matthew was working to uncover.

But he couldn't get them from her. He needed to get away from her.

He grabbed her hands and tried to dislodge them from his coat, but she hung on like a tick burying its head.

"Mrs. Maxwell, let go. There's nothing I can do to help you. Not like this."

"Exactly like this."

Dorothy Maxwell yanked on his coat, stretching up on her tiptoes, trying to kiss him.

Matthew twisted away in an effort to break loose without hurting her.

There was only one thing he could do. Get biblical—as in the story of Joseph.

Matthew ducked and twisted out of his coat, tearing fabric. He gave a final yank and pulled free, straightening just in time to ram face first into the porch post. He stumbled into the street and kept going. Didn't look back or yield to the cries behind him. He kept up a jog all the way down Main Street and to the security of the little box house by the railroad tracks.

Inside, Matthew slammed and locked the door then leaned back against it. Story, who had barked at his abrupt entrance, bounced around his feet.

He wiped sweat from his brow and found his forehead wetter than it should be. He lowered his hand to see the red of his own blood on the back of it.

He pushed away from the door and into the former sewing room. He fumbled at one of his mother's shelves where she had left a stack of scraps. He got one and pressed it against the cut on his forehead.

What he really wished for was his mother to bandage the wound and tell him he'd done the right thing and tell him what to do next.

He was in shock over Dorothy Maxwell's raw and brazen act. He needed coffee or a pen and paper or something.

He went back into the living room and sat on the edge of the sofa, resting his elbows on his knees and letting Story nudge her way to rest her chin on his leg like a warm hug. He stroked the top of her head.

"I wish all females were as easy as you, girl."

CHAPTER 53

Christopher Maxwell watched his wife walk up the road, stumbling on her own skirts. He let the curtain drop on their second floor bedroom window and downed his third shot of brandy.

He stood quiet in the semi-dark room with the note she'd left him. He listened to the front door open and close. She would come upstairs first, come to find her bottle that he'd smashed against the fireplace in their bedroom.

Her footsteps thumped on the stairs. When she was halfway up, he turned from the window, set his glass on the nightstand, and exited the bedroom to the hallway that overlooked the foyer below. The hallway was lit by cranberry wall lamps, but she wasn't looking up and didn't realize he was standing there until she reached the top of the stairs. She was dragging a brown jacket but drew it up to her chest when she saw Christopher staring at her.

"I got your note, dear."

Dorothy blanched as though she'd forgotten she left it. But color rushed back in her face just as quickly and she put on her cattiest smile.

"Then you know I'm leaving you. Matthew Teller is taking me away. He'll give me the happiness you were never capable of."

Christopher tried to laugh. It came out as a sneer. He held up the note, inches from her face.

"Teller is a fool, but he's not that big of one. You're lying, just like every word in this, saying how you two have been secret lovers for the past year and that's why he's out to destroy me. You're nothing but a little—"

She screamed over him, "You'll never be half the man that Matthew Teller is, and that's the God-honest truth!"

Maybe it was the sincerity of her words, the way she actually believed them, that tipped Christopher over the edge.

He took a mighty backhand swing at her face, whacking her hard and sending her staggering. There was nothing for her to grab as she fell backwards down the stairs. Her scream stopped halfway down but her body didn't as she flipped and flailed to the bottom.

Christopher froze at the top of the stairs, staring at the unmoving form of his wife at the bottom. He took a few tentative steps down then hurried to the bottom. He turned her face up, Matthew Teller's coat still tangled around her.

"Dorothy?"

He put his hand around her throat as he had once done in choking her. This time, he didn't feel the life of her blood pulsing beneath his hand.

From somewhere in the darkness of the house, a wholly evil voice said, "Well now. Isn't this just perfect?"

CHAPTER 54

The telephone rang. It was a foreign sound in the little box house, one Matthew wasn't accustomed to. Especially for it to ring so late in the evening. He pushed himself off the sofa and to the wall by the kitchen where he'd positioned the telephone within easy reach of any room in the house.

"Hello, Matthew Teller here."

The line crackled but no one said anything. Matthew repeated, "Hello?"

A raspy voice came over the line. "I know what happened between you and my wife. I want to get it straightened out privately, tonight. I have a newspaper to publish tomorrow."

It was the first time Matthew had heard Christopher Maxwell's voice over the telephone. It was no more pleasant than in person. Neither was the topic he was calling about.

Matthew contemplated the request. Was Maxwell planning to shoot him? Or did he really want to keep the embarrassing incident quiet?

The northbound Frisco train whistled. Daniel would be on it and likely stay the night with Matthew. He doubted Maxwell would shoot him in the presence of a U.S. Marshal, even an Indian one.

And Matthew had a newspaper to publish, too. He wanted to put the incident with Mrs. Maxwell behind him.

"I'll be over shortly."

When Matthew replaced the receiver on the wall mount, he cringed to see the blood he'd smeared on it. He would clean it up later.

He had to forgo a hat but in the kitchen he found the old work coat he used for tending chores. It was a warm evening, but he felt too informal without a coat.

There was something else he needed to take care of when he saw the man, too. Tell him he forgave him. Simple.

This hardly seemed the time to do it, but maybe it was the hardest time that meant the most.

Matthew went out the front door, leaving Story inside. On the porch, he observed a single figure reaching for the gate on the white picket fence in front of the box house. It wasn't Daniel.

The train whistle blew as Hannah Stillwater opened the gate and came through, having already spotted him on the porch.

"Good evening, Mr. Teller. Marshal Garvin asked me to give you an update on his investigation. He was watching from the train window, wanted to make sure I was safe." She smiled as she came up the porch steps. "He said to make sure you escort me…"

She stared at him, and Matthew knew he'd done a poor job at washing off the blood in the kitchen basin before donning his jacket. He imagined the cut on his forehead was pretty ugly, based on the lump he felt there.

Her eyes widened. "Are you all right?"

Hannah being there presented problems and solutions. He'd need to see her safely to the Monarch, but he also needed a witness at Christopher Maxwell's.

"Do you feel like taking a stroll?"

Hannah nodded and Matthew led the way down the stairs and through the gate. He asked Hannah to share Daniel's news. She told him how she'd been able to read Glenrose's lips enough to get a cursory description of the attacker. Daniel was convinced it was Clyde and was returning to Fort Smith to see what records he could find on the man.

"Now, would you please tell me what happened to you while I was away? I wasn't gone long and look at the trouble you got yourself into."

Matthew grimaced and paused under a streetlight so Hannah would be able to see his lips. "I shouldn't drag you into this and I'll take you on to the hotel from here if you want."

Leaving out as much detail as possible, Matthew explained what happened with Mrs. Maxwell, and how Mr. Maxwell wanted to straighten things out. Matthew ended with admitting it could be ugly.

Hannah's gaze didn't waver. "I am willing to go with you, Mr. Teller. If you trust me to be a reliable witness."

"Why would I doubt you?"

Hannah's lips tipped into a frown. "There is a man from my past, a former teacher, who ridiculed me for being deaf. He was fired for it and since then, has spent an inordinate amount of time making it difficult for me to keep a job. He wrote letters to my employers, accusing me of being a liar and thief. I'm sure he would have contacted you after you ran that article with my byline. You may as well know now before you position me as a witness for you."

Matthew didn't know why, but her story made him chuckle. She looked at him, quizzical.

He shrugged. "I'm just thinking how we're in the same boat, Miss Stillwater. Accused of doing things we'd rather die before doing. I'm not worried about your reputation. It's not as bad as mine."

She put a finger to her chin as if regarding him in deep thought. "You know, Mr. Teller, I shouldn't have worried about you hitting your head. I don't think anything could ever crack through that thickness."

Matthew laughed and offered her his arm. She took it and they continued their stroll.

When they neared the Maxwell home, Hannah spoke, her voice soft beside him, but she was close enough for him to hear her every word.

"You are quite a man, Matthew Teller. With quite a mission. I...I am sorry I left."

Matthew halted and turned to her. Her eyes were the Blue River—just as powerful and captivating and constant.

She opened her mouth to say more and Matthew held himself very still. She released his arm and slowly lifted her hands. She went slow, making exaggerated signs, her eyes pleading for him to understand the words she spoke.

He understood. At least, he hoped he did.

I am sorry I closed the door on you.

She held her hands open toward him, an offering. Matthew touched the back of her hand with his and felt his being change.

"Hannah..." His gaze drifted over her shoulder, toward Maxwell's home, seeking the nearest light source. He didn't want her to mistake anything he said in the dark.

But something was wrong.

The front door of Maxwell's home hung wide open, a single lamp illuminating some of the foyer's nooks and shadowing others.

Matthew glanced at Hannah, wondering if he should have her stay back, remembering the bullet Viona shot at his head in St. Louis. Instead, he motioned for Hannah to stay behind him as he went up the steps and peered around the door.

The lamp revealed no one sitting in the parlor. Sweeping his gaze to the right, Matthew saw the crumpled form of Dorothy Maxwell at the bottom of the stairs.

Matthew rushed forward, Hannah close behind him. He knelt by the woman and pressed his hand against her neck. He didn't need to. He could tell from the utter stillness of her body that she was dead.

Hannah knelt on the woman's other side, hand over her mouth.

Footsteps sounded on the porch and Matthew turned, still squatted. Hannah caught his movement and looked toward the door.

In stepped Christopher Maxwell, looking around quickly as though surprised to find his door open. When he saw Matthew, he whipped out a pistol.

Earl Reynolds appeared from behind Maxwell, horror and disgust immediately registering on his face.

Matthew wasn't sure if Reynolds' presence saved his life in that moment or if Maxwell was too cool and calculating to kill in blind vengeance.

Maxwell, hand shaking in fury, passed off his cocked pistol to Reynolds. "Keep him covered. I'm going for the doctor!"

Reynolds took the gun like he knew how to use it and kept it trained on Matthew.

"I knew you were a woman killer, you dirty Indian. And you! Step away from him." He waved the gun in Hannah's direction.

Matthew slowly stood, glancing at Hannah who was pale and trembling. She glanced at Matthew, raising her hand to brush loose strands of hair from her face. Her fingers twitched and Matthew caught her motion.

Thumb, middle finger, and index finger extended, making an L-shape. Two fingers tucked in and palm facing forward. Thumb on temple, move the index finger and middle finger down and up together.

The sign for *horse*.

Matthew stepped over Dorothy's body to get between

Hannah and Reynolds. "Take it easy, Reynolds. This isn't what it appears."

Behind him, he heard Hannah making tracks for the dining room. Good. She could reach the kitchen and back door from there.

Reynolds spotted her. "Hey! Come back here!"

Matthew held his hands up, palms forward. "She's deaf and scared. And she had nothing to do with this. If you'll just lower that pistol, I'll explain why I'm here."

"I can see the reason plain enough. At least she got one good swipe at you before you assaulted her."

The split in Matthew's forehead wasn't doing him any favors.

Matthew kept his hands out, thinking about the pistol in his waistband. But Reynolds did look like he knew how to use that gun. And he looked more than willing to.

"I knew from the first time I saw you that you had bad blood. Never known an Indian not to turn savage no matter how civilized you get. I'll see you hang for the women you've attacked and killed."

Matthew took a step away from Mrs. Maxwell's body, edging a little closer to Reynolds.

"I know it won't do any good to tell you this, but I didn't kill her. I got here just a few moments before you and Maxwell. I don't know what happened other than it was very convenient for him to call me over here and then for me to be found kneeling over his dead wife."

Reynolds sneered. "So, he called you over here, just like Carter sent you a telegram to come up there, and like Mr. Coxwell asked you to check on his wife? You're full of it, Teller. Christopher Maxwell called me not fifteen minutes ago and asked me to meet him at the *Dickens Herald*. He forgot one of the papers he was going to give me though, which is why we came back here. Just in time. Or not so much for her."

He motioned toward the body and Matthew took the moment of distraction to inch closer to him.

Reynolds jerked the pistol up, aiming square at Matthew's chest. "Take one more step, Indian. I sure would like you to."

From where he stood, Matthew could see out the window and down the street. There were some men coming at a fast clip. But it wasn't Christopher Maxwell and the doctor.

The few turned into a dozen and then more. Several carried lamps and one illuminated the face of John Bellanger. How long had he been in town?

Matthew didn't plan to stick around for the answer. He recognized a lynch mob gathering when he saw it.

The growing rumble reached Reynolds and he turned to look out the open door.

Matthew lunged for his gun hand, pushing it away as the gun went off. He jammed his elbow in Reynolds' jaw, ripping the pistol away. He sprinted down the hall to what he hoped would be access to the kitchen and back door.

Reynolds yelled and pursued him. Matthew hit the kitchen door, glancing back long enough to see Reynolds trip on the hall table, sending the lamp clattering to the floor. Flames shot along the trail of kerosene.

Matthew fled.

The new streets that had been added around Maxwell's home made it harder for Matthew to make a beeline for the box house, but he was able to weave his way through homes and business as the shouting grew louder behind him. They were pursuing, despite the fire started in Maxwell's home.

Matthew ran straight for the backyard of the house where he found Hannah leading Falama out of the barn, saddled and ready to ride.

Matthew didn't break his stride. He tucked Maxwell's pistol in his trousers with his own pistol, grabbed the reins from Hannah, and swung aboard. He reached down and grabbed her arm. She vaulted on behind him and he dug his heels into Falama's side.

They took off with a leap. They gained the south road and plunged into darkness away from the town lights before the bullets started flying.

CHAPTER 55

Matthew let Falama charge up the trail in the moonlit darkness at a full gallop. He'd brought his horse on this trail before, getting him accustomed to roaming the mountains with saddle and man on his back instead of as he had since he was born, running with a herd of wild horses on Blackjack Mountain. They hadn't done it in the dark though. Nor riding double.

Growing up on the Blue River with the stock of horses Matthew saw at the Stillwater homestead led him to believe Hannah could ride horseback. He hoped and prayed he was right as the horse shifted, gathered himself, stumbled, and surged beneath them up the mountain trail.

Skidding down a steep embankment, Falama lost his footing and went sideways. Matthew drew his head around and urged him on to regain his footing as they made for the other side of the embankment.

Matthew knew this area well. He and Philip used to hunt there when they were boys living at Uncle Preston's ranch.

When they crested the embankment, near the top of the low

mountain, Matthew reined Falama to a halt, circling him to check down the trail. The mob, on horseback, was gaining on them.

Matthew twisted in the saddle, motioning for Hannah to get off. He held his arm stiff while she used it to slide to the ground. As soon as she was off, Matthew swung off the other side and slapped Falama on the rump, sending him flying down the trail. The stallion would relish the chance to run free. Matthew didn't know if he would ever see him again.

Taking Hannah's hand, he pulled her through a patch of pines and brush to where the ground abruptly ended. They stood on the edge of a cliff.

The expanse yawned before them, the tops of 40-foot tall pines etched into the night sky view.

Matthew could feel the thunder of the wild riders closing in. He looked at Hannah, slowed his breathing, and mouthed, *Do you trust me?*

Her hair, torn apart in the ride, hung loose over her shoulders. She brushed it away from her forehead. "Yes."

Matthew groaned inwardly. He almost wished she didn't.

He released her, turned, and leaped off the cliff.

Hannah covered her mouth to press back the scream in her throat as Matthew Teller jumped off the cliff.

In a flash, she envisioned what her life would be like without him. It was suddenly something she couldn't even imagine.

Then she saw the hard sway of the pine tree across and below her. The moonlight illuminated its luscious evergreen branches, thick even at its top. Within those limbs, Hannah spotted Matthew Teller clinging to the trunk and waving wildly at her.

He wanted her to jump.

Hannah dropped her hands from her mouth and sucked in a breath. She glanced over her shoulder and saw the mob not far down the trail and coming fast. Though she was camouflaged by a patch of trees, they still might see her.

She trusted Matthew Teller.

Drawing in a fortifying breath, Hannah gathered her skirts and her courage. She leaped, letting go of her skirts, hands outstretched to grab for tree limbs as they thoroughly slapped and scratched her.

A strong arm wrapped around her waist and pulled her to the trunk of the pine. She hung onto it for dear life.

Her hair was in her eyes, and she couldn't see a thing. She stilled. The men must be passing about now.

After another minute, Matthew shifted and she realized he was still holding her tight against the trunk. She twisted around until her feet found a sturdy branch to brace against. He must have felt the pressure release so he loosened his hold. Still holding to the trunk, she tossed her head to get the hair out of her eyes and found him close.

She barely deciphered his words. "We are going to climb down, one branch at a time. I'll be partway below you."

He shifted to begin the climb down. She squinted to try and determine where he put his hands and feet. She followed carefully, noting how he stayed in a position to catch her if she fell.

It took several minutes to reach the base of the pine. As soon as her feet touched the ground, Hannah's knees gave way and she collapsed with a ludicrous giggle.

"I never thought I'd escape from a posse quite like that."

Matthew knelt in front of her. It was easy to see his face in the moonlight. He tried to smile but failed. He hadn't meant to put her in this kind of danger.

When he said nothing, she offered a smile. "It's all right, Mr. Teller. I'm all right."

He closed his eyes briefly then opened them and said, "There's a cave close where we can hide until those hot tempers cool."

Matthew helped her up and guided her to an opening at the base of the cliff. He held up his hand to hold her back while he made sure nothing else occupied the cave.

It was just deep enough for them to crawl into, and Hannah released a deep sigh once they did. They were safe.

CHAPTER 56

They sat still in the cave for half an hour. At one point, Matthew put his finger to his lips to signal Hannah to be completely quiet. He could hear horses and men shouting above them. The posse had found his horse and double-backed, looking for him.

They would never find them under this ledge, unless they jumped to the pine tree as he and Philip had done many times. The only other way the cave could be reached was to discover the path one mile away that led to the creek below, then climb up the steep path to reach the ledge.

The mob didn't linger at the cliff. Their sounds gradually faded and vanished. Hot tempers burned out fast once they lost sight of the object of their fury. They would regroup and restart the search in the morning. By then, Daniel should have heard what happened and would be on Matthew's trail.

Matthew shifted to stretch his legs out of the cave after the cramped position he had held. Hannah stretched out as well, sighing.

She signed to him, but he wasn't quite sure what she said. Something about leaving. He shook his head. "We better stay here the night, wait for Daniel to get back and clean up this mess."

She squinted and he could tell she couldn't see his lips well in the dark cave. He scooted close to the edge where the moonlight shined on his face. "We will stay here the night."

As he said it again, he realized what an inappropriate proposition he'd made. His cheeks burned hot, but he didn't know what else to do.

They could try to make it to Uncle Preston's, but the lynch mob might go there looking for him.

He wished he could warn his family, but if those men decided to cause trouble at the ranch, they would regret it. Preston and his sons and ranch hands were well armed and always on the lookout for trouble. They had dealt with outlaws crossing the Red River from Texas and trying to wreak havoc on the ranch. They were ready for most anything, even a lynch mob hunting Preston's nephew.

To his relief, Hannah nodded. "I thought we would. What I asked though, was if the men chasing us are gone?"

Matthew sighed. "Sorry. My sign language isn't progressing like it should."

"The fact you even want to learn is remarkable."

He wanted to become more fluent in the coming days. If there were any coming days for him.

Matthew drew his knees up to rest his elbows on them and clasped his hands together. His skin smarted from the pine bark cuts. "From the day I met you, I knew you were one of the most remarkable people I'd ever known. For the longest time, I thought it was just admiration I felt. I guess that's why I made such a fool of myself at the Monarch that night."

He swallowed. He had to stop talking.

Hannah took a shaky breath, eyes on his face in her searching way. He looked at the granite rock wall behind her.

More words spilled out. "I wanted to say so many things then.

How smart and courageous and funny you are. How kind and generous and wise. How amazed I was that you'd chosen to stay at the *Choctaw Tribune* after so much mudslinging and outright danger. And I wanted to ask you right. I didn't do any of it right."

"You can ask me again, Matthew."

He dared to meet her eyes, only for a moment, only to see if she meant it.

She did.

Matthew clenched his hands even as his heart clenched in pain. He couldn't ask her. Not now.

He was facing accusations of killing two white women, and attacking two others, and an Indian woman. His prospects for the future weren't promising.

But then, this wasn't in the future. Not yet.

He teetered on the verge of asking Hannah if he could court her. If he could marry her. If he could kiss her right there in the moonlight.

She would likely shut the door in his face again.

Matthew released his stinging hands and rubbed them on the sides of his trousers. His nerves were stretched tight enough to snap.

"I'll be back."

He pulled himself out of the cave and to his feet. He skidded down the steep incline, not finding the path and getting slashed in the face with tree branches. Once that stopped, he jogged to the bank of the creek. He knelt and scooped up handfuls of the icy mountain water to splash on his face. The cold burned the cut on his head and the fresher cuts from the mad dash through the mountain.

He brought up two more handfuls to dump over his head. The cold water ran down his neck and back.

Matthew sat, wondering how to contemplate a future that was nowhere in sight.

Hannah leaned her head against the cave wall in the darkness after Matthew Teller disappeared into the woods near the pine tree they'd jumped to. His absence left an emptiness around and inside her.

She stared at the moon in the complete silence of her world. She was the one who was foolish. Foolish to want this good man to take her into his life.

Yet Hannah prayed for it with all her heart.

She lowered her gaze from the moon and saw Matthew standing near the pine tree. He was waiting for her to see him so he wouldn't frighten her.

How, in a few months, had he learned how to be with her?

He approached and squatted in front of her. He offered his old work coat. "Try and get some sleep. I'll be over by the trail, keeping watch."

She accepted the coat and he rose quickly. Going back to the pine tree, he leaned against a head high boulder positioned above what she assumed was the trail they would eventually take to leave.

She found as comfortable a position as she could on the uneven cave floor and drew the coat over her. It smelled of horses, earth, and ink. It smelled of Matthew Teller.

CHAPTER 57

*D*aniel had never faced a lynch mob before, wearing a badge and expected to bring law and order. At least Grinning Green was there to back him up.

Daniel wouldn't mind if Green took charge, but his fellow marshal had yielded to Daniel's lead after they rode in at a gallop to Dickens.

When the train had stopped at Tuskahoma, the station-master rushed onto it, calling for the U.S. Marshals, saying a white woman had been killed in Dickens by Matthew Teller. Daniel and Green got their horses from the livestock car and rode back.

By the time they arrived in Dickens, the mob who had been out chasing Daniel's cousin had returned for supplies and fresh horses. Their tempers hadn't cooled.

Green and Daniel now stood on the porch of Christopher Maxwell's home after checking the scene of what appeared to be a brutal murder. The smell of smoke clung to Daniel's clothes. The hall had caught fire. It was a miracle the house hadn't burned. It could have taken the whole town out in the summer's dryness.

The mob had gathered at the porch of Maxwell's house, ready for the man to lead the hunt.

Daniel raised his hands for quiet. "Like I said, I'm not swearing in a posse of men carrying hangman nooses on every saddle horn. You all go home. I will find Matthew Teller myself and bring him in for questioning."

The crowd erupted, and one man jeered. "We know you're kin to Matthew Teller, and that the Choctaw Lighthorsemen never bring in a relative. You'll give him a fresh mount to ride out on!"

Daniel's hand itched to draw his gun and fire a warning shot in the air, let these men know he meant business. But he settled for crossing his arms.

"If you know who I am, then you know I am a United States Marshal, sworn to uphold the law even in Indian Territory. But the only way I can do my job is for you all to go home. Now!"

Shouts and shaking of ropes answered him. "We know Teller killed that woman!"

Christopher Maxwell moved from the shadows of the porch and to Daniel's side. Daniel started to order him to go inside the house, but Maxwell raised his hands and addressed the crowd.

"The marshal is right. This territory will be a state someday and we want to do our part to bring civilization to Indian Territory. That effort may cost me everything. It's already cost me so much."

Maxwell's voice cracked. He turned and went inside the house.

Daniel gritted his teeth. "We all want law and order and I'll see that takes place. I'll have Matthew Teller in custody by morning."

Daniel skipped down the porch steps and shouldered his way through the crowd that begrudgingly parted. Marshal Green followed, and they rode out of town toward the mountain where Matthew had escaped, Falama in tow. The horse had found his way back to the Teller barn.

Once they cleared town, Green whistled. "You did pretty fair back there, Dead Man Dan. Mighty big promise to bring your cousin in by morning, though."

Daniel didn't reply, didn't want to think of how his nickname was because he had never brought a man in alive.

CHAPTER 58

The first streaks of dawn cast shadows across Hannah's face as she lay sleeping. Matthew bent low so she would recognize him and gave her shoulder a gentle shake.

She shifted, yawning. Then her eyes popped open. He quickly put a finger over his lips. She quietly sat up and he mouthed, *Someone coming up the trail. Stay low.*

She nodded, his coat slipping down from her shoulders. Her hair was a tangled mess and there were dark circles under her eyes, pink whelps on her cheeks from the pine tree encounter.

She was beautiful.

Matthew crept back out of the cave and to the boulder, drawing both pistols from his belt. He pressed against the rock and watched the trail. From the racket he heard, there were at least two horses coming.

Matthew cocked the pistol in his right hand and steadied his aim with the side of the boulder.

A horse whinnied and the trail yielded Daniel.

Matthew rested his sore forehead on his outstretched arm, tension draining from his body. He straightened, uncocked and tucked away the pistols.

He turned back toward the cave where Hannah was watching him intensely. He finger spelled *Daniel*. Her features relaxed.

His cousin had spotted him and pulled up his horse, Falama in tow.

Matthew gave a wave. "I was wondering when you would show up, stranger."

Daniel dismounted, looking more grim than Matthew had hoped. He didn't blame his cousin.

He imagined the wild stories flying around Dickens, combined with the fact that Matthew had run. Daniel had a duty to fulfill.

Daniel dismounted but didn't accept Matthew's offered handshake.

"If you hadn't brought me to this spot that one time, I never would've found you. I guess you were expecting me."

Daniel's gaze shifted to look behind Matthew. Hannah came to stand beside Matthew, his coat still around her.

Daniel tipped his hat. "You all right, ma'am?"

"Of course."

Even Matthew was surprised at the defensiveness of her tone. He knew his cousin well enough to know that he wasn't worried about Matthew harming her. But she didn't know Daniel as well. He shifted his attention back to Matthew.

"You got to come to Paris with me. Get this mess straightened out."

"I was just waiting for you to bring me a clean shirt and my horse."

Daniel started to smile but it fell off. "Got half of that, anyway."

Matthew shifted to face Hannah. "You can ride double with Daniel."

He wanted to add that he needed to be ready to run again if they encountered trouble. She didn't need to be a target again.

Hannah slipped out of his coat, handed it back to him. "May I go to the creek first and freshen up?"

Daniel tipped his hat at her again, catching her attention. "Of course, ma'am."

When she disappeared from sight, Matthew found Daniel watching him far too closely.

Matthew stiffened. "Nothing happened last night."

"You didn't need to say that."

Maybe not. Still, Matthew felt he did. Daniel cocked a brow at him.

"I will say this, Matt. You'd ought to marry that gal, and soon."

Matthew frowned. "I've been suspected of killing two women and attacking three others. What chance do you think I stand of staying out of the hangman's noose?"

Daniel didn't respond. They waited in silence.

Hannah returned, hair redone, face washed, eyes shining with tears. She glanced at Daniel. "May we have a moment, please, Marshal Garvin?"

Daniel pointed a thumb over his shoulder. "I'll be with the horses. Don't be long, though. Everyone in Dickens is still pretty hot."

When he went down the trail again, Matthew turned to Hannah, bracing himself for what might be their last private conversation. Her eyes reflected that as they bore into his.

"Matthew, the marshal is your cousin. He...maybe he could help us. Maybe we could..."

Matthew lifted a finger and put it in front of her lips. His hand was steady, but inside, he trembled.

"Thinking of all the *maybes* will make us both cowards. I have to face this, even if it costs my life."

Hannah's eyes spilled out their tears. She touched the back of his hand.

"I am sorry. My father did not raise a coward. It's just..."

Matthew turned his hand and caught hers in a gentle squeeze. "*Holitopa chiahoke*, Hannah Stillwater." *You are truly beloved.*

Matthew was in the greatest fight of his life, the very fight for his life and his future. Now more than ever, he had to win.

CHAPTER 59

The coroner's inquest ruled that Dorothy Maxwell's death was not an accident. She was murdered. The one charged with her murder: Matthew Teller.

Matthew scratched down the facts in an attempt to write the *Choctaw Tribune's* next front page article. Ruth Ann said she would muster through writing the article about the inquest and he would let her, but he thought writing his own version might help him.

He didn't make it past the first paragraph before crumpling the paper and throwing it to bounce off the wall of the tight jail cell.

At the Lamar County Jail, Matthew sat perched on the edge of the cot with bedding that hadn't been washed. The prisoner before him must have been a drunk, judging from the stink of whiskey and vomit on the cot.

In the five days that Matthew had been there, he slept on the floor.

Matthew had written a long letter from jail to his brother in prison. It hadn't been his parents' dream for their sons to be writing letters back-and-forth from behind bars.

He wrote a letter to Nita. He had no address to send it to. Philip didn't either.

Now, he was left with nothing to do.

For the first time in an unknown number of years, Matthew was not busy. He had no work he could do and no willpower to even try. He was no longer striving. He wished it had been by choice.

However it happened, he was finally still.

He closed his eyes, regret washing over him. If he'd paced himself better, if he hadn't tried to squeeze the life out of himself, would he be there now? Sitting behind bars, a load of crimes he didn't commit leveled on him and weighing his soul to the gutter?

The jingling of his cell door being opened barely got Matthew's attention. He rose slowly from the cot, never having felt so much of his energy drained before. He offered Benjamin a handshake, but his brother ignored it and wrapped his arms around Matthew. Matthew returned the embrace with a grunt of appreciation.

Benjamin settled his larger frame on the bed next to Matthew, using it as a desk to open his briefcase. "I have more information for you. I'm giving copies of this to my associate here in Paris. You can trust Bruce Staples."

This was Benjamin's second visit to Matthew since Daniel arrested him. Benjamin and Ruth Ann had come straight down to Dickens when they heard the news, sending Caleb Gentry to take charge of the shop in McAlester. Ruth Ann was going to run the Dickens office to keep the main news flowing in the battle against the *Dickens Herald*.

Reynolds' latest headline read: *Civilized Choctaw Turns Savage. No Hope for Indian Territory Except Statehood.*

Benjamin had counseled Matthew about hiring an associate of his, Bruce Staples, a white lawyer there in Paris. That would be better than being represented by a full blood Indian in the murder case of a white woman, which moved the jurisdiction of the case from the Choctaw Nation to the federal court in Paris. And that was just the first charge.

After hearing evidence presented by a lawyer hired by Bellanger—likely paid for by Maxwell—Judge Isaac Parker issued a warrant for Matthew's arrest for the murder of Mrs. Bellanger. That was pending the verdict of this trial. The Tobusky County judge also issued a warrant for the attack on Sissy, despite the fact that she adamantly denied it was Matthew who attacked her. The police in St. Louis demanded to question him again about Viona. And the federal court in Paris was looking to charge him with the attack on Glenrose.

All thanks to the article Reynold's published through the *Dickens Herald*, tying Matthew to the crimes.

Civilized Choctaw Turns Savage.

As one of the deputies pointed out to Matthew: if found guilty of Dorothy's murder, he didn't need to worry about facing the other charges.

Della and Ruth Ann had been there to see him, Ruth Ann chattering nonstop while his mother held his hand. She was staying at the box house again to support her children in the fight by cooking meals and keeping the household running.

The only one missing was Matthew.

Benjamin pulled out three file folders and closed his briefcase to spread them on top of it. "I went over the details of the story you gave me and stopped your sister just in time before she erased some of our evidence." Benjamin opened one of the folders. "This is an affidavit from Mr. Bates as a witness that your telephone in the box house had blood on it and the wall, corroborating your story that you hit your head at the porch of the *Choctaw Tribune* and then went home, where you received a call from Christopher Maxwell. It doesn't prove innocence, but physical evidence like this can cast the shadow of doubt we need. Our second consideration is, since you did not kill Dorothy Maxwell, who did? Or was it an accident, that she fell down the stairs, drunk? The coroner confirmed she'd been drinking heavily that evening."

Matthew was only half listening to Benjamin, the same as he had been the past several days. He could hardly focus his mind on anything. Strategizing was pointless.

A strong hand gripped his arm and squeezed. Matthew looked up sharp and met the demanding gaze Benjamin settled on him.

"You will not give up. The case is not lost."

Matthew jerked his arm away. "We know what they did to your father with less evidence."

Benjamin didn't flinch. "My father followed the old ways of not defending himself after being accused. That is something I have learned from white culture. You have a right, a duty even, to speak up. If my father had, he might not have been sent to prison. Truth and justice are not always served, but we will not stop fighting for it."

Matthew splayed his hands over the sides of his head, leaning his elbows on his knees. His body trembled.

He whispered, "I want to live."

Benjamin rested his large hand on Matthew's shoulder. "She will wait for you. For now, we must fight."

Matthew must have passed out from exhaustion because he awoke on the smelly cot sometime in the night. He knew it was late night from the darkness and the quiet outside his cell window.

What woke him?

Someone was coming down the hall. A couple of someones, judging by the sounds.

Matthew rubbed his eyes and pushed himself upright, head

spinning. He blinked and his cell door opened for Leonard Coxwell.

The deputy next to him backhanded Coxwell's arm. "The rest of it."

"You'll get it when I'm done."

Coxwell entered the small room, looked around, and shuddered. Matthew didn't blame him.

Matthew yawned. "Wish I could offer you a seat and refreshment but…"

He waved his hand vaguely around the cell. He didn't know why he tried to make a joke. He wished someone had bribed the deputy to let Hannah visit. She was a witness and therefore not allowed to see him, and Benjamin advised her to not even write.

Coxwell crossed his arms and leaned back against the wall. "I came to thank you, Teller."

Matthew's mind finally placed Coxwell and he quickly stood. Did Coxwell believe Matthew had assaulted Sissy? Was he here to try and save the hangman some trouble?

Coxwell didn't look ready to commit murder, though his expression remained solemn.

"Thank me?"

Coxwell shifted his jaw. Whatever he wanted to say wouldn't come easy. "After the strain of the miscarriage, Eliza accused me of only marrying her for intermarriage rights. That angered me and tempted me to accept a business proposal that came my way after my marriage."

Matthew swayed. "Mind if I sit down? Jail is hard on a body."

"I wouldn't know."

Matthew sat sideways on the cot, feet on the floor as he leaned against the wall. It was easier to watch Coxwell's face from this position.

The man continued. "There are many opportunities in your peoples' nation. My people now, as you so clearly pointed out. I haven't been able to forget what you said. It made me regret what I did in D.C. I regret many things."

Matthew folded his hands over his midsection, willing his mind to focus. Coxwell had important revelations to share, that much he gathered. "What things?"

"I've done nothing illegal—being here makes me quite grateful I didn't—but still detrimental to the sovereignty of the Choctaw Nation. One of those was, agreeing to partner with Christopher Maxwell in several investments to grow the town of Dickens. I financed the telephone company."

Matthew sucked his lower lip between his teeth and bit it to keep from speaking.

Coxwell noticed and held his hands in front of him. "You have every right to be angry, Teller. At me. Everyone. I know you're innocent. I cannot prove all that Maxwell has done but I know enough to say he is the one who belongs behind bars. You're a good man. I do believe you're the only one in Indian Territory who has it all together."

Matthew bit his lip harder to hold in a laugh. Coxwell shrugged, embarrassed.

"What I'm trying to say is, you being a good man is why Eliza wanted you to go with me to D.C. It didn't work out the way she'd hoped, but it did eventually. I love her, Teller, and I intend to raise our children as responsible citizens of the Choctaw Nation. I have you to thank for that."

A jail cell was an awkward place to receive praise. Matthew accepted it with a brief nod, and did his best to fire up his reporter instincts.

"What do you know about the Palace in Hot Springs?"

Coxwell's expression closed up, almost by reflex. He stepped to the cell door and called for the deputy. Over his shoulder, without looking at Matthew, he said, "I know that Maxwell owns a large share in it and he'll blackmail and even kill to keep the secrets of that place. I wish I'd never gone there."

CHAPTER 60

When the first day of the trial was held, Matthew was seated at the defendant table with his lawyer, Bruce Staples. The Federal Court was much larger in size and intimidation than the Tobusky County Courthouse, where Philip's trial had been held. Not to mention it was packed with a couple hundred people looking for entertainment, thanks to the articles put out by the *Dickens Herald* and reprinted there in Paris.

The prosecution called its first witness.

Earl Reynolds.

The man settled on the witness stand and the prosecutor started off with preliminary questions, establishing Reynolds as a reputable reporter. Reynolds' past experiences in the west and Indian Territory with thousands of published stories billed him as a credible witness.

"When did you first meet the defendant, Matthew Teller?"

Reynolds settled his hard gaze on Matthew. "At the Enterprise Hotel in Dickens. He was rude."

"Can you elaborate?"

"I was taking dinner with the hotel manager, Blane Johnson. Johnson pointed out Matthew Teller when he came in, saying he was the publisher of the *Choctaw Tribune*. When Teller came up to ask the manager if he had seen a young girl who worked there, Glenrose Jessop, I tried to speak to him, but he ignored me and left through the kitchen. We heard hollering not long after and went outside. That was when we found the poor white girl bashed half to death. One of the other employees found a fountain pen by the girl. It had Matthew Teller's name etched on it."

Whispered gossip and comments rumbled through the courtroom and the judge banged his gavel. The prosecutor, Owens, said, "Now please tell us about the night of July 24."

"I received a message at my hotel room that there was a telephone call for me. I'd just returned from a civic meeting held in the hotel. I went down and it was Christopher Maxwell on the telephone, the publisher of the *Dickens Herald* for whom I had written articles. He asked to meet me at the *Herald* office, that he had information for me to review. He is also the one who gave me a great deal of information connecting Matthew Teller to attacks on four women this year alone."

The court room exploded in whispers and the judge rapped his gavel.

Bruce Staples bolted to his feet. "Objection, your honor. This is speculation on the part of the witness, and I request it be stricken from the record."

Owens interjected, "Your honor, I have the paper trail that Earl Reynolds received concerning these attacks and they are most relevant to this case. I will submit them with my next witness as evidence."

Matthew met Earl Reynolds' eyes. They both knew the most condemning part of his testimony against Matthew was still to come.

The questioning continued. "What happened when you met Christopher Maxwell at the *Herald*?"

"He was waiting for me at the door. He said he had forgotten one of the papers at his house but didn't want to leave me waiting. I went with him to the house. The door was standing open and when we went inside, we found Matthew Teller bent over the body of Dorothy Maxwell."

"And then?"

"Mr. Maxwell got the drop on the Indian before he could move. He handed the gun over to me, saying he would go for the doctor. A short time later, I saw Maxwell returning with the doctor and a posse. That's when Teller jumped me, got the gun, and ran for the back door. He pushed a burning lamp off the hall table to set the house on fire."

Matthew gripped his hands into fists. Bruce Staples whispered in his ear, "Did you?"

Matthew shook his head.

"In your opinion, Mr. Reynolds, was the crowd coming up the street overly threatening?"

"I'm not sure what you mean."

"Did they appear to be forming a lynch mob?"

Reynolds shook his head vigorously. "They appeared to be men righteously angry over the murder of a woman. They were coming to the defense of one of the leading townsmen whom they trust, one they recently elected as mayor."

"In your observation, was there any reason for Matthew Teller to run, other than guilt?"

Staples objected, but it was overruled.

Reynolds looked straight at Matthew. "The only reason he had to run was because he had just assaulted and murdered a woman."

"Objection, your honor!"

The prosecutor sat again. "No further questions, your honor."

Bruce Staples sidestepped the table and approached the witness stand.

"Mr. Reynolds, you stated that when you and Christopher Maxwell entered his home, you found Matthew Teller by the body. Was he the only one there?"

Reynolds furrowed his brow. "The deaf Indian woman who works for him was there, too."

"Why did you not mention that in your testimony?"

"It was irrelevant."

Now it was Matthew's turn to shoot out of his chair, causing people in the courtroom to gasp. The judge banged the gavel and Matthew reseated himself, glancing back to catch Hannah's eye in the packed courtroom.

She was seated with Della and Ruth Ann. He could tell from the look on her face that she had caught Reynolds' words. Matthew offered her the kind of look that assured her she was far from irrelevant.

Bruce Staples pressed, "For the record, Mr. Reynolds, the woman you referred to has a name. Hannah Stillwater. Now, please tell us the full story with her included."

Reynolds rolled his eyes. "Yes, she was there and at first, I thought she may have been part of it. But I've dismissed the idea. I didn't know at the time she was deaf and incapable of functioning on her own."

Matthew dug his nails in the arms of his chair.

Staples asked, "Do you believe Miss Stillwater witnessed the death of Dorothy Maxwell?"

"Objection, your honor."

"I withdraw the question. Mr. Reynolds, you gave us an illustrious list of your accomplishments as a reporter. In the...what was the number? 2,156 articles you've written related to the west, can you name one that featured American Indians in a positive light?"

"Objection, your honor."

Staples returned to the table where a stack of newspapers rested. He lifted them for the judge. "Your honor, I have 40 articles here as samples from the past 5 years of Earl Reynolds' reporting career. Every single one of them paints Indians as uncivilized savages. I'd like to submit these as evidence of the extreme bias of this witness."

"Objection, your honor. The witness is not the one on trial."

Matthew held himself very still, aware that the judge was observing him. The newspapers, all gathered by Hannah's brilliant work, was their strongest tactic of dismantling Reynolds as a witness. Staples had cautioned him it was a 50-50 chance the judge would accept them.

The judge shook his head. "Denied. The court is only interested in evidence pertaining to this case."

Matthew closed his eyes. Even if the evidence wasn't in the official records, at least everyone in the courtroom now knew Reynolds' history. Bruce Staples dropped the papers back on the table with a loud thump.

"No further questions, your honor."

As he seated himself, the prosecutor stood. "I call Christopher Maxwell to the stand."

CHAPTER 61

After Maxwell was sworn in, Matthew endured several minutes of the prosecutor leading the man to paint a picture of himself as a respectable founder of the town of Dickens, owner of the preeminent town newspaper, and mayor-elect. He ended the preliminary questions with painting a charming picture of Maxwell's home life with his wife, Dorothy.

Matthew was ready to stand and object.

The set-up questions finally ended, and Owens asked Maxwell to tell how he had called Earl Reynolds and met him at the *Dickens Herald* after leaving his wife reading upstairs in their bedroom. He said he couldn't remember if he locked the front door.

Maxwell's face was theatrically pinched. "I don't always lock up when I leave. Dickens has always been a safe town."

Safe for you, maybe. The thought rumbled close to Matthew's lips. He pressed them together, recalling how his office had been burned to the ground, how Maxwell had accosted his sister more than once, and the vicious attack on Glenrose Jessop.

Maxwell was behind it all.

The prosecutor checked his notes, then asked, "What happened after you met with Earl Reynolds at your office?"

"I had documentation about Matthew and Ruth Ann Teller that I decided to share with him. I mistakenly left one of the notes at home though, and asked Mr. Reynolds to go there with me. That's when we found the door open and..."

Maxwell clenched his fists. It was doubtful anyone in the courtroom except Matthew and his side could see through the act. Although Matthew had to admit, Maxwell looked genuinely distressed.

"Take your time, Mr. Maxwell."

Maxwell took a deep breath. "That's when we entered the house and found Matthew Teller with my wife. I...I didn't realize she was already dead. I thought she was only unconscious. After I stopped Teller from harming her further—"

"Objection, your honor."

"Sustained."

"That is, I suspected he had harmed her, and I drew my gun. I knew I needed to get a doctor right away and left the situation in Reynolds' hands. I ran toward the doctor's office, and met John Bellanger on the way. I had spoken with Mr. Bellanger before. His wife was murdered earlier this year and he suspected Matthew Teller as the killer."

"Objection, your honor!"

The objection was barely heard over the rumbling in the courtroom. Though many people in Paris had read the accusatory articles about Matthew in the *Dickens Herald*, the Bellanger story was news to most of the people there to watch the trial for entertainment.

When the judge regained order and sustained the objection, Owens said, "Please continue, Mr. Maxwell."

"I told Bellanger what happened, that is, what I thought happened, and he took off for the hotel where a group of men were still gathered after a civic meeting that had ended not long before. I went with him, realizing the doctor might be there still."

"And then?"

"Bellanger told the men what happened, and they rushed out to join us, including Dr. Anderson. The men there knew the vicious things Matthew Teller had written about me in his newspaper and, lacking local law-enforcement, they wanted to make sure justice was upheld. We went to the house and found it on fire. Some of the men stayed to put out the fire while the rest of us pursued Matthew Teller, but he disappeared in the mountains by horseback. We searched late into the night and then returned to Dickens for fresh horses. That is when Marshal Garvin, Teller's cousin, took over."

"I see. Let's go back to earlier. What was the information you wanted to give to Reynolds?"

Maxwell looked down at his hands, face flush. Then he looked straight at the jury box.

"Ever since the Teller family moved into Dickens, I've had to sidestep the advances of Ruth Ann Teller."

The courtroom rumbled with gasps.

"Objection, your honor!"

Matthew glanced back to see Benjamin on his feet, Ruth Ann urgently pulling on his sleeve.

The judge banged his gavel. "Order, or I'll clear the room."

Benjamin slowly reseated himself, tugging Ruth Ann's hand through his arm and covering it with his large one.

It was all Matthew could do to stay in his own seat.

Lies.

No one in the jury knew Ruth Ann, or Maxwell would never attempt such a blatant accusation. And anyone in Dickens would know Maxwell was flat out lying. At least, they should know.

Maxwell was a convincing man in print and in person.

The judge said, "Objection overruled. The witness will continue."

"Well, no one knew about this except her brother, Matthew Teller. He always thought I was the one making the advances."

"Did he ever threaten you about his sister?"

"Yes. He said he would kill me if he ever saw me with her."

"What happened on the night of March 13?"

"Well, I was hesitant when Miss Teller—Mrs. Dunn now—sent me a note asking me to meet her at the *Choctaw Tribune*. It was late, but she indicated it related to newspaper business, so I went."

Maxwell hesitated, adding drama to the moment. "I never wanted to bring this to light, but that night, Miss Teller propositioned me."

Matthew jerked and made it partway off his seat when Bruce Staples stopped him. Matthew was turned enough to see Peter and William out of their chairs and halfway to the witness stand.

Daniel, seated in the front row, jumped up and blocked them as the judge banged the gavel furiously. "Remove those men! I will have order in this court!"

Daniel said something low to his brothers-in-law. Marshal Green came up, too, and gestured for the door. Peter and William didn't leave without giving Maxwell a death look.

It took a few moments for the room to settle, and the prosecutor instructed Maxwell to pick up where he'd left off.

Matthew couldn't stop himself from taking satisfaction in Maxwell wiping his brow before the man recovered his composure.

"Well, I realized it was a set up when I turned and saw a man I didn't know taking a photograph of us. That's what I was taking to show Reynolds."

The prosecutor slipped something from his table and held it up. "Your honor, I would like to submit this photograph as evidence and share it with the jury, along with the paper trail Mr. Maxwell has detailing Matthew Teller's activities that show a violent history. The documents and witness affidavits also place

Mr. Teller at the location and time of attacks against a total of five women in Indian Territory, Arkansas, and Missouri."

"Granted."

While several pieces of paper were entered into the court record, Matthew watched the expressions on the jurors' faces as the photograph went around. Matthew didn't need to see it to know it was the one Maxwell had set up and taken when he accosted Ruth Ann. As far as the documents and affidavits were concerned, Staples had reviewed copies of them beforehand with Matthew. All were fabricated by Maxwell with grains of truth enough to make them believable.

The judge accepted the evidence and the prosecutor asked Maxwell, "How did you obtain a copy of the photograph? And why did you decide it was time to bring this to public light through Reynolds?"

Maxwell inhaled deeply through his nose. "The photographer sold it to me, claiming it was the only copy. He indicated he was double crossing the Tellers. I kept it locked away until...until the day I learned of my wife's affair with Matthew Teller."

A staying hand pressed down Matthew's shoulder. Bruce Staples held him firmly in his seat.

"What evidence do you have that there was a relationship between Matthew Teller and your wife?"

Maxwell's face looked pained, but underneath it, Matthew recognized his genuine anger. "My wife is...was...young and very beautiful. In her naiveté, she was lured by Matthew Teller, who used her infatuation to get even with me for the incident with his sister. Then he killed Dorothy for spite."

"Objection, your honor! The witness is presenting emotional and irrelevant statements to the jury."

The judge looked at the panel of twelve men. "You will disregard the witnesses' last few remarks."

Matthew shifted his jaw. The damage was done, and Maxwell knew it.

The prosecutor slid another file folder off the table and held it. "Your honor, I have the copy of a letter Dorothy Maxwell sent to Matthew Teller. It was found in his coat that was tangled with her body at the bottom of the stairs. I submit it as evidence."

Granted, the prosecutor read a disgusting note aloud to the jury, then, "Mr. Maxwell, did Matthew Teller ever say anything to you about your wife?"

Maxwell shifted. "Not in so many words, but even when he worked for me at the *Dickens Herald*, I caught him making passes at my wife when she came to see me. I guess it started back then and I didn't realize it."

"No further questions, your honor."

Bruce Staples hammered Maxwell with questions, trying to break apart his testimony.

When Maxwell was dismissed from the stand, he met Matthew's eyes. They both knew he was lying. It was Matthew and Ruth Ann's word against his, but separately. They couldn't corroborate each other and being siblings, Matthew doubted it would've done much good in the eyes of the jury.

And the eyes of the jury looked condemning.

Seated at the typesetting cabinet, Hannah's hands shook as she tried to form the next sentence on the trial article in the composing stick. Her fingers would not cooperate.

Before leaving Paris after the first day of the trial, Hannah had answered Bruce Staples' summons to visit his office. The law firm was familiar, almost a feeling of home though she'd only worked there a few months.

Mr. Shaw had stopped her, both elated and embarrassed to see her. After she left, he'd regretted firing her and wrote to her old college to investigate the accusation against her. Through that, he discovered the deception of Jackson Thomas' letter and wanted to rehire her. He just hadn't known how to reach her until her byline appeared in an article for the *Choctaw Tribune*.

She told him she was happily employed and wouldn't be returning to her old job as a typist in the law firm.

The visit with Mr. Staples was less vindicating. The grimness of the lawyer disturbed her. He asked her several questions again about that night and Hannah could tell he was debating about calling her as a witness.

She was top on his list, but after Reynolds' disregard because of her deafness, Staples was hesitant. They couldn't risk weakening Matthew's case.

If only she had time to write a convincing article exposing the mindset of people like Reynolds who believed she was "incapable of functioning on her own." She well knew where the philosophy came from—eugenics.

Eugenics was now destroying Matthew's chance at having a reliable witness to testify of his innocence.

Hannah looked up to see Hugh going to the back room, probably for more paper. Caleb Gentry had returned from the McAlester shop that Ruth Ann decided to close until after the trial. He was out now, collecting advertiser fees, something he abhorred. But he didn't make Hannah do it. He knew the accusing looks she was receiving around town after her flight into the mountain with Matthew.

Between the three faithful employees, they were trying to manage publishing and distributing a daily edition. The work felt like ocean waves crashing over Hannah. Disorienting. Gasping for breath. Fighting for life.

She secured the composing stick with string and prepared to set the sentence in the chase. But two figures appeared in the picture windows that made her shrink back. She ducked low.

Christopher Maxwell and Clyde stood outside the windows, staring into the seemingly empty *Choctaw Tribune*.

Hannah pressed a hand over her heart, recalling how Clyde had attacked her, and the fact that he might be the real killer of Mrs. Bellanger.

The two men stood side-by-side, facing the windows, looking like they'd arrived at their destination at the end of a long journey.

Hannah held her breath, squinting, wishing she could see their faces better through the dusty glass and distance.

Her traveling bag lay at her feet. She quickly dug into it to retrieve her stereoscope and a pin-holed photograph. Holding the stereoscope to her face, she raised just enough above the cabinet to watch the men. The stereoscope focused her eyes and mind on their words.

Maxwell was speaking. "There have been times you frustrated me almost as much as Teller, but I guess we're both finally getting what we wanted."

Clyde smiled. "I'll be there for the final moments of the crucifixion."

Maxwell turned his head and said something. Hannah couldn't make it out. Clyde responded by shrugging.

"I'll for sure be there when the trap door releases and Matthew Teller's neck snaps."

Hannah covered her mouth with her free hand, the stereoscope shaking in her other.

Maxwell flipped his coat back and hooked his thumbs in his vest pocket. "It's your hide. There *is* one thing that would complete this for me."

Clyde turned to him and said something. Maxwell nodded toward the picture windows. "It would be fitting if this building burned to the ground. I have a feeling it will tonight, don't you…?"

Hannah squinted, frustrated that she couldn't make out the last word he said. He seemed to have said the man's name, but it wasn't Clyde.

From the corner of her eye, she saw Caleb Gentry returning to the shop. He spied the two men at the picture windows and bowed up. Maxwell and Clyde caught sight of him, grinned, and moved on.

Hugh came out of the storeroom and Hannah nearly ran him over. "Excuse me, I'll be right back!"

She went out the back door, through the alley way, and carefully checked the street before entering it. She made a beeline for the Teller home. She knew the family would be gathered there, including Marshal Daniel Garvin.

A quick knock at the door brought the man she'd come to see. Marshal Garvin looked surprised. "Miss Stillwater, come in…"

"Actually, I came to see you, Marshal. Could you step out a moment, please?"

The marshal joined her on the porch, and she relayed the conversation she witnessed between Maxwell and Clyde, including Maxwell's threat to burn down the newspaper that night.

Marshal Garvin looked grim. "That's a smart bit of news. Marshal Green and I will see to it that it doesn't happen."

"There's one more thing. Right before they left, Maxwell called Clyde by a different name. I feel it might be his real one. But I couldn't quite make it out. Maybe you can help, especially if Clyde is a known outlaw."

"What did it look like he said?"

Hannah closed her eyes, bringing the image of Maxwell's lips to the forefront. If only she'd had a telescope instead of a stereoscope. She formed the word on her own lips, then said, "It looked like… Manny?"

She opened her eyes to see Marshal Garvin with his eyebrows scrunched, thinking. Then they loosened, and he stared at her.

"Banny? With a *B*?"

Hannah nodded, excitement leaping. "Banny, that was it!"

As quick as the elation came over her, it evaporated as she realized what Marshal Garvin had.

"Do you suppose Clyde is…"

"I intend to find out."

CHAPTER 63

The courtroom crackled with tension as it was called to order. Matthew took a seat along with the rest of the packed room, taking the opportunity to glance behind him and meet Hannah's eyes. She nodded, reassuring. She was as confident in her abilities as he was.

The judge said, "The defense will call its first witness."

Bruce Staples stood. "I call Miss Hannah Stillwater to the stand."

He turned and beckoned to her. Hannah rose and strode through the swinging gate of the three-foot carved railing, and to the witness stand.

Staples remained behind his table. "Your honor, I would like to demonstrate this witness's unique ability. She is deaf, but can read lips, even from a distance. I would like Mr. Owens to stand and say any phrase of his choosing for Miss Stillwater to repeat."

Before the judge could respond, Owens rose. "Objection, your honor. This is ridiculous, having a deaf witness at a murder trial."

Hannah was focused on him. "'Objection, your honor. This is ridiculous, having a deaf witness at a murder trial.'"

The audience chuckled and one man called out, "Let her testify!"

The judge banged his gavel and Hannah's eyes darted to Staples, and then the judge.

The judge glared at the audience, then the prosecuting attorney. "Objection overruled. This young woman is a qualified witness."

The prosecutor sat with an agitated sigh and Staples began. "Miss Stillwater, please tell us what occurred the day of Mrs. Maxwell's death."

Without hesitation, Hannah went through her day, including the train ride to Paris and how she interpreted Glenrose Jessop's words that Matthew was not her attacker—Owens objected several times throughout her monologue—then she proceeded into Matthew asking her to go with him as a witness to Maxwell's home and what they found when they arrived.

Staples yielded to the prosecutor, withholding his final set of questions for Hannah.

Owens looked bored as he remained seated behind the prosecution table. "Miss Stillwater, have you been deaf from birth?"

Matthew barely understood him, and Hannah narrowed her eyes at the man. "You are intentionally holding your lips in a flat line to prevent me from reading them."

Owens stood. "Is this better?"

"Yes."

"She has made my point, your honor. Life is only partly comprehensible for this young lady. She can only observe so much with her eyes and the rest passes her by. She cannot have full understanding of these proceedings, nor of what took place the night Dorothy Maxwell was killed. I request her testimony be stricken from the record."

Staples rose. "Objection, your honor."

The judge leaned forward and beckoned the lawyers to approach his bench. Matthew couldn't make out what they were saying. Hannah's attention was on Matthew, her eyes showing every emotion behind her calm mask.

This. This was why she'd run from him before. Why she couldn't trust him, trust anyone, to bear up under society's pressure to relegate her to the dark corners of the world where they thought people like her were only capable of communicating by grunts and begging for pity.

She had stood against that all her life. And now, she was facing her greatest test, one that she must pass if she had a chance at saving his life.

He gave her a nod to let her know he was standing with her, no matter the outcome of this day.

The lawyers returned to their tables and the judge spoke to Hannah. "Miss Stillwater, would you articulate your understanding of the purpose of this trial and your testimony?"

"Yes, your honor. This trial is to determine the guilt or innocence of Matthew Teller for the murder of Dorothy Maxwell of Dickens, Indian Territory in the sovereign Choctaw Nation."

The judge faced the tables again. "Please begin your cross-examination, Mr. Owens."

Owens stood behind his table, face serious. Matthew knew he was ready to break apart Hannah in another way.

"Miss Stillwater, the world must be frightening for a young woman like you. You are alone and vulnerable with your inability to communicate with normal people. But you made it to Dickens and Matthew Teller offered you a job and paid you well. What did he want in return for his kindness?"

"For me to perform a satisfactory job at the *Choctaw Tribune*."

"I see." He lifted a newspaper from his desk and read the headline: "'Indian newspaperman in questionable circumstance with deaf woman.' How do you explain this article that cited Matthew Teller as taking advantage of you while you were under his employment?"

"That is quite easy to explain. Christopher Maxwell is a good liar."

A mixture of grumbling and laughter echoed in the courthouse. The judge rapped his gavel.

The prosecutor shifted from behind his table and approached the witness stand, blocking Matthew's view of Hannah.

"Miss Stillwater, were you with Matthew Teller the whole evening on the day that Dorothy Maxwell was killed?"

"No, sir."

"No, you were not. In fact, there is a fifteen minute gap in which Mr. Maxwell left his home and returned. You stated in your testimony that Matthew Teller was bleeding and distressed when you arrived in Dickens, and you have no idea where he was ten minutes prior to seeing him, is that correct?"

Hannah's first hesitation. Then, "He told me..."

"That is hearsay, Miss Stillwater. Were you or were you not with him ten minutes prior to joining him for the walk to the Maxwell home?"

"No, sir."

Owens stepped to one side, allowing a clear view of the stand for Matthew. He swept his arm and pointed at him. "Are you in love with Matthew Teller?"

"Objection, your honor!"

"Your honor, my question is a legitimate attempt to uncover the bias this witness holds in favor of the defendant."

"Objection sustained. Keep your questioning to the realm of facts, not emotion, Mr. Owens."

Owens slapped the witness stand. Hannah didn't flinch. Matthew slid to the edge of his seat, willing her to look at him, and willing her not to.

"Emotion is the very essence of what we are dealing with, your honor," Owens said. "Revenge, jealousy, hate, love. The defendant was accused of having an affair with this witness and—"

"Objection!"

Owens raised a hand. "No further questions, your honor."

He returned to his table. Staples stood, breathed in a deep breath that seemed to calm the room and asked, "Miss Stillwater, would you please tell the court what you witnessed yesterday while working in the *Choctaw Tribune* office?"

As Hannah relayed Maxwell and Clyde's conversation, the judge had to call the court back to order more than once. Staples had instructed her to leave off about seeing the name *Banny*. Daniel was still working on that angle.

"What did you do after you saw the conversation, Miss Stillwater?"

Hannah took a breath. "I went to Marshal Garvin and told him what I saw. He said he and Marshal Green would lie in wait for the men."

Staples held up a piece of paper. "Your honor, this is a copy of the arrest report from United States Marshal Daniel Garvin. He and Marshal Green arrested two men who attempted to set the *Choctaw Tribune* office on fire last night. The men confessed they were hired for the job."

The prosecutor objected on grounds that this whole incident was unrelated to Dorothy Maxwell's murder. Before it was over-ruled or sustained, the back doors of the courtroom banged open.

Matthew looked back in time to see Daniel opening them wide for Peter, who rolled Glenrose Jessop into the courtroom in a wheelchair.

The judge banged his gavel and called for order. Matthew spied Glenrose looking around anxiously. So this was the angle Daniel had in mind.

Maxwell stood and headed for a side door. Marshal Green cut him off, grinning.

Glenrose's eyes widened, and she pointed to the opposite

corner. Matthew jerked to his feet. Even with hat pulled low, he recognized Clyde.

The man was clawing for a pistol hidden beneath his coat.

"*Don't!*" Daniel shouted.

In a split second, one man lay dead in the federal court.

CHAPTER 64

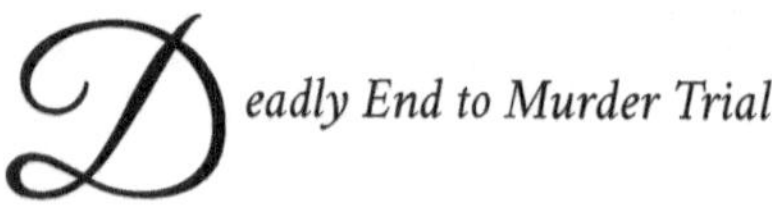

eadly End to Murder Trial

By Hannah Stillwater

A shootout occurred at the Lamar County Courthouse during the murder trial of Matthew Teller. A wanted criminal, Guy Banny, was identified in the courtroom by one of his alleged victims, Glenrose Jessop.

United States Marshal Daniel Garvin had been investigating attacks against several women spanning from Fort Smith, Arkansas, to St. Louis, Missouri, to Dickens, Indian Territory. Marshal Garvin garnered enough evidence to reconstruct Guy Banny's path to place him at all the attack locations and corresponding dates. When confronted in the courtroom, Banny drew a gun and was shot to death by Marshal Garvin.

Christopher Maxwell was also arrested in the courtroom. A warrant had been issued for his arrest from Fort Smith for conspiring to burn down the Choctaw Tribune *office. He is also accused of running an illegal prostitution ring spanning from Hot Springs, Arkansas to Indian Territory. The allegations include kidnapping, coercion, and enslavement.*

Upon his arrest, Maxwell gave a full confession to the crimes and also to the death of his wife. He claims that during an argument, he hit her and she fell down the stairs. He admitted to framing Matthew Teller for the killing along with confessing he had hired Guy Banny to kill Matthew Teller. But Banny went on his own quest for revenge in the death of his half brother, Jake Banny, former residence of Dickens.

The Choctaw Tribune *will continue reporting on the story as more facts emerge.*

~

Dickens Townsite Pending Annexation

By Matthew Teller

After much controversy, the annexation of the townsite of Dickens is still under question. Annexing would remove it from the authority of the Choctaw Nation. This would have grave consequences for the sovereignty of the Choctaw Nation as tensions mount over the proposed statehood and dissolving the sovereignty of the Indian nations within it.

~

Stormy Autumn Ahead

The Almanac predicts tumultuous weather as we enter a new season...

CHAPTER 65

*W*ind rattled the *Choctaw Tribune* building, vibrating the front door and warning of a severe September storm. Matthew leaned back in his desk chair, staring out the picture windows as the wind wreaked havoc. Business signs swung hazardously from their chains across the street, debris blew through the road and swirled.

Dickens. It had grown larger than Matthew imagined it would, and not in the way he hoped. When he established the *Choctaw Tribune*, he dreamed of having a wide influence across Indian Territory and even back east. They had achieved those things and more. Ruth Ann would argue that the *Choctaw Tribune* had attracted fine families and businesses to the town and helped shape it into what it had become. Perhaps so.

Matthew sat alone in the office. It was nearly suppertime on Saturday evening, and he was expected at the Ark. But he wasn't ready to go. He wasn't finished thinking in the quiet of the office, surrounded by the comforting scents of ink and newspaper.

He was learning to put aside "busy" in favor of regular rest, and quiet moments of contemplation like he'd done when he started his newspaper.

A lot of good had come out of it. And now, with Maxwell in jail and likely facing a hanging, it was the only newspaper in town. Matthew didn't take satisfaction in the way it happened, but at least it was finally over. He was finally out from under the shadow man's threat.

Matthew never dreamed Jake Banny had a brother. Standing over the body, seeing the man he'd known as Clyde, Matthew had whispered, "I don't know if it matters now, but I forgive your brother. And you."

Matthew's eyes wandered to the empty typesetting cabinet, along with his heart. Hannah had done so well in the courtroom and in the days that followed. She did her work efficiently and always seemed to be ahead of him. He didn't know how he would have survived all this without her.

He was fairly certain he was courting her now. They took evening meals together, either at the hotel or at the Ark. They sat in church and spent Sundays together. They went on a picnic with Lance and Amarillo, and another one with Leonard Coxwell and Sissy. They spent time on Uncle Preston's ranch, taking a canoe to the center of the lake and talking for hours about nothing and everything.

Matthew had never felt his soul as attached to another as he did Hannah.

Was it possible she felt the same? Had she come to trust him as one who would stand against anything, even how society treated her?

He leaned forward in his desk chair and opened his bottom drawer, the only one he kept locked. He pulled out the piece of paper with the notes on it because he was afraid he would forget what to say when the time came.

When would that time come? Everyone in his family adored Hannah. Her father had given his blessing. Matthew just had to find the right time and the right way.

The wind ceased rattling the shop. Matthew replaced the

paper and closed the drawer, turning the key in the lock. It was a good time to head off to the Ark—and to Hannah—while there was a break in the storm.

Matthew stood and halted. The wind hadn't just stopped. It had died completely.

In its place was another sound. The sound of the Frisco train barreling in from the north.

Except the Frisco was not due for another hour. And it had never made a sound quite like this before.

The hair stood up on the back of Matthew's neck, a chill sweeping him as a sudden, cold breeze crept beneath the door.

The sound of cracking wood and shattering glass a short distance away made him duck beneath his desk. At the same moment, the picture windows of the *Choctaw Tribune* exploded.

A tremendous wind screamed through the windows, sending newspapers into a wild dance. Matthew tucked himself beneath the desk, bracing his hands against the flimsy protection.

He didn't really care about his own protection. His mind was on someone else. But he couldn't reach her as the twister ripped through the town of Dickens.

CHAPTER 66

There was quiet and calm for several seconds. Then Matthew realized the ringing in his ears was blocking out other sounds. As the ringing faded, he heard shouts and screams, muffled but desperate.

How bad had the town been hit? How many people injured? How many killed?

Matthew pushed away his chair that had fallen on its side, blocking him under the desk, and crawled out. He stood and could hardly see for the darkness. The front of his building had collapsed.

Matthew fumbled for a match and lit the lamp somehow still secure on the wall behind him. He turned it up to high and glanced around. The *Choctaw Tribune* was fully intact.

The wind had blown out the chandelier and the other flames, and the hardwood floor was now covered in a carpet of newspapers. His printing press was unmoved.

He looked to the front again to see that the wall was still standing, sans the glass of the picture windows. The darkness was caused by the front porch posts collapsing. The porch roof covered the entire front.

Matthew blew out the lamp and went through the back store room and opened the door inward. A mountain of rubble filled his vision. The building in the alley behind him was a splintered stack of firewood piled in front of the door.

He had to get out. He had to find Hannah.

The Fullers. The Levitts. Peter. Had the twister hit the ranch where his mother was?

Matthew ran to the front again, slipping on newspapers as he went. He slammed into the front door and tried to yank it open. It was stuck, so he went through the window, barely avoiding the glass shards sticking out from the frame.

Matthew squatted and found a narrow opening in the A-frame shape the porch roof created. He began crawling through, the cries of people hollering for help and offering assistance in his ears.

He hit one spot where the corner post of the porch blocked his way. He gave it a push, but the creaking above him warned the roof would collapse if he moved it. He twisted to the left and found just enough wiggle room to squeeze out and roll onto the dirt road of Dickens.

He sprang to his feet in time for two men to bump into him as they rushed past. The scene before him was unbelievable.

Every building within his sight was flattened, crunched, or completely gone. Dickens was leveled.

People with torn and bloodied clothing rushed about, digging in the rubble, calling out the names of loved ones.

Matthew got his feet moving, running for the Ark.

As soon as the home came into sight, Matthew caught his breath on the primal scream in his throat.

The house was leveled.

Matthew charged into the rubble of what was once the front porch.

"Hannah!" he shouted.

But if she was alive, she wouldn't be able to hear him. He began calling for everyone else who had been in the home—the Jessops siblings, including Glenrose who was home now. Lance, Peter.

The board he stepped on gave way and his leg went through the jagged pieces. He forced himself to slow and listen for sounds, any minuscule cry for help. There was none.

Matthew heaved in a deep breath, scanning the debris. His eyes went round and across the open field, giving him a clear view all the way to the railroad tracks and his box house.

What had been his home since he started the *Choctaw Tribune* was a pile of rubble. His mother's sofa. His books. His home was gone.

Matthew didn't care. He swung his eyes back around the Ark. He whispered, "God, you have to help me find them."

He tried to move forward but the mass shifted beneath him. He caught himself. Broken glass sliced through his sleeve and skin.

He pulled a handkerchief from his coat pocket and wrapped it around the bleeding, glancing up again at the box house with the vague thought of his mother and the remedies she kept for healing.

The twister's path led north to south. He needed to get out to the ranch and make sure everyone was all right. He needed a horse to do that. He needed to do so many things at one time.

A quiet voice whispered in his spirit.

The cellar.

Matthew slid, crawled, and rolled his way off the debris to land on littered ground only to realize the Ark didn't have a cellar.

But his home did.

Would there have been enough time?

Hope leaped in his heart, and he began a mad dash for the box house. He arrived a few seconds later to see the barn doors of the half-destroyed structure hanging open and empty. He wanted to believe his horse had gotten out, the only animal stored there these days.

Matthew couldn't wrap his mind around the splintered wood of what had been his home as he bolted for the cellar doors. They were covered by what was left of his lean-to bedroom.

Matthew grabbed a board and ripped it off. He began ripping more off.

A dog barked.

Matthew froze. Story. Her bark came from inside the cellar.

"Peter! Lance! Are you in there? Is Hannah in there?"

"Matthew!" It was the voice of Lance Fuller. "You're alive! We're all in here but can't get the doors open."

Banging started underneath the rubble and Peter's voice, reverting to the squeakiness of a few years ago, squalled, "Get us out, Matt! It's crowded and it stinks."

Matthew released his terror with a laugh and went back to work removing the debris. When he got to the last layer, the doors pushed against it, giving him some help.

Then everything came loose and both doors flung wide open. Peter and Lance were on one door each, clearing the rest of the way as Story bounded out between them and jumped on Matthew.

He laughed again, scratching her behind the ears. "Good girl. That's a good girl."

Peter said, "She's more than that. She's the one that warned us the twister was coming. We could see it a ways off and ran straight for the cellar, warning people as we went. I kind of forgot about you, what with getting the women and children to safety."

Matthew gripped Peter in a bear hug, then pushed his cousin aside and waited anxiously by the door as Lance carried Glenrose out. Peter helped the rest of the Jessops and Mrs. Warren up. Hannah was last.

Matthew reached down and grabbed both her hands to pull her the rest of the way out and into his arms. She was shaking, but returned his embrace as she laid her head on his shoulder.

Daniel was right. He ought to marry this gal. Soon.

CHAPTER 67

The town of Dickens was destroyed.

Not in the way Matthew had wanted, but destroyed nonetheless. Even the First Baptist Church of Dickens and its shed with all of Hannah's pottery had been wiped out. Pastor Rand had been injured in his home, along with hundreds of others who suffered, and the 20 people who were dead after the enormous twister appeared in the northern sky and barreled into town.

Uncle Preston and his crew, unaffected at the ranch, came in to help with the rescues, injured, and cleaning up. The telegraph line was one of the first things repaired and Matthew ordered Peter not to leave the sounder. There were a great many messages coming in and out of Dickens and the lines of communication needed to stay open.

The telephone company was gone, and so were all of those lines. Only a single line from the telegraph kept Dickens in communication as people from all over, Choctaw and non-Indians alike, poured in to help the devastated town.

Almost immediately, Matthew worked to get a special edition of the *Choctaw Tribune* out. They needed the newspaper on trains going north and south, east and west, to report the devastation and send out calls for help and aid.

Caleb Gentry and Hugh Eberlin showed up. Matthew immediately put them to work at the press while he helped Hannah clean up around the press and put all the materials back in order so they could get into production.

Matthew brushed debris off his desk with one sweep of his arm. He moved his typewriter close and set to work writing.

He had plenty to write about with the telegraph constantly clicking and people discovering the *Choctaw Tribune* was a central place of communication.

The *Choctaw Tribune* printed flyers of individual needs for help and flyers to let everyone know about the church service Pastor Rand was holding in the field next to the church rubble.

By Sunday afternoon, the special edition was printed and sent off on the first train that made it through.

With everything in town leveled, Matthew opened the *Choctaw Tribune* for those around him to have a shelter for the night—the Jessops, Mrs. Warren, the Levitts, and Hannah. Peter slept with the telegraph, along with Matthew so that they could monitor it throughout the night. Uncle Preston set up temporary shelters raised from wagons and material from the ranch and hauled people out to the ranch as well.

Sunday night was long, but Matthew was up before dawn and at his desk again.

Over the next four days, the citizens of Dickens picked through the rubble. Many confessed they did not intend to stay in the town and attempt to rebuild. No one had deep roots there and the devastation was overwhelming.

There was a new town a few miles south that had been untouched, and there was a common sentiment that people preferred to move and start over there. The Levitts announced their decision to move north where there was a community of Jewish families.

On the fourth day, after the deceased had been buried and those with the most severe injuries taken to the hospital in Paris, Matthew stood in front of his desk, leaned back against it, facing his employees. Benjamin and Ruth Ann were there, along with workers from the McAlester shop.

Matthew had his hands propped on the desk behind him. Though he spoke to them all, he made sure Hannah could easily see him.

"We all know a lot of people have left the town for good. It doesn't look like she'll rebuild. That leaves us here at the *Choctaw Tribune* with a decision to make. We can stay and help this town get back on its feet for those who want to, or we can shut down and go to McAlester, or we find a new town to begin again."

Matthew looked around, waiting for input. Ruth Ann was the first. She moved to his side and tugged on his hand until he released it from the desk, and she held it tight, looking up at him.

"Matt, the *Choctaw Tribune* was never about Dickens, not really. Your ambition has always been for truth and justice. You can do that here or McAlester or anywhere. The location isn't important."

"I second that." This from Caleb Gentry. He had been a faithful employee the longest at the *Choctaw Tribune*.

Matthew glanced around to see nods from everyone. He squeezed his sister's hand.

"Well, if we're moving, let's make this the best edition the *Choctaw Tribune* ever published in Dickens. There's nothing more powerful than the press except God Almighty!"

Hours later, the print shop was a hive of activity. But today was about far more than the last edition of the *Choctaw Tribune* or the last days of Dickens.

Matthew kept one eye on Hannah and as soon as she finished setting type in an article he'd given her, he rose with a single sheet of paper shaking in his hand. He paused, took a deep breath, and stepped over to the typesetting cabinet.

"One more."

He laid the paper on her desk, but she stared at him. "Oh. I thought that was the last one. I don't know if I can get the set before the final page is ready to run."

"It's short. You can do it."

A smile teased her lips. "You're always very sure of yourself, aren't you, Matthew Teller?"

"I've been told I have a thick skull."

She looked down at the piece of paper and her humor was replaced by confusion. Matthew watched her scan the words he had copied from his Bible.

And God saw every thing that he had made, and, behold, it was very good.

She glanced up at him and he stepped around so that the cabinet was no longer between them. He slowly signed the verse from Genesis with an addition:

And God saw every thing that he had made, and, behold, it was very good, especially Hannah.

Hannah stared at him. Matthew pushed in. He wasn't sure he would ever again have the kind of courage he did in this moment.

Matthew went down on one knee and reached inside his coat pocket for the ring box. He opened it, keeping his face turned toward Hannah. She covered her lips with her fingers.

Matthew rested the box on his knee and signed, *You are everything there aren't words for. Would you honor me by becoming my wife?*

The entire shop behind him had gone silent. Matthew had always envisioned having friends and family close when he proposed, though printing the last edition of the *Choctaw Tribune* in Dickens wasn't what he had in mind. It still worked. At least he hoped.

He held his breath as a tear rolled down Hannah's cheek. She wiped it away, a luminous smile filling the still room.

"Yes, Matthew Teller. I will marry you."

Matthew quickly rose and slipped the engagement ring on her left hand before she changed her mind.

The room erupted with whistles and cheers. She whispered, "What did I do to deserve you?"

Matthew chuckled as he tipped her chin up higher with one finger. "I believe that's my line."

He pressed his forehead against hers. Yes. He wanted to kiss her. But once he began, he didn't want to have to stop.

Matthew stood in the quiet October breeze, his heart seized up in his chest at the sound of boots climbing the wooden scaffolding. The sound was reminiscent of the hanging he witnessed in Fort Smith shortly before Guy Banny threatened him in the court-house basement.

Daniel stood at his right side, rigid, mature, confident, gentle. Hannah was on Matthew's left arm, holding tight.

He had told her she didn't need to come, that she probably shouldn't, but she chose to be there. She wanted to walk with him even through this—the hanging of the man who had made Matthew look down the throat of hell more than once.

As the reverend at the top of the scaffold said a few words to Christopher Maxwell, Matthew fingered the letter in his coat pocket. It had come in two days before. He had memorized every precious line. Most of the words were misspelled, some were missing entirely, but he knew what she was trying to say.

Dear Uncle Matt,

I am not supposed to write you letters, but I am. Because I am your little bear. I want to see you again.

I love you.

Nita

Matthew had cried after getting the letter, then he had boarded the southbound Frisco to the Lamar County Jail where he walked in and told Christopher Maxwell he forgave him for everything the man had done to him.

Unlike Thaddeus, Maxwell hadn't rejected it.

He'd come to the bars and said, "That night, in that moment, I wanted to kill my wife. And I did. Because of you. You may not know this, Teller, but you've caused me hell, too."

The reverend stepped away from Christopher Maxwell and the last glimpse Matthew got of the man's face showed it was stolid.

Then everything happened at once. The hood was placed over Maxwell's head, then the rope. The hangman got in position, pulled the lever, and ended the man's life.

Only God could pronounce final judgment on his soul.

Hannah squeezed Matthew's arm, her face turned away from the scene. Daniel gripped his other shoulder and Matthew nodded.

Matthew turned away, guiding Hannah toward the depot. They would walk the three blocks there and board the train headed back to Hugo, Choctaw Nation, where the new shop was located. His journey was not over. It was only beginning.

Matthew had a wedding and a new life to prepare for.

AUTHOR'S NOTE

As with all my historical fiction works, the incidences portrayed in this novel draw a great deal from actual happenings of the time period. That said, I want to mention a couple of specific items:

The issue of town sites in Indian Territory is as convoluted and confusing as many of the events in that time period. I used historical documents to inspire the main plot of this story, but this novel is by no means intended as a legal study of the conflicts relating to the tribes, sovereignty, and the United States government.

While it appears gambling was illegal in Indian Territory during this time period, it was practiced in various ways both openly and in secret by all races.

The early life of Reverend Willis Folsom and his friend Tushpa (who later took the name John Culberson) is portrayed in my book, *Tushpa's Story (Touch My Tears Collection)*. Though Willis Folsom passed a year before this story takes place, I took literary license with the timeline to include a mention of this iconic man in the Choctaw Nation.

For the descriptions of the Blue River homestead, I relied heavily on Carolee and Wayne Maxwell's book, *Touched by Greatness*, the story of Choctaw scholar Charles McGilberry. Carolee's firsthand knowledge of her family's roots on the Blue River were invaluable to me in creating Hannah's homeplace.

The last name of Stillwater came from one of my readers, Cassandra Wessel. Family stories passed down to her talked of a Choctaw grandmother called "Stillwater."

For the characteristics and the grit of Hannah, I drew from
the life of Sue Thomas, a deaf woman who worked for the F.B.I.

GLOSSARY OF CHOCTAW WORDS

~

Chihowa: God

Chi hullo li: I love you

Chim achukma? How are you?

Chi pisa la chike: I will be seeing you / I will see you again

Halito: A friendly greeting

Ome: Expressing a ready assent, agreement or acknowledgment

Pashofa: cracked corn and stewed pork soup

Pokni: Grandmother

Yakoke: Thank you

Yaya: A Choctaw cry to grieve the passing of a loved one.

ALSO BY SARAH ELISABETH SAWYER

***Choctaw Tribune* Series**

The Executions (Book 1)

Traitors (Book 2)

Shaft of Truth (Book 3)

Sovereign Justice (Book 4)

Fire and Ink (Book 5)

Choctaw Tribune Boxset (Books 1 - 3)

Choctaw Heritage Standalone Books

Touch My Tears: Tales from the Trail of Tears

Tushpa's Story (Touch My Tears Collection)

Anumpa Warrior: Choctaw Code Talkers of World War I

***Doc Beck Westerns* Series**

Canyon War (Book 1)

Mission Bandits (Book 2)

Grave Robbers (Book 3)

Desert Captive (Book 4)

Ranch Feud (Book 5)

Bronc Buster (Book 6)

The Gunman (Book 7)

Ape Man (Book 8)

The Return (Book 9)

YAKOKE

Like each of my Choctaw Heritage Books, this one took a great deal of time, research, and input to finally bring it to life. I'm so grateful for all who came alongside me for this project:

My mama, Lynda Kay Sawyer, who never fails to encourage and push me onward in every book project.

My dear friend and reading pal, Catherine Frappier, who gave this book the editorial scrubbing it needed.

Mollie Reeder, who has listened to me gush about themes and characters in this book for years and years.

My brother, Doug Davis, for the constant flow of Choctaw historical information, including a catalyst piece for this story about the proposed Town Site Act.

Megan Baker (Choctaw Nation of Oklahoma Historic Preservation Department) for historical and cultural input, and all those on the Choctaw Nation Historic Preservation Facebook page for solid resources and suggestions. Yakoke!

Nick Brandreth, Historic Process Specialist at the George Eastman Museum, for the deep dive into photography development.

All of you faithful readers of the *Choctaw Tribune* series, thank you for giving me the heart and courage to continue on with each book.

All glory to God Who created me to be a storyteller.

ABOUT THE AUTHOR

SARAH ELISABETH SAWYER is a story archaeologist. She digs up shards of past lives, hopes, and truths, and pieces them together for readers today. The Smithsonian's National Museum of the American Indian honored her as a literary artist through their Artist Leadership Program for her work in preserving Choctaw Trail of Tears stories. She is the creator of the Fiction Writing: American Indians digital course. (FictionCourses.com)

A tribal member of the Choctaw Nation of Oklahoma, she writes historical fiction from her hometown in Texas, partnering with her mother, Lynda Kay Sawyer, in continued research for future works. Learn more at SarahElisabethWrites.com, Choctaw Spirit.com, and Facebook.com/SarahElisabethSawyer.